The DOOR KEEPER

STEEN JONES

In every world,
SJones

The Door Keeper

Copyright 2017 Steen Jones
thedoorkeepertrilogy@gmail.com

Copyright 2017 Royal JamES Publishing, LLC
royaljamespublishing.com

Front Cover Design: Meg Brim Copyright 2017
Book Design: Cindy C Bennett

Paperback Edition

No parts of this book may be reproduced, scanned, or distributed in any printed or electronic form without permission. Exceptions are reviewers who may quote short excerpts for review. Please write to royaljamespublishing@gmail.com for permission.

This book is a work of fiction. Any resemblance to persons, living or dead, or actual events is purely coincidental. The characters are products of the author's imagination and are used fictitiously.

A Royal James Publishing Book
Distributed by Royal James Publishing, LLC
www.royaljamespublishing.com

All Rights Reserved USA

Table of Contents

THE BEGINNING. 1
THE GALLERY OPENING. 9
THE SCHOOL PROJECT. 15
THE ITALY TRIP. 21
THE MEET CUTE. 28
THE TRUTH. 30
THE PICTURE. 38
THE UNCERTAINTY. 41
THE KEY. 46
THE NEW WORLD. 51
THE BUTTERFLAIRIES. 59
THE BROTHER. 66
THE SERENBES. 73
THE HISTORY LESSON. 80
THE PLAN. 88
THE RESEARCH. 94
THE OWL. 103
THE TRAINING. 110
THE PALUS DOOR. 116
THE PALUNS. 123
THE SCARE. 131
THE FRIEND. 137
THE ESCAPE. 141
THE RETURN. 149
THE NEW NORMAL. 155
THE NEW DREAM. 160
THE DECISION. 165
THE TENSION. 168
THE WEEK BEFORE. 174
THE TRIP BACK. 178
THE MEMORIES. 182
THE SURPRISE. 188
THE UNCLE. 191
THE DOOR MAKER. 196
THE DAY BEFORE. 202
THE DOOR HOME. 209
THE SUNS. 215
THE SHALLOW SEA. 220

THE FATHER.	225
THE WELCOME.	228
THE DINNER.	234
THE PAINTINGS.	240
THE BLACKSMITH.	248
THE FRIENDLY COMPETITION.	254
THE CONFRONTATION.	261
THE BURNING QUESTIONS.	269
THE JOURNEY.	274
THE BONFIRE.	277
THE SHOCK.	280
THE BETRAYAL.	285
THE OTHER SISTER.	291
THE DREAM THROWER.	296
THE PRODIGAL BROTHER.	299
THE REUNION.	303
THE FUTURE.	309
THE JUSTIFICATION.	312
THE REALIZATION.	317
THE WEDDING.	320
THE EPILOGUE.	326

ACKNOWLEDGEMENTS

ABOUT THE AUTHOR

The

DOOR KEEPER

THE BEGINNING.

I watched, powerless, as my mother continued to scream. She didn't look panicked or scared. Her scream was one of sheer determination, almost as if she screamed hard enough, or with enough force, she could prevent the oncoming tragedy. Of course, I knew this to be impossible, having dreamt of this moment hundreds and hundreds of times. These lucid dreams had grown harder for me to handle. Fully aware I was dreaming, but unable to stop it, or wake up, I was simply a forced spectator. My mother's hair dripped with sweat, and in between her labored screams, she shouted instructions to the doctor and nurse in the small white delivery room. In every dream, no matter the scenario, my mother always carried the authority in the room. I had to watch as her strength and resolve weakened. Until I heard my first cry and then her last.

Once I fully woke up, I let my eyes stay closed and allowed myself to feel the sadness. It was rare I allowed myself to feel it. I mean, technically I'd never met my birth mother. But this morning, for whatever reason, I felt particularly emotional about the whole thing. The dreams had gotten worse over the last year. I rolled over and checked my phone. 7:45 a.m. I missed when my body and mind allowed me to sleep until nine. Those were the days. I sat up slowly and felt an ache in my shoulder I hadn't felt yesterday. It was either sore from working late, or just the toil of turning thirty. I tried to massage it to ease the pain, but to no avail. Pulling on my sweatpants, I headed downstairs to make some coffee.

As I walked past Gabby's bedroom door, I saw that she hadn't straightened her room yesterday like she said she would. Gabby. My sweet little ten-year-old angel. My sweet little *messy* angel. Thankfully, my neighbor—and best friend—let her stay over last night since I had to work late. The house was quiet without her morning commentary. I made my coffee, noticing my favorite creamer was almost empty. I made a quick mental note to grab more. Once my coffee was doctored just right, I settled on the front porch in my favorite rocking chair. I stared across the sharp bend in the street at the geese settling into the lake. They honked at each other to move faster, itching to cool off no doubt. The air was already thick and warm, all the more reason to love North Georgia in the summer, my favorite time of the year. Already in a reminiscent mood, I allowed my thoughts to drift back to the first night I spent in this house.

Eric and I married a few months before we moved in. We were twenty years old, so young and in love. We were pregnant with Gabby almost immediately. When we went looking for a permanent place, we found this old farmhouse with barely any insulation and no dishwasher. Dark grey with white trim, the house was nestled between two small farms, the pastures laden with cows on either side of the property. The lake across the street provided a stunning view, and giant oak trees surrounding the house promised a colorful autumn. The grass was sparse due to the tree roots pushing up, and goose droppings from the flock of geese that took up residence in the front yard every morning. Eric insisted on buying this house because of the studio over the detached garage. I insisted on it because of the wrap-around porch. That was our relationship, disagreeing on why we agreed on everything. Of course, I could have painted anywhere, but he wanted me to have my own space. He was always so thoughtful that way. That first night, we had no furniture and no clue where the closest grocery store was, so we had pizza delivered and ate it in the living room on our mattress. We kept the mattress on the floor in front of the fireplace until we could afford an actual bed, and the heating bill for that matter. Remembering this, I couldn't stop the smile spreading across my face. I pulled the mattress into the living room several years later to surprise Gabby with a fun girls' sleepover night. She thought I was crazy, but of course, she loved every minute of it. It's rare to see her father in her, but that night, while eating pizza and watching movies in front of the roaring fireplace, I saw a spark of him.

My mind snapped to attention as I recalled I needed to run a few errands before Gabby came home later that afternoon. I downed the rest of my coffee and drudged upstairs to throw on some actual clothes. I decided on my usual wardrobe: jeans and a tank top, blueish grey to compliment my dark skin tone. I brushed my teeth hurriedly, ran my fingers through my black and quickly greying, short, asymmetrical hair. I decided several years ago to just let the grey grow out until it drove me crazy. It hadn't yet. It actually had a cool 'Storm from X-men' vibe happening. After I found earrings to match my antique pocket-watch necklace, I checked the soreness of my right shoulder one last time, rubbing the large bouquet of flowers tattooed there. My tattoo is one of my most favorite things. The vibrant, exotic collection of flowers was one of my first paintings as a teenager. I figured if I was going to give something a permanent home on my body, it should be something I treasured and of my own creation.

Running downstairs, I slipped on my flip flops and grabbed the keys. Today was definitely a convertible day. I was fortunate enough to have received a 1978 Corvette convertible from my adopted parents when I graduated high school, and I kept it for sunny warm days. Of course Eric and I bought a sensible family car when Gabby was born, but thankfully, I was able to keep the convertible since it was paid for. Running a little too fast toward the garage, I slipped on a couple of the thousands of acorns that littered my yard. Darn acorns. I reminded myself to price out an overhang to alleviate this problem. While I loved my beautiful big oak trees, the unbelievable number of acorns they produced was crazy! I steadied myself before I almost busted my butt again. I entered through the side door, and opened the garage. I slid into the silver beauty, and after turning the ignition, I backed out of the garage and did what every convertible deserves: put her top down. The morning sun hit my face. The black leather interior gets hot in the summer, but the heat never bothered me. In fact, I welcomed it. I slid my aviators on and spun out of the acorn adorned gravel driveway.

I needed to go to downtown Woodstock to pick up some remaining items I had to get for opening night, and to check on the painting placements at the gallery one last time before tomorrow. I drove down Arnold Mill Road, the long morning shadows of the trees flew past with my music turned loud. These alone moments in the wind were incredibly therapeutic. Once I topped the hill, I knew what was waiting at the bottom. As I hit the base of the hill and started toward the bend of the road, I caught a glimpse of it peeking out from behind some newly grown brush off in the field to my left. It was far enough off the road to not be obvious, but close enough for me to always notice. The door. A free-standing door on the edge of a field hidden among a wall of trees. It always struck me as being peculiar. It was obviously an old door, with different shades of green and some dark orange peeking through the cracked paint. It always captured my attention when I drove by. Such an odd, random place for a door.

※ ※ ※ ※ ※

When I got back into my car after buying the special light bulbs I needed for the gallery, I noticed a group of people gawking in my direction. I smiled politely, slipped on my glasses, and attempted not to hit them as I backed out of my parking spot. I'm used to it by now. The attention wasn't because I am pretty; I'm honestly rather odd looking. Maybe I should say I'm an odd conglomeration of pretty attributes thrown together like a Picasso portrait. Separately, they could be beautiful, but together, they just look weird. I have dark olive skin with large, light grey eyes. My hair, once completely black, has now turned mostly silverish-white with some black still popping out underneath. With a slim athletic build that's much taller than the average woman, throw in a couple facial piercings and the shoulder tattoo, well, you've got a real hard core Amazon chick, apparently. I was always entertained by the assumptions people made about me. I chuckled to myself. If only they knew how incredibly tame and boring I was.

I arrived at the gallery on Main Street, the gallery to be opened with my best friend, and neighbor, Danielle. It's housed above a coffee shop in downtown Woodstock, which used to be a studio loft we renovated over the better half of a year as our funding allowed. I opened the door to the homey gallery, laden with cushy couches and colorful, eclectic chairs. The smell of coffee wafted up the stairs, and coffee tables of all shapes and sizes were scattered around. The walls were brightly colored and resembled the set for the show 'Friends.' We decided on this comfy, cozy motif in hopes people would want to hang out here and browse the local painters' art after filling their coffee mugs downstairs.

"Eden, what the h-e-double-hockey-sticks are you doing here?" Charlie asked as he came up behind me, scaring me almost to death.

I turned to the young, tall, gangly kid with big light brown eyes, long, wavy, light brown hair and square jaw who stared at me. He wore his usual scoop pastel tank top and light pink cotton shorts. He held a hammer in one hand and a level in the other.

"I know, I know, Charlie," I said as I fumbled with the light bulbs. "I'm not really here. I just wanted to drop off these bulbs for the lights we wanted brighter." I lied. I honestly thought I would beat him there. Charlie is a local high school student we hired who worked part time after school for us over the renovation period. He had done most of the manual labor. Danielle took care of the accounting books and logistics, and I painted and curated the art. We were extremely thankful for him during this busy time. Plus, he was one talented artist with charcoal. I met him when I was a guest speaker in his high school art class. Weekend after weekend, we'd been surprised how this particular high schooler didn't sleep in on Saturdays like his stereotypical brethren.

"Seriously, Eden, everything is taken care of. Will you relax? I'll finish hanging the last few paintings and we'll be done. You've already told me where they go. Just go home and chill. Do something fun with Gabby tonight to keep your mind off all this junk."

When I realized he was serious, I relented and decided to go back home. He was right, of course. Everything that could be done had been. The caterers were scheduled the following afternoon to set up for the party, and everything else had been arranged. As I left, I stopped in front of the painting I did as a teenager that hung in the front of the gallery, the one that I had tattooed on my shoulder.

"That one has always been my favorite of yours." Charlie snuck up behind me, again. That crazy little ninja. "One thing I've always dug about your paintings is your great use of color. Anytime I try to paint or use colored pencils, everything looks dumb and muted. Your work is so bright and vibrant."

I always hated hearing an artist be self-deprecating. Although, being one most of my life, I understood the frustration with not being able to master certain things. So I grabbed his shoulders and walked him over to one of his pieces showcased in the corner over a lime green, tufted, antique couch. It was a beautiful charcoal drawing of a landscape, with detailed cascading hills and these amazing crooked trees with roots growing out from every branch. They almost looked inside out. So incredibly imaginative.

"Charlie, your work is some of the most brilliant I've ever seen. You have such a gift for realism. I could never create anything like this. We all wish we had what we don't. Just embrace your unique awesomeness, okay?" I tried to encourage him because he was still finding his voice as an artist. "Well, I'll leave you to it. See you tomorrow!"

"Thanks, Eden. Tomorrow night is going to be flippin' awesome." He smiled.

I walked back down into the coffee shop and grabbed my usual caramel latte for the road. This was the downfall of working above a coffee shop. Overload of sugar and caffeine—which reminded me to stop by the grocery store for my favorite creamer. While there, I bought Gabby's favorite ice cream for the evening. If you asked her what her favorite ice cream was, she answered the same every time—

any. But I knew the truth; she liked chocolate ice cream with chocolate chips and chocolate syrup. Same as me. We called it "triple chocolate overload."

Driving home, I looked forward to seeing Gabby and hearing all about her adventures at Danielle and Emmie's. Knowing Gabby, I knew to expect some dramatic turn of events that ended in either screaming in terror or howling in laughter. I hit the bend in the road and glanced to my right. And of course, right where I saw it last, was the door.

THE GALLERY OPENING.

While I straightened our small kitchen (complete with a dishwasher now), I heard her bounce up the porch steps singing Taylor Swift's newest single. She sounded extra sassy. I smiled. Gabby had such a beautiful voice. She rounded the corner.

"Hey, Mom, I'm starving. What's for lunch?"

"Well, hello to you, too, honey," I said while shaking my head. She came up and hugged me from behind.

"Did you have to work really late last night?" she asked out of politeness.

"It wasn't too bad. What did you and Emmie get into?"

"Oh my gosh, we had so much fun! We reenacted scenes from different movies and uploaded them on YouTube . . ." And then she entered her own little world, telling me all about the costumes they made from sheets and pillowcases, and the ice castles they built with boxes and paint. I absolutely adored her creativity. She made something amazing from just about anything. I turned around to give her my full attention. She motioned with outstretched arms, over-exaggerating some minute detail. Her eyes were wide and her eyebrows danced all over the place with myriad expressions, ranging from surprise to delight. She was incredibly stunning. If I were an awkward Picasso, she was one of Michelangelo's angels from the Sistine Chapel. Even already at this age, her skin was a shade lighter than mine, perfectly striking against her large, pale, ice blue eyes. Her hair was thick and wavy, a mane of dark chocolate that stopped right above her tiny little tooshy. She was already taller than average. I knew she would eventually be long and lean. Thankfully, she still had her pudgy cheeks to keep her face round which made me want to never stop kissing them. As I was trying to decide on how to get around the legalities of locking her in her room until she turned twenty-five, she got my attention.

"Mom? Mom, do you think we could do that?"

"Do what, sweetie?" I asked.

"You weren't listening . . ." she whined. "I wanted to ask Aunt Danielle and Emmie over for pizza and a movie night. Aunt Danielle said she wanted to talk to you about tomorrow."

"Yeah, that would be great. I'll text her real quick." And then I put on the best serious mom face I could muster. "But you better straighten your room, or there is no way Emmie is coming over. Seriously, Gabby, you were supposed to do it yesterday before you left."

"Yeah, yeah, yeah, Mom, sure thing," she yelled over her shoulder, heading upstairs before I could make her lunch.

"Gabby . . . Gabby . . ." No answer. "Gabriel Saunders! I'm serious this time. You better clean your room or I'm not calling Aunt Danielle!" It was an empty threat, and she knew it. The truth is that I really needed a fun girl's night. Between the stress of getting ready for the gallery opening and just trying to keep up with the daily grind, I hadn't spent any quality time with my best friend in a while. Danielle and her family had lived at the now faux farm next door to us for the past five years. We instantly connected due to our both being orphans. But while I found a loving family to raise me, she wasn't so lucky. She had a hard edge to her, one that served her well growing up in Boston, and served me well now as a business partner. I was the push-over, and she was the hard ass. Good cop, bad cop. We made a great team. Her husband was away on business a great deal, so Gabby and I spent a lot of time with her and her daughter, Emmie. More dinners, game and movie nights than I could ever attempt to remember. She really was my closest friend, and she never failed to tell me the truth.

🐾 🐾 🐾 🐾 🐾

"Enough is enough," Danielle said as she finished her last slice of pizza. "You haven't been on a date in over a year."

I just chuckled and grabbed another Coke. "D, you know as well as I do that there is absolutely no one I am interested in. Plus, it's not like I haven't been spending the last year trying to launch my dream business or anything . . ."

"Well, that's no excuse! Listen, I understand we've been busy. But the gallery is opening tomorrow, and you know it will practically run itself. You are running out of reasons not to date." She flipped her long, perfectly kept, highlighted hair over her shoulder.

"Don't forget about Gabby—"

"What about Gabby?" she interjected before I could finish the thought. "She would love to have a guy around here. If for no other reason than to expand her audience." She winked and looked over her shoulder at the girls playing in the living room. They were dancing along to a music video.

"Remember when we had the energy to dance like that for hours?" I asked her, not taking my eyes off the girls.

"I know. These days the only thing I can sustain for that long is a nap!" At that we both laughed.

I returned our empty plates to the kitchen, but I couldn't keep my thoughts from drifting toward Eric. I still couldn't believe it had been seven years since the car accident. One day he was here and the next day he wasn't. I had been a widow for seven years. Seven years . . . how can it seem like yesterday he was in this kitchen teasing me about burning dinner? I stared down at my feet and the cold tile under them, and was instantly returned to the time we decided to re-tile the kitchen floor over Labor Day weekend and it ended up taking two weeks. In the same breath, it also seemed like three lifetimes ago. It had been a long road to rewriting our normal, but finally Gabby and I had arrived here. It was easier for her, of course. She was so young, she didn't have much to compare life to. For me, it took much longer. Along the way I had a couple casual relationships. And by casual, I mean it never went beyond dinners or movies out. It all just seemed so complicated. And to be honest, I didn't mind being alone anymore. I think that was partially why none of the relationships ever progressed further. I had yet to find anyone I was willing to go through all the hard work of a relationship for.

"Hey, I noticed that your door handle is broken in the hallway," Danielle came up behind me, "and since you are refusing to date a man, you can borrow mine to come over and fix it, if you'd like. I'll share. Well, only his handy man skills that is . . ."

"Oh, shut up!" I snapped the dish towel at her.

"Come on, let's go dance with the girls and see how long we can last." D grabbed my hand and pulled me into the living room. About six minutes later, we were both sprawled on the couch, completely gassed.

The next night, the four of us found ourselves mingling with the rest of the city of Woodstock at our gallery opening. Wall Polish was a big hit. We invited mostly local business owners to gain the support of downtown, as well as the local high school art students to encourage their desire to show art there. Gabby looked adorable in a long, hot pink maxi dress with strappy sandals, her hair curled and flowing. She was in the corner drinking a raspberry lemonade with Emmie.

Emmie was the perfect contrast to Gabby with her short blond bob and light skin. Both were positively giddy the whole evening. D looked stunning with a short, one shouldered silver sheen dress, perfect for a fancy evening out. I, on the other hand, wore a gold and cream sundress with jeans and a pair of gold gladiator sandals. That was about as elegant as I got.

I sipped on my sugary iced coffee when I noticed Charlie standing by the green couch talking with someone, showing them his drawing on display. He was pointing and explaining when the man he was talking to started laughing. The stranger was unusually tall with broad shoulders. I'm honestly not sure why I hadn't noticed him before now. His presence seemed to take up the whole room. He had the same wavy brown hair as Charlie, but cut much shorter. The same eyes, but with a few creases at the corners. His square jaw was tight as he admired the drawing. I noticed that he looked particularly moved by it. He seemed too young to be Charlie's father.

"That's his older brother." D caught me staring at the stranger. "I've never seen him before, but I talked with Charlie earlier and he said his brother was coming in from out of town. Cute, isn't he?"

I grinned. "Not too shabby." Just as I said it, Charlie turned around and pointed in my direction. The tall stranger's eyes followed and met mine. Once he saw me, his entire demeanor changed. He shifted from relaxed and joking to what I can only describe as surprised and intense curiosity. With one eyebrow raised, I saw him mouth Charlie a question. His eyes never left mine. Charlie looked at me and shrugged his shoulders.

"Whoa, what is happening right now?" I had totally forgotten D was standing next me. "Heavens, he is staring you down."

I finally unfroze and turned to her and laughed. "Guess he's never seen a white haired, tattooed chick under the age of 60." We giggled and she asked me a question about the price of a painting in the other room. After I'd answered her, I turned to see if Charlie and his brother were still across the room. They were gone.

THE SCHOOL PROJECT.

Besides a tiny incident involving a teenager armed with a Sharpie drawing a detailed, provocative sketch on the bathroom wall, the rest of the gallery opening went without a hitch. The drawing wasn't half bad, and if it hadn't included certain male genitalia, I might have thrown an open frame over it and called it art. But it gave me an idea. I had Charlie bring some friends from his art class, and I invited them to deface the bathroom walls with Sharpies. I made a sign asking people to keep their drawing/words PG for our little patrons. Afterward, we kept Sharpies in a Picasso mug next to the sink. It actually looked really cool. I planned on repainting it every month or so to allow new patrons the chance to make their mark. Too bad I couldn't thank the little hooligan for the good idea.

I had just finished the sign for the gallery bathroom in my detached studio when Gabby came up the stairs.

"Hey, Mom, I have a project that is due next month, and I'm gonna need your help with it," she asked rather hesitantly.

"Next month? It's not like you to be so on top of your school work." I feigned surprise.

"Mom, don't be dumb." She rolled her eyes. But then they were soft when they caught mine. "It's a family tree. We are supposed to trace our relatives back at least three generations."

"Oh, okay." I realized what she was asking. "Sure, honey. I'd be happy to help you with that. I'll call Grandma and see what I can find for you." And, of course, now I understood her hesitation. Eric used to love this kind of stuff. He had his lineage traced all the way back to the 1800s. I, on the other hand, could only trace mine back to 1984. Not only is that not much of a family tree, it's barely a trunk, and definitely had roots missing.

There is a sweet naiveté with children, and I was no different. My parents told me I was adopted when I was six. While to everyone else it was obvious I was adopted, I was completely shocked when forced to comprehend what they told me. The fact that I had dark skin with light eyes, and both my parents had light skin with dark brown eyes meant nothing. What six-year-old understands genetics anyway? Sadly, for both my parents and myself, they had zero answers about my past. They couldn't tell me anything other than the city of my birth, the date of my birth, and that my birth mother had died just seconds after I entered the world. I found it odd until I became an adult. Obviously, my adoption was not handled through proper channels or there would be records, documentation, and information on my birth parents. Knowing my mother died during delivery kept me from digging into my adoption. Why try to learn more when there was only heartache to gain? Why try to find out about my family when they were dead? I knew deep down I couldn't ignore this forever, and Gabby asking questions made me face the unwavering, uncertain door to my past. Weirdly, up to this point I did not mind the unknown of my family history. However, my daughter's caring about it suddenly made it a priority.

Or, perhaps I had always wanted to know, and was finally brave enough to admit it.

As I picked up the phone I had a brief flash of my birth mother's face, screaming, clutching the hospital bed. I shook it off. This had to happen. It was time. I wasn't sure how my mom was going to react when I started asking questions, but I had nowhere else to go.

"Hello, Eden. How was the gallery opening? Your dad and I were so sorry we missed it."

"Hey, Mom. It was great. We are officially open for business. You sound much better. How are you feeling?"

Mom and Dad were supposed to come out to the opening, but Mom came down with a nasty virus. They lived in Charleston, South Carolina, too far to drive while sick. I knew they hated to miss it. They had always been so supportive of my crazy projects.

"Oh, I'm fine. Thankfully it passed quickly. How is Gabby?"

"She's good. She is actually why I'm calling. She has a school project that I am supposed to help her with . . ." I sucked in a quick breath and continued. "A family tree. She's supposed to trace her lineage back three generations."

There was a long pause on the other end of the phone.

Followed by even more silence.

"Mom?"

"Yes, I'm sorry, honey. Yes, sure, but you know that I don't really have much to tell you about your birth parents. At least no more than I have already told you."

"I know." I struggled for the right words so as not to hurt her. "But this is really important to Gabby. So I think I want to at least try and pursue this as much as I can. If you have time, could you retell me the story, and this time try to include every detail you remember? Maybe we will think of something we missed before."

"Okay, sure, I have some time before my appointment. Um, okay, I'll do my best." Like many adoptive parents in her place, I knew this was hard for her, so I let her ease into it.

"You know your dad and I couldn't have children and had practically given up hope of ever having one. We were approaching the age when we couldn't conceive naturally, at least without medical help, so we just decided to enjoy life and stop trying. We started traveling and doing mission work in different places around the world. We gravitated to the orphanages and hospitals in all the different cities we went to. It came natural with your dad being a doctor, plus it helped fill the void of not having kids of our own.

She told me things she hadn't before; the details about her eyes were new. I felt emotions begin to rise within me, a sudden ache to know this woman who gave me life, yet I never met. Suddenly, I became incredibly jealous my mom got to meet her. I fought back tears when she suddenly continued.

"We visited with her only once. A few days later we came back to check on her and she was gone, and there you were. The doctor on call when you were born told us that she had suffered from excessive hemorrhaging during delivery, and although they attempted a blood transfusion, it was not quick enough to save her life. You had barely survived. The labor was long and intense, and it was a lot of stress on your little body, but you pulled through. I asked to see you, and the nurse taking care of you brought you to me. You were so small, with beautiful black hair. But when you opened your eyes, I saw her. I saw your mother."

I felt as though I was grieving my birth mother for the first time. I felt the tears stream down my face. I saw her in my dreams, just as Mom described. I sat there, soaking in the silence, not sure how much more I could take—wondering if I had made a mistake, opening this door.

"There was a specific nurse that took care of you at the hospital. Apparently, she had befriended your mother during her stay. I asked what they were going to do with you, and she said she didn't know. There was no father's name on your birth certificate. Only that your mother's name was Ava Cherubini. That is the only information they had on either of your parents. I could tell that for whatever reason, the nurse was extremely hesitant to put you in the system, so of course your father and I offered to take you. Just as you were—undocumented. The hospital staff knew us well, and it seemed like the best option. So, that night, we took you back to Positano. A few days later, we flew back to the states and . . . you know the rest."

I tried to absorb everything she said. No father's name, only my mother's name. I already knew there had been no information about my father. But, Ava Cherubini. Her last name was new information. How had I never asked about it before? Eden Cherubini. My birth name.

"So is it safe to assume that my birth mother was Italian?" It was the only question I could muster.

"Well, it would seem so, from her name, but she didn't seem to know the southern part of Italy too well. From our visit with her she seemed like she didn't feel comfortable with her surroundings." Mom sounded as unsure as I felt. This was not much to go on.

"Mom, thank you so much. I know this isn't easy for you. You know I love you, right? Especially after hearing all of this. Thank you so much for being willing to take me in without knowing anything about me at all. You gave me such a wonderful life." Now, I cried tears of gratitude to the parents who raised me, who fed me, clothed me, taught me, and loved me unconditionally.

"Oh, Eden. When I saw your sweet little face, knowing what you went through to come into this world, that you had survived against all odds, I knew you weren't meant to go through this life alone. You gave us such a wonderful life, so thank you."

"I love you, Mom." Smiling, I was about to hang up, then one quick thought popped in my mind. "Hey, Mom, real quick. Who named me? Did you or Ava?"

"Neither . . . the nurse named you."

During dinner that night, I debriefed Gabby on all I learned from her grandmother. She took notes and asked some questions. Unfortunately, they were questions I didn't have answers for. After she was satisfied with her interview/interrogation of me, she went upstairs to go to bed. I opened my laptop on the couch and started the search for some answers. I found nothing on Ava Cherubini online. No records, birth certificates, marriage certificates, or even her death certificate. I searched outside of Italy. Nothing. I looked for the hospital where I was born. It closed over a decade ago. I shut my laptop and sat on the front porch.

The lake was beautiful, with the full moon glistening on the water. Lightening bugs popped in and out of my line of vision. The crickets sung their tune in summer harmony. I closed my eyes and envisioned the scene of my two moms sitting in a hospital room, talking together. The older, wiser mother who raised me, and the wild, young mother who birthed me. What I would have given to hear just a moment of their conversation three decades ago.

After a year of lucid dreams of my birth mother dying, Gabby getting this assignment, and now hearing the whole story from my parents' perspective, I decided I had to put the pieces of the puzzle together. I had to learn about my mother, if for no other reason than to find out more about myself and where I came from. I couldn't keep the door to my past shut any longer. With no twenty-first century trail to follow, I did the only thing any reasonable person does . . . I went back inside, reopened my laptop, and Googled 'cheap flights to Italy.'

THE ITALY TRIP.

A week later, I packed my suitcase with no definitive plan in mind. I had no clear leads either. I was going in blind, but it was an option, and that was enough. I double-checked my packing list, and Danielle popped through my bedroom door.

"I mean, this is perfect! You are going to go over there, meet a handsome, charming, Italian guy, and fall in love." Her smile and giggle were uncontainable. "Although, just make sure he is willing to move here, because I can't lose you to Italy." She paused dramatically and her eyes grew wide. "Oooooh, but if you did move there, it would be nice to have somewhere to stay when I come visit you once a month . . ."

At this point, I laughed along with her. "D, you are ridiculous. This is strictly a trip to investigate. I am NOT planning on a life altering 'meet cute.' But, I do promise to bring you home something involving high fashion. If you are really nice, it may even be a pair of something special," I said to change the subject.

"You got it. And don't worry about Gabby. She and Emmie are so excited to be able to spend the week together. They already have the whole thing planned. By the time you get back, they will be Internet sensations."

"Why does that not surprise me?" I smiled and threw a handful of clothes over my shoulder back into my closet.

🐾 🐾 🐾 🐾 🐾

After the almost thirteen-hour flight from Atlanta, I landed in Naples, Italy. I found my one medium-sized bag at baggage claim. Once again, happy with my decision to pack light. Finding my driver proved a breeze as well. We loaded up and drove along the Amalfi coast toward Positano. I thought it would be beneficial to follow my parents' vacation route, so I rented an apartment as my home base during my trip. An hour and a half later, we arrived at Villa Le Sirene. The owners met me at the car, and after customary double kisses, I turned and followed them as they led me to the door to the apartment. I was immediately taken aback. I instantly understood why my parents kept Positano as their Italian base on their vacations. Even after the beautiful drive from Naples, Positano was beyond anything I'd seen. I followed my hosts under a canopy of decadent smelling, deeply pink flowers. To my left, beyond the incredible garden that surrounded me, I saw the entire city splashed on the Italian hillside, like it had washed up from the sea.

We walked into the beautiful, spacious apartment, with a wooden beamed ceiling and colorful decorative stone tiled floors. Compelled, I walked to the opened French doors and out onto the veranda. Outstretched before me was the entirety of Positano. Colorful villas were stacked one on top of another. Right in front of the apartment, at the base of the hill, was an ornate old church called Santa Maria Assunta, complete with its golden dome steeple. The sun shone bright, and it seemed almost as though the dome was glowing. Below that, where the city met the sea, was Spiaggia Grande, the local beach. I saw people walking along the shore, eating gelato. The fresh and salty air felt intoxicating. The entire scene absolutely breathtaking.

Quickly unpacking, I decided to explore around town. Or should I say, explore up and down the town. With Positano located on the side of the hill, stairs took you to most destinations. I can, in all honesty, say I had never seen or walked more stairs in my life, but at every turn and around every corner was a new fresh perspective and view of the city.

I walked down to Santa Maria Assunta to take some pictures, wandering into the huge white and gold sanctuary. Everywhere I looked were golden gilded arches with golden cherubs looking down from their perches. Ornate paintings hung in the hallways that led to the smaller chapels off the main place of worship.

As I was taking a tour, the priest, Father Gregory, informed me mass was about to start. By the way he eyed my piercings, I could tell he thought it prudent for me to attend. Judgment aside, this was a once in a lifetime opportunity not to be missed. I settled into a wooden pew toward the back so I could sneak out if my stomach started rumbling and interrupting the ceremony, which wouldn't be the first time. The music crescendoed from the organ pipes, and the angelic voices of the men and women rose to match it. I let myself be taken away by the beautiful voices, even though I didn't understand the language. It somehow made it even more hypnotic.

Before I realized it, Father Gregory had taken the pulpit and started the readings. A bible, in English, lay next to me, so I did my best to follow along. He read out of Genesis, and best I could tell was talking about Adam and Eve and the original sin. As I tried to find the English counterpart to the Italian reading, I caught up to him after hearing my name in Genesis 3:24.

"He drove out the man, and at the east of the Garden of Eden he placed the cherubim and a flaming sword that turned every way to guard the way to the tree of life."

As he read the verse in Italian, I made the connection. 'Cherubim'—the angel God placed at the entrance of Eden—in Italian is 'Cherubini.' My mother's last name, the name I just came to know last week. I've been Eden Brown or Saunders my whole life, but suddenly, I couldn't think of anything but my given birth name. Eden Cherubini.

🌠 🌠 .🌠 🌠 🌠

Everything was the same: my mother sprawled on the delivery table, crying out in pain and sorrow, as well as frustration and determination. The hospital room was sterile and white. A young blonde haired woman held her hand, attempting to comfort her. My mother yelled to the doctor to save me, dripping in sweat and tears. I knew what was about to happen: I was about to be born, and she was about to die. Yet suddenly, with incredible force, my mother leapt off the table and swung a flaming sword, so hot I almost felt the fire . . .

I bolted up, sweating, unsure what to do with this new dream. I fell back down with heavy emotion and covered my eyes with my arm, remembering mass from last night. It must have made quite an impression on my subconscious. I rolled over and checked the time; it was noon here and six am back home. I climbed out of bed, made a quick cup of coffee, and settled comfortably on the veranda to shake the dream and make plans for the day.

The view was just as incredible this afternoon as it was yesterday. The wind blew up from the sea, carrying along with it the welcomed salty air. I reflected on yesterday and the newfound connection with my mother's last name. I wondered why I had never thought of it before. This wondering brought me back to my own daughter. I called her before she left for school.

After hearing about the latest developments in Gabby's circle of friends, and how many views her most recent YouTube video had, I grabbed a quick shower. Anxious to start on my first lead, I forwent makeup and drying my hair, ready to get to Sorrento. I left the apartment and bounced up the first flight of stairs to eat a quick brunch from Cafe Positano. After some delish Italian cuisine and a cappuccino, I jumped on the bus that would take me to Sorrento.

A quick thirty minutes later, I stood between a couple of street vendors, looking at Mount Vesuvius. Since I didn't have a plan, I decided to let the wind take me wherever it blew. I wandered the streets, passing by bustling tourists and locals trying to sell their handmade goods. Within the hour, I found myself in the older section of Sorrento, walking the narrow streets, visiting well curated clothing boutiques and small antique shops. I found an adorable dress that I bought for Gabby, as well as some fun trinkets for Danielle and Emmie. As I sat outside and ate my risotto at Fauno Bar in Tasso square, I watched people walking from all directions. It seemed the city's center stayed busy.

My mind wandered back to my seemingly impossible quest. What was I expecting to find? What was I trying to accomplish? Yes, I had a wonderful morning walking the colorful streets of Sorrento, but was no closer to any answers. I felt a bit foolish. I watched as a younger couple, tourists, stopped at railing on the other side of the square to peer over. As they pointed and pulled out their cameras, I quickly noticed more people peering over the edge. After paying my bill, I crossed the street and approached the railing.

Hundreds of yards below me, nestled in a deep green gorge, were overgrown ruins. A large square stone building was completely covered with dense green foliage, with a tall skinny stone chimney raised next to it. On closer inspection, I saw two small creeks come together to form a Y shape at the floor of the gorge. It was an incredible sight, and felt completely out of place in middle of the city's center. Perhaps Sorrento held some surprises after all.

After spending some time at the Church of San Francesco, named for St. Francis of Assisi, I made my way back to Positano. On the bus ride back, I thought about the monastery and Church of St. Francis. There was an incredible cloister in the middle of the grounds, complete with doors in every corner, and an exquisite garden in the courtyard. The stoned architecture was striking against the soft, colorful vegetation that grew in its center. As I walked under the stoned portico and through the arches, I read plaques containing detailed history of the buildings. I couldn't help but feel jealous of its painstakingly and accurately documented past.

Although my first full day in Italy did not yield any answers, I didn't consider it a total bust. I found some great gifts for my family and friends back home, and saw some beautiful places. But that was not why I'd come. I knew the possibility of any answers were probably in Sorrento. So the next morning, I found myself on the bus back to the city.

I had called my mom last night for some ideas. She had a great one. Once I was off the bus, I checked the directions she told me over the phone. I knew the hospital where I was born was no longer there, but I decided to go see where it once stood.

Walking up Corso Italia, I saw a woman standing by a flower cart. She was probably in her early to mid-sixties. She had greying light blonde hair pulled back in a loose bun to one side. She held a large, colorful bouquet of flowers that fell to her side, hanging upside down. She looked at me as though I was a ghost. I quickly smiled and kept walking, assuming she disapproved of my facial piercings or my tattoo. When I rounded the corner to head further north, I heard someone approach too close behind me. I turned around to find the woman just a couple feet behind me, staring at me, her eyes large and wide. She startled when I turned around.

"*Mi dispiace. Lei parla italiano?*"

"*Si, ma lo parlo solo un poco . . .*" I said slowly, letting her know I only speak very little Italian. "*Parla inglese?*"

"Yes, I'm sorry to scare you." Her accent was thick, and as far as I could tell, she was the one who looked terrified. She looked down at her feet fearfully. When she glanced back at my face, I saw something new, something different and yet something recognizable. I saw hope.

"Are you Eden Cherubini?"

THE MEET CUTE.

I stood there, frozen, looking at the woman in disbelief. How could she know me? Should I know her? How did she know my last name? I just learned about it a week ago. I could form no words to speak aloud.

"My name is Rosalina." She placed her hand on her chest and stared back at me expectantly.

"I'm sorry, Rosalina, do I know you?" I felt completely befaffeled—so much so, that I was pretty sure I'd just made up that word. This woman stared at me as though I was her long-lost child. A long-lost child. Suddenly, my mom's words replayed in my mind when I asked who had named me.

"The nurse." I exhaled the words as they formed in my brain. My eyes met hers.

Relief flooded her face. "Yes." She grabbed me forcefully and hugged me. The flowers she carried slapped me in the back of the head as she held me tight. She started laughing and let me go. She let the flowers drop to the ground, not caring about them anymore. Rosalina took my face in her calloused hands and studied it. I thought for a second she was trying to memorize it, then I realized she wasn't studying it, she was remembering it. Tears puddled at the base of her soft brown eyes.

"You look just like your mother," she whispered softly. Suddenly, I understood the full weight of the moment. I stood in front of my first, and perhaps only, link to my birth mother. She was her friend. She was there when she died, when I was born. Then, it was my turn to grab and hug her. We simply stood there, in the middle of a cobbled tiny side road, embracing each other; two complete strangers who meant the world to each other.

She invited me back to her villa for coffee. We walked along and made small talk about my visit there so far, and my life in the states. She asked about my parents, and I told her about Gabby. Once we got back to her place, she put on some coffee and we sat in her small kitchen at a table with a sunflower tablecloth. I was instantly struck by the intensity of the coming conversation, unsure how to begin. I decided to just dive in.

"Rosalina, can you tell me about mother?" I looked at her hesitantly.

"Eden, I have prayed for this moment for such a long time. I have waited over thirty years to talk about Ava. I have never spoken to anyone about her. Not even my husband."

I couldn't hide my surprise. "Why?"

"Because of who she was . . . and who you are." Her face became somber and her gaze shifted from mine. Then, as quickly as the moment came, it passed and she smiled as she continued, "If it's okay with you, I'd like to start at the beginning and tell you the whole story."

"Of course, please."

I inhaled slowly and closed my eyes. Allowing myself to feel the weight of the moment. It felt too good to be true. This was what I'd been waiting for, to learn about my mother. I knew that I would remember this moment for the rest of my life.

THE TRUTH.

The first time I met your mother, I was eating on the patio of a cafe in the center of town on my lunch break. Ava approached the Maître d, asking if she could eat. I listened to her explain that she had no money, but would work for some food. He rudely refused and shooed her away. As she turned to leave, she saw me sitting there, and our eyes met for a moment. I could tell she was very hungry, so I invited her to eat with me. Your mother was unlike anyone I'd ever seen before. Her hair fell down past her waist. It was an unusual color: silver, with a hue of purple, matching her light purple eyes. They reminded me of lavender. She had your face, with the same dark olive complexion. I remember she wore this long, white, simple flowing dress with small white flowers woven into her hair. I wondered how someone who looked so much like royalty had no money." She smiled while picturing my mother. I smiled, thankful for the beautiful picture she painted for me.

"That was the first of our many lunches together. We'd meet at the same cafe and I'd pay for lunch. She spoke perfect Italian, but seemed to have little knowledge about anything else. She always asked so many questions. She was curious about our traditions, religion, politics, and medicine. We'd have lunch together a few days, back to back, but then I wouldn't see her for a month. Then Ava would pop up again out of nowhere. At first, I would try to ask where she had been, or anything about her, but I quickly learned she was unwilling to talk about herself. I finally gave up and just let it be. This went on for over a year. Your mother and I would just eat, walk the city, and talk for hours. I taught her all I could about everything she was curious about. We visited cathedrals, museums, and even spent a weekend in Rome so she could see the historic sites. One day, Ava showed up and told me she was pregnant. She was beyond excited. She knew you were a girl, but had no idea what to name you. We walked the city, talking about baby names, and laughing at the bad ones. I believe Gertrude was on the table for a minute." She winked at me as I grimaced.

"After the day Ava told me she was pregnant, I didn't see your mother again for six months. I thought she was gone for good until she showed up to the hospital late one night. It was pouring rain, and your poor mother came in, soaked to the bone. She was in obvious pain, so I took her to the doctor on call and we had her admitted. She gave the last name Cherubini when we filed her paperwork. The entire time I had only known her as Ava. She'd been with us in the hospital for a couple of days when the Browns, your parents, came to volunteer. Ava liked Evelyn immediately. Later, Ava said that she knew your mom had a deep capacity and desire for love. I was so impressed she saw that in her. But Ava had that gift with everyone. She could see the gifts that people held deep within themselves, invisible to everyone else. A couple of hours after your parents left, Ava started having severe complications. She was contracting every few minutes with very little progress, and she refused any pain medication. That night, I stayed with her, extremely scared for both of you."

At this, Rosalina went quiet.

She closed her eyes and held the bridge of her nose. I gave her a minute, desperately needing one myself as well. Suddenly, my mind flashed back to my dream from the other night, and I could see Rosalina as a young woman, holding my mother's hand. She continued, snapping me back to the moment.

"At one point, while Ava was trying to rest, she jolted awake and grabbed my hand. Crying, she told me she had to tell me the truth before it was too late and the truth died with her."

Rosalina took a deep breath and looked me square in the eyes, "She explained that she was not from Italy. That she was not from here at all. She had come into this world through a Door. The best way she knew to describe where she came from, so that I could understand, was that is was another universe, another world. And her job, in that other world, was what they called a Door Keeper. Ava said that she was responsible for guarding the Door so no one passed through from her world to this one. She admitted she knew she wasn't going to make it through the delivery, and I had to do everything I could to save you, because you had a destiny you must fulfill. While I was trying to make sense of what she was saying, she pulled a chain necklace with a large ornate key attached to it from her bedside drawer. Ava had been wearing it when she came into the hospital. She grabbed my hand and gave it to me, telling me it was for you. But she told me not to give it to you until you were an adult."

"Wait," I finally interrupted, throwing my hands up, not able to take anymore, unsure I had heard her correctly—unsure of anything she had said since she started. A different world? A Door Keeper? I had a destiny . . . Did Rosalina hear herself? I had no idea where to start with this insanity, or how I could possibly take this seriously. So, almost laughing, I started with the most obvious question.

"She is from another world? I don't understand . . ."

"Eden, I didn't either, but I spent enough time with your mother to know that it was the truth. I didn't know what it meant, but nothing about your mother had made sense to me up to this point. She was so smart and quick, yet knew nothing about this world. She was curious, and would disappear for long periods of time."

"That doesn't prove anything except that she was flaky and unreliable," I argued, starting to get upset. Did Rosalina even comprehend what she was saying? She was talking about alternate worlds—the very things fairy tales were made of. This wasn't a movie, or the Chronicles of Narnia, for heaven's sake. This was real life. This was *my* life.

"I know this is hard to understand." Rosalina laid her hand on my shaking arm and tried to calm me down. "But if you let me continue, there is more to the story."

I did not believe a word . . . until I looked into Rosalina's worn face. It was the face of someone who had carried a deep secret for a long time, and I could tell it had been heavy, and she was bursting to get it out.

"Okay." I sighed.

"She gave me this." At this, she handed me a key on a chain. It was an old, large gold key that was made up of multiple infinity symbols intertwined at the bow, and two different bits pointing out from the key in opposite directions. It was one intense key.

"Your mother instructed me to give this to you after you turned eighteen. She said this was the key to the Doors. This was what allowed her to pass to different worlds."

"Different worlds, like plural?" I interrupted, on the verge of losing my composure.

"Eden, I know this is hard for you to understand, and I promise that I will try to answer as many questions as I can."

"I'm sorry Rosalina . . . go on," I said, unable to believe what I heard.

"After she gave me the key, she told me that her world was called Caelum. Her husband, your father, didn't know that she had come through the Door. She made a mistake coming here so late in her pregnancy, and once the contractions started, she knew that she wasn't going to make it home. Deliveries were different for them than they were here. Babies were born bigger, labors lasted longer and required different medicine and birthing techniques."

I didn't hear much after she mentioned my father. I'd never thought much about him. Once I knew he wasn't listed on my birth certificate, I never thought knowing him was possible. Now I was hearing that he lived in some alternate universe, or world.

I pushed back from the table, stood and walked to the kitchen window. It was open and the wind blew in, caressing my tear stained cheeks. I wasn't even aware I'd been crying. Staring out the window at the island of Capri, I suddenly noticed, and was drawn to, the people walking the streets below the villa. Here was a city of normal people, going about their normal lives, buying their groceries, sipping lattes.

One young girl walked with her boyfriend, laughing at something he said. I was one of those people twenty minutes ago. Twenty minutes ago, the most exciting thing about me was that I was an orphan. Now, I was apparently an alien of some kind, living in a world I didn't belong in. My mother was a Door Keeper, my father didn't know I was alive, and I had some mission I was meant to fulfill. Twenty minutes ago, I was a co-owner of an art gallery with Sharpies in the bathroom. I felt a sudden pain in my right hand, and looking down, I saw I squeezed the key too tightly. Staring down at it, I asked Rosalina without turning around, "What did you say when she told you all this?"

"Honestly, Eden, I believed her instantly. I know it sounds crazy, but she was in the direst circumstance of her life. I knew it wasn't a time for fairy tales or made up stories. This was the time for truth, her eleventh hour, and she knew the only way to save you was to tell me everything she could to help during the delivery."

"Okay, so let's talk about that." I decided to try and focus on one thing at a time. "What exactly happened during the delivery?"

"First, Ava explained you were much bigger than the doctor thought. Most babies born in Caelum weigh an average of ten to twelve pounds and are born very slowly. Labor and delivery normally take around forty-eight to fifty-six hours. She knew she wouldn't have as long here without the medicine they have available there."

I couldn't help but flash back to Gabby's birth. She was ten pounds on the nose, and her delivery was a nightmare. Took over twenty-four hours, and she sustained multiple injuries upon delivery. She spent several nights in the NICU, and I had a very difficult time recovering myself.

Rosalina continued, "Ava warned me we needed to do whatever we could to speed your delivery up, but under no circumstances could we perform a C-section. You would have died immediately. Apparently, there were crucial functions the delivery process serves in your ability to breathe properly. So, to try to speed the labor along, we did all we could think of to fast track progression naturally. I walked with her around the hospital, and she drank basil and oregano tea. While we those days together, she told me about her world, their language and customs.

"They have kings and queens who rule, and within Caelum there are kingdoms made up of islands. There are features of her world that aren't present in ours. For example, the colors are completely different in her world than ours. Everything is brighter in Caelum. She explained it as if there were a filter or film over her eyes here. It sounded like heaven to me.

"She told me some of the most amazing stories of her adventures in other lands, and for a reason she couldn't quite pinpoint, this world of ours was her second favorite place to be. We barely slept over the next couple days. I stayed by her side the whole time. I simply couldn't bear to leave her alone. You have to know, Eden, that she was so brave. Her only thought was to save you. It was one of the most beautiful and touching things I've ever witnessed. Multiple times the doctor wanted her to start pushing, but she knew the longer she could hold out, the better it was for you. She listened to her body, until she knew she could no longer." At this, Rosalina started crying softly.

"When she knew it was time, Ava grabbed my hand and thanked me. She implored me to do what she asked, and looked me square in the eyes, communicating her trust. Then she told me goodbye."

At this, Rosalina covered her face with both her hands and began to weep openly. I put my hand on her shoulder, and we sat there together for a couple of minutes in silence. I realized Rosalina and Ava were more than just casual friends. Especially more than my parents thought. Rosalina was the only person in this world who truly knew Ava, and was there for her at the most important moment. And for that, I was indebted to her.

Rosalina regained her composure and resumed. "After telling me goodbye, all of her focus was on delivering you. She refused all medicine so she could focus and feel everything. She could sense if you were stressed or in trouble, and she needed to be able to feel it all. Clutching my hand, we began to push. It took over four hours of sweating and screaming and every ounce of strength and will that she had, but that night at 9 pm, you were born. I immediately put you in her arms, knowing she had only a minute or two left. She sang to you, a song I'd never heard, in a language that I assumed was her own. After caressing your cheek, and kissing the top of your head, she passed. I immediately took you from her arms because I noticed you were struggling to breathe. We cleaned you up and gave you some additional oxygen. I stayed with you until you were stable. The doctor asked me what Ava had wanted to name you. She had not yet decided. Knowing your story, and where you came from, I did the best I could think of. I told him Eden."

Everything swelled up inside me. Confusion, fear, overwhelming grief, love, wonderment . . . It was all consuming, like a nightmarish fog filling every square inch inside me, heavy and thick. I had never met my mother, but over the past thirty minutes, I'd come to love her fiercely. And yet, I felt angry and betrayed that she would leave me alone where I apparently didn't belong—on the other side of her Door. However, through the dense fog of emotion, a slight light pierced through the darkness. Knowledge and information, both of which had eluded me until now. I knew I would likely spend the rest of my life trying to process this information, but some things seemed to fall right into place. The puzzle pieces that felt so isolated from my life were now pieced together, and I had part of my family tree, giving me roots from which I could stand.

Yet, all the burning questions still remained.

THE PICTURE.

That night, I sat on the veranda at the villa in Positano. Rosalina offered for me to stay with her, but I needed to be alone. I needed to process, or at least attempt to process all I had heard earlier. I stared at the full moon's reflection on the ocean water for hours. None of this made sense, yet I wanted to believe it so badly. Not knowing what else to do, I went into the villa and found the journal I bought for Gabby the day before. The best way to work through this was to write it all down.

The beautifully lit golden steeple and the laughter of the restaurant patrons below me melted away as I spent the next several hours putting my feelings and questions on paper. I found no shortage of words as they poured out me. The rest of Positano fell asleep long before I put my pen down. I slept better than I had in over a year, dreamless.

Rosalina and I planned on spending the next couple of days together. She wanted to tell me the stories of my mother and spend some time with me, as I did with her. I arrived back in Sorrento just in time for us to have lunch at Cafe Latino, her and Ava's usual meeting spot. We spent the sunny afternoon laughing and teary-eyed as she recounted stories of their friendship. We talked about my journaling the night before, and she listened intently as I vocalized some of the feelings I was working through. Rosalina was gracious and understanding with me.

That afternoon we ventured out of the city for a wine tasting tour of a local vineyard. She recalled Ava loved learning about wine and the process to make it. Rosalina and I walked through an open field, lined with rows of grapes clinging to the vines that held them, sipping on an expensive glass of Chianti. She chuckled at one point telling me that of all of the wines Ava tried, her favorite was a simple Moscato.

"She said it reminded her of her favorite tea. I laughed at her and said she must like her tea strong."

Later that night, we went to a restaurant called Excelsior Vittoria. Sitting on the spacious veranda overlooking the marina below, she reminisced of the night her and my mother had spent there.

"We'd met earlier that day, of course, Ava showed up wearing the most beautiful dress. It was an empire waisted, one shouldered, emerald tunic dress. She looked like a Greek goddess." I smiled at that. Already knowing Rosalina rarely exaggerated, so it truly must have been beautiful.

"I joked with her that she always made me feel underdressed, and I'll never forget her response. She handed me a linen bag and said, 'Rosalina, it is time you feel like the queen you are!' I opened it to see the most amazing deep royal blue silk I'd ever seen. Eden, she had brought me a dress. Of course, at the time, I didn't know it was actually from a different world." Rosalina's eyes sparkled as I watched her recall the moment.

"So of course we immediately went back to my apartment and I tried it on. And Ava was right, I felt like a queen. It tied around my neck and plunged down to here!" She gestured to her sternum area and started laughing, "Of course, my girls were much perkier back then . . ." I almost choked on my Moscato, laughing when we both noticed the waiter had walked up at the perfect moment. They had come here that night, both adorned in their regal dresses, and had a night to remember. I tried to imagine them there, sitting a table eating and laughing, carefree. It wasn't too hard to do, being there myself with Rosalina. As if she sensed what I was thinking, she whispered, "Being here with you feels like being in a time machine." She reached into her purse and pulled out an envelope.

"I have something for you, Eden."

I took the envelope carefully and opened it. On the back of a 5x7 picture, the words "Me and Ava at Excelsior Vittoria" were handwritten. I took a deep breath and turned the picture over. There she was; standing tall with a beaming smile, her arm wrapped around a younger version of Rosalina. Ava looked just as Rosalina had described, and just like she looked in my dreams. Her long thick hair was loosely braided and pulled around to her front, falling down below her waist. She had what looked like dark green vines woven through her hair that matched her dress. She was stunning. Her eyes were wild and bright, a lavender color just as Rosalina said. I'm not sure how long I sat there staring at the picture, tears in my eyes, before Rosalina spoke again.

"You are so much like your mother, not just your appearance, but your posture. The easy way you laugh. And despite all of the hardships you have endured and confusion you are working through, I see that joy and positivity always win with you." Rosalina's hand was on my hand. She squeezed and added, "That . . . the ability to radiate joy is what makes you special and unique, not where you are from."

Those would be words I'd cling to for the rest of my life.

THE UNCERTAINTY.

I sat on the veranda at Le Sirene, back in Positano, a couple of days later. Rosalina and I had spent some wonderful and memorable time together. I'd almost forgotten about all of the crazy Door Keeper stuff. But, of course, it began to bubble to the surface again when I was alone. After hearing about my desire to start journaling, Rosalina was kind enough to give me her own diary from over thirty years ago. It was a beautiful gift, being able to read about my mother from her point of view. This personal account of her was unexpected, and more than I could have asked for. I glanced back into the villa at the long blue dress that hung on the door. Rosalina had kept it all these years. She confided she only wore it that one night at Excelsior Vittoria, and she knew my mother would have wanted me to have it. I couldn't bring myself to try it on. Somehow, it would have made everything feel too real. I took a sip of coffee and skipped ahead to read more about my mother.

"I'm at a loss. It's hard for me to imagine a world without Ava. Mine or hers. She has been gone 2 days, already it feels like so much longer. The only thing reminding me of the short time is her daughter, Eden. So new and fragile. I don't know what to do. I want to take care of her so badly. I see so much of Ava in her, and selfishly I don't want to lose her. But I'm scared and alone. I don't

think I can raise her by myself. But, I made Ava a promise, and I'm just not sure how to fulfill that promise. I want to do what is best for sweet Eden. I just wish I knew what that is. I can't put her in the system here, but what other options do I have? God, what do I do?"

I looked up at the Amalfi Coast. Storm clouds rolled in. They were thick, dark, and ominous. I couldn't help but feel like it symbolized the oncoming shift in my life. How could it go back to the way it was? The wind picked up and whipped the scent of the salty air through the apartment. Rain fell far out on the horizon, reluctant to come to shore. I picked up the key that hung around my neck and studied it. Infinity symbols intertwined to form a larger intricate pattern. I rubbed my thumb over the bits, wondering how old it was and what kind of power I held in my hand. Whatever Door this key unlocked had the most intense locking mechanism. I'd never seen a key like this before. I let it drop to my chest and went back into the villa to splash some water over my face. Different worlds. Doors, plural. My mind couldn't stop replaying the conversations I had with Rosalina. I decided to go for a walk. I grabbed my now completely ordinary looking house key and left everything else behind.

As I walked down the first flight of stairs down toward the coast, I recalled the nearly memorized journal entry of Rosalina's about my parents taking me home.

"I feel so torn and divided. I'm relieved and yet devastated. I found a loving home for Eden, but I had to say good-bye. The Browns came to visit Ava today. After hearing she had died, they asked to see Eden. Of course, they fell in love with her as quickly as I did.

There was too much of Ava in her not to. They offered to take her, off the record. Of course, there was no record anyway. I knew this was the answer, but letting her go was so much harder than I thought possible. I feel like I've lost my friend all over again. And now Eden is gone. What if I never see her again? What have I done? I didn't want to give them the key . . . .How could I have explained? What was I supposed to say? Who will believe me? I'm not even sure how to feel.

"I wish there was a way to let Ava's husband and family know what has happened, that Eden is okay. She never told me where the Door was, and even if she did, what am I supposed to do? I feel so helpless. I hope I did the right thing. The most upsetting thing is that I may never know."

I'd spent nearly every day with Rosalina since the day we met. I spoke to her about this journal entry, and questions she might still have about her decision thirty years ago, assuring her she did the right thing. We talked all about my life in Georgia, and my wonderful childhood. She saw pictures of Gabby and the new art gallery. We discussed having a great love, losing it, and figuring out how to get back on your feet again. If nothing else, I gave her the closure she deserved for giving me an incredible life with a loving family.

I was thankful for my life. It had been full of unconditional love, joy, and security. I never once felt like an orphan. I never felt alone, scared, or even unsure of my standing in the world. My parents taught me to be secure and confident in who I am—or at least, who I was.

But now who was I?

As I reached the beach, the wind picked up in strength. I kicked off my flip flops and walked to the shoreline, allowing my linen pants to soak up the sea water. I realized that was what was so unsettling to me. I had spent my entire life secure in who I was, feeling confident in what made me different from those around me. I embraced the things others considered odd. I knew all of those things about myself and I'd never questioned them. Now, I couldn't help but question everything. I always knew I was a little different than those around me, but now I felt nothing like those around me.

Who am I? What am I?

For the first time in my life, I had no idea. My feet sunk deeper and deeper into the sand. My mind flashed back to the conversation I'd had with Rosalina a few days before about what she'd done with Ava after she died.

"She asked me to cremate her as was their custom in Caelum. They didn't bury their dead there. So, I had her cremated, and I spread her ashes on our favorite beach to visit together. She loved the ocean, and told me it reminded her of home." It was funny to think about how I had never met my birth mother but we were so similar. I'd always loved the ocean, but now I knew it would always remind me of her and the home I'd never seen.

I felt the grains being pulled out from underneath me. My footing became increasingly unsteady. The waves crashed against my knees and the rain finally came ashore. I allowed it engulf me, along with all of the random thoughts swimming in my mind.

My mother was from another world; a world on the other side of a Door. My father may or may not be alive in that other world. I, apparently, had a destiny.

I raised my chin toward the sky. The cool rain felt refreshing hitting my face. I felt so lost and numb the storm could've swallowed me whole and I wouldn't have noticed.

I stood in the rain for what seemed like hours, rolling over everything my mind would allow. It was not lost on me how my mother gave her life so I could have mine. Her face consumed every fiber of my being. I thought about the picture Rosalina had given me. It made me wonder—how I had dreamt her face for a year before ever seeing it? How I dreamt young Rosalina before I'd ever met her? It was a mystery how I could see so vividly into the past, but like all of this new information I'd learned, I had to believe there was a purpose.

Another face popped into my mind. My sweet Gabby. How did all of this affect her? Did this mean she was otherworldly too? Probably, but I couldn't tell her. How could I expect her to understand what I couldn't? Ava died doing what was best for me. I could bury and forget all of this nonsense, if it would be best for my own daughter. But I wasn't convinced it was.

As I stood there on the Spiaggia Grande, the rain falling on my face, my thoughts drifted back to a time a few years ago when Gabby and I got caught in a rainstorm with the top down in my convertible. I smiled to myself when I remembered how hard we laughed. We drove down Arnold Mill, racing back home as fast as we could, but we finally had to pull over on the side of the road, at the field with the Door, to put the top back up.

The Door in the field. The one that led seemingly nowhere. Everything snapped into focus.

I was wrong. I could not bury this. I knew it was time to go home.

THE KEY.

I flew home with a lot more baggage than I'd left with, though no one would notice on the surface. On the plane ride home, I decided on a believable story I could tell Gabby. Obviously, I would leave out the "mythical worlds only accessible through magical Doors and keys" part for the time being. I would tell her about Rosalina. I could tell Gabby how she recognized me on the street, and how we spent days talking about Ava. This alone would give her wonderful, new information about my mother without revealing the unbelievable stuff. It would also explain the blue dress and my newfound friendship with Rosalina. I'd explain how she and Ava met, and what a special friendship they shared—one that spanned over a year.

I hated lying to Gabby, but there were still so many unknowns that the whole truth was something I didn't even know how to explain. I mean, was this really how a mother/daughter conversation was supposed to go down? "I'm sorry, Gabby, but in order to finish your family tree project, we will have to find a magical Door somewhere in Italy, use this older than dirt key to open it, and then explore another realm/world to find my father, who may or may not be alive."

Yeah, I'd stick with the simpler story. At least I had the picture to show her, which was a gift we'd both treasure. However, I would need to keep Rosalina's journals a secret.

Once I arrived at the Atlanta airport, I was ecstatic to see Gabby, Danielle, and Emmie. I threw my arms around my sweet baby girl and lifted her up, swinging her around. She had grown up so much since I'd been gone—or maybe I was the one who had done the growing. In the car, all three girls fired off questions faster than I could answer them.

"What did you bring me?"

"What was your favorite food?"

"Did you eat a lot of gelato?"

"How good looking were the men?"

"Was it as hot there is it is here?"

"What did you find out about your mother?"

"What did you bring me?"

I couldn't help but laugh and answer their questions in the same shotgun rhythm.

"What did I *not* bring you? Mushroom ravioli. Too much. Absolutely. Not nearly as humid. I met a nurse from the hospital where I was born. And I brought you shoes."

At the mention of the nurse, they fell quiet. They wanted to know more, but I told them I would tell them the whole story when we got home. The remaining drive we talked about the beach, the church I toured, and the amazing food. They asked me to tell them things in Italian, as apparently I was a quick study—a trait I assumed I inherited from Ava.

Over a dinner of Danielle's Italian specialty, spaghetti, I told them about Rosalina, how she recognized me because I looked like Ava, their friendship, and a few of the "safe" stories that I had read from her journal. I explained the story about the blue dress. It was more difficult than expected to explain how Ava died during childbirth. They hung on every word. Retelling it for the first time, I realized how amazing the story actually was, even without the magical Door to another world. A woman who was present during my birth thirty years later recognized me on the street of foreign city because I looked like my mother. I showed them the picture of Ava and they agreed it wasn't as farfetched as one might think. Besides the length of our hair and my facial piercings, we looked almost identical. As I looked at Gabby I saw Ava in her, too. To see Gabby's face light up when she saw her biological grandmother was incredibly special. Thankfully, the news and picture filled their appetite and no deeper questions were asked.

After tucking Gabby into bed, I grabbed the key from Rosalina, my mother's key, and got in my car. It was a warm night, the moon full, so I put the top down and drove to the only place I had been thinking of for the past thirty-six hours. Once I saw the Door peeking from behind the trees, I slowed the car down to a crawl and pulled off onto the side of the road. Stepping out of the car, I walked around to the front, and sat on the hood. I pulled the key out from under my shirt and took it off my neck, rubbing it on the worn-down sections. My mother had used this key. How many Doors had she opened with it?

I looked at the Door on the edge of the field, seeing it clearly in the moonlight. Is this why I was so drawn to this Door? If Rosalina was right, could this Door lead to another world? I wanted so badly to try the key, but I also knew that if this key did work, then whatever was waiting for me on the other side of the Door was not something I wanted to tackle tonight. I stared at the Door as I got back in the car, and chills slowly covered my body.

What I could not have possibly known was that as clearly as I could see the Door, he could see me. He was watching me. And, although he could not tell exactly what I held, he knew enough to guess what it was, and why I was there. He knew I was a threat, and now, I was on his radar.

ℒ ℒ ℒ ℒ ℒ

My attempt on the Door would have to wait as I went into the weekend with Gabby. We had lost time to make up for. After eating lunch at our favorite restaurant on Main Street, we checked in on the gallery. Wall Polish got two more bookings for art shows, and if I hadn't been carrying the key and thinking about my mother, life might have felt normal.

The weekend closed helping Gabby finish her family tree project. She decided to include Ava, but also to include my adoptive parents' family "trunks," too. We used my art studio over the garage to paint a tree on a large canvas for her to use. It was a lovely way to spend our Sunday together, but it did little to distract from the key now hidden in my top dresser drawer.

The next morning, as I watched Gabby get on the bus, the minor distraction turned into a complete hijacking. The only thing I could think of was the Door and the key and my Door Keeper lineage. Before I knew it, I was right back on the side of road, staring at the unknown, with the worn, old mystery key in tow. I walked across the street and started to cut across the field, feeling every blade of grass as it beckoned me. Stepping closer, I could see the Door's intricacies, beautiful markings never noticed from the road. The hinges were attached to a tree, and the Door itself was built into two different trees. Someone had either grown these trees around the Door, or built the Door to fit into the trees. Either way, it was impressive. The Door was multiple shades of green, some parts having faded under the sun. Some of the green paint chipped off to expose a dark, bold orange beneath. I noticed rectangular inlaid panels, giving the Door an odd sense of depth. The handle was a dark bronze-ish golden material. It matched the key perfectly. My heart began racing. As I approached the Door, I pulled out the key. They were definitely made of the same material. At this, my heart beat loudly in my ears. Could all of this be true? Could this Door take me to a different world?

Completely distracted, I never noticed the small cameras attached to the trees about fifty feet on either side of the Door.

I held the key up to keyhole and paused.

Was I about to do this? What other world would it unlock? What answers to my past lay on the other side?

I inserted the key and turned slowly, as far right as it would turn. I pulled on the Door.

Nothing.

I tried turning it the other way.

Nothing.

I tried right, one last time.

Nothing again.

I should have known. Feeling foolish, I slowly began pulling the key out, but suddenly felt it catch, and in that instant, it felt like the key was made for my hand. *That's right*, I remembered, it had *multiple* bits. Maybe I had to turn it multiple times. Where it caught, it allowed me to turn it even further right, and pulling it out more slowly, it allowed one last turn. I pulled on the Door. It opened. In that moment, I knew nothing would ever be the same. My life as I knew it was over. This was a step closer to finding out more about Ava and whatever destiny she referred to. I felt nothing other than my heart, beating in my throat.

Inhaling deeply, I pulled the key out, put it around my neck, opened the Door and walked through it.

THE NEW WORLD.

It took me a moment to adjust. A slight thin film developed and slid over my eyeballs. I blinked a few times to make sure that whatever had just happened didn't impede my eyesight. It felt natural, although I'd never experienced anything like it before. I turned to see if the Door was there, and thankfully, it was. It looked the same as the other side, but was built into the trunk of a large, overgrown, twisted tree. I looked up and followed the enormous tree as it disappeared behind a dense fog overhead. After inspecting the Door, checking the key fit, and feeling confident I could re-enter back into my own world, I turned around slowly to take in my new surroundings.

Everything was dry and dusty. A thick heaviness permeated the air, almost as though it was slowly solidifying around me. I felt every square inch of air that touched my skin. I realized my body sensed the change before I did, and that must be why my eyes formed a barrier. I was suddenly grateful they had. I began to find breathing extremely difficult. The air seemed to sit in my lungs, unmoving. Before I panicked, I stripped off my tank and wrapped it around my mouth and nose, pulling the bottom through the arm holes and tucking it snug, yet loose enough to allow air to flow. It seemed to filter the air enough for my lungs, for the moment.

I looked at the land that stretched before me. While dry and desolate, it was breathtaking. There were rolling hills as far as I could see, with large trees seemingly strategically placed every hundred yards or so in every direction. It looked as though they were all equally distanced apart. They grew tall and twisted as the one did behind me, nothing like what grew in north Georgia. They, too, all disappeared behind the intense cloud cover overhead. Besides the trees, everything within my view seemed muted and barren. I couldn't see any colors other than varying shades of brown. I looked closer at the enormous trees. As the trees grew taller, they had more and more root-like branches that sprouted into the dense fog above. Some fell straight down into the ground. As much as this all was new and incredibly exciting, it had a twinge of familiarity.

As I shook the eerie feeling of recognition, I decided to explore this new world before me. Then I froze with an intense realization that I had just entered another world through a Door, with a key that I had inherited from my mother. Had I just become a Door Keeper? Was this the first step toward fulfilling my destiny?

My first step proved more difficult than I thought. The weight of the air around me felt like attempting to move through sand. It was much easier to pull my foot up and out than it was to push it back down. Huh. Attempt number two was no easier. Trying to understand my surroundings, I raised my hands up and straight out, in the shape of a T. Then completely relaxed them only to watch them slowly drift back down to my sides. It was one of the oddest sensations. It took them about six seconds to fall completely. Completely intrigued, I decided to put this new gravity to the test. I stiffened my body and tried to fall backward. I actually had to push myself backward, which is completely counterintuitive. The air shifted around me, with no additional pressure from any direction. Fascinating. It took about ten seconds before I hit the ground. Getting up was another story. It took me over a full minute to stand back up. The slower I moved, the less pressure. The last experiment I tried was to jump. Unsuccessful. I couldn't gain any momentum. Only my legs rose with the rest of my body staying in place. My feet made it about a foot off the ground, but I stayed there for a second before they slowly began to drift back down to the earth beneath me. Now that was crazy. It also gave me another idea. I bent my knees and raised my feet up toward my body then tried to stand up, and as I landed about a foot off the ground, I quickly attempted it again. It worked, and there I hovered two feet off the ground. I furiously tried to start walking as though I was walking up stairs.

Before I knew it, I was at least ten feet in the air. I was still under the tree that the Door was built into when I noticed one of the root like branches about twenty-five feet in front of me. I knew if I could get to that branch, I could rest a bit. This was exhausting work. I slowly climbed the invisible stairs to the branch and sat down. I was now about fifty feet above the ground. I could see the Door at the base of the tree where I came through, and looked up to see that the dense cloud cover started about one hundred more feet above me. If this was something I wanted to attempt, I would need an easier way than defying this crazy gravity much longer. My legs were burning as it was. I noticed a branch that came straight down through the cloud and into the ground. If I could get to it, I could climb it the rest of the way. Ignoring the rational voice in my head that maybe this wasn't a good idea, I slowly and painfully made my way to the branch.

As I climbed higher and higher, I noticed a slight shift of gravity. It seemed a little easier to move, but still stable and supporting me, which my aching muscles greatly appreciated. Finally, I came upon the edge of the never-ending cloud. I reached out and cupped some of the moisture in my hand. It was borderline solidified, almost like a gel. Curiously, it was dry. I had gone this far, and it seemed silly to turn around now, so I pushed through head first. I climbed the branch for what seemed like forever, holding my breath, unsure of the gel-like fog.

When my head reached the clearing, I felt the immediate difference and no longer struggled to breathe. I untied the shirt around my head and flung it over my shoulder to keep climbing. Ah, sweet, fresh air. I inhaled deeply to fill every square inch of my lungs. Revived, I finished climbing and saw a wide branch to sit on and recoup. As I rested my weary body, I quickly slipped my shirt back on. When I looked around, I was shocked. It was a completely different world up here than it was below.

The sky was clear and a yellowish peach. All of the tree branches were intertwined to form pathways in every direction. Flowers bloomed from most of them in almost every color imaginable. I saw all kinds of unnamed flying creatures, plus butterflies, bees, and birds of all size and shape. None of them took notice of me. I stood slowly, got my bearings, and started walking. Besides the branches in all directions, it was hard to imagine I was walking in a tree. Every animal looked hard at work, busy carrying pollen or making nests. I took notice of a large flock of tiny birds moving in unison, as though they were a school of fish flying through the air. I passed a large diagonal branch with hundreds of chrysalides hanging from it. They looked like glass ornaments hanging on a Christmas tree. I was trying to take in all the sights and smells when a branch cracked to my left. I quickly cowered behind the closest large tree trunk and tried to see the culprit, but saw nothing. Maybe I was being paranoid, being in up in a tree in a new world I'd never been to and all. But a couple seconds later I heard it again, and knew something or someone was there.

"Hello? I know you're there. I'm not here to hurt you," I said in the sweetest tone I could muster.

Nothing.

"My name is Eden Cherubini, and I'm a friend." I had no idea why I used that name.

Someone peeked out slowly from behind a branch. Once she saw my face, she must have decided that I was trustworthy, because she flitted up and over the branch in one swoop, landing perfectly on the branch below. She stood with her arms on her hips and her head tilted to one side. She was studying me, as I was her. She was only a child. Her hair was a curly reddish pink, and her skin was so light, it was almost translucent. She had incredibly huge bright green eyes that took up almost a third of her face. Her mouth was small, her lips were pursed at me as though she disapproved. Her body was petite and extremely slim, and it wasn't until she lifted her arms above her head that I noticed her thin wings. They resembled what you would see if you looked into a large bubble, with multi-colors floating through them. As she gracefully moved her arms back and forth, the wings carried her to me with little effort. She landed a couple of feet beside me on the same branch. She was only about three feet tall, and wore no clothes, but had no visible parts of which to be embarrassed. I noticed that her arms and legs were stained with color, almost as though her limbs were painted with watercolor. That answered my modesty question. She startled me when she spoke.

"Hello, Eden, my name is Lolli. Welcome to Terra Arborum, Land of Trees." Her voice sounded like music.

Land of Trees made sense. I realized she was waiting for me to respond, so I said the only reasonable thing you can say to human-butterfly hybrid.

"You are so tiny . . ." Realizing I might have offended her, I quickly added, ". . . and so beautiful!" She laughed at me. Her laugh resembled bells.

"Well, hello, Eden, it is nice to meet you." She stuck her tiny hand out in an offering of peace. I reached out and gently grabbed her hand, afraid I would break it. She was so intensely delicate.

"You seem to know a lot about my customs," referring to the handshake, "and you speak English?"

Her voice rang quietly and beautifully, "Well, of course we have our own language, but you are not the first celestial I have met. Are you a Door Keeper from Caelum or Earth? Forgive me, you have traits of both."

I wasn't prepared for that. I had barely begun to comprehend where I'd come from myself, much less to be able to explain it to a . . . what I can only describe as a butterflairy. So, I gave it my best shot. "My parents were from Caelum, but I was raised on Earth . . . in Earth. On Earth?"

Lolli smiled as me sweetly. "No wonder I had such trouble placing you. I thought for sure you were from Caelum, but then you spoke English so perfectly. Plus, the Doors for all of the other worlds are hundreds of miles away."

"So you are a Door Keeper?" I asked her in shock.

"Well, no. We do not have Door Keepers here. We all are aware the Doors exist, but would never dream of going through them. We are an extremely fragile and peaceful people. We would not last a day in your worlds. Plus, our wings are only strong enough for our own gravity. We trust all of the Door Keepers in the other worlds to keep us safe and protected. We provide them help with agriculture issues and special foods in exchange for their protection. We have lived here for thousands of years without a problem or danger."

I suddenly wondered if my being here was a danger to them. I didn't have long to ponder it before Lolli flitted up and gracefully flew around me. She stopped at my tattoo.

"Oh, these are beautiful! When did you visit us before?" she asked in her singsong voice.

"I've never been here before. This is the first time I have come through a Door."

She looked at me, surprised. Her long thin eyebrows almost leapt off her face. She pursed her lips at me again. "How is that possible?" She pointed at my tattoo. "This flower right here is only grown here, in Arborum."

How was that possible? I painted my tattoo based on several different dreams I had of fields of flowers growing up. How could I have known about these if they were here? She grabbed my hand and started flying slowly, pulling me alongside her. She started humming a beautiful song. She rotated between whistling and humming, a soft song, then crescendoing into what sounded like an epic ballad. I started to notice animals following us. Butterflies, birds, and large bees closely followed. Suddenly, I saw more butterflairies appear. I realized she wasn't singing. She was speaking to them. This was her language, and it was as enchanting as she was.

We rounded an abnormally large tree trunk when I saw them. Stretched out before us was an expansive field of thickly interwoven branches covered with the flower from my tattoo. It was a light turquoise, large hibiscus-looking flower with a smaller white rose-type flower growing out of its center. People always assumed it was two different flowers, but I had painted it to be one. The air smelled so sweet. I walked toward the field and looked around. I asked Lolli if I could pick one, and she agreed. I plucked one from a branch, and held it by my shoulder. A perfect match. Amazing. Sticking it behind my ear, Lolli smiled at me.

"We call it a Serenbe." I looked around and saw all of the little butterflairies watched me with smiles. What world had I stumbled into? As unsure about it all as I was, I knew I increasingly did not want to leave.

THE BUTTERFLAIRIES.

Before I knew what was happening, I was flying through the dense air to Lolli's home. On either side of me a butterflairy held my hands. Because of the different gravity, it felt like we flew a hundred miles an hour with the wind moving around my body, but of course we were moving much slower than that. Within minutes we arrived at Lolli's home. Well, more like a tree hole. I climbed in the best I could, and looked completely disastrous next to Lolli's graceful movements. It was very small, cozy and warm. The room was incredibly simple with only a chair made of limbs, a matching table, and one large rolled up blanket. The blanket looked like it was large flower petals sewn together. She shared a space with some unusually large fireflies that lit the space in a warm, yellowish-green glow. Looking from one side to the other, I realized that if I were to stretch out my arms in either direction, I'd touch both sides. And I knew I couldn't stand up without bonking my head or injuring some of the fireflies.

Lolli offered me some tea made from the nectar of the Serenbe flower. I gladly accepted her sweet gift of hospitality. With the first sip, I was instantly transported back to Italy, drinking Moscato wine, with that familiar sweet bite. Hadn't Rosalina said my mother preferred Moscato because it reminded her of her favorite tea? Was this tea what Ava was talking about? Unsure how to process this, or if I was dreaming it, I just relaxed and enjoyed the tea. It was incredible. Sitting there, in her tiny tree hole, Lolli began to tell me about her people and their land. She tried to teach me what they called themselves in their native tongue, but I chuckled and told her there is no way I could ever pronounce that. I jokingly informed her that I had nicknamed them butterflairies, and she seemed to like it, as least enough to keep using it for my benefit.

    The butterflairies led simple, peaceful lives. They lived completely off of nature and its provisions. They nurtured and cared for the trees, pruning and cultivating them, using even the dead and broken branches, as they could be of use. They considered themselves botanists with a major in floriculture and crossbred flowers to discover new and beautiful creations. The Serenbe flower was created by one of their leaders, and named for her, over five hundred years ago—clearly, they lived for an exceptionally long time. Lolli was fifty years old, and only about a quarter into her lifespan. No one ever died from anything other than old age in Terra Arborum. She explained that butterflairies were asexual and only laid one egg per lifetime. Lolli hoped to have her daughter in another fifty years.

    As I sat there and listened to Lolli tell me all about Terra Arborum, I was in complete awe. It was fascinating to hear how they lived, and their customs and traditions, and how they were so vastly different from the world I came from. I couldn't help but wonder if this was how my mother felt spending time with Rosalina. Sitting here, drinking the Serenbe tea with Lolli, I tried to imagine my mother sitting here with us, gushing over all the little details. I'm sure she would have asked to see the hatching field where all the eggs were laid and protected until they hatched. I assumed my mother had to have visited here since I recognized the tea from here as her favorite, but I needed to know for sure.

"Lolli, do you have Door Keepers come through often?" I asked casually.

"No, definitely not. I have only ever seen one, other than you." Her voice rang softly. "It was my only time ever seeing a man. Men are interesting looking creatures." She grimaced.

I laughed, "Yes, they can be for sure. I was just curious if my mother had . . . Wait, what man?"

"It was the Door Keeper for your world, Earth. He seemed young for your species, maybe what you call . . . a teeneeg . . . a teenager?"

Interesting. This was something that I hadn't even considered. If there were Door Keepers to protect the Doors, and they were particularly protective of Terra Arborum, then I wondered why I made it through. Why didn't he stop me? "How long ago was this?"

"I think it was about fifteen years ago. But my friend, she met a woman Door Keeper from Caelum about forty years ago. Maybe that was your mother?"

Suddenly the mysterious male Door Keeper seemed less important. "Is your friend still alive?" I asked too enthusiastically.

Lolli's singsong laugh filled the air. "Yes, she was only a decade or so when she met her. She is now my age and lives in a tree a couple of hours north of here. I would be happy to take you to her if you would like."

I almost crushed a firefly in my haste to go. I was beyond excited, until I tried to calculate how long I'd been here already. If we made that trip, it would be after nightfall when I returned home. That is, if time even worked the same here. Gabby would be worried sick, and I could never do that to her. I wished my cell phone had reception in this crazy tree world so I could call Danielle and explain. But explain what exactly? My new butterflairy friend that lived in a tree and was over fifty years old, but only looked twelve, had a friend that met my mother forty years ago when she visited their magical land through a Door. With a laugh, I realized not having cell reception wasn't my biggest problem in this scenario.

I was about to explain to Lolli that I couldn't make the trip today when a loud gust of air swirled into the tree. I covered my ears. A large shadow covered the entrance of the tree. Lolli's eyes widened and grew bigger than normal, if that was even possible. She didn't look scared or upset, just surprised. She flew out of the tree and I heard her speaking to someone. Then, I heard a deep male voice. That's odd, I thought she said there were no men.

"She is just visiting, Strix. She has been very kind and friendly."

"Well, the last time I spoke with the Door Keeper, he did not mention a woman," I heard the incredibly deep raspy voice answer her.

"She is not an official Door Keeper—"

"What?" the deep voice interrupted. "Then how could you bring her here? How could you treat her as a guest, when you know very well that she is unwelcome and could bring danger?"

"If you would just talk to her, Strix, you would see that she is no threat."

"Very well, bring out the celestial."

I was suddenly extremely concerned. He was right, I'd come here uninvited. I shook when Lolli came through the opening and landed in front of me.

"You have no reason to be afraid, Eden. Strix is just very protective of us. His bark is worse than his bite, as your saying goes." I smiled, still unsure, and clumsily made my way out of her home.

I was completely unprepared for what stood before me.

THE DOOR KEEPER

The first thing I noticed were his talons. Maybe the fear in me noticed those first. They clutched a branch a few feet in front of me. As I slowly made myself look up at the face of the being who considered me an intruder, I involuntarily shuddered. In front of me stood a giant owl. He had to have been over nine feet tall. His eyes were bright and dark yellow. They bore into mine as he spoke.

"You are right to be scared." His raspy boom of a voice echoed in my ears.

"Stop frightening her, Stix. She is not a threat, and you should stop treating her like one." Lolli stood next to me and took my hand in hers. Her bravery was encouraging, and also a little humorous.

I finally found my voice. "Sir, my mother was a Door Keeper. She died when I was born. I'm sorry to intrude in your beautiful land, but I am just trying to learn and understand where she came from."

Strix's face softened. "Ah. Yes. Your mother was Ava. I'd recognize her face anywhere, especially in yours." He opened one wing and bowed with the other. "I had the pleasure of meeting her on several occasions."

"You knew my mother?" I blurted out before I could stop myself.

"Yes, but I am confused. She was Caelum's Door Keeper. Why do you speak English?"

At that, Lolli filled Strix in on my story. I was thankful for her interjection as I became overwhelmed by it all: sitting on a branch in an old twisted tree, watching a tiny butterflairy animatedly explain why I was there to a giant owl. If I hadn't lived it over the past few hours, I would have thought I'd lost my mind. Maybe I had. Maybe I had fallen in the field and hit my head on a rock and was dreaming this whole thing. I suddenly couldn't wait to tell Rosalina that she was right. These places existed.

After Strix knew my story, he offered to tell me about my mother. He noticed the Serenbe in my tattoo and the one behind my ear, and told me that it had been my mother's favorite flower. At this news, I couldn't contain my joy. This entire time, I'd been wearing a piece of my mother on my shoulder, and didn't even know it. He told me stories of their flying adventures, and how Ava used to go with him on his check-ins. Strix flew from one side to their land to the other every other month to check in on all the animals and butterflairies (obviously, Strix didn't use that term). He told me about the time Ava tried to show them how to make fire and almost burnt an entire tree down. That was the last time she tried to teach them anything from other worlds.

After almost an hour, and three Serenbe teas, I knew it was time to go. I had to pry myself from the amazing company. I had lived my whole life completely disconnected from my birth mother, and now I knew two of her friends. Strix offered to fly me back down to the Door. I hugged Lolli as we said our goodbyes, knowing we would definitely see each other again. I climbed up onto Strix's back and grabbed onto his reddish-brown feathers to keep from falling off. It was like trying to grip silk. He spread his wings and took off toward the tree with the Door. His wings moved through the air, loud and methodical. The rhythm of it relaxed me. I held on as Strix effortlessly whizzed through and around branches with ease. I recognized the place I had first met Lolli when Strix made a sharp dive and cut down between two large branches through the dense cloud cover. Knowing what was coming, I managed to strip off my shirt again and somehow not fall off. Strix slowed down before we exited the cloud and I tied the shirt around my mouth and nose again. When we finally came out of the cloud into the world below, I could see the tree with the Door. Not impacted by the denser air,

Strix came to a stop right in front of it. I slid slowly off his back, and thanked him for his hospitality and the flight of a lifetime.

He smiled and wrapped his giant wing around me. "I am truly sorry to hear about Ava's passing. Please feel welcome to visit us anytime. It was a pleasure to get to know you, Eden." With that, he turned and flew up through the clouds. As I watched him disappear, I looked out at the twisted trees one last time. I wanted to remember these beautiful root branched trees. They almost looked inside out.

I grabbed the key and put it in the Door, being careful to stop at each bit and turn it so it would open properly. Happy that it worked, and suddenly aching to see Gabby, I turned the knob and opened the Door. The air felt fresh and warm on the other side. I closed the Door behind me and pulled out the key. I yanked my tank off of my face and slid it back on. Replacing the key around my neck, I turned around and came face to face with a huge man. He forcefully grabbed the back of my neck before I could react, and after a quick sharp pain, everything went black.

THE BROTHER.

When I came to, I was in a dark room. I couldn't see anything until my eyes began to adjust. I knew I was sitting in a chair with my hands tied behind my back. I tugged on my feet and felt that they were tied to the chair as well. Duct tape covered my mouth, and a splitting headache reminded me I was very much alive. As my eyes continued to adjust, I attempted to take in details of the room. It was large and open. To my left, I saw a door with light shining through the crack at the bottom. I heard two men arguing; one shouted and the other seemed to interject, only to be shot down. I used all my energy to concentrate on their conversation.

"How could you do this?" The voice sounded horrified. "How is this *okay*?"

"What did you expect me to do?" The deeper voice sounded much calmer.

"How about *not* kidnap her?" the other snapped back.

"I did not kidnap her. I have to question her. You have to admit, this is unprecedented. Cut me some slack, man, we're in unchartered territories here."

"Well, we'd better go check on her, for heaven's sake, she's probably awake." The annoyed voice got louder as the sentence progressed.

I heard footsteps drawing closer and the door opened. Two tall figures entered. One walked behind me and grabbed a chair, and the other walked to the far side of the room and stood with his back against the wall. The one leaning on the wall reached for the light switch. It was so bright, I grimaced and squinted as my eyes readjusted to the light. Once I regained my vision an immediate shock reverberated through my body.

"Charlie?" I tried to yell through my duct taped mouth. He glanced up at me apologetically. It all hit me like a flood. The charcoal drawing over the green couch in the gallery were the trees from Terra Arborum. That was why it felt familiar; I'd seen them in his artwork. He looked to the man now crossing my line of vision who dropped a chair in front of me. He sat and faced me with a poker-face glare. It was Charlie's older brother. Despite his handsome features, my body remembered how his hand had clamped on my shoulder, and the feeling of helplessness shot through me again. I narrowed my eyes and glared right back.

"At least take the tape off so she can go ahead and let us have it. 'Cause trust me, she's gonna." Charlie half smiled at his brother.

The intimidating stranger looked at him, then back at me wearily. "If I take it off, will you relax so we can talk about what happened?"

I kept my glare, as to appear brave, raised one eyebrow and then proceeded with, "Mmmph, uu hhinnk hhhaat, ooo kkaabbbyyy."

"Point taken." The man relented and removed the tape from my mouth in one quick motion. I winced.

"I'm so sorry, Eden," Charlie whined.

"Charlie, what the hell?" I yelled. Anger fueled me with adrenaline.

The stranger fired back, "Don't you worry about Charlie. You worry about me."

"You," I said glaring at Charlie, ". . . you are *so* fired. And as for you," I turned my attention back to my abductor. "You big oaf, I don't know who you think you are, but—"

"Where did you get this?" Charlie's brother cut me off. He was holding up my key. I glanced down to see it missing from around my neck.

"Give that back, you—"

"Big oaf?" the man finished, almost laughing. "I'm sorry, Eden, but I fail to see what you're going to do about it. Now, we can either sit here and talk about this like adults, or I can leave you for another hour or so until you're ready." He sat calmly and stared me down. I noticed the Serenbe flower that had been tucked behind my ear was squashed on the floor.

"My flower!" Not able to contain my hurt, I blurted, "you stepped on it with your fat foot! That was special to me."

"More special than this?" He dangled the key in front of my face.

I desperately wanted my key back, so I chose to take a deep breath and play whatever game this was.

"Okay. You obviously know who I am. Charlie, I assume this is your brother. Do you have a name?" I looked at him with wide eyes and spoke to him like was a child. Very adult of me, I know.

He smiled at my sarcasm. "James."

I returned his smile with an over-the-top fake smile of my own. "Well, James, the key was a gift from a friend."

"Did your friend tell you about the Door, too?" he asked a little more intensely.

"No, she didn't." I sighed, too tired to keep up with the charade.

"Then how did you know the key worked with the Door?"

"Just a hunch." I shrugged.

By now I had fully inventoried the room. It was a large 20x20 foot space with a couch and mini kitchen to my left. It took me a minute to understand what I was looking at to my right. There was a wall with about a dozen monitors that looked like surveillance. I noticed the Door from the field covered from several different angles and distances. This was where he watched the Doors.

"*You* are the Door Keeper?" I exhaled in complete surprise without meaning to.

"What?" Charlie immediately responded.

"How do you know that term?" James looked surprised.

At that moment, I realized I was in no danger. This guy was just as shocked as I was about the fact I had a key and had just come out of another realm. He protected Terra Arborum and the butterflaires just as they had warned me he did. I was equal parts relieved and nervous, unsure how to make him understand I wasn't a threat. I was also keenly aware that he held the fate of whether I could visit Terra Arborum again, and in order to, I needed to be on his good side.

"Oh, boy. I think we have a lot to talk about. Why don't you untie my hands and I will tell you the whole story." I changed my tone and lost all traces of sarcasm. I looked at him and Charlie with all the sincerity I could muster. He eyed me suspiciously. I quickly added, "Seriously, I'm sorry for acting bratty. This whole Door Keeper, keys, and butterflairies thing is all very new to me."

"Butterflairies?" James and Charlie asked in unison.

"You know, the winged people who live in Terra Arborum," I replied seriously.

James' face relaxed with laughter. "Well, your name for them is certainly easier to pronounce." At this Charlie smiled. The tension in the room vanished. James cut the tape around my hands and feet. Charlie brought me some coffee that tasted just enough like the

Serenbe flower for me to ask about it. The nectar was part of their gift in exchange for protection, just like Lolli had said.

As I sat in the room with Charlie and James, they explained the house we were in was on the property of the Door. I also found out time passed the same in Terra Arborum as it did here. It was only around noon, which was a great relief. Gabby wasn't worried or waiting for me. As I became more confident and comfortable with my surroundings, I began to tell them parts of my story. Starting with the family tree project, I laid out my visit to Italy, Rosalina, the key, my mother, and the story just kept flowing. I wasn't even sure that I should be telling anyone any of this, but I couldn't seem to stop myself. I explained that I had always noticed the Door, and then launched into my time in Terra Arborum. It was such a great relief to tell my story to people who would understand it, and even believe it. James admitted to seeing me parked on the side of the road by the Door the night I returned home. The first night I had the key. He was walking the perimeter of his land when he saw and stopped to watch me.

"Although, that wasn't the first time you caught my attention," he said, looking at me intently. I remembered the first time I saw him at the gallery opening. He had looked at me just as curiously then. He knew I wasn't from this world even before I did.

"What gave it away?" I asked.

"I knew when I saw your tattoo. There are less than a handful of people alive in this world who have ever seen that flower. But honestly, once you've been around Doors and different worlds, you just learn to sense the different types of presence you feel when encountering someone new. In some worlds, like in Caelum, the inhabitants look a lot like us. But in others, they look like completely different creatures." He paused and looked at me. "Didn't you always feel different? I don't mean this to come off wrong, but your features are so unnatural for here, between your skin and eye color, and your hair."

"Geez, James, you basically just called her a freak," Charlie scolded him.

He blushed and apologized for the first time since our encounter and I smiled. "I promise, I didn't take it that way. I understood what you meant. I did always feel different, like I didn't really belong. But I knew I was adopted from an early age, so I just always wrote it off as that. Honestly, feeling different has become as natural to me as breathing."

I asked the brothers why they thought I was drawn to the Door. James explained that he's known where most of the Doors were since he was a young boy, but that there is an energy that surrounds them, and that Door Keepers tend to pick up that energy. That even if he wasn't aware of a Door, he could detect its location based on that alone. And he guessed because I had passed through it before, granted in utero, my body and mind recognized it. That was why he didn't have to guard the Doors too intensely, because the average person would never have noticed it. Arnold Mill Road had been there over twenty-five years, but people had traveled that path for hundreds of years, and I was the first to ever approach it—besides kids running across it, playing in the fields. In fact, of all the Doors that he watched, this one was the one he had to watch the least. Until now, he added with a grin.

Throughout our conversation, I noticed Charlie growing grumpier and grumpier. Finally, James asked him what was wrong. "Well, I'm actually kind of mad at myself for not seeing it. I've been working for you for almost a year and I didn't put two and two together. How did I miss it?"

"Well, Charlie, I've been living in this world for thirty and didn't figure it out. Cut yourself a break," I replied with a chuckle.

"Yeah, but I've heard all the stories. I've lived with Door Keepers my entire life," he replied, upset with himself.

"Speaking of that," I had a sudden thought, "any chance you have any artwork from other worlds? I'd love to see them if you do."

"That depends," Charlie said wryly. "Am I still fired?"

THE SERENBES.

It had been a week since my trip to Terra Arborum, and Charlie, James, and I agreed I needed some time to process everything. Unfortunately, the visit through the Door did little to answer any questions I had about Ava's predicted destiny for me. All it did was stir up more questions that I didn't have time or energy to address.

D and I had some new artwork to install at the gallery, and Gabby had her weekly singing and drama classes, and I had to act like I was still living in a normal world without the possibility of entering others. Responsibilities like teaching painting classes at the community center, laundry, and homework with Gabby stole my focus and attention. I begrudgingly fell back into business as usual the day after leaving James and Charlie's house.

However, my responsibilities ended every night as I put Gabby to bed. And every night since the "Door" day, I sat on the front porch, drank a glass of wine, and replayed the scenes from start to finish. After returning from Italy, I began journaling every day. It was a wonderful way for me to work through my feelings and allow myself to comprehend this new life I had accidentally entered into. Plus, after reading Rosalina's journal entries about my mother, the idea of having it all written down to share with Gabby one day made it feel less like lying to her.

One specific night I wrestled with the realization that of the few Doors that existed in this world, Eric and I had moved within seven miles of one. What did that mean? Was I destined to find the Door? If I was, then why did I have to travel halfway across the world to Italy to discover they existed? I wanted to call Rosalina and tell her everything, but something stopped me. I knew she would believe me, and that she would be a great comfort, but I couldn't make myself call.

Most nights, I simply stared at the stars, wondering what night looked like in Terra Arborum. Did they have stars? I imagined what the world looked like with all the giant fireflies flying around at night. I wrote about when I met Lolli, and what it felt like when the wind engulfed me while flying on Strix's back. I had to go back. But my responsibilities here, in this world, weighed heavily on me; like a brick tethering a balloon to the ground.

*****

My phone vibrated and I sat my paintbrush down to check it. James. Again. I ignored it like I had all the other times. Poor Charlie had come up to Wall Polish a couple days ago, and I practically chased him out of the gallery. I just couldn't handle it. I wasn't sure why I avoided them, but I couldn't bring myself to see or talk to either of them. Whatever it was, it was the same thing keeping me from calling Rosalina. I slipped my phone back into my pocket and re-dipped my brush into the light blue paint.

Painting was another outlet I used to process everything. Writing was my way to record, and painting was my way to remember. The only thing I was completely sure of was that I didn't want to forget any of it. I was upstairs in my studio, in the middle of painting one of the branches from Arborum with chrysalides hanging off of it when I heard someone open the door downstairs in the garage. Danielle called this morning wanting to borrow my car, so I hollered, "Up here, sweetie!" Feet sounded coming up the stairs.

"Sweetie, huh? I didn't know our relationship had reached that level, yet."

My paintbrush paused on the canvas and I closed my eyes. Dang it.

"You know, not answering your calls should have clued you in," I said slowly as I turned to see James standing in the doorway, holding a large bouquet of Serenbes. He smiled when he saw my surprise as my eyes locked on the beautiful flowers.

"I felt really bad about crushing your flower. I knew it meant a lot, so I thought I'd attempt to make it up to you." He smiled genuinely and then chuckled. "But honestly, *sweetie*, you didn't have to dress up for me." He grinned at me.

I looked down at my painting clothes and laughed myself. I wore a pair of over-sized dark blue cotton overalls with a white tank underneath. My hair was thrown up in a bandana. I looked like I should have been riveting sheet metal in the 1950s, not to mention I had paint over most of my exposed skin.

"What can I say, I'm a messy painter."

"You're a talented painter. That is amazing. It's been years since I've seen above the cloud cover in Terra Arborum, but I'd recognize that anywhere," James said, inspecting my painting.

"James, I know you're not here to critique my work . . . so why are you here?"

"Easy, you weren't returning my calls. Charlie said you haven't spoken to him since last week, other than to make him leave work early. I wanted to check on you. Are you doing alright?"

He looked at me too intensely for my own comfort, so I distracted myself with cleaning my brushes. "I'm fine. It's just a lot to digest, and I'm taking my time working through it."

"I know it's a lot to digest, that's why I'm here. I thought it would help if you had someone to talk to about all of this."

"James . . ." I looked at him, frustrated, not knowing what to say.

"Eden, I've had my whole life to wrap my brain around this craziness. You've had two weeks. I know we had a rocky introduction, but I can help you. You need a friend. Trust me, this is not something to work through alone."

"Well, I've had a lot of experience being alone. It's comfortable, and it's easier for me." It was getting harder for me to push him away with us standing in the same tiny room. Not to mention that he knew and understood some of the most complicated things about me, things even I hadn't worked through, yet.

"Listen, Eden, it may be easier, but it's not better. Look, let's go put these Serenbes in water and talk over some ice cream."

I shot him a surprised look.

"Don't look so shocked. Charlie has worked for you for almost a year. You are an open book. I personally like Neapolitan."

"Well, there will be none of that garbage in my freezer," I relented.

A few minutes later we were in the kitchen. I put the flowers in a vase I found under the sink.

"What am I supposed to say when Danielle comes in here and sees these flowers?"

"Well, they'll most likely die in a day or two, anyway. Our air lacks necessary nutrients to sustain it as long as it lives there. Plus, she may not even notice since you have one on your shoulder. I meant to ask you about that . . . if you'd never been to Terra Arborum, how did you know about Serenbes?"

"I'm not sure. I dreamt about them as a kid. They were beautiful and unusual, and so I painted them. Then fell in love with the painting enough to get it tattooed a year after Gabby was born," I answered while handing him a bowl of chocolate ice cream with chocolate chips.

James took the bowl, rolled his eyes at me and took a bite. "Huh, not bad. Guess it'll do." It was my turn to roll my eyes. "So what did your husband say when you got your tattoo?"

I shot him a surprised look. "Well, you're just jumping right in, huh?" We settled on the front porch in a pair of rocking chairs.

"Well, I'm not going to lie. I'm curious about you and your past."

"What happened to me being an open book?" I asked.

"Charlie never felt comfortable asking about it. And you may be open about your fave desserts and movies, but you seem to be a hard nut to crack about the serious stuff."

"That's because no one likes to relive pain," I answered, staring down at my bowl of ice cream.

"I'm sorry, Eden, I didn't mean to pry. We don't have to talk about it." He paused for beat. "Listen, I haven't told you any of my story. I think it's only fair that you learn about me before I hear any more about you."

James spent the next hour telling me about how he came to be a Door Keeper. His given name was James Musgrove. The first Door Keeper in his family was born to Mary Musgrove in 1736. Mary was a Yamacraw Native American who was an interpreter for James Oglethorpe, founder of the colony of Georgia. Mary and James had a brief affair after her first husband died. She gave birth to James, named for his father, before she remarried a different man.

Part of Mary's job was to maintain peaceful relations between the settlers and the Native Americans. She traveled with her son all around the colony to maintain the peace. Oglethorpe took very good care of her and her son financially, especially after her second husband died.

When her son, James, went out on his own, he used his wealth and status to travel further into the colony, exploring. His relationship with the Creeks and Cherokees allowed him access to lands beyond where the settlers had traveled. Eventually, he came across a legend told to him from a local chief about a Door that led to a mysterious land.

James became obsessed with finding the Door, and after twenty-five years of searching every square mile he traveled, he found it. He purchased the land from the natives who owned it, and it had been their family's land since. Although it took him another decade to figure out how to actually open the Door, James told me jokingly that was a story for another day. The eldest son of the family had carried the job title since then. Over ten generations of Musgrove's had protected the Door.

James had been the Door Keeper since he turned twenty, twelve years ago. He inherited the job from his uncle. James' father, Jay, died when he was a teenager, so his uncle had to fill in until James was of age. The Musgrove's owned so much of Northern Georgia, they had slowly been selling small pieces of it at a time to fund their operation ever since. Over the past 250 years, the Musgrove's were charged with guarding two additional Doors. Again, another story for another day.

James looked out over the water. "You know, most days I feel normal. I have a semi-normal life, nothing out of the ordinary ever happens. I travel a bit, keep track of certain people, and watch the Doors. Then, you parked your car on the side of Arnold Mill Road and everything changed. It all became real again. It's been over fifteen years since I've traveled through a Door. We aren't supposed to, you know. We are charged to protect the Doors from anyone passing or attempting to pass through. And you waltzed onto my land and just walk right through one. Some Door Keeper I am."

"James, I'm sorry. I didn't think to ask what all of this might have meant for you. How were you supposed to know someone else had a key?" Out of motherly instinct I reached my hand out and covered his, but was startled to feel something . . . unnatural for me. I quickly removed it and looked away.

"Eden, as shocked as I was to watch you walk through that Door, I hadn't been so excited and amped up in a long time. I have only ever met one Door Keeper in my life, other than my own family, and let's just say he wasn't half as pretty as you." He smiled as he looked at me.

Sitting there uncomfortably, I looked at my phone, and realized what time it was. Gabby would get home from practice any moment. I stood up and thanked James for the flowers and the chat. Thankfully, he took the cue and stood to leave. After shaking hands, he turned to head to his car as Gabby's ride pulled in the driveway. They passed and greeted each other.

"Who was that?" she asked, staring at the puff of smoke his jeep left from the gravel driveway. "He's handsome." She giggled and bounced off into the house to start her homework.

"He's trouble," I mumbled to no one in particular.

THE HISTORY LESSON.

After spending the next morning at the gallery, I decided to go to James' house. I wanted to hear more about his job as a Door Keeper, and all that it entailed. After all, learning about his job might give me some insight into my mother's.

The feeling that flooded me as I drove down the hill and around the curve overwhelmed me. I glanced to my left to see the Door that had changed everything. I visualized what lay behind it. The trees . . . the cloud cover . . . Strix and Lolli. A rush of excitement coursed through me as I realized I was one of only a few people that knew it all existed.

James' driveway was past the Door on Arnold Mill about a quarter of a mile. He had told me he owned the surrounding fifty acres. I turned down the overgrown gravel road and slowly proceeded to pass under a tunnel of intertwined trees. After about three minutes, I was beginning to wonder where the actual house was. Last week after my "abduction," he brought me back to my car on a trail through his property on foot.

When I finally reached the house, I was surprised. I hadn't paid attention that day, being distracted by my experience with the butterflairies and kidnapping and all. It was an oversized barn that had been converted into a two-story house. It was stained dark brown with cream trim. It looked like it had the original barn doors, complete with the large X's across the front. The large iron weather vane even looked original perched on the tin roof. The top floor had a large picture window with a warm glow emanating from within. There were beautifully manicured coral colored rose bushes along both sides of the front doors. It was the only feminine quality on an otherwise masculine house. A woman's touch. I hadn't noticed a ring on James' finger, and he hadn't mentioned being in a relationship, but now I wondered if there was a woman in his life.

Suddenly feeling anxious, I got out of my convertible and walked toward the front door, knocking just a tad too enthusiastically. The door slid open along the rolling track above it and James stood there, grinning, taking up the entire doorway.

"Glad you changed your mind," he replied, looking relieved. I had almost chosen not come, struggling with all of this new information.

"Well, I decided there is never a better time to learn the truth than the present."

"I don't believe you," he said as he ushered me into the house. "I think you just couldn't stand your curiosity anymore." I huffed under my breath because he was right. He placed his hand on my back and guided me toward the kitchen, and I felt that familiar twinge again. "This way."

Walking through the house, I inspected its contents to see if anyone else lived there. Some books were sprawled across the kitchen counter. High school chemistry. Definitely Charlie's.

"Would you like anything to drink?" James asked, snapping me back to the present company.

"Sure, a glass of water would be nice." I decided to jump right in. "Your roses are beautiful, does your wife grow them?" I turned my attention to the window over the sink, feeling silly to have brought it up. When James didn't answer, I turned around to find him a foot away from me, holding a mason jar of water.

Looking at me a little too intensely, but with a hint of a smile, he answered, "You know, Eden, you could just ask if I'm married."

I blanked for a second under the weight of his gaze.

"If that was what I was asking, I would have." I raised my chin, trying to save face. "I just like your roses." I was lying and he knew it. Thankfully, he graciously relented.

"I've never been married," he answered my original question, but not without a slight smile. "The roses were my mother's. She passed away ten years ago, about five years after my father died." Sadness rounded his eyes.

"I'm sorry, I didn't know." I was not expecting this, and certainly wasn't sure how to proceed. "We don't have to talk about it, if you don't want to." I recalled how he had graciously steered the conversation away from Eric when I didn't want to talk about him yesterday.

"No, it's okay. It was a long time ago. I'm sadder for Charlie. Our mom died when he was seven. He never really knew my father, and doesn't remember too much about our mom. I was sixteen when my dad died, so when my uncle stepped in, I didn't take it very well. We don't pass the baton until the eldest son turns twenty. But of course, as a naive teenager, I thought I could manage it all. I didn't handle the transition very well, and now, looking back, I feel like Charlie suffered the most from my frustration and anger. I still carry that, unfortunately. But I eventually came around, when Uncle Thomas started to train me. Once I officially became the American Door Keeper, my uncle left, and I helped Mom raise Charlie."

"Wait, American Door Keeper?" I asked. "What exactly does that mean?"

"Why don't we take this upstairs, and I can show you," he said with a wink.

"Geez." I couldn't help but roll my eyes. "Very subtle, James. Lead the way to your *office*."

🙢 🙢 🙢 🙢 🙢

James explained he had three Doors he was responsible for guarding: two in North America, and one in South America. He was assigned to the two in North America by the Door Maker. Each world has its own Door Maker. He was responsible for overseeing the Door Keepers, and upkeep and maintenance for all of the Doors. The Door Maker's job was passed down generation to generation, as was the Door Keepers. He was the only one who had full knowledge of all the worlds, their inhabitants, and the rules and laws that govern the job of a Door Keeper. The Door Maker was also the maker and maintainer of the keys. The Earth's Door Maker actually lived in Italy. I wondered if that was a coincidence, or if it was more than that?

The Musgrove family had been Keepers of both of the North American Doors since the discovery of the Door in North Georgia. As soon as the Door Maker discovered the Georgian Door had been found, he gave James Musgrove the keys to the Doors, and the location of the one in the Midwest. The family inherited the Door in Brazil when its Door Keeper died without an heir. Thankfully, it was only about fifty years ago, when planes and other technology made keeping track of a Door on another continent possible. James split his time between the Doors, spending slightly more time in Georgia for Charlie's sake.

He showed me the other two Doors in his surveillance room. The Door in Brazil was located in a city called Arraial do Cabo, 100 miles east of Rio de Janeiro, on the coast. From the previous Door Keeper, his family inherited the land that surrounded the Door on the beach. Because Jay, James' father, couldn't be there year-round to guard the Door, he decided to build a little beach cottage around the Door to camouflage it. No one would ever think anything of it when they saw it. Of course, I noticed the intricate details of the lock and hinges. It appeared to be made of the same metal as our keys. The Door itself was large, made of a weathered wood with rod iron embellishing in every corner. Quite a beautiful door for a quiet little beach side shack. But to the naked eye, probably nothing out of the ordinary.

The other North American Door was located in Santa Fe, New Mexico. It was a paneled wooden door, each panel carved with different geometric shapes. It was stained variations of light to dark, with a pop of turquoise color in all the grooves. It was a beautifully carved piece of art, built into an orange adobe mud wall that bordered a garden. Of course, James' family owned the house and adjacent garden. Anyone who tried to access the garden through that gate would be naturally disappointed when the Door would not open.

After brewing some coffee, James and I took a seat on his back porch and delved deeper into being a Door Keeper. I was surprised to learn that James had not gone through any of the Doors except the one here in Georgia. Even then, he had only gone through once, in defiance of his uncle, when he was a teenager. I remembered when Lolli told me she had seen a teenage boy years ago. She had seen James. I smiled when I pictured her face as she mentioned how odd men looked. I tried to imagine what James might have looked like as a teenager. I'm sure he was gangly, like Charlie.

"Why in the world, no pun intended, have you not gone through the other Doors?" I asked in shock, more than one time.

THE DOOR KEEPER

"Eden, there are rules to this job. Rule number one is that we guard the Doors so no one passes through, including us." James exhaled.

"But you open the Door to get supplies from Terra Arborum," I retorted.

"That's totally different. We exchange services, and I never actually enter through the Door. I just open it, and grab what they leave," he answered, seemingly impatient. "Why do you keep asking me?"

"I don't know," I said honestly. "I'm just wondering why, if that was the number one rule, my mother broke it so often. I mean, she visited Rosalina dozens of times, and who knows how many times she visited Lolli's world."

"Well, that wasn't always the rule . . ." James said slowly.

"What? Why are you just now telling me this? What changed?"

"I'm not sure. My uncle told me that about twenty-five years ago, the Door Maker contacted my dad and told him that he was no longer to pass through the Doors into the other worlds. It was hard for my dad to take. He loved traveling and visiting his friends in the other worlds. He would even go with other Door Keepers and travel to their worlds. It was by far the biggest perk of the job." He smiled and continued, "As you'd imagine, my family likes to explore. He didn't take the change very well. My mother said she thought it contributed to his death."

"How did your dad die?" I asked as gently as possible.

"We aren't sure," James responded. His gaze left mine, and he stared off into the trees. "He left on a trip to check on the Brazil Door and never came back. My Uncle and I have searched every square inch of the property and all the major cities around it, and found nothing. We finally gave up after Mom died and had him declared dead." He sat there for a minute without saying anything. "My mom never gave up hope that he was alive. I would argue with her and try to help her accept the truth. I can't help but wonder if I'd just let her believe and let it go, she wouldn't have had the heart attack." He looked at the roses that grew along the back side of the house, mirroring the front.

"So that is why you put so much care and work into her roses," I said, more of a statement than a question. "You are honoring her because you feel responsible." I put my hand on his to attempt to comfort him. I wanted to remind him that I understood . . . but somehow, I felt that he already understood what I was trying to say. "It's not your fault."

"I know, but knowing that doesn't make it any easier."

We sat there for a few minutes in silence. I felt a sense of kinship with James, understanding what the loss of a parent felt like. But I also think I had it easier. I never knew what I'd lost. I didn't grow up with Ava, being loved and cared for by her, or being taught by her. I didn't have to be haunted with all those memories. I thought about his father, and how hard it must have been for him to stop visiting his friends in the other worlds. I wondered why the rules changed, and if my own mother could have abided by them. From the little I knew about her, I don't think she could have.

"Maybe he couldn't either!" I suddenly blurted out.

"What?" James jolted at my sudden outburst.

"I was just thinking about Ava, and if she could have kept the rule and not gone through the Doors. And I don't think she would have. I don't think she could have. She cared for Rosalina too much. She even risked her own life, being pregnant with me, and came through the Door in Italy."

"I know where you're going with this, Eden, and I've already thought about it. Even if he did go through the Door, there is no way he could still be alive. If he was, he would have found a way to come back through."

"James, I know you don't want false hope, and I promise that is not what I'm trying to do. I'm trying to help you find closure. What if, at the very least, we could find out what happened to him?" I ask hesitantly.

"But the rule . . ." He considered with a furrowed brow.

"James, I've already broken the rule. I'm not afraid to break it again." His eyebrows raised, dissolving the deep crease in his forehead between his eyes. A smile slowly formed as I saw him considering this option.

"Like I said, Eden, everything changed when you parked your car that night, and I saw you through the trees."

"Oh, come on, James. We both know everything changed when you saw me at the gallery opening. My being the Caelum Door Keeper's orphan daughter was just a bonus." I winked.

"Ha! Touché." He grinned.

THE PLAN.

"So, we're thinking about wearing matching dresses. Do you think that is too little-kiddish, or okay because we are best friends?" Gabby stuffed her mouth with pizza. It was the last Friday night before school let out for the summer, and we had set up a little picnic by the lake in front of our house to celebrate. She was talking to me about the awards ceremony their class was having for graduating 4th grade next week. Of course, she and Emmie were in the same class.

"Honey, you are *never* too old to dress to match your best friend," I say and wink at her. The longer I can keep her a little girl, the better for me and the rest of the world—every world, for that matter.

"You are coming, right?" she asked dramatically. "I think I'm gonna get the art award again this year." She grinned from ear-to-ear. I loved she was as interested in art as I was at her age. I was also proud of her immense talent. She had an incredible imagination and determination to create whatever she thought of—a rare gift. She could think in three dimensions so much better than I could at her age, or even now in fact. I wondered if she would take an interest in sculpture. I could see that.

"I wouldn't miss it. Danielle and I are already planning to have breakfast together, then coming to cheer y'all on." Then I add playfully, "And we've already planned our matching outfits, so I'm pretty sure that means we are better best friends than you and Emmie."

"Oh, Mom, don't be ridiculous." She rolled her big blue eyes and flipped her hair over her shoulder. "That's impossible!"

I smiled at her. Once she stuffed her face with another bite of pizza, I dove into the main reason I had suggested the picnic.

"Hey, sweetie, I was thinking . . ." I wondered how to navigate this next part without raising any questions. "I have a little surprise for you. Grandpa and Gigi are driving down next week to come to visit for a bit. They wanted to come to your awards ceremony and see Wall Polish, since they missed the opening. What do you think about going back to Charleston with them for a week or two for a little quality time with them, all by yourself?"

"What?" she exclaimed with glee. "Really? That would be *so* much fun! Are you serious?" A piece of pizza flew out of her mouth and landed in my lap. We both howled with laughter.

"Well, you are ten now, and quite grown up." I smiled. "I would drive out later and we could all have some time together in South Carolina. Then, once we reach our perfect shades of tan, we can come home."

"Oh my gosh! Mom, that sounds amazing. I'm *so* excited. Can I run inside and call Emmie and tell her? She is *not* going to believe it."

"Sure thing, honey." I watched her run off toward the house. One down, and one to go.

I knew Gabby would be the easy one. I was lucky I had something in my back pocket that I knew she had always wanted to do, and wouldn't question when I offered it. Thankfully, my parents were already planning on coming down to visit, and were almost as excited as Gabby was about spending some alone time with her. Yes,

I knew Gabby would be easy. Danielle, on the other hand, would prove more difficult.

I sat on the blanket and looked over the lake. The geese were on the far end, forever honking at each other to keep it moving. I smiled as I let myself relax into the sunset, until I remembered the daunting task before me. How was I going to disappear without raising any questions from my best friend? My story couldn't contradict anything I told Gabby, who, luckily, I didn't have to explain why I wasn't going with her to Charleston the whole time. Again, super fortunate I had something she was so excited about that distracted her from the truth. Then, in a moment of inspiration, I knew I had the same thing for Danielle.

🐾🐾🐾🐾🐾

We sat on one of the couches in the gallery, and Danielle's face was flushed with excitement.

"When did this happen?" The words rushed out of her like a dam breaking.

"D, don't get too excited, it's still new. We're just getting to know each other."

"But you are actually interested in someone. This is huge!" Danielle could barely contain herself. "You'd better tell me everything. Start from the beginning."

I took in a quick breath and proceeded to tell her the story I'd concocted for my cover. I knew with D it was important to incorporate James into the story. Chances were good that she would see us together at some point. I hated lying to her, but it was easier than the truth.

"A couple days after I got home from Italy, my car overheated on Arnold Mill and I pulled over to let it cool down. Apparently, I was parked on James' property. He came to check on me and make sure everything was okay. We recognized each other from the Wall Polish opening, and he offered to get coolant for the car, so we walked to his house and, while talking, realized we had a lot in common." That part was not a lie of course. "We've hung out casually a couple of time since then." I noticed that Danielle looked a bit shocked.

"Girl, why didn't you say something?" she asked.

"Honestly, D, I wasn't expecting anything to come from it. I didn't even answer his calls for a week." I shrugged my shoulders, revealing another truth. "But he was persistent. He even brought me flowers in person to convince me to go out with him." I giggled a bit, just for dramatic effect. Geez, I wonder where Gabby gets it from.

"Wait, what kind of flowers were they?" she asked, more in a gossipy way than a 'did he bring you flowers that do not exist in this world' kind of way.

"They actually looked a lot like my tattoo," I replied, still a bit impressed that he had taken the time and energy to get them from Terra Arborum. I wondered if Lolli picked them for him.

"Ooooh, that is a very good sign. It shows he is observant and thoughtful. He might actually be a Keeper."

"D, you have *no* idea," I answered, smiling. Yeah, a Door Keeper. I added for good measure, "I'm not planning on telling Gabby until I know whether or not it could even turn into anything. I don't want to confuse her or get her hopes up, like I have obviously already done to you."

Danielle's cheesy grin was hard not to adore. But I knew once I told her this info, it would satisfy any absence from the gallery, any missed calls, or unanswered texts. This story also allowed for James and me to be seen around town together without raising any questions. My mind drifted to my conversation with James on the phone when I explained my plan to him.

"Wait, so I have to pretend to date you so we can prepare to sneak off to Brazil and try to find information about my dad's death? You know, Eden, if you wanted me to ask you out on a date, all you had to do was say so." I imagined him winking, per usual. All teasing aside, he knew it was the easiest explanation for us spending a good amount of time together. Charlie was all set up to work my time at the gallery while we were training and gone. With Gabby's trip scheduled, James and I had a little over two weeks to get ready for the trip to Brazil, and about a week to actually walk through the Door.

We needed to collect information about the Brazilian Door, and what may lay beyond. We also had to train, as best we could, based on what we learned within that time frame. The one thing we knew for sure was that it was not a peace-keeping world like Terra Arborum. There were no treaties or arrangements. We couldn't go to the Door Maker; he would never allow us to pass through. We had to get the information another way. Thankfully, his father kept journals, too, but it would require us digging through mountains of them to find the information that we needed. It was the best place to start.

"Are you guys hanging out tomorrow? Is that why you have Charlie scheduled to work in the morning?" Danielle asked, snapping me back into the moment.

"No, Gabby and I are going to White Water. Actually, since you aren't working tomorrow either, would you and Emmie like to go? We have two free buddy passes we haven't used yet." White Water is the local water park that Gabby and I had season passes to each year.

"You sure you don't want to take your new boy toy?" D asked, grinning.

I grabbed the pillow beside me and smacked her in the face with it. "Honey, he hasn't earned the right to see me in a bikini yet!" We both laughed.

THE RESEARCH.

The Monday of Gabby's last week of school, James and I started digging through his father's journals. Charlie was out of school for the summer, so he helped us get through more writing faster. I was surprised James told Charlie about our plan. After he explained that he needed Charlie to look after the Doors while we were gone, I understood. He couldn't very well ask his uncle to fill in. His uncle would have never agreed to our plan. It had to be the three of us, and we had to do it alone.

I looked through Jay's logs of the Brazilian Door for anything out of the ordinary. Any visitors or repeat visits by tourists. I didn't want to intrude in James' family privacy by going through his father's personal journals, so James and Charlie went through those. It was like combing through Rosalina's journals, except for the excitement when finding parts about Ava, or in this case, about what lay behind the Brazilian Door. About three hours into our scavenging, Charlie came across the first entry about the land beyond the Door in Brazil.

"November 10, 1989. This week was a hard visit to Palus. My allies among the Paluns are dwindling, either being killed or going into hiding. General Sapp is determined to squash our alliance with the leadership of Palus. For my own safety, I stayed with the rebels

in their camps, but I am unsure if they will still stay intact until my next visit. Sapp's strategy of scaring the rebels into submission is most definitely working. I wouldn't return if I didn't think Squash's life wasn't in danger. But if Sapp ever found out he was the Door Keeper, all would be lost, and everything we worked for towards peace within their world, and well as this world, would be in danger."

James, Charlie and I looked up at each other with wide eyes. None of us expected that. Not only did it not give us very much detail of the world itself, it also revealed a hostile army. Granted, it was over twenty-five years ago, but the information still left a somber heaviness that hung in the room. We knew if we were going to go through with the plan, we had to find out a lot more information before leaving. Over the next two days, the three of us pored over books, every hour or so yelling out a new detail we could use to prepare for our trip.

Me: "He left his 'boots caked with mud outside the Door by accident' and it caught the attention of some passersby."

James: "It says here, 'Squash, of course, couldn't notice my new haircut since he can't see, but yet he notices when I wear a new deodorant. That sloth's nose.' A sloth?"

James: "This is weird, 'I had to postpone my trip to see Squash till tomorrow. I couldn't get my phenylephrine.' What is that?"

Charlie was our go-to researcher. He opened the laptop and asked for the spelling. His answer sound more like a question. "Eye drops to dilate your eyes?"

"I found something . . ." one of us would yell out at random times.

James: "'I had to go to the doctor yesterday because of the painful rash from the unknown foliage I fell in a couple of days ago in Palus.' Yikes, looks like we'll need some good clothes."

"Whoa, this is new." James exhaled, nose still in the book. "'This morning I asked Squash's family about how sloths can exist in our world so differently than in theirs. They told me about how their original Door Keeper let some of the persecuted sloths escape to our land to make a new life. Apparently, they mated with some lesser species and the originals died off, which is why our world doesn't have traditional ground sloths anymore.'" He looked up at me. "Ground sloths? If my memory serves me correctly . . . aren't those huge?"!

"Already on it." Charlie had already searched and was reading. "'Ground Sloths are a diverse group of extinct sloths. The term "ground sloths" is used as a reference for all extinct sloths because of the large size of the earliest forms discovered.' Does that answer your question?" he asked, eyes wide.

After all the journals had been looked through, we surmised it to be a muddy place inhabited by oversized sloths, who may or may not be able to see. Regardless, it was obviously dark enough for James' father to need to dilate his eyes, and the land contained foliage that could irritate our skin. We also knew that up to the time of his dad's death, the Palus Door Keeper was a sloth named Squash. Oh, boy. Also, we found nothing else about the civil war being fought at the time of that specific journal entry. Who won? Who lost? Was it still dangerous? Jay's journal set was incomplete. James knew there were some earlier journals from when he first became a Door Keeper, he just didn't know where they were.

On Wednesday, I had to pull out of the world of research so I could spend some quality time with my parents and Gabby for a couple of weeks. After days of reading about a seemingly fictitious world, it was nice to rejoin the one I actually lived in.

My parents arrived at my house a little after lunch to be there when Gabby got home from school. After settling them in the guest bedroom, we sat on the front porch and caught up on recent events. I'd already told them a lot about my trip to Italy, but as parents do, they wanted to hear it all again in person. It was fun to be able to gush about how much I loved and appreciated the Italian countryside, especially the city of Positano. Most importantly, we talked about my new friendship with Rosalina, the picture of my birth mom, and I shared with them one or two of the stories she told me about her time with my Ava. My mom asked if I felt any closure about Ava, and I answered her the best I could.

"You know, Mom, I'm not sure if I'll ever feel closure. The fact that I have any information about her at all, though, is really comforting. I know she belonged somewhere and had a family. I know she was kind and loving. And really, even though I'm not sure if I'll ever know more, that is enough for me." *For now*, I added in my head. Technically, all of that was true. All of that was enough to satisfy me, for now, especially considering I was attempting to help James find his closure at the moment.

As we finished up our sweet tea, Gabby's bus stopped in front of the house. She squealed with delight running up the driveway toward Gigi and her grandpa. After hugs and kisses, we piled into Grandpa's truck and headed into downtown Woodstock. My parents were itching to see Wall Polish. I intentionally distracted myself as we passed by James' land and the Door that led to Terra Arborum, attempting to stay in the present for the moment. We parked the car in front of the coffee shop below the gallery, and as I opened the door, I smacked right into James, leaving with his freshly brewed cup of coffee. Lucky for me, his reflexes were faster than my clumsiness. His face lit up when he saw I was the culprit, and his smile broadened when he noticed the rest of my family behind me.

"Well, hello, Eden." His eyes moved from mine to my parents.

"Hey, James, excuse us, we were heading upsta—"

"These good-looking people must be your parents," he interrupted, before I could even attempt to avoid an introduction.

Scrunching my face at him before I turned around, I smiled and said, "Yes, this is Edward and Evelyn Brown. And, of course, you've met Gabby."

My parents both shook his hand and Gabby added, "Hello handsome man from my porch!" She giggled and ran upstairs.

Dang it, Gabby.

James raised his eyebrows at me then added, "I like her, she's a smart girl." He smiled at my parents. "Well, I'll let you guys get up to the gallery. You should be very proud of Eden, she has put together quite a hot spot for downtown. We all love spending time up there." With that, he waved and walked to his car park down the street.

As we walked up the stairs, I turned around and made sure both of my parents heard me. "He's just saying that because his brother works at Wall Polish."

"Are you sure he's not just saying that because he has a crush on you?" my dad asked, laughing.

"Dad! That's ridiculous. Trust me, he is in his own world, if you know what I mean." I smiled at myself. I quickly turned the conversation away from James and to the gallery. "Y'all take a look around and I'll catch up in a second. I'm gonna go check in with Danielle."

After checking in with her, and making sure my schedule was cleared for the next couple of weeks, I caught back up with my parents and Gabby. Gabby was showing them the bathroom with the Sharpie artwork everywhere. They thought it ingenious that I turned a teen prank into a creative outlet. My dad even drew a cute little picture of a Bulldog. We finished touring the gallery and walked around downtown. We visited all of my and Gabby's favorite boutiques and antique shops. After dinner on the roof of our favorite Cantina, we sat in the park square and ate gourmet cupcakes and ice cream from a little shop called Cupcakealicious. It was a beautiful night, and so refreshing to spend time with my family. My parents were so easy to be with, and, of course, Gabby served up all the entertainment we could possibly need. If Rosalina could see moments like this, she would never worry about the decision she made. This little world of mine was truly full of love.

Driving home, it was impossible for me not to look at the Door as we passed by James' property. I knew what awaited me. I put Gabby to bed, and my dad settled in the recliner to watch some baseball. Mom and I took some coffee and sat on the front porch. We sat in silence for a while before she finally spoke up.

"You know, initially it bothered me you were looking to learn about Ava."

"Mom . . ."

"No, let me finish," she interjected. "But after a couple of days, I began to understand. I began to see it from your perspective. Quite honestly, I started to think about Ava myself. She was so . . . different. Something about her spirit, for starters. I can't really explain it, but something about just knowing her, even for a day, made me feel special, like I got to witness something no one else did. I know that must sound crazy."

"No, Mom, I promise it doesn't," I answered, feeling a pit deep in my stomach for the woman who raised me from birth.

"It's just . . . I don't blame you for wanting to feel that, too. I see her so much in you. And I recognize that feeling. Like knowing you, I've got a special insight that no one else has." Her eyes began to look watery.

"Oh, Mom. Thanks for understanding." I smiled at her.

"You know, Eric used to always say that to me," she added, out of the blue.

"Say what?" She surprised me bringing him up.

"He used to tell me that he felt so special that you chose him. That he got to experience life through a lens that no one else got to experience. He said you were 'something unique to this world'."

At hearing that, I closed my eyes and allowed a couple of tears the permission they needed to flow. I missed Eric. He was so aware, and he hadn't known it. He knew me and understood me when I didn't understand myself. He gave me Gabby. No one would ever be able to fill the hole he left when he died.

As if sensing what I was feeling, my mother added, "Please don't be afraid to open yourself up again. Don't deprive someone else from feeling what Eric did. You are special and unique, and someone would be very lucky to have a front row seat to it all."

Knowing she was talking about James, but incredibly touched by her words, I didn't push back. "Thank you, Momma." I smiled at her.

No matter what I learned about Ava or where we came from, nothing would change how I felt about the beautiful and wise woman who sat next to me. We sat together in silence, listened to the crickets, and watched the lightning bugs fly over the lake.

The next day was Gabby and Emmie's awards ceremony and last day of school. My parents, Danielle and I all had breakfast together, then made our way over to the school. When Gabby won the art award for her class the third year in a row, we all stood and cheered.

It would have embarrassed any other child in her class, but her smile was unsurpassable. She and Emmie wore their matching dresses, so naturally that invited a ridiculous number of pictures of them together and with their friends, classmates, and teachers. After it was over, we all went back to Danielle and Emmie's house and ended up spending the day together, playing games, and ended it with pizza and a movie as per usual. It was a wonderful day of laughter and celebration.

The next ten days consisted of training with James off and on, and time spent with my parents and Gabby. Thankfully, Gabby dragged her grandparents all around Atlanta doing some of her favorite things. We went to concerts in the park, Stone Mountain for the laser show, and to Six Flags Over Georgia. There were a few days that they took Gabby to do things without me, freeing up some time for James and me to work on my weak cardio. But until Gabby left, we couldn't dive into anything more intense, so for now, James and I ran together.

Most mornings, I would wake up early and we would run the length of the road I lived on. We ran in silence because I was out of breath most of the time, but I found the silence comforting. There wasn't a need to fill the empty space between us, him simply running next to me was enough to push me to not give up. While I never looked forward to the burn in my legs, I did look forward to his quiet presence beside me.

One of the days I had free, James suggested I go back to Terra Arborum to try to get more information about Palus from Strix. I was surprised that he suggested it, but I knew it was a good option to learn more. However, I was shocked when he told me he wouldn't go with me.

"Eden, we only have a limited amount of time. We have too much to do, so we need to divide and conquer. You go talk to Strix, and I'll work on getting all of the gear we need." I knew he was right, and I was so anxious and excited to go back to Terra Arborum and see Lolli that I didn't ask any more questions. The next day, I grabbed my key and the little purple box I had wrapped carefully a few days ago, elated to see my butterflairy friend again.

THE OWL.

This time, having permission to enter and the proper gear, entering Terra Arborum was far more fun. I didn't have all of the anxiety I did last time, so I enjoyed every second. I heard the familiar click of the Door closing behind me, and felt my eyes instantly create and slip the protective film over them. I put on a half face respirator I used for painting with harsher chemicals to help filter the foreign air. With all the extra cardio training, making my way to the cloud cover proved an easier task as well. Before I knew it, I was standing under the peach colored sky, inhaling the fragrance of every flower imaginable. It had been less than a month since my last visit, but it felt too long.

I immediately started walking in the direction of the tree that I knew that Lolli was in. If I could find her, she could get me to Strix. I rehearsed what James and I had discussed for my line of questioning to get information about Palus. Strix, and anyone in Terra Arborum, would not want to have anything to do with a potential breach of Doors. I would mask my line of questioning with desire to learn more about my Ava, James, and the Door Keeper's worlds. I was preoccupied, watching a large flock of hummingbirds flying together, when I heard the sound of bells behind me.

"Are you looking for Lolli?" I turned around to see a beautiful butterflairy identical to the others, but with a short, dark purple pixie cut.

"Yes, I am. My name is Eden," I introduced myself.

"I know. I remember you from before. My name is Vi. Lolli will be delighted to see you. Would you like me to take you to her?"

"Thank you, that would be wonderful." On our way to Lolli's tree hole, Vi told me she was over 100 years old, which was difficult to believe considering she looked Gabby's age. When we arrived at Lolli's tree, she fluttered out of her hole, surprised to see me. She embraced Vi, then me, barely coming up to my waist. She stepped back and smiled, her eyes bright.

"Eden, you've come back. And you have met my mother." My eyes darted back and forth between the two butterflairies. Incredible. Vi looked the exact same age as Lolli. They invited me in for some Serenbe tea, and we talked for an hour about the hatching process and the mother-daughter relationship in Terra Arborum. I couldn't wait to give Lolli the gift I'd brought her. I knew how much she loved drinking tea, so when I was shopping in a boutique back home, I found an adorable tiny hand-painted tea cup and saucer. She absolutely loved it. I finally got the courage to ask if I could see Strix during my visit. Lolli sent word for him by singing/talking to a tiny blue bird. About thirty minutes later, I heard the familiar whooshing sound of his oversized wings outside of Lolli's place.

Climbing out, my foot caught on a root, and I fell out of the hole onto a soft bed of feathers. Strix had caught me.

"Well, it's lovely to see you again, Eden." The giant owl lifted me back onto my feet with his huge wing.

"Hello, Strix, it's nice to see you, too." I thanked him for his assistance. "I was wondering if you had any time to talk about Ava. I've been wrestling with all of this over the past month, and I thought since you knew her, you might help me make sense of some things."

"Of course, Eden, I'd be honored to tell you more about your mother." Strix bowed. "If you have some time today, why don't you come with me on a short run I have to make. I have some friends a couple hundred miles away that need some assistance, and I planned on going today."

"That sounds perfect, thank you." I turned to my gracious hosts and said my goodbyes for the moment. After I climbed onto his back, Strix spread his wings and bolted up into the open sky.

I watched as the treetops grew further and further away, until it almost looked like solid land beneath us. I was surrounded by a warm glow of soft light bouncing off the few clouds within touching distance above me. I only saw green treetops in all directions as we flew away from the sun.

It was completely silent, the only sound the occasional whooshing of my new friend's wings cutting through the air. I was mesmerized by the beauty and stillness around me when Strix broke my concentration.

"What would you like to know, my dear?"

"Well, I have a confession to make. I'm not just here to ask about Ava. I had a run in with James Musgrove."

"James . . . well, I haven't seen him in years. I knew his father and uncle fairly well. I was very sorry to hear about Jay." He paused and continued, "It's very difficult, the Door Keeper life. I'm afraid that there are immense dangers when you deal in traveling to other worlds."

This might be easier than I thought.

"Well, that's what I wanted to ask you. After losing my mother and hearing about James' father . . . I'm not sure this is something I want for my life. I mean, it doesn't seem as though every land is like Terra Arborum."

"Absolutely not, Eden. There are very dangerous lands that you must fear. There are lands where being a Door Keeper is the most important job there is."

"Like Palus?" I felt bold.

"Palus? Why would you ask about Palus?" Strix countered.

"Well, James shared some of his father's journals with me, and Jay wrote about the war and his friend, Squash. I guess I just wondered what happened with all that."

"Squash. Squash was another dear friend of mine. He was the type of Door Keeper I mentioned. He was extremely important in keeping Terra Arborum safe. There was a civil war in his land years ago, one that threatened our protection as well as the safety of other lands. I was aware that Jay was helping him fight. All I know is the war ended and we are still safe. But I never saw or heard from Squash again, and I'm not sure what happened to him. I have tried to make contact, but he has never responded. In fact, I have heard nothing from Palus since."

I decided that was enough information for the moment. I didn't want Strix to get suspicious, so I changed the subject.

"How old are you, Strix?"

"Four hundred and fifteen."

"What? That's incredible, you don't look a day over three hundred." I laughed. Strix's laugh sounded more like a bark.

I looked out to my right and saw a large, open, brown space in the tree tops with strategically spaced dots. It almost resembled an acre-sized nest. I asked Strix about it, and he told me it was one of the hatching fields, where they cared for their eggs. We steadily continued to climb until we ascended through the cumulus clouds that hovered above us. Once we broke through the clouds, the expansive deeply pink sky stretched out before us. I couldn't help but spread my arms out on either side and soak in the sun's rays. It enveloped me like a warm blanket. The only thing that could have made the moment any more perfect was if Gabby was with me.

It turned out that Strix's friends were bright red flamingo-type birds that needed help moving their home to a new tree. So, stick by stick, we relocated the family of flamingos. It was not a terrible way to spend an afternoon, and not a bad test for my cardio. By the time Strix and I left to head back to my Door, I had forgotten all about my recon mission. It wasn't until we were a few minutes from Lolli's home that I remembered to probe some more about Palus.

"So, how are the world's different? How is Palus different from here?" I asked without pretense.

"Eden, why are you asking these questions?" The giant owl turned his head completely around to look at me, freaking me out and almost making me fall off.

"Geez, Strix, warn me before you do that!" I took a deep breath. "I'm just curious."

He didn't answer right away. Instead, he dipped below the clouds and shot down to a nearby open field of flowers that looked like multi-layered, overgrown violets. He shrugged me off his back and turned to face me. His deep glowing eyes bore down into mine. I stared at my own reflection in them while I noticed his bushy eyebrows lower. If I hadn't just spent the afternoon with him, I would have been terrified. But to be honest, I no longer felt completely safe.

"I am an owl, Eden. I am very wise and *very* observant. Your heart rate is elevated, as it has been every time you have asked about Palus. So I will ask you one more time, why are you curious about it?" His voice was stern.

With a deep pit in my stomach, I knew I couldn't lie again.

"Strix, I'm sorry. We just didn't want to put you in the middle. You are a peace keeper, and we did not want to ask you to do anything you felt uncomfortable with," I said honestly.

"We? You and James?"

I nodded. The giant owl lifted his face toward the sky and sighed. His huge feathered chest rose and fell as he exhaled. "Do not tell me what you are planning. But if you want to ask me questions, I will tell you what you need to know. A parent's bond is not one easily broken. I cannot blame you or him for wanting closure." He was much smarter than I thought, and I felt terrible about lying to him. I lunged out and hugged him tightly.

"Thank you, Strix. You are a wonderful friend," I mumbled into his brown silky feathers.

"You're welcome, Eden. Now tell me," he held my shoulders with his wings, "what do you need from me?"

🦉 🦉 🦉 🦉 🦉

Once I returned home, I called James and relayed all the information I'd gotten from Strix. His intel, along with Jay's journals, suggested we were walking into a thick, marsh-like, jungle landscape. The trees were entwined and dense, so there was hardly any light. We'd have to be prepared to trudge through some deep mud, all the while keeping our skin covered so we didn't expose ourselves to any poisonous plants. James assured me he would have everything we needed in time for us to leave in a week.

That night, my parents, Gabby, and I had a special dinner celebrating the end of their visit. It had been eventful and full of excitement. They were recounting their day at one of the local lake beaches, when my Dad asked how my day was. *Well, Dad, I spent the day riding on the back of a giant owl and relocating an eight-foot nest for a couple of red flamingos . . .* wasn't going to fly, pun intended that time. Instead, I answered, "It was good. I ran errands and got some things I've been needing for the gallery." Unfortunately, the lying never got easier.

The following morning, Gabby and I packed up her suitcase with all her essentials for the ten day vacation with her grandparents: swimsuits, dresses, her favorite movies, and dolls. I knew I was going to miss her like crazy, and couldn't help but wonder if what I was about to do would impact her more than I was letting myself believe it would. I kissed her cheeks and cried when she left. She was my entire life. And quite honestly, I hated that she couldn't be a involved in a growing part of it. But I knew that protecting her from all of this was imperative at this point. I also knew it wouldn't be forever.

I pulled myself together and grabbed my key from the top drawer. It was time to get to work.

THE TRAINING.

"At least we know we are not walking into a war zone."

I shrugged, not really feeling at ease. James and I were planning our training schedule for the week. I realized I was fortunate during my first visit to Terra Arborum, especially considering I had no idea what I was walking into.

"I can't believe I just walked right through the Door off Arnold Mill without an inkling of what was on the other side. I can't imagine if it had been a different world, especially with all of this information about Palus. I was really lucky."

"I don't even want to think about it. But, yeah, you were lucky," James replied as he unrolled a leather pouch exposing half a dozen scary knives. "Terra Arborum is the only peaceful world that I know about, the rest are hostile to outsiders."

James handed me one of the knives to practice, and showed me how to handle it properly. I wished we could take guns, being a decent shot and much more comfortable around guns than knives. James explained that with the past unrest with Palus and their desire to conquer other worlds, we wouldn't want to give them any reason to restart the fire, but we needed to be prepared to protect ourselves if the need arose.

I was uncomfortable with the knives, and couldn't help picturing stabbing myself by accident when trying to fend off an enemy. I told

James as much, and he assured me I had no idea what I was capable of until the situation arose, that by blood, Door Keepers have some unique and special gifts that don't manifest until the moment they're needed. Maybe he was right, but it did little to ease my fear.

Charlie came home after work and we all had dinner together. It was nice to actually get to know him outside of the gallery. He was a funny kid, with an incredibly quirky sense of humor, making me laugh a lot. Of course, I already knew these things, but it was all framed differently now. Now, we had a much deeper connection. We both understood and knew things that 99.9% of the world didn't. We shared the knowledge of loss, and the hope of opening a closed Door. I'd already felt like I had an older sister type relationship with him, and now it was magnified. Charlie was helping me clean up the kitchen and load the dishwasher while James put together our next training exercise.

"You know he likes you," Charlie blurted out, handing me a bowl.

"Well, he should, I'm quite a catch . . ." I kept a serious face, taking the bowl and scraping the contents into the trash.

"Eden, I'm serious." He turned and faced me squarely. "He doesn't date women. How can he? How do you explain to someone what we know? I mean, he's gone out with women . . . look at him. Good looks run in our family." He finally relaxed, pointed to himself and grinned. Then he sighed. "But with you, it's different. He can be himself. I've never seen him so relaxed with someone other than me or my mom."

I thought about that and how what Charlie said made sense for me, too. I didn't date, either. With Eric dying and having Gabby in my life, it seemed like an insurmountable obstacle. Or at least an obstacle I didn't care or have the energy to overcome. Maybe until now. But I still wasn't sure what Charlie wanted from me.

"What do you want me to say, Charlie?" I asked honestly, still staring into the now empty bowl I was holding.

"I want you to tell me you will give him a chance. Listen . . . I know you don't date either. I know Gabby's father died and you are super independent. I just don't want you to write James off as any other guy, because he's not. And if he is pursuing you, it is because he can see himself with you. He's not just looking for a piece of tail."

I burst out laughing. "Charlie, trust me, if someone is pursuing me, I know it's not because they are 'looking for a piece of tail'. And feel free to *never* use that terminology around me again." I could barely contain my amusement.

"Well?" he asked me, still serious.

"Well what?"

"Will you give him a chance?" he persisted.

"Charlie, if you are asking me to date your brother, I can't answer that. I'm honestly not sure how I feel about being with someone. Do I have feelings for him? Maybe, but it's been a long time since I've actually been in a relationship. And I'm super comfortable with what Gabby and I have going on. It's easy."

"Well, it may be easier, but easier isn't always better." He looked down at the sink.

"Your brother said that to me." I remembered when he came and brought me the Serenbes after I'd ignored him.

"My dad used to say it. And it's true." Charlie locked eyes with me again. "I'm not asking you to date him. I'm asking you to allow him to pursue you without shooting him down. Just give him a chance to win you over. And believe me, I understand that you shouldn't be won easily. I know that you're special, and you have a lot to consider with Gabby. I just want you to stay open to it."

I was slightly overwhelmed at his words; first, because he echoed what my mother told me the week before, and second, because he sounded so mature for seventeen. It was obvious James had done a great job raising him, and taught him a healthy respect for women. I sank the plate under the dishwater and held it there to soak, but I turned to look Charlie square in the eyes.

"Thank you for that, Charlie. I promise you, I will remain open. Believe it or not, you're not the first person to ask that of me. I appreciate you looking out for me and Gabby. You're a sweet younger brother. James is very lucky." I gave him a little side hug because my hands were still buried in the sink water.

"Um, do you guys have something to tell me?" I heard James tease us, standing in the doorway to our backs.

"Actually, yes, James. I have decided I'm a cougar and have set my eyes on your brother as my prey." I made a funny face and rolled my eyes for emphasis.

Charlie elbowed me to play along. "Yeah, Eden, don't tempt me . . . you are one hot, albeit older, *'piece of tail'.*" He could barely get the words out without howling with laughter.

"Charlie!" James looked horrified by his words.

"It's a long story, James. Don't worry, I don't think he'll ever say *that* again." I turned toward the little hooligan and flung sink water all over him in retaliation. James jumped in and grabbed his head under his arm and squeezed until Charlie cried uncle. After we all calmed down and finished cleaning up the kitchen, Charlie headed upstairs to work on a drawing, and James and I went out to the garage. It was another moment of peace, feeling right at home with these two.

Knowing we were about to head into a world where we may not be able to see very well, we decided the best way to train was to put ourselves in a similar situation. We suited up and headed out onto his property as the sun set. Our goal was to walk the entire perimeter of his land without any aid or additional light source. Within twenty minutes, the sun had completely set and it was dark. James' property was heavily wooded, so it was initially tough to get our bearings. As the time passed, my eyes adjusted. After ten minutes, my eyes were like night vision goggles. I walked ahead of James and heard him struggle behind me.

"Are you alright back there?" I yelled over my shoulder.

"How are you not having issues?" he asked as he tripped over a fallen log.

"How did you *not* see that log?" I teased and waited for him to catch up.

"You could?" he asked, surprised, stumbling up beside me.

"I can see almost normally. Everything just looks a little grainy. Like I'm looking at an old photograph." I thought about my eyes being the first thing to adjust in the other world.

"Didn't you say your eyes adjusted in the other world first? That they sensed the change in air pressure before you even did?"

"Yes, I was just thinking that, too. It's about time I do something useful for this trip," I said, smiling. Of course, James couldn't see that.

"Okay, let's try to see how far we can get together. I'll walk behind you, and you try to be my eyes. We've got to learn to work together." Now that we knew we would have a pair of eyes in Palus, we adjusted our strategy a bit.

After a couple of steps, we knew him walking behind me would not work. He repeatedly stepped on me with his long stride. After adjusting him to walking next to me, we made much better pace. For the next couple hours, we walked around in the dark. James placed his right hand on my right side, walking on my left side with his arm crossed behind my back. James was left handed and I was right handed, so it allowed both of us to have access to our weapons if we needed them. I guided him when there was an obstruction in his path or turns that needed to be made. We quickly realized we would need to be quiet while we navigated to avoid being detected, so we worked on hand signals and taps to communicate. It took practice, but James and I were quick studies. Over the darkness of night, we learned to anticipate each other, and to communicate without talking. It was surprisingly therapeutic and comforting, like our running together, listening to the crickets chirp and the squirrels jumping from limb to limb, walking side by side with someone you fully trusted. We later jokingly dubbed it the Palus tango.

After calling it a night, well past midnight, I drove home. As I lay in bed, staring at the ceiling, I wondered how I had never noticed that my eyes adjusted to the dark so easily before. I wondered what else my eyes could do. They do change color sometimes randomly, and I couldn't help but wonder if there was a reason for it. I closed my eyes and let my thoughts drift. I thought about what it felt like to train with James and practice with knives earlier that day. I thought about how it felt when he grabbed my arm and showed me how to twist my opponent into a vulnerable position. I remembered how his tall frame leaned over mine as his arm wrapped around my chest. I could still hear how he laughed when I made a joke about the size of his boots swallowing mine. It was not the first and, I had an inkling, it would not be the last time I fell asleep thinking of James.

THE PALUS DOOR.

Our flight was scheduled to leave Sunday morning, and we'd trained nonstop leading up to our departure. The plan was to land in Rio, then drive to Arraial do Cabo. James normally stayed at the tiny beach house Jay had built around the Door, but we were obviously not planning to use it much. Our plane tickets were open ended since we weren't sure how long we would be. Saturday was spent packing and going over final details. I left James' house before dinner so he could spend time with Charlie and I could be alone with my thoughts.

    I grabbed some junk food at a drive through, and drove up interstate 575. Top down and music blaring. The sun was low in the sky casting long shadows and creating sunbeams peeking through the trees. It was still warm, but had cooled off from the earlier scorcher during the day. I couldn't shake the feeling in the pit of my stomach that something ominous was in our future. We were about to cross a line that would change everything, even more than it already had. I grew closer to James every day, and I couldn't tell which scared me more: the unknown behind the Door, or my feelings for him. I pulled off the highway into the overlook parking lot. After grabbing my food, I sat at one of the picnic table overlooking the foothills of the Blue Ridge Mountains.

Biting into my burger, I thought about Gabby and how my actions in the coming week would affect her. How long could I keep this up? How long could I hide this growing part of my life from her? Everything in my life hinged on her, and while I knew that all of this was part of what would make her feel complete one day too, I had to be safe and careful of how to give all of this information to her. After finishing my dinner, I pulled out the now worn notebook I'd been journaling in the past month, recounting my time with James and Charlie this past week. I wondered about the motives behind this trip. Why was I so fixated on finding James' dad? Perhaps it was just easier to focus on his problems rather than face my own.

I allowed my mind to replay the conversation I'd with Rosalina the night before. I'd finally forced myself to call her and tell her everything that had happened since I left Italy. Rosalina was important to me, and the best connection I had with Ava. If I wanted to remain close to her, I needed to fight my natural tendencies to pull away. Plus, I wanted someone other than seventeen-year-old Charlie to know our plan and where I was if anything happened. She, as any good surrogate mother would, brought up many of the questions I was attempting to wrestle through this evening. I felt an overwhelming peace after talking with Rosalina, almost as though I had talked to Ava. Unfortunately, it was all too fleeting. Here I was, less than twenty-four hours later, already questioning my decisions again. Was I prioritizing James over Gabby? Because that was *not* something I could consciously do. My body felt at war with itself. My head saying one thing, and my heart another. I also knew that every new world I entered gave me a better understanding of Ava and her life. Deep down, I hoped Palus held some answers for her as well as James' father. As I sat there on the side of the road and watched the sun set, I realized I'd never be able to move on until I knew for sure.

I had made my decision, and I needed to stop second guessing myself, determined to put all my energy and focus into what lay ahead tomorrow.

🙢 🙢 🙢 🙢 🙢

My alarm sounded at 5:30 the next morning. I woke up to realize I'd had another dreamless night. I hadn't dreamt of Ava's death since Italy, and couldn't help wonder what that meant. I stumbled out of bed and headed to the bathroom to shower, brush my teeth, and throw on some mascara. I ran my fingers through my wet hair, walked to my closet and put on some comfy flying clothes. I hung my key around my neck. There was no way I would let it out of my sight. I grabbed my bag and practically fell downstairs, never having been a morning person, especially before coffee. I sat on the front porch, watching the sun rise, when James pulled in my driveway. He had the top off his jeep and asked if I was okay to ride that way. I assured him there was no better way to dry my hair, or to fully wake up. Toward Atlanta we drove.

"What did you end up telling D about going out of town?" James inquired as we boarded the plane at Hartsfield Jackson International.

"I told her you invited me to a cabin with some friends of yours in Tennessee for a couple of days." I shrugged.

"That's just ridiculous. I'd never ask friends to come along. I prefer quality one-on-one time," he teased.

"Well, it's a good thing that it is a fictitious trip." I chuckled. "I hate lying to her. But the truth isn't an option."

"Yeah, this part of the job sucks. Lying to the people you care about. I'm really thankful I never had to lie to Charlie. And I'm genuinely sorry that you have to lie to Gabby." He looked at me earnestly. I appreciated his sincerity.

We landed in Rio around lunchtime and found our rental car. The drive along the coast was gorgeous. I was almost sad the drive was over when we came up on James' beach house . . . and its Door.

The Door itself was originally freestanding. A hundred years ago, this part of the country wasn't settled, so it wasn't a big deal. But as cities started popping up, the Door Keeper at the time added a fence and garden around it before James' father added the cottage. It was a one bedroom, one bathroom micro-house with the tiniest kitchen. The entire thing was probably 750 square feet. The outside was painted a light creamy color with coral accents. The shutters and front door were a bright coral. James explained that coral was his mother's favorite color. I remembered the roses at his house were the same color. His father used to bring her with him sometimes so they could get away together.

As I walked into the house, the first thing I noticed was the backside of the Door. It was the same as the side facing the beach. Weathered stained wood with intricate rod iron embellishing in every corner. It obviously remained locked at all times. I'm not sure why it shocked me, realizing the Doors looked like regular doors and had two sides. I asked James which way we entered Palus through. He told me Jay built the house so he could enter from inside the house and not arouse suspicion. I pulled the key out from under my shirt. Perfect match. James walked back out of the house, so I followed him. He exited the front door and walked around to the back of the house facing the beach. The wind blew and the breeze felt lovely on my face. The view was spectacular.

"You know, if we weren't planning on storming an unknown world armed with scary knives and trudging through mud, I'd thank you for bringing me here." I kept a straight face while staring at the crashing waves.

"Don't forget, this was your idea," James said and looked over at me. "And don't for a second think that we can't change our minds." He straightened and moved closer to me. "We could just stay here and enjoy the view."

I looked up at his golden-brown eyes peering down at me. He tenderly stroked my arm. His eyes never left my face as he used his other hand to tilt my chin to look at him directly. I felt like I was looking at the sun, warmth caressed every inch of my face. My heart raced wildly as he whispered, "We don't have to do this. Just say the word and we can stay here."

For a brief moment, I felt desire rising up in me. It started in my gut, but quickly began to burn throughout the rest of my body. I knew the longer he held me in his gaze, the quicker my resolve would fade. My body was at war with itself again. My brain immediately panicked. His eyes betrayed that he was about to kiss me, and I realized that if he did, everything would change, and I wasn't ready for that.

I pulled back and uttered hesitantly, "As beautiful as the view is, we haven't spent the last month preparing for a vacation. We came here to find out what happened to your dad, and I intend to see it through."

Disappointment flooded his face. He dropped his hands to his sides and sighed. "Okay. Let's get to it, then."

We went back inside and prepared our gear and reviewed our plan. The main goal of this trip was to locate Squash if he was still alive. We would look for his hideout close to the Door. We knew that Palus' technology was limited, so he would have to have a place close by to watch it. Strix mentioned to me that Palun people—sloths—could not see, but had amazing sense of hearing and smell. Our first task would be to camouflage our scent. Our second task was to search the surrounding area within 100 yards of the Door in all directions. If we found nothing, we would re-enter our world to regroup and make a new plan. If we did find his hideout, we would go from there.

We both put on our protective clothes, including utilitarian boots and gloves, grabbed our packs with our gear, and walked to the back of the house. I pulled out my key and asked, "Do you want to do the honors?"

"Thank you kindly, ma'am, but by all means, ladies first." He smiled and spoke with a deep southern drawl. I grinned back and inserted the key, this time knowing what to listen for. I felt it catch, turned right. It caught again, another turn right. One last time, another right. The knob turned all the way and it opened. I had become my mother's daughter. For the third time, I pulled the key out, placed it around my neck and opened the Door.

To walk straight into a wall of vines.

I looked back at James who looked on with surprise. I pulled and tugged and opened a small enough space to squeeze through the dense jungle wall. Once through, I stepped into a thick layer of mud. I could barely see, but I knew within a few minutes my eyes would adjust. The mud on the ground was thick and deep. There was a dense ceiling of vines and trees intertwined above me, preventing any sunlight from permeating. I looked behind me as James squeezed his tall frame through the small opening I created. I noticed the couch we were just sitting on in the beach cottage through the vines. The air was hot and sticky, but manageable.

"Thank you, hot Georgian summers," I whispered to myself.

James straightened up behind me and whistled softly. "Holy crap. This is crazy."

"Rookie," I teased.

We quickly closed the Door and found it was built into a stone wall, overgrown with surrounding trees and vines. Satisfied we were alone, we hit the ground to cover our scent. I slathered mud on and through my hair, coating it as thickly as I could, slicking it back. For a brief moment, I was transported back to the Home Depot parking lot when I noticed the group of people staring at me. Who knew the tame Amazon looking woman was actually turning into a legit bad ass Amazon chick? I smiled at myself as I rubbed the thick mud on my face like a mask, and my eyes began to adjust. By the time I had rolled around and covered myself head to toe in Palus mud, I could see almost perfectly.

The trees above and surrounding us were skinny and looked more like vines. I reached out and touched one to feel they were covered in a papery bark. I peeled it right off and crumbled it like a thin onion peel. That was the best way I could describe it, a long dark onion. The leaves were all long and heavy, drooping off the trees. Swamp as far I could see, which amounted to about ten to twenty feet in any direction. I turned around to see James finishing mudding up. I stifled a giggle. He looked like the swamp thing, all covered in gunk, trudging toward me in slow motion.

He whispered, "I know you aren't laughing at me. Just because I can't see you doesn't mean you don't look ridiculous, too."

"Touché, James. Touché."

THE PALUNS.

James took his position on my left side and wrapped his right arm around my waist, just like we'd practiced. We slowly made our way through the dense jungle. I was armed with a small machete to cut through anything standing in our way. Even with my keener sense of sight, I could only see about ten feet ahead of us. Once we paced about a hundred yards from the Door, I used a bright yellow chalk and marked one of the larger tree vines as a marker. If a Palun came across our markers, we didn't want to leave behind any evidence, and chalk seemed to be our best bet. We turned around and walked back toward the Door to repeat the process until we had searched all the land surrounding the Door. For the better part of an hour, James and I quietly made our way through the swampy Palus landscape. My left hand gave him silent instructions while my right cut down vines obstructing our way as we danced our Palus tango.

We were almost a quarter way through our search when I saw something out of the ordinary. Several yards to our left was what looked like a horizontal roofline cutting through jungle vines. I chalked the tree directly in front of me so I'd know where we left off if we needed to resume our search and this didn't pan out. My guesstimation was that we were around fifty yards west of the Door back to our world. Satisfied with my bearings, we made our way to the structure.

As we approached, I observed that it was a small square wooden house with an A-line tin roof. I gave James the ready-signal as he drew his knife. His right hand gripped my waist a bit tighter. When I glanced in his direction I saw his eyes were closed and his breathing was slow and deep. He looked incredibly calm, and I felt like a nervous wreck. Thankfully, he couldn't see the wild panic in my eyes as we headed toward the house. I looked in the window and saw an empty chair and table, and a huge wooden bed frame lacking the normal mattress and blanket. The house was clearly abandoned. Looking at all of the bare furniture made me wonder if sloths got cold. I whispered to James that we were clear.

To be safe, we followed our plan to position James in front of the entryway. He opened the door slowly and entered with his knife drawn. Once he was convinced we were alone, I closed the door behind us.

James asked me to describe the room. I listed the details of the structure, and that I could see no evidence of anyone being here recently. Spider webs were everywhere, and nests in the corners of the room. He asked me to open the only window. Perhaps if Squash couldn't see, he would listen to watch the Door instead. I opened the window and we sat in silence to better take in our surroundings. Within a minute, we heard what sounded like running water. With no better lead before us, we decided to explore the direction of the sound.

After walking for what seemed like an hour, (though it was likely less than half that time) I spotted rushing water through the trees. The river was wide and fast, and looked like it opened up the jungle roof so there was more light. Once we got to the river, I understood why the jungle was so dark. The sky was a deep yellowish green, the color it turns at home before a storm. The sun was high in the sky, a perfect white yellow circle, and it was all kinds of eerie through the yellowish green haze.

"Wow, I can see a little," James whispered, catching me off guard. We marked a larger tree at the edge of the jungle and the river so we could track our steps. James decided we should follow the river downstream and I agreed. I felt safer by the river, at least more so than in the dense jungle.

After following the river for the better part of the day and just seeing more of the same, we knew it was time to head back up river to the tiny wooden home and regroup. When James and I turned to retrace our steps, a shadow caught my eye on the other side of the fast moving river. I was ahead of James as this point, so I signaled to stop. I saw the shadow stop behind a tree. My heart pounded out of my chest.

"James," I could barely get the words out, "we aren't alone." I nodded toward the other side of the river and took a few steps forward.

"Damn it." He exhaled when he saw the figure mirror me. "My bet is that he's not alone either."

"What do we do?" I asked as calmly as I could.

"Just what we talked about. Appear as nonthreatening as possible. Put up your machete and I'll hide my knives. Keep heading up the river and whatever happens, we cannot be the first to attack. We don't want to be seen as being aggressive. Unless of course, they attack first." He grinned at me and was obviously loving this. What had I gotten myself into?

He grabbed my hand and, no longer attempting to go unnoticed, we made fast time up the river. But a few minutes in, we heard rustling behind us. James stopped, looked me square in the eyes and mouthed, "It will be okay." He put his hands up in the air. I followed his lead . . . scared through my bones.

The next thing I saw was tattooed in my mind forever. As James and I stared intensely into each other's eyes, his trying to calm mine, and mine wild with fear, my peripheral vision caught giant sloths coming out from behind every tree in every direction. There were at least twenty. Most stood taller than James and I, and all of them were armed with huge machete-type weapons, but much more menacing. The blades were at least three feet long with upturned, curved, notched edges, attached to an ornate handle at least four feet long. Once surrounded, the sloths sat the ends of their weapons on the ground with the blades pointed up in our direction. We were enclosed in an intimidating circle of weaponry. I noticed the massive creatures lacked typical clothing, but donned military warfare; utilitarian belts with smaller knives and axes draped over every soldier's shoulder. The metal circle parted to welcome their leader.

He was about seven feet tall with a large, dinosaur shaped body. His feet were square and wide, his legs short. The sloth's back, laden with gear, arched over to reveal that he must walk on all fours a great deal. At the moment, his disproportionately long thick arms were sitting on the ground in front of him, hiding his huge claws. Like the others, his fur was a light brown that hung longer on his torso and head than on his arms and legs. His dark mouth was downturned and disappeared under his large snout. He had only one eye, and a long, deep scar running across his face where his missing eye once belonged. I was not sure what was more intimidating, his face or his glare. He walked into the circle and straight up to James. He looked down on him in disgust. James spoke first.

"We do not mean you any harm," he said confidently. "We are just visiting—"

He was interrupted by the leader's deep growl. It was loud and sounded like a cross between a tiger's roar and a dog's irritated bark. His words were not from our world, but it was obvious he talked to his soldiers as they moved in unison to his instructions. Four sloths broke their positions. One grabbed my hands while the other bound them behind my back. The same thing happened to James. The sloths' giant claws dug into my arms, their long nails more like talons. I grimaced at the pain of their uncoordinated work. James quietly asked if I was ok, and the sloth leader hit his face with the back of his hand.

I looked on in horror. I couldn't believe this was happening, and I was powerless to stop it. Just like one of my dreams, but it was real. What was going to happen to us? What had I done? James looked back at me with blood dripping down a cut above his eye and barely nodded to let me know he was okay. One of the sloths who tied my hands grabbed them forcefully and pushed me forward. I tripped over a branch under my feet, and trudged behind the others. We were led back upstream, and I could hear the loud stomping feet of the sloths leading James behind me.

The first thing I thought was if this had been the world I had entered into when I walked through the first Door back in Georgia, I would be alone and completely unprepared. I pictured Lolli's face and the sweet Serenbe tea, such a far cry from being handcuffed by giant hostile sloths. I longed to be standing in front of that green Door with the cracked and worn paint off Arnold Mill Road, on either side of it. At least I knew both sides of that Door were safe. The idea of feeling safe felt worlds away.

I heard James cough and as I started to turn in his direction, I saw it: the tree we marked at the river's edge. He wanted to make sure I noticed it. After about ten minutes past the marked tree, I could tell the sun was beginning to set.

Thoughts between missing Gabby and James and I surviving rushed through my mind. I was keenly aware that we would be at a distinct disadvantage if James could not see. I attempted to slow my breathing and calm myself. I was already so scared, and now we were losing the only advantage over the sloths we had. I started breathing slowly out my mouth and in through my nose. My heart rate slowed. I thought through the items in my backpack. Was there anything I could reach or use if an opportunity presented itself? There was the chalk in my pocket and a tiny propane tank hanging off my pack. We packed it last minute in case we got stuck here and needed to eat without attracting attention. Those were the only things I could reach if the sloth weren't holding my hands. My knives and everything else that was useful were inside the pack and inaccessible. My eyes adjusted as the sun continued setting, but I knew James had already lost his ability to see. We moved further away from the river and deeper into the swampy jungle. My feet sank in the deep mud, and the sloth behind me pushed me along impatiently. I found myself shivering in the cool air. There was a huge bonfire in the middle of the clearing, and sloths gathered around, warming themselves. I had been shivering for the past hour, but I hadn't yet actually felt the cold. Fear will do that to a person.

As soon as we entered the clearing, everyone stopped and stared. Sloths started growling at each other. The closer we got, the fiercer their reaction. By the time we had entered the circle of torches, they were all barking and throwing their enormously long arms in the air and pounding the ground. I froze when I saw the aggression in their faces reflected in the light of the fire. The sloth leading me forced me down on the ground about seven or eight feet away from the bonfire. I was thankful for the temporary moment of rest and warmth. James was thrown down beside me, dried blood now caked on his face. The sloths continued yelling at each other, ignoring us, which gave James and I a moment to recoup.

He leaned in and whispered, "The propane tank. Can you reach it?"

"Yes, but I don't think dinner is a good idea, James." I thought he had lost his mind.

"Listen, we have to get out of here. This isn't good. We need something to create a diversion so we can try to get away. If you throw the tank in the fire, it might give us a chance." My hands were tied behind my back, in the perfect spot to grab it. But it would be close to impossible for me to hit the fire with my hands bound. We had no other option, so I decided to attempt James plan. I slowly slid the tank out of the side pocket and tried to reposition myself to throw it with some accuracy.

I turned my body to face James so I could throw with my right hand. I looked deep in his eyes, inches from each other, as the bonfire light danced on our faces. My mind was still as I took a deep breath, and threw the small tank with a strength that both our lives depended on.

Once I threw it, I saw a wild look of determination on James' face. He was attempting to free his hands. How could that possibly be when I could barely wiggle mine? When we heard the tank land in the coals in the fire, James lunged his body on top of mine to protect me from the imminent blast. For a moment, the world, at least this one, moved in slow motion. I hit the ground, feeling the weight of James body on mine. The look in his eyes was perfectly balanced between panic and hope. I heard the hiss, then massive explosion, from the tank in the fire. I watched a giant ball of fire rise behind him. I felt him desperately searching for and withdrawing a pocket knife. Somehow, he had actually freed himself from the sloth's bindings. Surprised I could hear anything over the ringing in my ears, I heard the faint chaos of the sloths. James flipped me over and cut my hands free with the knife. In one swift motion, he hoisted me to my feet by my backpack with his other hand.

I couldn't believe we were free. But hope was dashed when I was again face to face with the sloth who had tied my hands. Knowing we were fighting for our lives and for Gabby and Charlie back home, we could not afford to lose. James miraculously pulled the small machete from my bag when he was lifting me up and had placed it in my hand. Grabbing it tightly, I swung it up with as much force as I could muster and cut the sloth across the chest. He stumbled backward toward the fire and, in the midst of him faltering, I saw the remnants of the explosion behind him. Most of the camp was trying to put out the fires that had spread. Not only was it chaos, but a community of furious sloths searching for the two with targets painted on their backs. James had used his deadly knife skills behind me to defeat a sloth. Perhaps there was hope. He reached out to grab my hand for us to run. As I reached for James' hand, a sharp pain hit my face. James yelled and lunged toward me, only for his body to then fly in the opposite direction. I tried to find my bearings, but the giant sloth reared his hideous claw back and brought it around, hitting my left side. I felt the ripping of my skin and the crunch of my ribs as my feet left the ground. As I flew backward through the air, Gabby's face flashed before me, and I cried out in pain. Everything went black before I even hit the ground.

THE SCARE.

I was sitting in the passenger seat next to him. Seemingly, no time had passed; he looked exactly the same. He was singing, quite terribly, to our song by Aerosmith, "I Don't Want to Miss a Thing." We danced to it at our wedding. Eric was driving his SUV with the windows down. The air was warm, and he had his arm sticking straight out of the window as though he was trying to catch every bit of air he could. It reached his favorite part of the song, and I noticed the joy building in his face. He loved to serenade me with this song. I could even smell the familiar scent of the air-freshener he always used. Lemon. He always loved the clean smell of lemon. I realized he didn't know I was there or could see him, because although it was my first time having this dream, there was a devastating sense of deja-vu. Even before it happened, I knew. The music swelled, and I watched in horror as he closed his eyes, getting swept away by the lyrics at just the wrong moment. I heard the horrendous crunching of metal before I saw anything. The smell of burning rubber filled my nostrils. It all happened in slow motion, his body being thrown and tossed like a rag doll, even while harnessed in his seat belt. His body being crushed as the car enclosed around him.

The first thing I felt upon waking was the pain in my side. It felt like it had been ripped open. The next pain was the sting in my right eye and, before I even tried, I realized that I couldn't open it. It had swollen shut. My ears faintly heard a mixture of ringing and buzzing. When attempting to let out a groan, I was unsure if it even escaped my lips. I think I felt someone under me . . . or were they above me? Was I sitting up or laying down? I had no idea. Maybe I heard someone saying my name. Eden? Eden, can you hear me? No. No I can't. Maybe? Yes, I think I can. Inner dialogue in my head couldn't be a good sign. Next time it was a little louder.

"Eden, please, can you hear me?" Whoever it was sounded desperate.

"Yes?" I tried to say the word.

"Thank God." Relief. I sure didn't feel relieved.

Attempting to open my good eye, I began to make out a man looking down on me. James. Why was he shirtless? He gently lifted my head and placed it on something rolled up and softer than the hard rock surface the rest of my body was lying on. I tried to sit up and he stopped me. Actually, the pain that ripped through my left side stopped me.

"Whoa, Eden, don't move. I need to check out your wounds first. You got hit pretty bad." I felt him check my side. "Okay, the bleeding seems to have slowed down so that's good. I'm gonna wrap it in my shirt so we can keep the bleeding to a minimum, but I don't want to apply too much pressure in case your ribs are broken. How does it feel to breathe?" He looked at me, his face coated in concern.

I tried to take a deep breath. "Holy cow, it hurts, but not as much as the stinging."

He hinted at a smile. "Good, then hopefully they are just bruised. Let me help you sit up. But move slow, okay?" As he helped me up, I noticed he was quite beat up himself. He had long scratches all along his torso, and his right shoulder had a deep gash across the top that looked like he had already attempted to attend to it. The cut on his face had reopened. If I looked anything like he did, we were quite a pair. After I sat up, he wrapped my torso in his shirt to act as a bandage. He sat next to me, exhaled slowly, and we welcomed the silence.

I took a moment to assess our surroundings to find we were locked in a cell of some kind. We sat on a rock floor with grey brick walls. There was a large door on the opposite wall made of bars. I noticed candlelight farther down the hallway but there were no lights in the cell, so I realized that James could not see very well.

"Do I look as bad as you do?" I ask, exhausted but jokingly.

"Girl, it's not good." He looked toward me and smiled. "But pretty bad-ass if I say so myself."

"Ha! *Ouch*." I immediately regretted trying to joke around. James grabbed my hand.

"I'm so sorry, Eden. Is there anything I can do?"

"Any chance Door Keepers can go back in time? I'm really regretting not taking you up on your offer to stay in Brazil and enjoy the view." I let my head rest on the wall behind me.

"Yeah, the sun and sand between our toes does sound appealing right now." I could hear him smile. "Dang it, you're not going to look half as good in your bikini now that your side is all ripped up."

"James, you are so lucky that I am immobile right now, or I would kick your butt." I sighed, since laughing was out of the question. "Seriously, James, I'm sorry. This is my fault. This was such a bad idea . . . what's going to happen to us?" I started to cry. I'd run out of any strength to mask my emotions any more. The tears started to flow. What will happen to Gabby?

"Eden, please don't cry," James pleaded.

"James, we are both seriously hurt. I can barely move. We're in a jail in some crazy world, and have no idea where we are. I miss

Gabby, and now I'm afraid I may never see her again. I don't want her growing up without me." I was full on sobbing.

"I won't let that happen," James replied forcefully. He placed his hand on the side of my face. "Ever since I met you, Eden, my life has been turned upside down. But the one thing I know, the one thing I am absolutely sure of, is that you make it better. Since meeting you, everything has felt right: every step, every risk, every decision. I feel, for the first time in my life, that I am actually living. I'm doing what I was made to do. You have made me come alive." And with that, he kissed me.

In that moment, I was done. I was done trying to keep James away. I was done being afraid. I was done trying to stop the inevitable. James had brought me alive, too. He had awakened something in me that I thought died in that crash a long time ago. He awakened my desire to not want to be alone anymore. I wanted him in my life, and I did not want to be without him any longer. I gently caressed his face as I kissed him back with every emotion that had flooded me since we met. Since the first time I saw him at the gallery opening. Since that afternoon we fought in his surveillance room after he knocked me out. Since that day he brought me the bouquet of Serenbes to apologize. Since the moment I wanted to kiss him the first time on the other side of this blasted Door. Our lips parted and we rested our foreheads against one another's. Breathing heavily.

"I'm sorry I've been so afraid to let you in," I confessed.

"Eden, don't apologize. You have been through a lot in your life. You have Gabby to think about. And honestly . . ." he paused, ". . . it was worth the wait."

I smiled at that. "I thought, after Eric died, that I would never be with anyone again. I didn't want to be with anyone ever again. It was purely selfish. I just didn't want to make room for anyone other than Gabby or myself. But I want you to know, that has changed. I feel the same way about you."

James smiled. "I knew you did. I just had to be patient for you to realize it, too. Would you want to tell me about Eric? I'd love to hear how y'all met."

I smiled, knowing he was just trying to keep my mind off of our current situation. "We were high school sweethearts. After my parents adopted me, they moved to Atlanta to raise me. We moved around a decent amount, but finally landed in Cherokee County my sophomore year of high school. I was a junior and Eric was a senior when we met. I had gone to prom with a guy from another school, and had a photo album with me. You know, back before social media and everything." I smiled and continued. "He was sitting at this table with some other guys that were passing around the photo album, and when he started looking through it, he noticed I was sitting at the table with him. He immediately came over and started a conversation with me. He was dating some other girl at the time, but obviously broke it off when he realized how incredible I was."

James laughed at that. "Smart guy."

"Anyway, we dated off and on for a couple years, and got married when I was twenty. We were pregnant with Gabby within a couple months. Life was perfect. We were in love and had a beautiful baby girl. Then, seven years ago, when Gabby was three, Eric went out of town for a business trip." I paused, trying to phrase the next part. Even injured in a different world didn't make the magnitude of what happened to Eric any easier, especially after having that dream. "While gone he was hit by an elderly woman who had fallen asleep behind the wheel."

"I'm so sorry you had to go through that," James whispered.

"You know, I've never been angry about it," I realized out loud. "I mean, I've never been angry with the woman who hit him, or God for taking him away. I've just felt sad that he wasn't able to watch and see Gabby turn into the beautiful young woman that she is becoming." My heart sank deep in my gut when I started to realize that I might not either.

"We are going to get out of this, Eden, I promise." James read my mind once again. "They have left us here for a while, which means they probably don't know what to do with us yet. That's good news."

"Well, I would love some good news right now."

As soon as the words left my mouth, we heard the clanging of the barred door. James wrapped his arm around me, hurting my ribs a bit, but I was too thankful for the comfort to care. Two guards crouched through the door and stood on either side as a huge sloth, who moved painstakingly slow, entered the cell. He looked down at us, and stood silent for a moment. He grunted and barked, and the other two sloths left. He sunk down low, putting his face within a foot of James' and mine. I could smell his breath, and it was not pleasant. It was obvious that this sloth held our fate in his hands, we could tell by the authority he carried with the other sloths. He grunted faintly, almost like a hum. And then in perfect English we heard, "I would recognize that smell anywhere. Jay . . . where have you been?"

THE FRIEND.

We were speechless. The old sloth continued speaking slowly and deliberately. "Jay, how could you be so careless as to get caught? Why did you not wait at the house? I still follow protocols. And who is this woman with you? I know you would not risk bringing Beth here."

I sensed James further tense up at his mother's name. This was Jay's friend, this was Squash. I jumped in because James seemed frozen.

"Are you Squash?" I asked hesitantly.

The large sloth jerked his head towards me. "Yes, little lady, I am. And who might you be? You smell wonderful." Before I could answer, James found his voice.

"Squash, I'm James. Jay's oldest son."

"Oh, well, I should have known." His face looked sad. "I assume since you are here, and he is not, that he is not alive."

"No sir, he isn't. He died about fifteen years ago. That's why we are here. We're trying to find out what happened to him."

Squash plopped on his backside. "Fifteen years. I was not expecting that. I am truly sorry, son, but I have not seen your father in well over that. I am not quite sure the timing of the last time we spoke. Those were difficult and dangerous times for me."

"Would you mind telling us anything about the last time you remember talking to James' dad?" I questioned. I was still in complete shock we had actually found the Palus Door Keeper, or rather he had found us. The adrenaline pumping through me helped ease the pain I was fighting on my face and in my side.

"Yes, ma'am, of course. We were in the middle of a civil war here in Palus. It is common knowledge here that there are Doors and other worlds, but most of the Paluns were content with things the way they were. However, a General rose through the ranks and was hellbent on finding the Doors and the Keepers of them. What initiated his agenda, I never knew. Over the years, he collected quite a following, and those of us that opposed his plans rose up. At the time, I was a nobody. I was a simple Palun without rank or title. But, as the Door Keeper, I led those who were with me. Obviously, they had no idea who I was or what I did. Only my best friend, Frye, knew who I truly was. Times were getting hard, and we were losing the war, fast.

"The last time I talked to Jay, he was planning on coming to bring me additional weapons for the rebels. While trying to hold on until your father could come back, Frye and I decided to go out scouting to make sure our current camp location was safe. We got tracked down by some of General Sapp's men. They enclosed and we fought them off. But Frye was badly wounded. Both of us knew he would not last the day. He told me to let him take the fall as the Door Keeper. If General Sapp thought the Door Keeper was dead and had taken all of its secrets with him, he might give up his plight to find the Doors. I held my friend as he died in my arms. I knew he was right, and that this was our only chance to end this brutal war without even more death. To ensure his sacrifice wasn't for nothing, I buried the key and took Frye's body to General Sapp and turned him over as a traitor. The act gave me access to join Sapp's army, and I've spent the last decade rising through the ranks to keep an eye on the leadership and make sure that my secret stayed just that. It is a good thing, too. You would be dead by now if I had not intervened."

"So is General Sapp still in charge?" James asked with a furrowed brow.

"No, sir, he is dead. But his son is. You met him earlier by the river," Squash gravely answered. "He is not a big fan of yours; you injured some of his soldiers. But, he trusts me as his father did. I advised him his best course of action was to make examples out of you two, which he plans on doing. But that is why you have been left undisturbed for the moment. They are planning your punishment. And if I am going to get you out of here, we are going to have to be creative. Where is your key?"

"We hid them in our backpacks once we knew we were being followed," I answered.

"Them? You have more than one?" he asked with curiosity.

"Squash, meet Eden. Her mother was the Door Keeper of Caelum," James introduced. I could feel the energy in the room shift.

"Caelum. What a beautiful place, or so I've been told. Your people are rare beauties. No wonder you smell so good." I couldn't help but chuckle. Squash continued, "I am assuming you have been to the house I built by the Door."

"Yes, we have been there," James replied.

"Can you get back there if I can get you to the river?" the old Sloth asked.

"Yes, sir." I was thankful we marked the trees.

"Okay, you are almost two hours' trek north of the Door. If we can get you to the river, you can swim down it in a fraction of the time. If I can get your packs to the house before you, you stand a chance. I am going to leave and take them there myself. I will arrange to have you transferred first thing in the morning to our other campsite for flogging and interrogation. Sapp Junior would not question that. The route they will take to transfer you will allow you access to a bridge. Do whatever it takes to jump it and get yourselves into the river. We sloths are terrified of the rushing water. We are too heavy and uncoordinated to swim, so that will buy you time to get ahead of them. Here is a knife to use to free your hands once you are in the river. Don't attempt to use it before; it may alert the guards if they hear you cutting the rope. If you do not escape at the river, you will not make it. The general will most definitely have you executed, and I am afraid I could not stop it." Squash put the small knife in James' pocket.

"Thank you, Squash." My gratitude overflowed.

"Eden, Jay was one of my best friends. I would do anything for him or his family." Squash smiled, as much as a sloth could, at least. Then he suddenly added, "Plus, we can't allow little Sapp Junior to know that the keys to the Doors and Keepers are still out there and in play. It would reignite the civil war. As far he knows, you have traveled from a far-off place. He has not put two and two together yet."

"Squash, once we are gone, we will not return. The secret will leave with us." James promised.

"Ok, now comes the hard part. James, I'm going to have to beat you up a little bit. If the general finds out I have been here and have not left you hurting, it might blow my cover," Squash apologized.

"I understand." James grimaced at me and stood up to take the hit.

I watched on with my one good eye as an ancient giant sloth backhanded my new boyfriend with his huge claw, then gave him a big bear hug.

THE ESCAPE.

After Squash left our cell, we were left reeling. We found who we were looking for, but were no closer to finding out what happened to James' father. I began to feel that way about every Door I passed through, they seemed to open nothing but more questions. Now that we had an ally on the inside, we knew our chances of getting home had improved. We still had a long road ahead of us. Neither of us was in great shape to fight for our lives, but our spirits had lifted dramatically. Squash said he'd make sure we were left undisturbed until our transfer so we could attempt to get some sleep, plan our escape, and gather up all the strength we had left. We spent the time sleeping on and off, and trading stories about Charlie and Gabby. Simply talking about her, and picturing her face, strengthened my mind and my body. I missed her so much. I felt my innate desire to do whatever it took to get back to her taking over.

I had to fight the temptation to get angry at myself for risking my relationship with her. As much as I said this trip was for James, to help find information about his dad, I knew better. This was about me and my longing for adventure and to fulfill some bigger destiny. I was selfishly hoping to learn more about Ava. Since the day I met Rosalina and found out about my mother and her true identity, I had dreamt of the purpose she was sure I was to fulfill. In this moment, though, I grappled with how I was so stupid as to risk the most incredible blessing I have at home for something in another world that may or may not exist. Why did I think I could possibly need anything more than her? She is my everything. She has always been my everything. And I felt guilty for admitting to myself that I even thought about wanting more than to just be her mother.

But was it wrong for me to want more? I wasn't sure. My biological mother wanted more. But looked what it cost her. It cost her life, with me. Knowing me. I could never sacrifice that with my sweet Gabriel. She was a part of me. I wondered if there was a balance? I had already started to figure out that being a Door Keeper was much more than just adventure. It was protecting people at all cost. It was watching over those who can't protect themselves. It was guarding a treasure that deserves to be guarded, or keeping the evil out. I understood why Door Keepers were so important. After seeing lands like Terra Arborum and Palus, it was difficult to imagine them co-existing. Perhaps Ava didn't sacrifice herself for the sake of adventure, perhaps it was something larger. She told Rosalina I had a destiny. I wondered if part of that destiny was being separated from my true family. I then wondered, if I had to, could I make that same sacrifice? I didn't know. Maybe I was too selfish. Could I be a good mother and be a Door Keeper, if that was the destiny my mother talked about? I was completely terrified to try to answer these growing questions that plagued me.

James and I both startled someone approach the cell door. We weren't sure if Squash had been successful sending our backpacks to the safe house, but there was nothing we could do but follow the plan. As the sloths dragged us from the room, I hollered as pain shot through every inch of my torso. Adrenaline quickly took over as I raised my eyes to be face to face with General Sapp's son. As he grunted and exhaled, his stale breath entered my nostrils. He quickly turned and immediately walked down the hallway. Crap. We didn't expect for the general's son to be our transfer. As soon as we walked out of the cave type structure, which had been our prison, I saw the sun had already risen. Still in the dense swampy jungle, I realized I was the only one who could see. But it didn't take long for us to hear the river so we knew we were heading in the right direction. Seeing the break in the trees up ahead, I knew we were close. I felt my heart pulsing throughout my entire body, and then it sank when I my eyes landed on the bridge, towering above the river. I started breathing slowly again, as I had this whole trip, to attempt to calm myself. It was important to stay aware and alert. This was it, our only chance at escape. I went over the plan again and again in my head. We had rehearsed it in the cell last night and again this morning. We tried to plan for any contingencies. Squash assured us the river was deep and calm enough to carry us, but I wasn't looking forward to the fall, and hoped my ribs could withstand the impact.

By the time we arrived at the bridge, James had the knife readied to cut his rope after we were in the water. After the signal, I was instructed to go ahead and jump into the river with my hands bound to ensure I got off the bridge. James was in much better shape to fight off someone if necessary, but my ribs put that out of the question. I needed to get into the water without a fight. James was to jump in, hands free, and cut my ropes once in the river. I was a decent swimmer and could keep a level head under water. Plus, I could hold my breath for a good amount of time, so I knew I could hold on until James got to me. I prepared my lungs for a long hold as we took our first steps onto the bridge. The bridge was an old wooden bridge painted a deep green, like everything else I'd seen up to this point. It was about fifteen feet in the air, high enough to startle me, but not high enough to keep me from jumping. Time seemed to slow to a crawl as my foot took its first step onto the rickety wooden slats. I knew I could trust James with my life; maybe it was an innate Door Keeper thing. We were each other's only hope. We crept across the green structure as our future lie below. After we hit the middle of the bridge I took a long deep breath, closed my eyes, said a quick prayer, and waited for James.

    I heard him headbutt the soldier behind him, followed immediately by an angry sloth's growl. I fell to the ground, disorienting the soldier walking behind me just as James kicked him as forcibly as he could. My body caused him to trip and fall, allowing me a half second to jump before Sapp Jr figured out what was happening. The huge weight of the sloth, falling over me, crunched my already damaged side. I exhaled through the pain in my ribs and sucked in the largest breath they would begrudgingly allow as I flung my body over the rail. When I hit the water, the pain in my torso was blinding, but the water enveloped my body like a warm cushion. It helped me relax, which allowed me to regain my composure. I tried opening my eyes under water, but it was no use. I couldn't see anything. I had no concept of up or down, so I remained as still as I could. Thankfully I could feel myself begin to float upward, giving me the direction I needed to kick. I couldn't hear if James had hit the water yet or not because of the rushing water. I began to kick as hard as I could upward. I was losing air, and needed to find James or the surface quickly. The dull ache in my side reminded me that all of this was very real. Just in time, I suddenly felt James' large hands grab mine and begin to cut the binding. Thank God. My hands were free within three seconds, and James pulled me to the surface.

    We were already out of sight of the bridge, and we knew it was unlikely the sloths would follow us overboard. The water was moving fast, but we could float with the current. Not too long later, I saw the marked tree come into focus, and we used the little energy we had left to swim toward shore. James reached land first and grabbed my hand to pull me toward him. We climbed up the bank, battered and bruised, but alive. We knew we didn't have time for anything but running, so I held his hand as we entered the jungle, abandoning the blind tango we had so carefully rehearsed for so long.

My entire body ached as we made our way to the house. I hoped our packs were there with our keys. I pictured Gabby dancing in my living room and my energy surged. She was twirling and singing, her hair flowing around her, creating a beautiful swirl of light chocolate. Her voice was beautiful and angelic. I will get back to her. I must get back to her. I pushed on and, before I knew it, we were back at the house. I busted through the front door with James behind me to find Squash sitting on the bed. He startled me and I yelped. James pulled me behind him and swung his knife.

"Hold on there, son, it is just me," Squash said in his slow drawl and put his huge claw out in defense.

"Squash, what are you doing here?" James asked in disbelief.

"I just had to know that you made it through. Here are your packs. You better get your keys and get out of here. I will take you back to the Door."

James and I opened our packs to get our machetes and keys out. I pulled mine out and put it around my neck. Squash walked toward me.

"Do you mind, m'lady?" he asked me, motioning to the key. I placed it in his hand.

"It is amazing. That we are all so different and yet all connected by this one little thing. People have fought and died to even see one of these, much less be in possession of one. The Doors connecting and separating us are imperative to our survivals—to all of our worlds' survivals. Take great care of this, Eden." And with that, Squash gently hugged me and licked my forehead. Totally catching me off guard, I stifled a laugh. Then he turned to James.

"You need to know that your father loved you very much. You, Charlie, and your mother were his life, even more than his job as a Door Keeper. He did his job to protect you. You take care of that knife I gave you. It was the last thing your father ever gave me. I am so sorry about his death. I hope you can find some answers and some peace. Take good care of Charlie. Peace be with you, my friend." They embraced.

As Squash closed the door to the house behind us, we heard rustling about a hundred yards toward the river. He looked at us and motioned for us to run.

"Squash, if they know you're here, they will know you helped us," James pleaded.

"James, go. Lock the door behind you. You and Eden will be safe. It's time I pay the price I should have years ago." His face looked peaceful, as though he had been ready for this. I wondered if he had left it out of the plan purposefully because he knew what our reaction would be. "It's my final act as this world's Door Keeper. I'll fight them off and give you plenty of time." He growled forcefully. I looked on in horror as I realized my new friend's life was about to end.

"Go!" he hollered. James grabbed my hand and we ran side by side. Branches hit our faces, scraping our arms and legs, but we were too close to stop now. We heard the barking, fighting, and growling start within seconds. We rounded the stone wall and I fumbled to grab my key. I was sweating and my hand kept slipping. We could hear a loud howl in the distance. Oh, Squash. I closed my eyes and breathed. I inserted the key, turned, click. Turned, pulled back slowly, click. Tree limbs were breaking with the oncoming sloths. I turned it again, click. The loud stomping of their feet quickly advanced. The door opened and we both fell through the wall of vines. James shoved the door closed with his foot, stood up and locked the door. He turned and fell back against the Door exhaling in relief.

I looked up at James and immediately felt the weight of everything we had just gone through. He looked like we had literally just gone to war. We had. He stood there, still shirtless, his chest heaving with every breath. His entire top half was scraped and bruised. His face was swollen and bloodied with mud still dried and clumped in his hair. His pants were ripped from the fight at the campsite. A couple of tears streamed down his face. I knew he was mourning Squash and the lost hope of news of his father. I felt my own tears flowing down my face freely. We had made it. I would see Gabby again. It was impossible to even process everything that had just happened. I still couldn't believe it.

I collapsed onto the soft carpet, feeling every bruise and cut on my own body. James slowly bent down and sat next to me. I noticed his face relax as he looked over at me, arms perched on his knees. Then, thankfully, I saw a hint of playfulness develop in his eyes.

"Good heavens, girl. This is the first time I've really been able to even see you. You look absolutely terrible." He slightly smiled at me. I reached up and touched a deep cut on his upper lip. It would most definitely scar. At this point, though, I felt like my whole face would scar. I leaned in and kissed him softly.

"James," I say over-sweetly, "I was actually just about to recommend that you steer clear of the bathroom. You do *not* want to see yourself in a mirror right now."

"What do you say we go soak ourselves in some salt water and attempt to clean out some of these scrapes before we head to the hospital?" he asked with a serious face.

"Enjoy the view for just a minute?" I considered. "Sure, a little salt in the wounds never hurt anyone." He smiled as he helped me up carefully. We peeled off the little remaining clothes we had on, James down to his underwear and me down to my bra and panties. We walked down to the ocean and cautiously entered the water. I felt the sting in every single scrape. It was painful, but not intolerable. Thankfully, the ocean was calm so we could ease in slowly. As I went under the water, I welcomed the intense burn on my face and sides. Something about it felt good. Healing. Cleansing. I was thankful to be alive to feel it. I ran my fingers through my hair to remove some of the filth. I came up out of the water to be greeted by James. He wrapped his large, muscular, scraped and cut, but now clean arms around me, and hugged me ever so gently. We were home. We were safe. Through the stings and pain, I already felt like wounds were beginning to heal. Honestly, pain never felt so good.

THE RETURN.

James was right, I looked dreadful. We came in from the ocean and painstakingly put some clothes on so we could go to the hospital in Rio. I stood at the mirror and barely recognized myself. My right eye was swollen shut and already discolored to a deep purplish blue. A wide gash about two and a half inches long ran through my eyebrow and down, barely missing my eye. It was a souvenir from Palus that I would wear the rest of my life, no doubt. I lifted my shirt to look at the left side of my long torso. Bruising had already begun around the three perfect, deep slices running diagonal down my side. The bleeding had already stopped, but I needed a lot of stitches. I wondered how I would explain this to Gabby. It looked like I had wrestled a bear. That would be more believable than the truth.

After a quick visit to the hospital to get sewn and stapled back together, we ate for the first time in almost twenty-four hours. James and I decided on a believable story to explain our injuries to everyone. When we arrived back to the house on the beach, I put my purse down and stood there staring at the Door; the Door that led to the world where we almost died. James came up next to me and put his hands on my shoulders.

"You okay?" he asked gently.

"Yes . . ." I answered slowly. "I'm not quite sure what to feel." I stared at the brown wooden door. "What do you think is happening on the other side?" I asked suddenly.

"That's a good question." James left my side and walked toward the door and stood in front of it, crossing his arms. "I don't know about you, but I don't want to find out."

We sat outside watching the sunset, planning the next couple of days. It was Monday night and I told Gabby I would drive out to meet her in Charleston sometime that weekend. We also knew once we got home to Woodstock, Danielle would be on me for details about the trip. James and I knew our arrival home with these injuries would cause quite a stir, so we decided it would be best for me to call home and inform D about our "accident" so she would be prepared for our ghastly looking appearance. I called Gabby to tell her I would be driving out on Saturday, which would give my face the week to begin to heal. We booked our flight home for Thursday morning to give us a couple days to rest.

James and I spent the next few days resting on the beach and drinking well-deserved margaritas. We laughed and relaxed. It was a complete departure for us up until this point. It was nice not to strategize or carry the heavy issues we'd dealt with over the past few weeks. We may have looked beat up, with half of our bodies covered in gauze, but our minds and spirits felt healthy. We enjoyed the silence in moments, and talking about lighthearted things in others. We bought fresh caught fish from the local market, and James grilled it out on the back deck. It was nice to just be fully present. I hadn't felt fully present since before the morning Gabby brought her family-tree assignment home. After going to Italy, I'd thrown normal out the window. A beach and margarita? Yes, it was extremely overdue.

By the time we landed in Atlanta, all of our minor scrapes and scratches were almost healed. Only the large wounds remained. Thankfully my hair covered most of my badly, now greening, bruised and cut eye. The swelling had gone down in James' lip, we weren't quite as jarring to people. He was right about our looking bad ass though. We would chuckle as people would give us a wide birth when we walked by.

James dropped me off at the house later that afternoon. He kissed me goodbye and I watched as his Jeep rounded the corner and drove out of sight. He and Charlie would have a lot to talk about tonight. I turned to go into the house and stopped short. It sounded corny, but I knew I would enter this house a different person. So much had changed this week. I had seen things, experienced things. I had faced fears and conquered them. I had opened myself up again. Rosalina would be proud, as I definitely had a part of Ava in me. I had fought a giant sloth, for heaven's sake. But all I could seem to ask myself was, "What does this all of this mean for me as a mother?"

That night, Danielle brought dinner. I was grateful she accepted the story about the fall down the mountain without any reserve. However, she did get a few jabs in, making fun of my appearance. I at least got to be honest with her about my feelings towards James.

"So tell me, and don't you dare leave out one tiny detail, how was it?" she asked with wide eyes, leaning forward in her chair.

I laughed. "Tell you about what, specifically?" I teased her.

"About the kiss, you goon!" She was practically yelling at me.

"Well, we were sitting in . . . the hospital room, waiting on the doctor. It was cold and gloomy and we were both in pretty bad moods." I remembered the feelings before we kissed. "I was upset that we had gotten hurt and mad we had taken the risk, and he just leaned over and kissed me." I smiled at the memory.

"How? How did he kiss you?" she emphasized.

"It was soft . . . and tender. We were both pretty banged up. But I could feel all my reservations melting away. It didn't take but a moment for it to get more intense, though." I smiled at her as she fake swooned and fell on the couch.

"Why were you so nervous about him? I still don't understand why you were so hesitant to date someone." She propped herself up on her elbows facing me. She looked like a teenager.

"I don't know. It's hard to explain. I think it was just that I was so comfortable the way things were. And the older I get, the more I appreciated that feeling. I liked routine, and to know what lay ahead . . . and ever since I've met James, my life has turned upside down. It made me all very nervous." She had no idea how much this was true.

"I don't think it's boring. I get it. I feel the same most days." She sat up and smiled at me. "Besides, Eden, not everyone is built for adventure."

I had to pretend cough to stifle my laughter. "That's for sure."

꧁ ꧁ ꧁ ꧁ ꧁

I obviously couldn't wait to see Gabby. Her face was what got me through everything that happened in Palus. Saturday morning I loaded up my car with the bare essentials and made my way to Charleston. After the initial shock of my appearance, everything was smooth sailing. My mom, Gabby, and I spent some wonderful time together walking downtown, shopping, and eating gourmet food. We laid on the beach and built sand castles. Gabby had such a wonderful time visiting her grandparents that we talked about making it more than just a yearly trip, and she was thrilled.

So much had changed over the past week; I knew I needed to tell Gabby about James if we were going to give a relationship a shot. I was hiding so many things from her, and James was *not* going to be one of them. We were driving home back to Georgia when I finally got the courage to bring it up.

"So, Gabby, I wanted to talk to you about something." I wasn't a hundred percent sure how I was going to tell her. "Do you remember the handsome man from the porch?" I smiled when I remembered her calling him that at the coffee shop.

"Yeah, sure. What was his name?" she asked absently.

"James. Well, we have become pretty good friends," I added carefully.

"Is he your boyfriend?" She was teasing me. I laughed out loud.

"Kinda. What do you think about that? How would you feel if I had a boyfriend?"

"Well, I have one, too, so I think it's okay," she said sheepishly.

"*What*?" I reacted overdramatically. "*Who*?"

"His name is CJ, and he is so funny. He shares his chips with me every day at lunch."

"Well, well, well, how long has this been going on?" I asked, poking her side with my free hand.

"About a month. It's no big deal, Mom, I've had lots of boyfriends." She rolled her eyes. "But don't worry," she added, "I'll never kiss a boy. That's disgusting!"

"*Ha*! Can I get that in writing please?" I joked, raising my eyebrows. After a few seconds of laughing, I tried to steer the conversation back to where we had started.

"Would it be okay if we went over to James' house for dinner tomorrow night? He invited us over for spaghetti."

"Sure, that sounds fun." She barely skipped a beat. "You think I could bring my iPad and we could make some videos over at his house?" she asked enthusiastically. She loved finding new locations for her homemade videos.

"I think that would be awesome. He has a lot of land that you can explore and play in." My mind went to the door on his property.

My imagination suddenly drifted to Gabby playing with Lolli up in the trees in Terra Arborum, and I had an overwhelming desire to tell her everything, about all the adventures, my new friends, and the other worlds.

"Mom? Are you okay?" Apparently, my face wore the tension I was feeling. I looked at her and relaxed. Her big blue eyes were filled with concern.

"Of course, sorry, honey. Why don't we stop for some lunch? I'm starving," I said in an attempt to cover myself.

"Can we go to Chick-fil-A? They have a new milkshake I can't wait to try." I smiled, excited to try it myself. I loved her so much, my little mini me.

THE NEW NORMAL.

It felt good to get back to my normal. I'd missed it. The last ten years, I'd had a single focus and goal: Gabby. I had learned to live over the past decade with a one-track mind. Ever since I'd boarded that plan to Italy and received my mother's key, I'd felt split right down the middle, and ever since I'd met James, my life had felt torn in two. Both sides seemed not to want to co-exist and I needed to find a way for them to. I slowly realized that I couldn't go back to the way things were. I was a Door Keeper, and while I had no idea what it meant for me, I knew it meant something more than simply running an art gallery in Woodstock, Georgia. I had fallen in love with James, and I had no idea what that meant for me and Gabby, but I knew it looked different than the past seven years.

I definitely had some things to work through and figure out. As I walked upstairs from the coffee shop and passed the painting mirrored on my shoulder, I stopped. I stared at the flowers and wondered what else they could represent. The Serenbe from Terra Arborum sat next to a large opened peach and coral flower. Again, one I'd never seen one in this world. The flower was a light peach with darker coral edging and spots that resemble a watercolor painting. The petals were thick and looked like those of an open rose, but the center was an oversized deep yellow/gold color, and looked more like the center of a sunflower. I looked down at my body. That was the flower that was placed on the front round part of my shoulder. The first one to be noticed. I wondered . . .

※ ※ ※ ※ ※

Later that day, Gabby and I sat at the table with Charlie and James. Gabby was delighted to find out Charlie was James' brother. Charlie had hung out with Gabby for me multiple times at the gallery through the building process. After a nice dinner, Gabby convinced him to go outside and make some videos, although it didn't take too much convincing. After James and I cleaned up the kitchen, we sat in his living room and cuddled on the couch.

"I could get used to this, you know."

"Get used to what?" I answered.

"Dinner with you and Gabby. She and Charlie having fun together. It feels like we are a normal family." He traced the slowly healing large scar that now ran through my eyebrow and down under my eye.

"You'd better be careful; you can scare a girl off with talk like that," I teased him.

"Oh come on, we've been through too much for a little serious DTR talk to scare either of us off." James raised his eyebrows.

I couldn't help but laugh. "True. I agree with you, this does feel easier than I thought it would."

James and I picked an older movie to watch as the kids played. I relaxed into him on the couch. He was right, this felt good. He had his arm wrapped around me, and I started playing with his fingernails. Neither of us could get ours completely clean since our traipsing through Palus. I traced the edges of his large hands, feeling the hard calluses, and running my fingers along the lines in his palm. It felt so great to have this. Someone to just be with. I didn't realize how much I'd missed it. Maybe I'd relied on Gabby too much.

Maybe it wasn't fair for her to be my whole life for so long. I couldn't help but start to imagine what our life could look like together, what our future would hold.

Before long, Gabby was asleep, and Charlie took her upstairs to sleep in his room so we could debrief together about our trip the week before. He came back down and settled into the chair across from us, anxious to hear my side of the stories. I hopped up to grab a glass of wine from the kitchen and heard a knock at the door. As I opened the door, I heard Charlie yell, "Hurry up, Eden, I've been waiting all week for this!" I laughed as I turned to face the opened door. Shock resonated through my body when I saw the stranger before me.

He was tall. At least as tall as James. The stranger was muscular, but lean and cut. With short silverish white hair, closely cropped around his nape and ears, longer toward the top. His skin was a dark olive, almost the same shade as mine, only slightly darker. His eyes were wide and a crazy mint green. He stared at me like he'd seen a ghost. Honestly, our stares mirrored each other. Neither of us said a word, and suddenly his eyes narrowed and a scowl creeped across his face. I watched his jaw clench tight, and before I knew what happened, he threw his arm up and hit me across the chest with his forearm, pushing me against the wall. I yelled as my side throbbed in pain from his attack. He had pinned me against the wall as I did my best to fight back, but to no avail. He was too strong.

His face was inches from mine when he growled at me, "Who are you?" in an accent I didn't recognize. I looked back at him, pleadingly. The pain was excruciating. Before I formulated an answer, I saw James out of the corner of my eye. He smashed the stranger in the face with his fist. The man's arm loosened his grip and Charlie tackled him. James pulled me out of the way and helped Charlie get the man under control and bound. The white haired stranger cursed. Charlie wrapped the intruder's hands together with a lamp cord and stood him up in front of me. We stared into each other's eyes. The man looked more confused than angry at this point.

"Whoa. That's weird," I heard Charlie exhale. I looked at him and his eyes were wide. I turned to James who looked curiously back at me.

"What?" I huffed, gripping my side in pain, not having any idea what was going on.

"Your eyes . . . they changed color," Charlie barely whispered.

"Impossible," the stranger said and looked at me intently.

"Get him upstairs, above the garage. We don't want to wake Gabby, if we haven't already," James ordered. Charlie grabbed the man and took him up to the surveillance room. James sat him in the chair in the middle, just like he did me when he thought I was someone I was not.

The man was obviously agitated, but he looked more confused and upset than angry or defiant. I pulled a chair up in front of him and sat down. James warned me to be careful. For whatever reason, I wasn't scared. The man eyed me carefully as I looked him over. I saw a chain that went underneath his shirt. I asked if I could look at his necklace. He nodded slightly. I sensed James tense up as I gently took hold of the chain around the man's neck and pulled it to reveal what I seemed to know was there all along. A key. He spoke.

"I know who you are. I was sent here to take you. We know what you did. You violated your sacred oath as a Door Keeper, and you will be punished for it." He was looking at me but talking to James, and James didn't seem surprised.

"I didn't think we could get away with what we did without a visit. How did you find out so fast?" James questioned him. I looked at James in shock. He didn't warn me about this at all.

"The Door Maker contacted us when you passed through. Your key is tracked and monitored," the man answered.

That's why he wanted me to go to Terra Arborum to talk to Strix. He knew that I wasn't being tracked or monitored. I was immediately angry he didn't tell me about this danger, but I was too intrigued by the stranger to deal with it right now.

"What's your name and where are you from?" I asked him before James could say or ask anything else. The man stared at my tattoo then back into my eyes.

"You can call me Marek." I watched his eyes turn from the mint green they were when we met to a light greyish blue color. They turned to my eye color. I was completely fixated on this man.

"Marek, my name is Eden, and my mother was a Door Keeper from a place called Caelum. She died when I was born." I wasn't even sure why I was telling him this. What did I expect? His face remained stone, but his eyes seemed to dilate and suddenly his face softened. He didn't speak for a good sixty seconds.

The tension in the room built until I thought it would explode.

"My father, Samuel, ruler of Caelum, sent me for you, James." Marek's eyes never left mine. "He was the one that instituted the law forbidding Door Keepers to pass through the doors. He created the law after his wife, my mother, Ava, passed through the door to Earth and died with her unborn child over thirty years ago."

At the mention of my mother and father's name, something rose up in me, something foreign, something new. Something I couldn't understand or explain. But as it bubbled within me, my eyes turned the same color as Marek's, my brother's, was currently turning. A soft shade of purple.

I think Rosalina had called it lavender.

THE NEW DREAM.

The two large rocks we stood on were equally faded. Once upon a time, bright veins of purple, blue, and green hues coursed through them. However, as the years passed, they had turned soft and pastel, now resembling the sky right before the sun sets. She stood across from me, on her large rock, concentrating on the task ahead of her. Her silhouette dark against the deeply orange and yellowing sky. Her arm twisted behind her back, and her hand gripped a round flat stone, gently rotating it in her palm with her fingers. She turned her head to look at me, and a couple pieces of her long hair blew across her face as she smiled. Then, she turned her focus back to her target. We stood in the middle of a huge lake, surrounded by mountains on all sides. I saw the glistening of the suns reflecting off the lake behind her, setting in the distance. She pulled up her leg and dipped her body back. Her arm almost completely outstretched behind her before she whipped it around her body. Everything was fluid as I watched what I was waiting for. Right before she released the rock, her wrist flicked in just the perfect way sending it skipping across the lake's surface. Perfection. She turned and grinned at me, her large eyes bright with excitement. Her hair danced out behind her as it caught the wind. Someone called my name behind me, and the figure before me broke into a million pieces and floated away. Tiny, silver pieces, as thin as paper. They flew through the last remaining sun's rays, like pieces of ash. I watched, painfully, as the memory of her floated across the lake until I could no longer see the tiny particles.

I opened my eyes. A sudden chill ran through my body. Where was I? I heard my name called again as it had in the dream. I was outside of my house, and stood facing the lake. I turned to see my brother had already crossed the street and made his way to me. He was barefoot and only wearing blue striped pajama pants.

"Eden, what are you doing out here? Are you alright?" His light mint green eyes looked heavy with concern. His eyebrows were scrunched in the middle like mine get when I'm worried about Gabby. Gabby. I closed my eyes and saw her grin at me as she did in the dream.

"I'm fine, Marek. It was just another dream," I say with my eyes still closed. I neglected to tell him that I had just woken up and apparently slept-walked out here. I'd been having the dream ever since my brother arrived, but had yet to find myself outside upon waking.

"The one with Gabby?" I nodded. Marek looked out over the lake and rubbed his bare arms. His left arm was covered in a sleeve of tattoos. Beautiful script in his native language. Our native language. "It's getting colder here. Is it already time for your next season?"

"Ha, this is Georgia, Marek, there is zero predictability. Who knows, we may skip fall altogether and go straight to winter." I shrugged. It was the first cold night we'd had, hinting at the beginning of fall. I had a sudden thought. "Have you ever experienced a winter?"

"I did once, about ten years ago. A world called Iskrem. Your Door to it is Norway. I hated it, the cold was so brutal. Our people are not accustomed to such low temperatures."

I shivered. "Let's go inside. All this talk of cold weather is making me freeze."

As we crossed the elbow shaped bend in the road back toward the house, I thought about the past couple months. Gabby had started school, 5th grade, a few weeks ago. Next year she'd be going to middle school. I pushed the thought from my mind as soon as it entered. I looked over at Marek, my brother.

It had been a little over three months since my brother had broken down James' door and entered our lives. I'd loved having Marek stay with us. It'd been incredible, hearing about Caelum, and his life as our father's Peace Keeper. While Marek was not technically a Door Keeper, (that role is traditionally for women in Caelum) his role within our father's regime required him to cross worlds as the need arises. He is the only one legally allowed to cross through the doors, and only to keep the peace. I assume that by peace, my father meant separation. If there was any infraction, or boundary crossing within the Door Keeper community, Marek was responsible for taking action. At this point, I was still unsure about what action it was he was supposed to take. I tried not to think about it since James and I were the violators.

The night that Marek arrived at James' door, we spent the entire evening trying to figure out how to proceed to keep everyone safe. We finally just decided for Marek to buy some time by sending home a fake story to his (our) father to explain a delay in returning with James. We wanted to make sure that we came up with the best plan possible. Plus, he wanted to spend some time getting to know me and Gabby before returning home to Caelum. We knew we were on borrowed time. That, eventually, we would have to discuss it and decide on the best course of action. But for now, we were all procrastinating the inevitable return.

We also had to come up with a cover for Marek for everyone in my life, including Gabby. It was painfully obvious we were related, there was no scooting around it. We used Rosalina as our alibi. We told everyone after I had visited Italy, Rosalina contacted my brother to inform him of my whereabouts. She didn't tell me about him because she was not sure he wanted to meet me. Marek easily slipped into a thick Italian accent for everyone other than myself, James, or Charlie. Gabby was on cloud nine to learn she had an uncle. They'd immediately hit it off. Most of the time I heard her screaming in delight as Uncle Marek chased her all around the house, then tickled her until she could barely breathe. Most of the time they walked into a room, she was hanging off of him like a jungle gym. They'd become inseparable. Marek spent most of his time with me at the gallery, or brushing up on this world's technology. One day, he spent over four hours at the Apple store learning about the latest iPhones and tablets. However, I noticed very quickly that he avoided James whenever he could manage. He always offered to watch Gabby, or take her for ice cream, if the boys were over. James was equally as skeptical of Marek. As much as I tried to force them to take the time to get to know each other, both men resisted. I felt strained from the tension, but the joy I felt from suddenly having so many people so close in my life outweighed everything else.

We were back inside the house when I said goodnight to Marek, and began to walk upstairs when he stopped me, gently grabbing my arm.

"Eden, your dreams are becoming more and more frequent, and I know you were sleepwalking tonight. In our family, the unconscious mind is very connected to our waking one, many times seeing things before they happen. I think it's time we meet with

James to discuss our next move." His eyes turned purple, as they normally did when we discussed Caelum.

I sighed, not wanting this moment, or the past three months, to end. But at the same time, knowing something unstoppable was on the horizon. "I think you're right. I'll call James in the morning. We can head over there as soon as Gabby and Charlie have left for school."

THE DECISION.

The wind whipped my hair against my face. The cool morning air felt refreshing as we drove in my convertible to James' house the next morning. Marek sat next to me, his chin pulled toward the morning sun.

"I'll miss this car."

"What, no convertibles in Caelum?" I teased, knowing they would never allow or have technology like this.

"Closest we have is horseback . . . it's just not the same." He shrugged.

We drove past the door in the middle of the field, the one that led me into my first excursion into another land. I couldn't help but smile when I pictured Lolli's face. We took the next left into James' long tree covered driveway. After parking the car, Marek did not move to get out.

"You okay?" I asked.

"The last time I drove up this driveway, everything changed. When you opened the door and I saw you, Eden . . ." He trailed off and looked down toward the floorboard. After a minute, he looked up at me. "Months before we met, I started having dreams about you. Dreams of us sitting around a huge bonfire in my favorite place where I played as a kid. A secret place I'd never shown anyone. You looked just like you look now. I always got so angry when I had the dream, because I knew you were dead. I thought it was an alternate life I was seeing, maybe the way our lives could have been if Mom hadn't left Caelum that day. When I saw your face after the door opened, I just knew you weren't real. I got so angry thinking I'd slipped into the dream again. I never could've imagined the dreams were actually telling me that you were alive. I'm sorry I never told you. I just wanted to make sure that at some point, I did."

We sat in silence for a few minutes. I looked at my older brother, unsure what to say. I wasn't the only one who had lost everything when my mother died. I reached over and gave Marek a hug. "I'm glad we found each other, too, broseph." He laughed and pushed me away.

🙢 🙢 🙢 🙢 🙢

"Eden, there is *no* chance you are going without me." James was furious. Marek had suggested we go back to Caelum alone.

"James, we have no idea if you could even handle the environment. Marek said it's extreme—" James cut me off before I could finish.

"That didn't stop you coming with me to Palus," he said, obviously upset. I had not seen him this angry before.

"James, all Eden is saying is it would be safer for you to stay here with Gabby."

"This is not your decision, Marek!" He stood in frustration and slammed his hands on the table. "Eden and I have faced worse odds before, and as long as we stick together, we'll be fine." James was getting too worked up.

"Babe, just sit down for a minute," I pleaded. Although it had only been five months knowing James, the bond that formed between us was tightly woven. Facing death together and coming out the other side will do that to a couple. Thankfully, I could see James attempting to calm himself. He sat, and I took his hand in mine. "I will not go without you if you want to go. It was just a suggestion. I just don't want to put you in another situation like I did in Palus. Especially not unnecessarily. Plus, let's not forget that Marek was under orders to bring you back to my father for God knows what. I just don't want to put you in any danger."

I felt an odd, tangible sensation tingle on my left side coming from Marek's direction. It was almost though I felt a wave of guilt wash over me; but the guilt wasn't mine. I glanced over at my brother as he stared at the table, his jaw clenched. James regained my attention, his voice much calmer.

"Eden, I appreciate your concern. But we've been in this together from the beginning, and I want it to stay that way. You went to Palus to me to help me find information about my father, and I intend to go to Caelum with you to find yours." He looked into my eyes earnestly. I smiled back at him and nodded. I loved having him on my side. He made me feel brave in the face of so much uncertainty.

We both looked at Marek. He glanced up uncomfortably and looked from me to James and back again. It was obvious he felt uncomfortable with this idea.

"Okay," he said hesitantly, "it's settled then. We all three go together."

We spent the next two hours creating and going over details of the plan for our trip to Caelum. Arrangements for Gabby, the story of why we were going to Italy, and our plan once we arrived in Caelum. Once everything was clear, and we were ready to put the plan into motion, Marek finally relaxed and looked at me with a glimmer in his eye.

"Eden, it's time to go home."

THE TENSION.

"Wait, so you are going to meet your dad?" Danielle's dark blue eyes were wide. We sat on my favorite green tufted couch in the gallery, sipping on coffee. We enjoyed the slow early mornings together at Wall Polish, and usually used the time to catch up with each other before the after-breakfast rush.

"Yeah, apparently he lives somewhere in Tuscany. Marek hasn't seen him in a long time, so it might take a while to track him down, but I think we will find him." I'd practiced the lie so many times I actually started believing it.

"I swear, your life has become more exciting and dramatic than a soap opera." D exhaled slowly. "I mean, seriously. A new boyfriend, dangerous accidents, brothers appearing from nowhere, and now an estranged father. Eden, your life has become primetime material." She sipped her coffee.

"Tell me about it. It's starting to wear me out." I half smiled at her.

"How are things with James? What does he think about all of this?"

"Things are going great with James." My full smile returned. "He's been so supportive. You should have seen his reaction when I suggested Marek and I go to Italy alone. It's wonderful to have someone to go through this with. I can't imagine going through the past couple of months without him."

"I'm just happy to actually have someone to double date with now." She beamed.

Over the past summer, Marek gladly babysat for Gabby and Emmie so James and I could spend some time with Danielle and Patrick. D's husband had been home most of the summer, so it was nice we could all four spend time together. It felt normal; which, after stumbling into this insane world of Door Keepers, was lovely.

"Well, let me know if I can do anything to help you with Gabby while you're gone."

"Actually, we're taking her with us. Rosalina really wants to meet her, and I still feel bad about leaving her here last time."

"Oh my gosh, does she know yet? She is going to flip out. Wait, doesn't Rosalina want to meet me? Or I could come babysit so you can have some romantical time . . . for heaven's sakes, when do I get to go to Italy?" She strung every word together like a giant run on sentence. I couldn't help but laugh at her.

Danielle and I spent the rest of the day at work together, cleaning and going over the calendar for the next month. The gallery was running smoothly and, thankfully, required little maintenance. Wall Polish had become everything we hoped it would be. Many local artists rented it out for shows, and most of the coffee shop patrons used it as a social meeting place, in turn drawing more artist's interest.

Later that night, James and Charlie came over for dinner so we could talk to Gabby about the trip. I was in the kitchen with Marek preparing pesto chicken pasta when I heard them come through the door. I turned to see James' large physique taking up the entire doorway. He smiled at me in a way that made my whole body feel warm.

"James." Marek slightly nodded his head.

"Marek." James returned his gesture.

"Charlie. Good to see you again." Marek held out his hand, and Charlie grabbed and shook it overenthusiastically.

"Thanks, Marek. Listen, dude, super sorry again about the whole fighting thing and tying you up with a lamp." Charlie scrunched up his face, looking as uncomfortable as the room felt. "How's your jaw feeling? Is it alright?" Marek's chuckle relaxed the room. Charlie had grown even taller over the summer. His arms and upper body had filled out a bit so he didn't look so gangly. He'd also shaved his head, which made him look much older than the seventeen he was.

"No worries, Charlie. We all regret some actions from that day." He glanced at me apologetically.

"*James!*" Gabby came barreling into the room and jumped into James' arms.

"Hey there, Gabbs!" James gave her a bear hug. "Missed you, girl. How was your week at school?" He put her down and took her hand, leading her into the living room. Charlie followed them and I watched Marek eye them as they left the room. He gazed on even after they were out of sight.

"He's good to her," he said quietly, not turning around.

"Yes, he is," I answered to the back of his head. "He's good for me, too."

"I don't think he should come with us." He slowly turned around to face me.

"You said that before, but what I want to know is, why?"

His eyes changed color. "You don't know what it's like back home. It's different. Him being there will be very complicated. I'm under orders from our father. If he goes with us, I can't guarantee his safety."

"And you don't know what it was like in Palus. We saved each other. He makes me stronger, Marek."

"Well . . . I don't trust him," he replied honestly.

"Well, he doesn't trust you either, but guess what? You don't have to. You both just have to trust me. Because I'm not doing this without both of you." I lifted my chin to look my older brother squarely in the face. He looked down at me and his eyes and face softened.

"Yes ma'am." He faked a deep southern accent, then turned back to finish making dinner.

Over the past few months, Marek and I'd fallen into quite a rhythm in the kitchen. The chicken pesto pasta was a big hit with everyone. About halfway through dinner, I brought up my earlier conversation with Rosalina.

"So, Marek, I set everything up with Rosalina earlier today, and all of the arrangements have been made." Then purposefully sounding as casual as possible, I dropped the good news. "We all leave for Sorrento next week." Everyone sat still and slowly looked at Gabby. Her eyes were wide. I added for dramatic effect, "And, Gabby, I've already informed your teachers that you'll be missing school."

"*What*? I get to go to Italy?" Gabby squealed in delight. "Are you serious? Oh. My. Gosh. I'm *so* excited. Are we all going?"

"Not *all* of us . . ." Charlie pouted. He had only argued the plan for a couple of hours until James told him he'd consider the week training for his apprenticeship as Door Keeper. Charlie knew how long it would take for him to be fully trained, and he might as well start now. Most DK's started training at eighteen.

I launched into the story we had prepared for Gabby. "So the plan is for us to go stay with Rosalina. Remember my friend I met there that you've talked to on the phone?" Gabby nodded excitedly. "Well, we're going to go stay with her while your Uncle Marek,

James, and I try to find your grandfather." Grandfather. Just saying it surprised me. Gabby's next question did as well.

"Will I get to meet him?" she asked.

All the adults in the room looked at each other. Marek was the first to answer.

"Gabby, I haven't seen your grandfather in a long time. I'm not sure where exactly he is or if he is even still alive." He lied easily. "We just want you to come along so you will be close by in case we do find him."

The truth was we wanted Gabby close in case anything crazy happened. We needed to know we could get to her quickly if things went wrong.

"Also, Rosalina really wants to meet you in person. She said Skype isn't real life," I joked to ease the new tension. I added for good measure, "Rosalina even mentioned maybe taking you on a special trip to Venice for a couple of nights to go shopping."

"Oh! Isn't that the city with all the boats?" Her eyes light up again. "That sounds amazing." And then, whispering to herself, "Very grown up. I'm a not a little girl anymore."

"So you keep reminding me," I mumbled under my breath.

That night I sat in bed, attempting to journal my feelings. Six months ago, Gabby was my only family. Now, I was risking her again for the sake of meeting family I'd never met. I underestimated the danger in Palus, and I hoped I wasn't doing it all over again with Caelum. But Gabby and I both deserved to know the family I left behind and where we came from. It might never happen if I didn't do it now. I hated lying to Gabby about finding Samuel, but unless he was willing to leave Caelum to meet her, the truth would have to wait. She wasn't ready for this Door to be opened. This Door was more like Pandora's box. I would have never thought I'd feel this way. Up until this point, I'd always valued the truth, no matter the consequence. But experiencing everything I had in the past few months, the need to protect and shelter those I love had made everything turn varying shades of grey. My world used to be so black and white. Now, with my worlds becoming plural, nothing felt either.

I felt as conflicted as I did before we left for Palus. Except this wasn't for James. This was for me and Gabby. This was our family, our heritage. Plus, I didn't want to lose Marek in my life. If having him here was any indication of what could be waiting for me in Caelum, I was all in. It wasn't like finding my brother filled a hole, it just made me feel fuller. Overflowing. If finding my father would do more of the same, it was an easier decision.

The main thing that plagued me was the uncertainty between Marek and James. Why did they distrust each other so much? What was I missing there? Not to mention the fact that James was wanted by my father. And I had a deep pit-in-my-gut feeling that he had very ill intentions.

THE WEEK BEFORE.

The week leading up to the trip to Italy, I didn't see James much. He and Charlie spent most of their time together preparing for Charlie to be alone. There were protocols and systems to be put in place in case anything went awry when we were gone. I spent most of the week at the gallery, and trying to help Gabby get ahead in some of her classes so the time away wouldn't affect her grades. Marek was gone most days getting gear and things he wanted to bring home to Caelum. At night, Gabby, Marek, and I ate dinner together and practiced Italian so Gabby could learn a little of the language before the trip. Again, the normalcy and routine of it all relaxed me. Gabby and I had adjusted quite well to the increase in our little family. She welcomed Charlie, James, and Marek into our lives as though she had always expected them. I was surprised at how well we'd both adjusted. I can't even remember why I was so adverse or nervous about the idea of entering into a relationship with James. I was already at a place where I couldn't imagine it any other way.

We booked our flights on a Friday night so Gabby could go to school, and we could travel overnight, arriving in Naples the next day. That Friday morning I sat on the front porch with my coffee and opened my computer. I clicked the name that had changed my life forever: Rosalina. Her bright, smiling face popped up on my screen.

"Well, my dear, shouldn't you be packing your bags?" Her thick Italian accent was music to my ears.

"Rosalina, I've been packed since yesterday. This trip couldn't come soon enough." I smiled.

"I hope you are planning to actually spend some time with me before you gallivant off on your big adventure."

"Gallivant?" I laughed out loud.

"Yes, gallivant. I watch American television."

"Ha-ha, yes, of course. We plan on staying with you a couple of days to make sure Gabby gets settled before we leave. Also, Marek has some business to attend to before we go through the Door."

"Well, this is just almost too much. I can't believe after all this time, I'm talking about Doors, Door Keepers, and Caelum again . . . it's just so much fun!"

"Well, Rosalina, after all you have done for me, and Ava, I'm glad you get to be a part of it, too."

Her face changed as she asked her next question. "How are things going between Marek and James?"

"Not much different," I replied honestly. Rosalina had been my only confidant about the growing tension I felt between my boyfriend and brother. I continued, "They haven't seen much of each other this week. Both are trying to tie up loose ends before we leave tonight."

I filled her in on the conversation I had with Marek in the kitchen the week before. I concluded with my biggest fear. "He still won't tell me what our father wants with James. Which, of course, worries the heck out of me."

"Eden, it doesn't sound like it's James he distrusts. I think he doesn't trust himself. James just happens to represent the one thing he is torn between: his allegiance to your father, and his newfound allegiance to you." I took a minute to process her wise words. She continued, "Has James talked to you about his feelings towards Marek?"

"Honestly, he hasn't. He told me when Marek first arrived that he didn't trust him, but hasn't said much about it since. I think he knows how much Marek has come to mean to me and Gabby. But I know from the way he avoids him that he still feels the same way."

"It will all work itself out. It always does with family. Just don't avoid the conflict. Sometimes, working through it is the only thing that can bring the peace." I smiled at my mother's friend, once again thankful that she found me that day on the street in Sorrento.

"Thanks, Rosalina. I can't wait to give you a hug tomorrow."

"And I can't wait to meet Gabby, James, and Marek."

"Oh, trust me, they can't wait to meet you either. After all, they have you to thank for all of this." At that, she pretended to give me kisses on both cheeks and we disconnected.

Rosalina was right. Whatever was going on with Marek was internal, a battle within himself. There was nothing I could do to ease it or change it. I just needed to let him work it out for himself. It sucked, though, considering I was never good at remaining passive.

Later that evening, I moved all of our luggage onto the porch while Marek and Gabby played inside the house. The sun was setting above the lake. My mind unconsciously raced back to the first time Eric and I had come to look at this house. We'd come around this time, late summer, at the end of the day. Setting the suitcase down, I walked off the porch and across the street. I stood there, staring off over the lake as the sun's last rays glistened across the rippling water. I was instantly transported back to that moment, over ten years ago. Almost as though I'd traveled back in time, I felt Eric come up beside and place one hand on my lower back and one on my growing tummy. We both had stood there in silence, admiring the beautiful view, until he spoke.

"This is it, Eden. This is the place our little Gabrielle will grow up," he said.

I looked over and saw him like it was yesterday. His eyes level with mine, dark brown with black glasses framing them. He smiled at me crookedly, exposing his imperfectly perfect teeth. That day, at that moment, we hugged and made the offer on the house.

Now, I stood there and felt the tears well up inside me, unwilling to fall. I wished Eric could have watched Gabby grow up here, could see her playing with her uncle. I wished that he could have watched me discover the truth about who I was. I'd been gifted so much, and had so much to be thankful for, but for a brief moment, I allowed myself to grieve all that I had lost.

"Eden?" I about jumped out of my skin.

"Dang it, Marek, you almost gave me a heart attack!" I yelled dramatically.

"Sorry. Any reason I keep finding you out here by the lake?" he asked.

"I was just thinking about Eric, wishing there was a way he could have seen all of this." I shrugged.

"I wish I'd had the opportunity to him," Marek said thoughtfully, turning his attention toward the lake. "Anyone who contributed to that sweet angel inside the house is due my gratitude. Not to mention that he was there for you when the rest of us couldn't be."

I smiled. "Well, you are all here now. And I'm sure Eric is super grateful to you for it."

"Come on, Eden, we have a plane to catch."

THE TRIP BACK.

Charlie and James came and picked us up just a few minutes later. Charlie dropped us at the airport. Charlie and Marek's awkward goodbye made Gabby and I giggle to ourselves. James just rolled his eyes as Charlie gushed over Marek and tried to give him a hug that resulted in more of a rejected tackle. As we made our way through security, I looked back to see Charlie waving widely and yelling, "Arrivederci!" I wished at that moment he could have come with us. Charlie would have made our trip that much more entertaining.

Gabby turned and, mimicking his gestures. yelled back, "Arrivederci, Charlie!"

James looked over his shoulder at me and smiled. It was the smile that melted me a little more each time.

The flight was uneventful and we landed after sleeping most of the time. Gabby had made friends with the flight attendants and left the plane with all sorts of little goodies, including a sleep mask and one of the travel bags from first class. As we walked through the airport, I saw the sign being held up first.

"EDEN CHERUBINI"

I followed the arms holding the sign to see Rosalina attached to them. I smiled and cut through the crowd, excited to see my mother's, and now my, friend. Her light blondish, greying hair was in a loose braid tucked into a bun. Her face lit up when she saw us, and embraced me as she had when she first recognized who I was. She quickly pushed me aside rather comically and scooped up Gabby, who squealed in delight. I watched Rosalina set her back down on the ground and hold Gabby's cheeks in her hands, kissing her whole face.

"You are so beautiful, *molto dolce ragazza!*"

"What?" Gabby's face scrunched up.

"Oh, that means 'very sweet girl'." Rosalina laughed. She stood up and looked at James first. "And you . . . you must be James," she said, her eyes bright. "*Dio mio. E un bell'uomo, vero?*" She looked at me.

"*Si lo e,*" I replied, smiling. I winked at James who stared back at me with his eyebrows raised. I whispered to him later she had told me he was very handsome.

"Marek, you are most definitely your mother's son." She had turned to my brother and reached out for his hand. "You and Eden could be twins."

"Thank you, Rosalina," Marek's accent thickened as he spoke to her, "and thank you for bringing me and my sister together." He lifted and kissed her hand.

"Oh my!" Rosalina exclaimed while blushing. "We should be on our way, we have quite a drive ahead of us before we get to Sorrento."

We picked up our bags and loaded up in Rosalina's rental car. I adored watching the drive through Gabby's eyes. She was enamored by the beautiful beaches and little towns we passed through. Almost the entire drive she was oohing and ahhing. I couldn't fault her, the coastline was just as breathtaking as my first trip was months ago. A little over an hour later, we arrived in Sorrento and were unpacking our bags in Rosalina's quaint villa. After we had settled, Rosalina made us some dinner and we sat at her kitchen table with the sunflower tablecloth, the place where I first learned the truth about my mother and where I was from. We ate, laughed, and enjoyed the gorgeous view of the far-off island of Capri.

🙰 🙰 🙰 🙰 🙰

She looked at me and grinned slyly as a sliver of her hair whipped across her face. I saw the determination in her eyes as she refocused her gaze on the lake stretched out before her. I looked behind her back, knowing what I would see before my eyes arrived there. She held the rock gently, slowly turning it round and round within her grip. The two glowing orbs of light descending behind her as they approached the mountains. The warmth in the air surrounded us like a blanket. I looked at her target, calm and glistening, begging to be disturbed. She lifted her leg and leaned her upper body back in a fluid motion and as her arm reached around, gracefully flicking her wrist at just the right moment to send the rock skidding across the glass-like water. I felt such a deep sense of pride as we both watched the rock skip along the surface, sending beautiful circular ripples from every contact point.

"Eden . . ." I heard my name softly called from behind me, and as she turned her head to look for whoever called my name, it happened. Her inevitable combustion into a million tiny silver ash-like pieces. I reached out toward the floating embers as if to try to catch them and put her back together.

"Eden . . ." He sounded closer this time. "Babe," he said. I opened my eyes to see James with a concerned look sitting on my bed.

"James, what's wrong?" I asked and sat up quickly.

"I was going to ask you that." He placed his hand on my wet cheek. "Were you having a nightmare?"

"Kinda. Not sure if it's just a weird dream or a nightmare. I'm okay, though. What time is it?" I asked groggily and yawned.

"It's early, but I have a surprise for you. I know this trip is for Caelum and for you to go home, but I couldn't resist the opportunity for us to make some memories together before all of the craziness starts. Gabby is going to hang with Rosalina. Would you come with me today?" He stood and reached out his hand as an invitation.

"What did you have in mind?" I grabbed his hand and grinned.

"How about we take in the sights and just enjoy the view?" I couldn't have imagined a better way to wake up.

THE MEMORIES.

After getting dressed and ready for the day, I headed outside to meet James. Gabby was still sleeping, and I didn't see Marek up yet either. In the kitchen, Rosalina had already started making a lovely smelling breakfast. Her long hair was loosely braided and fell down the center of her back, her light green apron tied with a perfectly quaffed bow. She stopped with the spatula in her hand and turned her head toward me, winked, and went right back to cooking.

"I'll see you tonight, sweetie. Have fun." Although I couldn't see her face, I knew she was smiling.

"Thanks, Rosalina. Give Gabby a kiss for me."

Ready to begin whatever James had planned for us, I bounced down the steps of Rosalina's apartment and walked out the front door into the quiet morning. James stood looking into the window of the chocolate shop across the street with his large brown leather bag thrown across his shoulder. I took the moment to appreciate that I had someone to be with, someone to have adventures with. I was thankful it was someone who I could be myself around. James had seen me at my most vulnerable. He'd seen me afraid, in pain, brave, and content. And now I got to spend time with him, in Italy, one of my favorite places in this world. Excited to get our day started, I

THE DOOR KEEPER

crossed the cobblestone street and walked up beside him. I intertwined my hand in his as he smiled down at me.

"So, what are we going to do today?" I asked.

"Well, we are going to start by heading to the Marina," he said with a sparkle in his eye.

We strolled through Sorrento, hand in hand, and before long we made it to Tasso square. Just six months ago, I sat at a table outside of Fauno Bar, people watching. Before James, Marek, Caelum, or even knowing Door Keepers existed. As we walked through the square, I pulled James over to the railing.

"Take a look at that." I leaned over the railing and pointed.

"Wow, what is it?" he asked, following my lead.

"I did some research when I got home from my first trip. It turns out it's an old set of ruins called "Valley of the Mills." The larger building was originally a watermill that dates back to 900 AD, and has been abandoned since the mid-19th century. Water used to flow down through the valley, and the mill powered the entire city."

"It's beautiful," James replied in awe. "Look at all those green ferns. They have completely taken over the buildings."

"Yeah, apparently the humidity down there is really high and makes for a great environment for them to grow," I said, admiring the seemingly forgotten buildings at the bottom of the gorge.

"How did you find this?" James asked suddenly.

"I don't know, I just saw people stopping and looking over the rail, and had to know what was down there. It intrigued me so much. I couldn't wait to show you when I found out we were coming back. It just looks like it doesn't belong, and I kinda relate." I grinned.

"Huh." James' eyebrows were crinkled in the center.

"What?" I looked at him.

"Nothing . . . I just get what you mean." He shrugged. "You ready? Marina Piccola is just down the street."

As we turned to leave, a tingle ran up my spine. Shaking it off, I wrapped my arm in James'. We arrived at the marina a few minutes later, walking down the hill toward the brightly colored boats. James led me straight to a beautiful wooden speedboat docked on the farthest pier. It was a gorgeous dark stain with white leather interior. He climbed in first, then helped me in. The early morning fog was beginning to lift, and the cool air whipped through my hair as he maneuvered us out of the marina.

He drove the boat south toward the island of Capri. The sun broke through the clouds, instantly warming the temperature. Water spraying from the sides of the boat created little rainbows. Before long, we made it to the island's cliffs. The rock faces were tall and steep, plunging deep into the bright blue waters. James slowed the engine, and we slowly made our way around the island. He finally found the spot he was looking for. He pulled up close to one of the smaller cliffs, and I saw a metal hook sticking out of the rock face. He turned off the engine and tied off the boat.

James opened his large leather bag to reveal a small woven basket and a thermos. As soon as he unfolded the linen cloth that lined the basket, I smelled Rosalina's kitchen. Chocolate croissants, my favorite. I peered in to see about half a dozen of them, still hot. We spent the morning sitting on the bow of the boat, eating chocolate croissants, strawberries, and drinking caramel cappuccino from the cafe below Rosalina's apartment. With a full belly and the warm sun on my face, I reached my maximum contentment level. Feeling bold and happy, I stripped off my clothes, wearing my swimsuit underneath, and dove off the boat into the clear turquoise Mediterranean. The water felt refreshing and surprisingly warm engulfing my skin. James joined me, and after a quick dip, we climbed back onto the wooden vessel and continued on our journey.

We drove just a little further west and came upon some buoys near the mouth of a small cave. James shut off the engine and dropped anchor. He signaled to a man in a small rowboat who came over to pick us up. I still had no idea what was happening. As soon as we entered his smaller boat, I noticed we were heading toward the mouth of the cave.

The skipper smiled at my confused look and said, in his husky thick Italian accent, "*Buongiorno*, welcome to Grotto Azzurra, Tiberius' sacred sanctuary. If you do not mind lying down in the boat while we enter the cave. *Grazie*." I looked at James who just smiled at me.

"I'd say we listen to the man." He laughed as he laid down next to me. I quickly followed suit and watched our skipper pull us along by a chain attached to the cave walls. I stared up as the ceiling of the cave appeared above me, hovering only about three feet above us. Suddenly we were engulfed in total darkness, except for the radiating blue glow emanating from the waters below. We sat up as our skipper started to sing an operatic tune that echoed off the walls, providing the perfect acoustics. It was mesmerizing. The only light in the cavern was provided by the sun's rays reflecting the bright azure color from the clear water under us. I had never seen anything like it. It felt less like floating on water and more like entering another world, which of course I had some experience in. I leaned over the side of the small rowboat and ran my fingers along the surface of the magical blue glow, unsure if this could be the same water I just swam in. It didn't seem possible.

Within minutes, our tour was over. We had to crouch back down as we exited the Blue Grotto, and our lovely skipper took us back to our boat. As I climbed back aboard, I saw other boats driving up for a tour of their own. James paid the man before he left to take the other tourists on their magical adventure.

"Thank you, James, that was incredible," I said, still staring at the mouth of the tiny cave that held such wonder.

"Of course." He smiled. "I'm just glad we got in before the tourist rush so we could experience it alone. I knew you would like it."

After our encounter with the Grotto Azzurra, we turned south to loop around the island and, after passing under the stone archway of Faraglione di Mezzo, a huge rock formation off the coast of Capri, James turned the boat back toward the mainland. It didn't take to long for me to realize we weren't heading back to Sorrento. I reclined, enjoying the beautiful coastal views that popped out behind the cliff face and enamored me as it had the first time. Positano. The view from the water was even more amazing. The colorful villas were all stacked upon one another on the cliff, almost as though they were chiseled from its stone. Two breathtaking hills of buildings, side by side, with the Santa Maria Assunta nestled in between. I couldn't take my eyes off the perched city as we made our way to its shores.

James pulled the boat into a small pier area, and we docked right next to the Spiaggia Grande. It was already after lunchtime so we walked straight to one of the local beach bars and ordered pizza and limoncello. We ate on lounge chairs and let the salty air wash over us. Only every hour or so would the looming quest we had ahead of us nag at my consciousness. I was so thankful for the distraction. I told James as much, and he reminded me we still had the whole day here.

After finishing up our pizza, James joked that it would give us fuel for the adventure he planned for next. We hopped on a bus that took us to a little village called Montepertuso, just down the coast. When we got off the bus, one of the locals pointed us toward a large pierced cliff jutting out over the ocean. We walked out and saw a magnificent aerial view of Positano below.

"This is the tail end of the 'Walk of the Gods'," James said. "We don't have time to do the entire thing, and the path leading to Positano is a hard trek, but I've heard it's worth it. You in?"

"You kidding me? If I can't do this, I'm not fit to be a Door Keeper." I laughed. "Let's do it."

I followed him down about a hundred million steps as we slowly made our way to Positano. He was right, though, passing through olive groves and watching the view change with every step was well worth the journey. Once we got back to Positano, we rested and had a coffee break at a cafe that was next to Villa Serene, where I'd stayed before. We teased each other about our aching bones and our inability to age gracefully.

After feeling fully refreshed, we spent the next hour or so shopping, attempting to find Gabby a present worthy of my absence—although I was sure Rosalina was spoiling her rotten. Once I was satisfied with my gift, James spoke up.

"Ok, now it's time to find you a dress." He sounded weirdly excited.

"A dress . . . for what?"

"Dinner. I made us reservations at a special place." He grinned.

"Heavens, James. Today has been amazing, we seriously don't have to do anything else." His boundless energy amazed me. Not aging gracefully, my hiney.

"Trust me, Eden, *this* is why we came here today."

"Okay . . . now I'm kind of excited. This dress, should it be casual or fancy?" I asked sheepishly.

"Fancy. Definitely fancy." He winked and my heart fluttered.

THE SURPRISE.

The day had already become one of my top ten best, and I couldn't imagine it getting any better, until I saw the restaurant. La Sponda was a pristine white backdrop to the lemon trees and garden of colorful flowers that adorned every pillar and archway. The bright red exotic flowers and white roses grew like wild vines up and around the ceiling. With no walls, there seemed to be no divide between the restaurant and the outdoors. The entire space was lit with candles. The waiter later told us that over four hundred candles lit La Sponda every night. The maître d sat us under one of the archways overlooking the city, now glowing as the sun set behind it.

"You look beautiful." James eyed me over his champagne glass.

"Thank you. You picked it out." I smiled slyly. The dress he bought me was a light cream, flowing maxi dress with spaghetti straps and a semi-plunging neckline—the kind only someone with a small chest can pull off modestly. Thankfully my hair curled somewhat decently from the salt water swim earlier in the day, and a bobby pin with a cream flower tamed the wild tuffs of hair behind my ear. James looked dashing in a light blue button down and dark grey slacks. His skin now darkened on his forehead and cheeks from a day on the boat. His light brown eyes glistened with the candlelight glowing around us.

We enjoyed an incredible evening with some of the most delicious food I'd ever eaten, and champagne flowed generously. We laughed, sharing stories from our childhood, dreams about our future, and talked seriously about whatever Caelum might bring. Around dessert some beautiful music began to play from the oyster bar above us. James held out his hand in yet another invitation. I placed my hand in his, once again gladly accepting.

He held me close as we swayed slowly to the soft rhythmic music. He smelled like the ocean and sun we had been basking in all day, and I couldn't stop the smile spreading across my face. As if sensing my joy, he looked down at me and chuckled.

"What?" he asked. "Do I smell bad?"

"No, absolutely not. You smell like our day today. Perfect."

"Well, good, because showers were the only thing I didn't plan for us."

"James, I don't want to wash anything away from today." I pulled back and looked into his warm brown eyes.

James moved his hand from my lower back to my face. He rubbed his thumb along the deep scar that ran through my eyebrow and down next to my eye. I felt the smoothed out yet hard calluses on his hand from his love of being outside.

"That's good, because I don't either. Whether it's Palus mud or the Mediterranean, I want to smell like whatever we do together. Because anything we do together is worth remembering. Eden, I want to marry you. I want to be with you always, whatever the adventure, whatever the world." His jaw tightened, and I got lost in the longing in his eyes, for just a moment. l would have happily gotten lost there forever.

He reached in his pocket and pulled out a deep bronze golden ring. "I know you don't love over-the-top jewelry, so I had a friend make this from my father's old key. A key to the door that brought us together."

I couldn't form words. Anything I tried to say got stuck in my throat. Inscribed inside the simple band was the phrase, "In every world."

"Eden, I want Charlie, me, you and Gabby to be a family," James said as if trying to convince me. As though he needed to convince me to love him, or trust him, or adore him any more than I already did.

"James . . . I . . ." I became overwhelmed with everything I felt. I looked in eyes and saw all I needed to see. "I have never wanted anything more."

I smiled through the tears that flowed. His face lit up as he placed the ring on my finger. A ring made from the metal that bound our worlds together now bound us together. It was just perfect. We stood there, kissing under the bright moon that looked on from above.

Then, as beautiful the moment was, a darkly comical thought crept through my mind that I couldn't shake. I pulled away from him and suddenly burst out, "Wait, so you *didn't* get my father's permission?" We both laughed, but also silently understood how much more complicated things were than either of us wanted to admit. Yes, we were in this mess together, and now it was time we faced it.

THE UNCLE.

We came in well after midnight, and everyone was asleep. I had missed my sweet angel, and knowing the next day was my last with Gabby before we left for Caelum, I crept into her bed to snuggle. I slept sound and dreamless next to my little girl. I woke up the next morning to her playing with my hand and its new piece of jewelry.

"This is pretty, Mom," she said sleepily.

"Thanks, sweetie. Good morning, how did you sleep?" I asked, rolling over.

"Good. Rosalina and I had fun yesterday. We spent the day at a beach! I was so tired, she made us walk everywhere." Her eyes were wide.

I chuckled. "Walking is good for you. And I'm glad you had fun."

"Where did you get this?" she asked, still fiddling with my ring.

"James gave it to me yesterday," I said. She smiled. "Gabby . . . he asked me to marry him." Her bright ice blue eyes grew wide. They reminded me of the Grotto Azzurra.

"He did? Mom, I'm so happy! I love James." I smiled as she tackled me in a giant hug, almost knocking me off the bed.

"I'm so glad, honey. He loves you, too." Her hair smelled like flowers.

"Wait, so is Charlie gonna be my brother now?" she asked with a wrinkled nose.

"No, James and I getting married will make him your uncle," I explained.

"So, now I have two new uncles. Charlie and Marek. That is *so* awesome." She sat up and jumped out of bed.

"I hope Uncle Marek thinks so . . ." I mumbled under my breath.

"Oh my gosh, I'm gonna have a dad." She spun around and faced me with a grin spreading across her face. She stood in front of me in her character pajamas, her hair cascading perfectly over her shoulders to her waist. Her eyes couldn't contain her joy or excitement over this new revelation, and it was infectious. That was my favorite thing about Gabby, her ability to change the mood in a room simply by inhabiting it.

"That's right, sweetie. James is excited for us to be a family." I sat up, taking in every moment with my beautiful daughter. She came back and sat on the bed.

"Mom, I'm so happy. You're happy, too, right?" I smiled down at my little mini me and tucked a tuft of hair behind her ear.

"Gabbs, I couldn't be happier." She gave me another bear hug.

Suddenly she belted out, "Oh my gosh, let's go tell Rosalina, she's going to be so excited. She told me yesterday that she liked James." The last sentence was said as she bolted down the hallway. I hopped out of bed and put on a robe, following Gabby to the kitchen.

"Good morning, Eden." Rosalina's singsong voice echoed as I entered the kitchen. She held a cup of coffee toward me. "Gabby tells me you have some good news."

"Gabby, why don't you do the honors?" I barely got it out when Gabby jumped in the air with arms stretched out above her.

"*Mom and James are getting married!*" she cried out.

"What is this I hear about me getting married?" James entered through the other doorway behind Gabby.

"James!" She turned around and hugged him fiercely. He scooped her up and she laughed as he sat her on his hip. "Jame . . . Dad . . . that feels weird." Her face scrunched.

"Why don't you just keep calling me James for now? We have plenty of time to figure all of that out." He kissed her on the cheek and then walked over to kiss mine.

"Good morning, hon. Good morning, Rosalina. Whatever you are cooking smells incredible." He sat Gabby down at the table covered in plastic sunflowers and, after grabbing a cup of coffee, sat with her.

"Thank you, James, and congratulations. Now, let me see the ring." Rosalina giggled and reached for my hand. She peered down at the band and her breath caught. She looked up at me with a knowing look.

"Is that the same metal as the key?" she whispered. I nodded. I should have known she would recognize it. She held onto my mother's key for over thirty years.

"It is absolutely perfect." She smiled. "James, you did well."

Rosalina was right, it was perfect. I stared down at the little promise wrapped around my finger when it hit me. A huge swell of emotion entered the room. It felt dark, angry, and concerned, yet with traces of happiness and joy. It was conflicted, torn between fear and hope. I knew he'd entered the room before I looked up from my ring. He stood in the doorway, jaw tight and eyes hard. They turned purple, then slowly back to his usual shade of mint. Although I'm sure it wasn't visible to anyone else in the room, I felt him inhale very slowly and unclench his fists.

"Good morning, Marek," James said politely while sipping his coffee.

"Congratulations, you two." Marek's eyes never left mine.

"Thank you, brother." I held his gaze.

"I know you're spending the day with Gabby today, but I need to steal you away for an hour. We have to meet with someone important before we leave on our trip tomorrow," Marek said flatly.

"Okay." I looked at Gabby and James. "I'll be right back, you guys. Make sure you leave some of this yummy breakfast for me." James looked at me with a hint of concern, but I smiled and kissed him on the forehead as if to say, *let me deal with him*.

*   *   *   *   *

Within minutes, we walked side by side down the streets of Sorrento in silence. I finally couldn't take it anymore.

"You had to have seen this coming," I said, agitated.

"Of course I did." His tone had relaxed. "I just hoped it would be after Caelum. This makes everything much more complicated."

"Because of our father," I added.

"Yes." Once again, telling me nothing more.

"Well, just the threat of 'complication' doesn't scare me anymore, Marek." I was getting frustrated. "You either tell me of a legitimate threat, or stop bringing it up."

Marek stopped mid-stride, and turned and faced me, his face full of concern.

"King Samuel has laws. James broke them and for that, he'll expect him to be punished. He's never made exceptions before, and I'm not sure you will be enough to change his mind. Honestly, I have no idea how he will react to you even being alive. I'm sure he will be beyond happy. But depending on his reaction to all of this, I can't guarantee James will come out unscathed. Believe it or not, I actually like him. I may not fully trust him, but he loves you and Gabby, and that I do trust."

"Thank you. Okay. So we just need to convince Samuel to make an exception. That is something I can work with." I smiled and placed a hand on Marek's arm. "Everything will be alright."

"I wish I believed you." Marek looked grim. "You'd better take that off." He nodded at my ring, "The Door Maker doesn't take kindly to people messing with his metal."

"The Door Maker?"

"Yes, the only one in this world that knows everything about every world. I think it is time that you two finally meet."

THE DOOR MAKER.

When Marek and I turned the corner, facing the Church of San Francesco, I laughed out loud. Of course, this ancient building would be the perfect place for the Door Maker. No wonder I was drawn to it last time I was here. Nestled next to the meticulously kept public gardens, this church and its adjoining cloister was one of the oldest and most revered buildings in all of Sorrento.

"What?" Marek asked, surprised.

"I came here. Last time, before I met Rosalina. I spent some time here." I stared at the intricate white architecture displayed in front of me.

"That doesn't surprise me. He, and this place, has a strong pull to us. It's his energy, it acts as a magnet. Let's go."

※ ※ ※ ※ ※

I wasn't sure what I'd imagined when I thought of the Door Maker, but I'm pretty sure it wasn't who I was staring at. Maybe I envisioned an old Italian monk who had dedicated his whole life to his craft of door making. Maybe we would've interrupted his meditation or something. Instead, I stood behind a huge burly man, bent over, wearing coveralls, the top half unbuttoned and hanging loosely around his waist. Dark, curly hair popped out the top of his white tank top, and he was elbow deep in soil. A huge chain of keys dangled from his side, jangling every time he moved. His hind quarters almost rivaled the size of the ginormous oak tree he was planting under. We stood in the garden, in the middle of the cloister that I had grown so fond of during my last visit. I didn't remember seeing this man, and definitely wasn't sure how his energy could have been what drew me here.

"You gotta be careful when planting around an oak tree. Its roots are powerful and greedy. They'll kill anything that encroaches on its territory." His voice was booming and deep, muffled by the hole in the ground he dug.

"Thanks, Gio, I'll remember that when tending my garden back home," Marek responded sarcastically.

"Ah!" Gio bellowed as he sat up and turned to face us, while simultaneously plopping on his big butt. "I knew someone important was going to visit me today." Gio had a large mop of dark brown curly hair with a matching full beard. His face was flushed and red from the excursion of planting, but his eyes were bright and excited. He laughed rather loudly. "I'm so happy it's you." He held his hand to my brother and, ignoring the dirt caked on every square inch, Marek hoisted him up. They embraced in a rather violent looking bear hug.

"I wondered when you were gonna pass by on your way back home."

"Well, I ran into someone worth delaying my trip." Marek stepped back and presented me like he was Vanna White. Gio's eyes grew wide.

"Ah, yes. I see. Very merited delay, indeed." Gio stepped forward and grabbed my hand. He raised it slowly and placed his other huge, dirty hand on top of it. "Aren't you an unexpected and yet very welcomed surprise." He kissed my hand. "I am Giovanni, Door Maker of this fine world. And what do you, beautiful daughter of Caelum, call yourself?"

"I'm Eden," I answered. "Marek's sister."

"Of course you are!" Gio boomed. "That is undeniable. But what is deniable is how you could be alive." His voice softened as did his eyes. "I searched for you for months after your mother's passing."

"She was adopted and taken to the states." Marek stepped in for me. "Alright, Gio, you can let her go, she's not going to run away." My brother laughed and pulled on Gio's arm that still held my hand tightly. The Door Maker gazed at me, completely enamored.

"Oh, Marek, she's gonna change everything," he said, suddenly turning away.

"I know, that's why we are here. Can we go to your office for some privacy?" Marek looked around at the growing number of tourists entering the garden.

"Of course, of course. I'll clean this up later," he said, gesturing widely at the gardening tools. "Follow me, my friends." He led us through one of the large arched doors located in the corner of the cloister. We walked down some steep stone circular steps and finally into an underground cellar, full of gardening equipment and other cleaning supplies. He unlocked a door off to the side using one of his many keys. I noticed several that resembled the key I used to enter Terra Arborum and Palus. I walked through the smaller doorway that Gio had to squeeze through into what I recognized immediately as his "office." It was a large space complete with both a woodworking and blacksmith area. Metal castings and related tools were housed on shelves, and a giant stove I assumed he used to melt the metal sat in the center of the room.

"Marek, Eden, would you like some tea or coffee?" Gio walked toward a little kitchenette.

"I would love some tea."

"Yes, my dear, of course." He brought me a cup made of wood with intricate carvings. It was beautiful. Before I even took my first sip, I smelled the sweet nectar of the Serenbe flower from Terra Arborum. I decided not to say anything for fear of letting him know I'd been there. This was, after all, the man who tracked and reported border infractions.

"Now, Marek," Gio plopped himself into an oversized recliner, "what can I do for you, my old friend?"

"Well, Gio, we're planning to return to Caelum in the morning. I'm afraid that I haven't done the best job explaining the different worlds, laws that govern the worlds, or the impact her return will have on them, to Eden. Of course, not that she would listen to me . . ." Marek cut his eyes over to me and rolled them subtly. "I was wondering if you could give her some context."

"Well, I have a wedding I need to prep the garden for this afternoon, so I don't have too much time." Gio was looking at his calendar. "But I can give you the quick version so you might better understand."

Gio spent the next thirty minutes informing me about the cycles of the worlds, how there are cycles of war and peace, and just like in any one world, those cycles are based heavily on different generations and pivotal events. My mother's death was one of those events. He neglected to say if it was one that led to peace or war, and I honestly didn't want to ask. Before Ava died, travel between worlds was allowed for Door Keepers only, but after she never returned, King Samuel became fearful and mandated that it was no longer. He instituted laws against it to protect all of the worlds from each other. When I questioned what gave him the authority to make such a rule, Gio explained that Caelum was the oldest known of all the worlds.

Whomever ruled Caelum ruled all the Door Makers and Keepers, which was why his home base was so close to Caelum's door. Most Door Maker's set up shop around their access point to Caelum.

Gio also explained the science behind the doors and the portals—at least as much as can be explained or comprehended by our finite resources. He walked me around his little shop, explaining to me about the different woods and metals he used for the doors. Depending on the world the Door opened, Gio would use a combination of woods from both worlds. All of the metal he used for the keys, locks, knobs, hinges and decoration came from an old world he, and most Door Makers, no longer had access to. He shrugged when I asked him why, but I knew better. There must have been a reason for the shutout, but at that moment, it was the least of all my questions.

The portals between worlds are slight overlaps of energy fields. They exist regardless of a Door's presence, but the Door is what allows us to control who has access to them. He told me a story about a poor man who accidentally discovered another world just walking through the woods. It took him days to find the exact right spot or portal to go back through to get home. That is actually how the Door Keeper in Russia got his job, he literally stumbled into it. He also added that a new portal or world hadn't been discovered in over three hundred years. He laughed that he doubted there were any more. I thought back to James' story he told me about his family history as Door Keepers. I wondered if that world, the world of Terra Arborum, was the last portal on Earth to be discovered. Of course, I knew that world itself was much older, another fact I didn't share with Giovanni.

Before Gio wrapped up his history lesson, he added, "Your arrival in Caelum will most definitely be a pivotal event that will turn the tide one way or another. Ava's and your assumed death put all of the worlds on a teeter totter, just barely balancing. Your return will plunge us into either war or peace. And, Eden, only you can determine which."

A heavy and dooming presence hung in the air.

"Well, friends, I have some toilets to plunge, and chairs to set out." Gio jumped out of his chair, laughing like we had just been discussing his chore list, not the impending fate of our worlds. I looked at Marek, desperately needing more answers, knowing they would not come. He simply looked back at me with a half-smile saying, *I told you so.*

THE DAY BEFORE.

My encounter with the Door Maker left me on edge, but I refused to allow anything to come between Gabby and my last day together for the next week. James could sense my uneasiness, but he also could tell I didn't want to talk about it, so he resigned to let it go . . . for the moment. Rosalina, Gabby, James and I decided to go tour Pompeii and Mount Vesuvius for the day. Gabby and I had watched a documentary on it a few months back, and Gabby was fascinated by the story. I was afraid it would have scared her, but she wasn't shaken so easily.

James and I walked hand in hand, keeping an eye on Gabby as she darted from place to place, oohing and ahhing. The temperature was smoldering hot despite being early fall, although none of us besides poor Rosalina seemed to mind. We had a wonderful time learning about that historic day in 79 AD, and touring the different parts of the city. Gabby's intrigue was infectious, and I found myself getting swept up in it all.

However, after lunch, the looming shadow of Gio's prophetic speech slowly crept over me like an impending eruption from Mount Vesuvius. The irony of our visit to Pompeii wasn't lost on me. Unforeseen destruction. A city functioning like every other day until a single event changed everything. Suddenly, it was hard to breathe in the entombed city. I broke away from our tour group and retreated to a secluded spot. Retreat. Seclusion. Why were those always my first reactions? I leaned against a giant pillar and took a deep breath, feeling afraid. I'd convinced myself that going to Caelum was just about finding my family. Deep down, I knew it was more than that, but somehow Gio's words confirmed it and brought it all up to the surface. Gio's little prophesy had given a name to my biggest question: my destiny. What had my mother told Rosalina? That I had a destiny to fulfill. Is that what she meant? Immediately, I realized that for one of the first times, I didn't want to be alone. Screw seclusion. Screw trying to be brave alone. I was part of a team now, and James deserved to know the truth. He deserved to know what he was getting himself into. I turned to go find him—and smacked right into his huge chest.

"Eden, what's wrong?" Apparently, I had a wild panic in my eyes. Everything from the morning spilled out of my mouth like word vomit. Marek's concerns, meeting Gio, his speech, and fact that the worlds are teetering between war and peace, and that somehow my return would shift the balance one way or the other.

James exhaled. "Well . . . hell. This was probably the worst place we could have come today."

I busted out laughing.

"Yeah, I didn't really think it though." I sighed.

James grabbed my hand.

"I'm sorry, James. I'm still trying to figure out what it looks like to be in a relationship. I'm so used to protecting Gabby and dealing with things alone. But I don't want to live that way anymore. We're a team, and I need you. I don't know what is in store for us, but I know I am stronger having you with me."

"Eden, as long as I am breathing, I will be standing next to you, facing whatever obstacle you are having to face."

"Thank you." I rested my head on his shoulder, already feeling better. The moment reminded me of the day he came to my house with the Serenbe flowers. He was so patient with me. Gabby ran up full speed, Rosalina huffing trying to keep up behind her.

"Mom! James! I saw the place they took baths together. How gross is that?"

"Gabbs, you smell gross . . . you could use a bath. Here, let me go throw you in theirs." James picked her up and tossed her over his shoulder. She started squealing in laughter and protest.

That night, we all shared a meal together that Rosalina and I cooked. Gabby spent most of the time filling Marek in on all of our adventures at Pompeii and Mount Vesuvius. Marek seemed to have relaxed since our visit to the Door Maker. Maybe now he felt I understood the gravity of what was about to happen, or maybe he was just hiding it better. After dinner and homemade gelato, we played cards per Gabby's request. Marek kept pretending to cheat, which would throw Gabby in a tizzy, which threw the rest of us into tizzies. There was nothing funnier than getting Gabby all riled up and competitive. We played and laughed well past her bedtime. My announcement of that fact was received poorly from everyone in the room, adults included.

After her pajamas were on and her teeth were brushed, I climbed into bed with her to whisper our prayers and her favorite poem. She loved when I whispered in her ear, saying it gave her "the tingles". She informed me it was her turn to say the poem tonight. Gabby had heard the Edgar Albert Guest poem in a car commercial and she instantly liked it, so we both memorized part of it. James even had as well over the past couple of months. We recited it every single night before bed. She pulled the covers up around her face and started:

THE DOOR KEEPER

> Somebody said that it couldn't be done
> But he with a chuckle replied
> That "maybe it couldn't," but he would be one
> Who wouldn't say so till he'd tried.
> So he buckled right in with the trace of a grin
> On his face. If he worried he hid it.
> He started to sing as he tackled the thing
> That couldn't be done, and he did it.
>
> Somebody scoffed: "Oh, you'll never do that;
> At least no one ever has done it;"
> But he took off his coat and he took off his hat
> And the first thing we knew he'd begun it.
>
> There are thousands to tell you it cannot be done,
> There are thousands to prophesy failure,
> There are thousands to point out to you one by one,
> The dangers that wait to assail you.
> But just buckle it in with a bit of a grin,
> Just take off your coat and go to it;
> Just start to sing as you tackle the thing
> That "cannot be done," and you'll do it.

I smiled at her, incredibly grateful to have that poem in my head. I had an inkling I would be quoting it to myself over the next few days. Leaning down and whispering, I prayed over my little angel. It felt different leaving her this time. I didn't know what to expect when James and I left for Palus, but this time, I knew. I knew that after this trip, one way or another, nothing would be the same. I would meet my father. I was returning to the world my mother was from. Apparently, where I . . . where *we* belonged. How could that not change everything? I kissed Gabby on the forehead and she smiled sleepily up at me.

"Goodbye, Mom."

"Goodbye. sweetheart."

"I hope you find your dad. I love you and I'll miss you." She blew me a kiss. My heart melted.

"I love and will miss you, too, sweetie. I'll see you when I get back." I blew her one back. "Goodnight." Before closing her door, I watched her roll over and get cozy in the bed. I loved her so much. I couldn't stand leaving her, but I knew going home was just as much for her as it was for me. Whatever awaited me would one day await her. Whatever fate, or destiny, or family, it was all hers as much as it was mine. I soaked in every square inch of her perfectly round face, then gently closed the door.

I walked past Marek's room, and he was talking to James about the climate in Caelum. He and I had already gone over what to expect tomorrow, but he needed go over a few last details with James so he would be mentally prepared. I made my way toward the kitchen when I saw Rosalina standing out on her terrace. There were two glasses of wine sitting on the ledge. I joined her through the opened curtains.

"One of those for me?" I joked.

"*Si, amica mia bellissima.*" Rosalina smiled.

I laughed, "Ah, wine and flattery will get you everywhere." We sat on the terrace overlooking the Mediterranean Sea and the Island of Capri.

"Rosalina, you might have the best view in all of Sorrento."

"That's the beautiful thing about the Italian coast, my dear, all the views are the best." She sipped her wine. "How are you feeling about tomorrow? Earlier today, I sensed some tension."

"There was, but I think it's okay now. Marek and James don't always see eye to eye, and they have no problem telling each other when they don't." I rolled my eyes.

"I think it's interesting . . ." Rosalina said, half aware.

"What's interesting?"

"Well, both James and Marek love you, fiercely. It's easy to see that. Obviously, they love you very differently. You have a deep emotional connection with your brother despite you not growing up with him. There is no decision of love or connection, it just is. I can almost watch you both have conversations without words." I nodded, agreeing. "But you and James . . . your relationship is not necessary or required, but a choice. That choice has changed you both for the better. Together, as a unit, you seem unstoppable."

"What are you trying to say?" I asked, leaning forward.

"I think those two boys represent the worlds you belong to. Caelum is your home, your family. Earth is your heart, your love. I'm not sure both can co-exist together. I mean, there is a reason that there are doors between them, and Keepers to guard them."

"I've never thought of it that way, but the past few months have been great."

"Yes, but both of them knew that this day was coming. They knew that these past few months weren't permanent. I'm afraid there is a choice to be made. You have to decide what you want to do after you go to Caelum. Does it become your home, or does Earth remain your home?"

My brain began to hurt. Rosalina was asking me all of the questions I didn't want to ask myself. Is that what this was all going to boil down to? Me choosing between worlds? I'd never had a choice before. My mother left before I was born, my adopted parents chose me, Eric dying and raising Gabby by myself, all of those things happened to me. The only decisions I'd made had been since Rosalina gave me the key and since I'd met James.

"I'm sorry, my dear, I didn't mean to upset you. I just worry about you. After all, I do feel this is all my fault." Rosalina had deep creases around her eyes from years of smiling, despite the current look of sadness.

"Your fault?" I looked at her, stunned. "Rosalina, you have given me one of the greatest gifts of my life. Sure, it's complicated. But what good things about life aren't?" I gestured inside of the house. "Two of the people that came here with me wouldn't be in my life if it weren't for you. Some of the biggest questions I have ever had were answered the day we met. Please don't ever apologize for that." I continued thoughtfully. "You're right. I will have to make a choice. But for the first time in my life . . . I get to. I get to decide my fate, or destiny, or whatever. I'm not just a bystander, having it all decided for me."

"Ha!" Rosalina chuckled. "You look like Ava when you get all determined. Even Gabby reminded me of her tonight when she got upset at Marek for cheating." She smiled and sipped her wine. "I have to thank you, Eden, for finding me. These past few months have added years to my life. Being with you, Gabby, and Marek have made carrying Ava's secret for all these years completely worth it. Perhaps this was my destiny, to pass on what Ava left for you and Gabby. I feel completely honored to see her legacy live on, and to be a witness of all this insanity: Doors that lead to other worlds and magic lands. I swear, no one would believe it." She laughed.

"Rosalina, I think that every single day." I raised my glass. "To fulfilling our destinies!"

"Cheers." We clinked glasses and sat in silence, watching the moon's reflection as it danced across the sea.

THE DOOR HOME.

I recognized the place immediately. I stood on the giant, beautifully faded rock in the middle of the quiet lake. Mountain peaks touched the dusk sky all around me, tall masses of lush green, harsh against the bold pinks and purples painted across the clouds. I looked over my shoulder to face the suns, feeling the heat, and watched them slowly sink behind one of the mountains. Subconsciously, I turned the flat smooth round rock in my hand behind my back. I looked back to my target. Outstretched before me was the untouched mirror of water. My goal was seven—no, eight skips. I smiled as I looked at her. She stood on the other rock a few feet from me. She admired me with love and pride in her eyes. She knew I could do it. So I refocused and reset my body like she taught me. I reared back and made sure I flicked my wrist at just the right moment. The rock sailed and bounced and bounced three . . . four . . . five . . . six . . . seven . . . eight times. Ah, I did it! It was perfect. I excitedly turned to her, unable to contain my smile. Her face was glowing in the last rays of the suns. Her lavender hair was long, and gently tossed in the wind.

"Eden." I heard my name called.

And poof she was gone. I was awake.

Wait . . . what was that?

"Eden," James whispered and cupped my head with his large hand.

"You slept through your alarm. It's six."

"Sorry, I'll get ready. Give me a few minutes." I sat up. He was already dressed and ready to go.

"I'll go make some coffee," he said as he left.

I got dressed and went into the bathroom to finish getting ready. I didn't understand the dream. I assumed it was me and Gabby, but this was not that. It was me and Ava. I was younger, Gabby's age. I looked into the mirror at my reflection. I'd brought the picture of my mother and Rosalina, so I went and got it out of my bag. Holding it up in the mirror against my reflection, I saw her in me. We had the same long nose and angular face. The same oversized, slightly droopy eyes and high defined brows. Her lips were fuller than mine, but we both had the same large, crooked smile.

I ran my hands through silver and black hair, tucking the short, left side behind my ear, letting the right side fall down, framing my face. My large grey eyes only required some mascara and I left my skin alone, knowing what I was in for later that day. I wore a cream, two-piece swimsuit with a loose fitting grey tank top and lightweight linen skirt. I brushed my teeth and did one last look over before I left the bathroom, grabbed my pack and walked to the kitchen. Marek and James were already waiting on me, coffee in hand.

Marek wore a pair of linen shorts and a white button down. James was in a pair of beige shorts and light blue V-neck. We were all adorned with Teva sandals and backpacks full of gear. As we sipped our coffee, the room hung quiet with a sense of excitement, nerves, and uncertainty all jumbled together.

"Alright, sister, you ready?" Marek said, his eyes subtly turning light purple.

"Not sure I'll ever be, big brother." My eyes mirrored his, I felt them change, now used to the once strange sensation.

"Well I sure as hell am!" my fiancé said excitedly.

Ha, leave it to James to break the nervous tension. We all laughed, even Marek, and dumped our coffee. Walking out the front door, I turned to look back up at Rosalina's to see her standing on the terrace, watching us leave. I whispered, "Take care of Gabbs for me."

"I will." She mouthed as she lifted her hand with a sweet smile.

We walked silently in a line following Marek through the quiet dark streets. The sun was just beginning to rise and had yet to awaken the city. We were on Corsco Italia when we made our turn onto Via Fourimura.

I should have known. Of freaking course.

"You know where the door is, don't you?" Marek asked without turning around.

"Yes," I answered, shaking my head.

"Where?" James asked.

"*Vallone dei Mulini*. Valley of the Mills. The place I showed you when we first got here." How could I not have seen that coming?

"Sure, that makes sense." James obviously feeling the same as me. "How in the world do we get down there?" he asked.

"There is a way, we just all have to be on our game." Marek kept walking.

We passed a couple of old hotels overlooking the Vallone dei Mulini, and a minute later the deep gorge sank next to us. We walked along the green fence into the vast black space below, too dark still to see the actual mills. A huge stone parking structure was across the street was labeled Autoparco Vallone dei Mulini. We passed the parking garage, and built into the stone wall was an old beat up wooden door. There didn't seem to be any way to open it until I saw Marek reach for a little pin pad on the right. He entered a seven digit code and I heard a click.

"Is this it?" James whispered, even though there was no one around.

"No, but this allows us access to the valley," Marek responded as he slowly pushed the door open. Once through, he relocked the door using the code. Then we proceeded to walk down stone steps in a tunnel until it opened into the valley below. The only way down was step by unsteady step along the cliff face. We took our time and made our way slowly down into the valley. The sun rose and the sky above us was turning the colors of my dream. My confusing dream. *Not now*, I reminded myself, focus on the task at hand.

It was difficult to focus when each step down brought me closer to answers. Closer to my heritage. Closer to my destiny. Closer to war or peace.

Once we made our way down to the ravine floor, the sound of running water from the two streams racing to get to the sea echoed off the valley walls. The stairs stopped at a fern covered, narrow, arched bridge that crossing would take us to the abandoned ruins. Marek explained that there were three buildings that were used, up until the 19th century. A water turned wheat mill, a saw mill, and a public washhouse for women. As we came up on the largest of the buildings, it was barely visible through the dense jungle-looking ferns. Marek said they were called Phillitis Vulgaris, very rare to this world, and once we entered Caelum, we would understand how they came to be here. It was one of the most intriguing sights, these old buildings, concrete and colorless, covered in the most vibrant of greens. It was as if the ferns were unsatisfied with man's design and took it upon themselves to create beauty where it lacked. The combination was breathtaking.

We approached the smallest of all the ruins, the bathhouse. We entered through an opening that used to be a door, and through the empty archways to the far end. There were large pool-like holes that used to contain water, and stone seats and cutouts along the walls. Nothing was left that wasn't stone. We turned a corner and there it was. At the far end of the smaller arched room was a matching wall. The Door leading home was perched in the very center of the wall about three feet off the ground. There was a small circular ledge, and matching stone steps leading up to it. There was only one small arched window and the rays from the sunrise outside cast a bright pink hue across the floor.

"Whoa." James exhaled.

"Yeah." It looked as surreal as the moment felt. I reached to my chest and clutched the key that would open the Door to take me home. The intricate wooden Door in front of me was the same shades of grey as the stone surrounding it, worn in some places more than others. Hints of a bright golden yellow color seemed to seep through the vertical slats of wood. Around the edges of the arched door were metal accents that I couldn't tell were vines or branches. One larger branch of metal arched and split into smaller branches across the middle of the door, drawing your eye toward the large round lock in the center, curving to match the other arches in the room.

"It's beautiful. Did Gio make this?" I asked in awe.

"Ha, no." Marek laughed. "I'm not sure how many of his great grandfathers ago did." He looked at James and nodded. "Eden, I think we should give you a moment to go through alone." He must have already spoken to James about this because he just nodded in agreement.

"Alright, babe. I love you," James said as he turned to me, taking off my pack. He wrapped his giant strong arms around me, giving me my favorite bear hug. "Enjoy this moment. We'll be right behind you." Tears beginning to puddle in my eyes. The smell of his skin relaxed me. Taking my key from around my neck, I climbed the stairs. Standing in front of the Door, I barely kept my hands from shaking. My entire body buzzed. My heart pounded as I felt the key enter where it was made to go. This key hadn't been used in this Door for over thirty years, and it seemed to know it. I could've sworn the metal squealed with delight as I turned it. Ever since I found out the truth about who I was and where I was from, passed through my first Door into Terra Arborum, and met Marek; I had imagined this moment a thousand times. Thousands of times I dreamt of what it would be like to pass through the Door into Caelum, my family's home. As the locks clicked into place, I felt the energy from the world beyond the Door rush through it, and through me. I pushed the Door open and walked through. My world's suns bathed me in their glorious and blinding light.

THE SUNS.

T he only way I can describe how it felt was . . . that moment you ease into a perfectly hot bath, your body involuntarily inhales and exhales in relaxation.

I heard the rushing water stop as I closed the door behind me, not worrying about locking it since my brother and finance were waiting on the other side. Water. I stood in shallow warm water, maybe six inches deep. I couldn't see anything, yet I *felt* everything. My eyes were open, but saw nothing other than blinding white goldish light. It's hard to explain. They weren't hurting or straining, they seemed to be adjusting—very, very slowly.

The air around me tickled every square inch of my skin, like my hands when holding a warm mug of hot chocolate. It was hot, but not uncomfortable, more like when you've been cold and suddenly find yourself warming by a fire. Whatever the light source was, I raised my arms up toward it to soak it all in. If felt incredible. It felt right. My skin soaked up everything around it, and the tingles spread slowly through the rest of my body. I inhaled deeply and exhaled slowly. Salt water and sweet fruit filled my nose. Still unable to see anything, I reach down and slip off my sandals. My feet sank into soft sand. I wiggled my toes and smiled, I must be standing on the shore of an ocean. A very warm ocean. I felt the very slight current of the shallow waves lapping over each other. As my face turned toward my feet, a small glint of light flickered in my line of vision. It was even brighter than whatever had blinded me. I looked up and saw that tiny flickers were glistening everywhere. What was happening? Suddenly a slow fading of color crept and seeped out from seemingly nowhere outstretched before me. The lightest and most crystal turquoise green I'd ever seen. It grew bolder with every passing second, and the glitters of light bounced everywhere. Above the glistening turquoise developed a blue color, spreading like watercolor across the top half of my vision. My eyes were adjusting, finally.

Once all the colors and my vision had fully developed, I noticed I stood in the middle of an ocean as far as I could see in all directions. The water was completely clear and the sand perfectly white beneath my bare toes. The cloudless sky above me was the brightest of blues, framed by the light source that I felt still creeping over my skin. Or should I say two light sources. Caelum had two suns. One larger, the other smaller, higher up and to the right of the larger.

The shallow water was constantly in motion, like how the waves pulled back from the shore just before another hit, but there were no waves. Just the smooth overlapping of ebbs and flows in all directions. I took a few steps out and turned in a circle. The water shimmered and sparkled all around the freestanding Door. And I thought that the Door off Arnold Mill Road looked out of place. Arnold Mill Road. Georgia felt a million miles away. Then, as if right on cue, James slowly stepped through the Door. The water rushed through it and down the steps behind him into the abandoned building. It looked like a black hole since my eyes had adjusted to the light here.

"Holy crap, it's bright!" He wore the darkest pair of Ray-Ban's I'd ever seen. I smiled at him as he walked toward me hands reached

THE DOOR KEEPER

out, blinded. "Holy crap, it's hot," he added and I couldn't contain my burst of laughter. I grabbed his hand and pulled him to me. Behind him Marek stood with his eyes open, his face tilted toward the suns. It was obvious they had the same effect on him as they had on me. He was soaking it in.

"How's your skin feeling?" I asked James, curious if it was affecting him the same way.

"Feels like it's on fire." He grimaced. "It's manageable, but I'm glad Marek gave me that cream. I can't imagine if he hadn't."

"What cream?"

"A cream made from the milk of a cactus plant that grows here." Marek walked up behind me and handed me my backpack. "It will protect his skin from burning while he's here."

"Your eyes have already adjusted," I said, more of a statement than a question. His pupils had almost all but disappeared, his eyes now giant mint disks. I wondered if mine looked the same.

"This is your first time, so I knew it would take a little bit longer for you," he answered, gesturing around. "What do you think?"

"I think I've never seen colors like this before. It's incredible." I smiled.

"Eden . . . your skin." James tried to take off his sunglasses and yelped, "*Nope*! Nope, can't take those off." I glanced down and he was right, my skin had already turned about two shades darker. I looked at Marek and could almost watch his darken right before my eyes.

He looked at me thoughtfully, and then answered James' question while still looking curiously at me. "Our skin has always absorbed sunlight better than other skin types. It was designed to." Marek had a weird look on his face.

"Now I know why I always hated winter." I nodded, admiring the new golden bronze color.

"What?" James' face contorted under his dark glasses. "What just happened? What did you say?"

"What was what?" I looked from James to Marek, who now had a big smile on his face.

"You're speaking Caelun," Marek answered.

"What?" Both James and I said simultaneously. James added, "What is happening?"

"She is speaking Caelun," Marek repeated.

"That's what you just said," I answered, completely confused.

"No, *that* was English." He looked back at me.

"They both sounded like English!" I almost yelled, not understanding what was happening.

Marek walked over and took my shoulders in his hands. "Your brain is hardwired for Caelun, but English is your first language. It's like a switch you flip in your brain. Caelun will sound like English to you because it is what you recognize and your brain processes, but you can speak either you wish now. I told you about your skin in Caelun, and when you heard it, your brain switched and answered me in Caelun, even though you didn't realize it."

"Okay. So how do I go back and forth?" I asked, not sure what language I had asked it in. Judging by James' face, it was Caelun.

"Just look at James and think English before you speak. Your brain will program itself to translate based on who you are speaking to."

"Seriously?" I tried to think English and turned to face James. "Did you just understand anything he said?"

"Every word. *He* was speaking English." His eyebrows raised behind his sunglasses.

"What the heck? This is going to drive me crazy!" I threw my hands in the air.

"You'll get the hang of it." Marek laughed and started walking away from the door. "Come on, we have a little hike before we get home."

THE SHALLOW SEA.

It wasn't long before I realized that the vast ocean never got deeper. The shallow sea stayed about six inches deep, crystal clear water with a hint of the brightest turquoise hue to it. The ebb and flow of the overlapping shallow currents were consistently licking at my ankles. Even after about an hour of walking, when we finally got our first glimpse of land, I wasn't hot. The air was so dry that the heat felt light. Again, hard to explain, considering we were surrounded by water.

The freestanding door wasn't the only thing we saw in the middle of the ocean. We came across a few beautifully large trees, secluded and alone, yet flourishing under the bright suns. One was so big around, all three of us wouldn't have been able to wrap our arms around its trunk to touch each other. There were about half a dozen huge swan-like birds resting under its shade. I gave them a double take when I realized they were the same color and shade as the water. The light turquoise colored birds were large and graceful, most of them floating peacefully, only one looked perturbed we came close. He was up on his legs, flapping his wings at us and honking. Marek gave him a smile and a nod.

"Are those giant swans blue?" James asked behind me. Marek chuckled.

"Yes, we have actually passed at least twenty of them, you just haven't noticed because they blend in."

"Wow."

"They're amazing." I exhaled as I watched another join them, gliding under the long branches and landing in a perfect skid across the top of the shallow water.

Not long after that, we came across a fruit orchard. Rows and rows of endless fruit trees sprawled out before us, each one rising from the sea. We walked straight through, and the sweet smell overwhelmed every one of my senses. Apples, oranges, mangos, peaches and so many more. I asked Marek about the salt water, and he told us the salt content was low and the trees adapted thousands of years ago. Walking under the lush fruit while my toes sank in the soft sand felt wrong and right all at the same time. I imagined Gabby climbing the trees and jumping limb from limb.

After passing through the ginormous orchard, the first sight of land sprawled out before us. Mountains rose in the distance, high into the clouds that formed over the land. There was no beach. The end of the sea was more like the end of a lake. I noticed a small village just off shore. I became nervous, knowing we were close. As we approached the coast, Marek stopped and pulled out two lightweight golden cloaks with hoods. He instructed us to put them on so no one would recognize us as outsiders. I didn't love the idea of covering my skin from my newfound favorite weather, but I knew we needed to enter undetected. James and I threw them over our shoulders, raised the hoods, and walked into the village.

The roads were artistically placed flat stones that created beautiful patterns. The buildings were immaculate hand built construction that included bricks, rock, and hand planed wood beams. Marek told me that Caelun people took great pride in their creations, and their towns were considered such. The line between nature and Caelun-made items blurred in the most beautiful way possible. Some buildings were built into the hillside, and some in and around trees so as not to disturb their growth patterns. The first Caelun I saw was a small child, no more than the age of five, running across the street in her bare feet, light golden hair flowing out widely behind her, laughing and playing. I watched a woman with long, white, braided, hair and dark skin weaving a colorful tapestry outside her front door. I noticed that most of the buildings were places of work as well as homes. Men and women bustled around, buying and selling goods. Apparently I read in Caelun as well. We passed a bakery, fruit stands, a blacksmith, and brick makers. Although everyone noticed and acknowledged Marek with a reverent nod, no one seemed to care about the two strangers traveling with him, which allowed me to simply take it all in. All of the Caelun people had dark skin, light eyes, and almost whitish hair. Some women's hair were colored a light pastel, but all wore it long, even the men. Most of the men we saw had their hair tied back or braided, and wore only long lightweight skirts. Many had tattoos, but most of them I saw were gold. James was walking next to me, and I heard him chuckle.

"I don't think I could pull off one of those," he joked, referring to the skirt.

"Shoot, I think you'd look good. Of course, I'd hate to see you hide two of your best qualities, those tree trunks you call legs." I reached for his hand. Even though I couldn't see his face, I could feel him smile.

"Even though we are used to the heat, it's good to wear lightweight clothes that provide air flow. You will see soon enough; even your t-shirt and shorts will begin to feel claustrophobic." Marek joined in the conversation.

"You're the only man I've seen with short hair," James said without asking.

"I'm also the only warrior in the village," he replied simply.

"Warrior?" I looked at my brother. "I thought you were a peace-keeper?"

"Here, they aren't that different."

I suddenly was aware that if that were true, my father's idea of peace might be a little different than mine.

On our left, a young boy helped an older man load up a cart with bricks, a large horse grazing, waiting patiently for his load to be ready to move. The horse's coat had a beautiful silver sheen with a long flowing white mane. Other animals cooperated with the inhabitants of the village, everything from birds to cows, and species of animals I'd never seen before. We turned up the main street toward a larger house on the hill. We walked up stone steps lined with peach trees on either side all the way up the path. I deeply inhaled the fresh scent of the lovely fruit. Marek pushed open the two large stone doors to reveal a large courtyard of more fruit trees and colorful exotic flowers everywhere. An older, familiar looking woman was tending a flower bed when we entered.

"Marek!" she exclaimed, got up, and rushed toward him. She was wearing a light grey Grecian-style dress with a longer train. Her hair was long and braided into a high ponytail. It was a shade darker than her dress, with a few white streaks.

"Vera." My brother embraced the woman, and my body turned cold as she turned her ice blue gaze upon me. A flash of fear and terror engulfed her face as her eyes locked onto mine. Within half a second she recovered and attempted to replace it with something else, but not before I could register what she was trying to hide.

"It's impossible." Her voice was deep and husky.

"I know. I was just as shocked." Marek smiled. I imagined Vera wasn't smiling inside, at least not based on what I first felt when she saw me.

"Does your father know?" she asked him.

"I'm Eden." I outstretched my hand, ignoring the question, and anxious to explore what I sensed from this familiar stranger. She looked into my eyes with a forced smile and took my hand in hers.

"It's an honor to meet you, Eden. I'm Vera."

No one said anything for a beat as we stood in the middle of the courtyard.

"I'll take you to your father immediately." Vera turned her attention back to Marek. "He's already so happy to see you, and this news shall surely send him over the moons." She picked up the train of her dress and turned to lead us down the main hall.

"Okay, guys, here we go. Aunt Vera will lead the way. She is mother's sister." My aunt. That is why she looked familiar. Her face shape was the same as Ava's, but the similarities ended there. Her features, while beautiful, were harsher with an edge to them. It was obvious that Marek or James hadn't picked up on any of what I felt when my aunt first saw me, and I now became increasingly nervous to meet any more of my estranged family. I hoped my father was happier to see me than my aunt was.

THE FATHER.

Every part of my body twisted in nerves. I wasn't sure how my father was going to react to me, much less James. He and I walked side by side, following my brother, who followed my aunt. We entered a large living space with white stucco-type walls and dark wooden beams highlighting the architecture. There were huge open windows and skylights to allow the suns' ray to fill the space. Brightly colored artwork starkly contrasted the white walls. Most of the paintings were vibrant flowers and landscapes. An oversized Serenbe flower caught my attention toward the back of the room, along with a group of men sitting around, talking. I heard the booming laughter of the man in the center of the group, telling a story.

Before my eyes had even fully settled on him, I knew he was my father. His hair was snow white and hung down, brushing his shoulders, heavily layered and swept back away from his face. His skin was dark, with a very short, closely trimmed white beard. His eyes were greyish green, the perfect combination of mine and Marek's. He, like the other men, were shirtless, with a wrap skirt tucked up and through his legs. For comfort, I guessed. His deep voice carried through the room, and his laughter was easy and light. I watched him curiously as I waited for my emotions to implode. But they never did. I wasn't sure what to think or how to feel about this stranger in front of me. He noticed Marek and his white teeth spread into a large smile that stretched all the way to the corners of his eyes.

"Marek!" His voice boomed. "I've missed you, son. What has kept you away so long?" He jumped up, arms outstretched. He crossed over half the distance to where we stood when he stopped, dead still, his arms dropping to his side.

His eyebrows furrowed, not in anger, but in question. He was extremely tall, and his barrel chest inhaled and exhaled slowly. He took his time, as though he was trying to rationalize what he saw. Giving in, I looked at his eyes. They were two puddles of unshed tears, thick and glassy. He slightly shook his head.

"Ava?" He sounded like he wasn't getting any oxygen, despite the deep breaths he took.

I lowered my hood.

"Eden," I answered, then heard the audible gasp in the room from Samuel's guests.

"Eden?" His eyes questioned Marek, and I saw him nod slowly just out of my peripheral vision.

"Eden." He closed his eyes, and the stored tears flowed fast down his cheeks. He walked toward me, reaching his hand toward my face. He stopped short, looking afraid to touch me.

"Where have you been?" he whispered.

"I . . . I . . ." I wasn't sure how to explain, or what to say. Thankfully, Marek stepped in.

"It's a long story, Father, one we can't wait to share with you. Perhaps we can let Eden and her friend get settled, and when we are alone, we can have dinner and discuss it." My brother nodded toward all of the guests glaring from their seats.

"Of course." My father nodded, and looked back to me. "Of course. Please, Eden, Marek will show you to your room. But, first . . . may I?" He reached his arms out to me, an invitation for a hug.

"Sure." I nodded and smiled.

Tears steadily flowed down his cheeks as he placed his hands on either side of my face. He studied every square inch. Emotions flooded his eyes as he did: relief, joy, recognition, sadness, and curiosity. When he could take it no longer, he pulled me into a strong embrace. He smelled like lemon and lavender, and I wondered if lavender reminded him of Ava, like it did me. Hugging me tightly, I felt the resolve of a man who had lost everything and refused to lose it again. He wept, and the full weight of what he had lost fell on me. I finally felt emotion rise within my chest, and couldn't stop my own tears. He loosened his grip long enough for me to glance back at James, who was wiping a tear from his eye. Wishing I could have given him the same moment with his own father, I was still incredibly thankful he was here with me.

My father pulled back and cleared his throat.

"Marek, please show Eden and her friend to their rooms, so they can freshen up and get ready for dinner. Vera, please let the cook know how many to prepare for, a welcomed feast for our reunited family. My daughter was lost and she has come back to me. Tonight, we celebrate her return!"

THE WELCOME.

"Did you understand any of that?" I asked James when we walked to our rooms.

"Nope, not a single word." James smiled. "But you really didn't need to understand the language to appreciate what just happened." He grabbed my hand. "That was awesome."

"Eden, here is your room." Marek opened a door into a small room overlooking the shallow sea. I looked at James, nervous to split up so soon, especially before we had a chance to address his violations with Samuel.

"It's alright, Eden," Marek said, noting my concern. "James is staying with me. I'll keep an eye on him. We will deal with everything tonight. Don't worry."

"It's fine, honey. I'll see you in a bit." James kissed me on the forehead and followed Marek out of the room, leaving me alone, and not completely at ease.

I walked to the large open window and took in the view in front of me. The entirety of the shallow sea stretched into the horizon. The two suns were high in the afternoon sky. The giant fruit orchard covered the right side of my view, springing up from the sea. Perfect rows of colorful trees, and when the wind blew up the coastline, I thought my head would explode from their sweet aroma. I closed my eyes and inhaled slowly, attempting to pick out the different scents, but they had jumbled together like a fruit cobbler. A flock of giant swans floated out in the water, only visible by the water disturbance they left in their wake.

I turned back to the room I stood in. It matched the rest of the house so far, white walls with dark wood beam accents, beautiful and artistically placed stones beneath my feet. The bed was covered in a brightly colored woven tapestry, not unlike the one I saw being made when we walked in.

Above the bed was another painting, one that I recognized immediately. I stood there in shock for over a minute, suddenly aware I wasn't breathing. It was the same one—the flower from my tattoo, the one next to the Serenbe. Different shades of peach and coral, thick petals surrounding a dark gold seeded center. I walked closer to the oversized painting and inspected it. The same veins of color running through the petals, the dark edging, the same pattern of seeds overlapped in the center. I looked down at the bottom corner and a tear fell down my face slowly as I saw it. I saw her. She was an artist. Even her signed name was a work of art. It looked like an uppercase "M" with a line straight through the center. But I saw it immediately, her signature, Ava's signature. I ran my finger over her name. It felt surreal to see it tucked in the bottom right corner, in the exact same placement I signed all of mine.

"She was a very talented artist." I turned around to a tiny little woman propped on an ornate wooden cane in my doorway. She bowed as low as the cane would allow, then walked into my room very slowly. She was one of the oldest people I had seen so far in Caelum. Her hair was a light rose color and twisted up in a million braids piled on the top of her head. She wore a wrap dress the same color as her hair, with white embellishments on the edges. Deep smile lines adorned her face, and the creases around her golden eyes increased as she spoke.

"Your father insists on displaying her art. I do not blame him. She was the best artist in the village. We would all trade for her pieces." She was looking out the window absentmindedly. She continued, turning toward me.

"How rude of me. My name is Wynn, and I am the Skin Specialist."

"I'm Eden. It's nice to meet you."

She held out her hand. "Come with me, Eden, we are going to pamper you just a bit before your dinner tonight." She smiled, deepening the creases on her face.

I followed Wynn down the corridor as she explained to me that a Skin Specialist was an important job to our people. They were responsible for skin care health, but also the adornment and decoration of skin, which apparently was common practice in Caelum. She led me into a large room that smelled delicious. The ceiling was tall, and the first thing I noticed were about half a dozen shallow tubs built into the floor. It reminded me of the old Italian bathhouse we walked through to get to the Caelun door. Marek and James entered the room through a door on the opposite wall.

"Oh, good, you are all here. Let's get to it then." Wynn clasped her hands together.

"Get to what?" I asked, confused.

"Oh, man, I've missed this. It's been months since I've had a proper bath." Marek smiled, looking down at the tubs.

"Proper bath?" I scrunched my face.

"English, guys?" James looked exasperated.

"Oh, sorry." I thought English before I spoke. "Marek is saying we are going to take a 'proper' bath. I have no idea what that means."

Wynn then took us all over to a wall of shelves and colored ceramic bowls filled with heavenly smelling goodness. I translated what she said to James after she instructed us to smell different bowls and pick two different scents. She informed us that our nose would pick what our skin needed and craved to be its healthiest. I took her word for it. I happily picked peaches and honey. James picked chamomile and the sap of a cactus—the same thing Marek had him use as a form of sunscreen. Marek picked Eucalyptus and mint.

Wynn made us all tea using the ingredients from our bowls, and a sweet younger woman, whose hair and dress matched Wynn's, filled the baths with a thick milky substance. Wynn's daughter was named Shay. Turned out their family had been the Skin Specialist for generations, the craft passed down for years. I watched in fascination as Wynn and Shay filled the tubs and stirred in the ingredients that we had picked. The golden honey drizzled thickly onto the already peach colored creamy substance. I was all too ready when Wynn announced my bath was ready. I stripped down to my swimsuit, already feeling weird about bathing with my brother and boyfriend, and not needing nakedness to add to this already awkward situation.

Anything other than pure bliss melted away as soon as my foot entered the bath. The texture was a thick cream that coated my skin and enveloped it like a hot blanket. I wanted to eat it, it smelled so good. I sat, leaning back, amazed at how instantaneously any and every anxiety fell away.

"Geez, what is with Caelum and loving everything that is hot?" James laughed as he eased into his bath. I laughed.

"Oh, yeah, that's what I'm talking about." Marek sighed as he got in his tub.

None of us said much of anything after that. We relaxed in our tubs for almost an hour before Wynn told us we could get out. The cream cooled only slightly and had begun to harden on our skin. We dry rubbed the substance off to reveal new, refreshed, glowing skin underneath. Shay then proceeded to pull out a gold paint, asking permission to paint me. The boys moved on to something else while I stayed behind and got "tattooed" by my new Skin Specialist.

She started with my actual tattoo and outlined all of the flowers in the gold paint, which made the entire thing look even more beautiful. She then replicated the intricate flower outline pattern down the rest of my arm and up across my shoulder, upper back and chest. She continued up my neck, fading the painting out around my jawline. It was an incredible job, and her steady hand impressed me. I told her as much, and she blushed, admitting my mother was one of her artistic inspirations. Shay was in her mid-twenties, and had been her mother's primary body painter since she was only five. She was very shy, and kind, and I was thankful to have already made a new friend in my homeland.

Shay then introduced me to the village's hair guru, Arie. She did most of the people's hair in the village. I realized quickly that everyone had a specialty and a job that was passed down from generation to generation. Arie's family had been the hair stylists here for a thousand years. She explained to me that everything is done with plants, from the products to the colors. Marek told me that the Caelun people valued nature, but I had no idea it was this extreme. Because my bath had been peaches and honey, they decided to continue with that theme. Arie made a concoction in a bowl complete with fruit and flowers, and slathered it on my head, then whipped it up in a canvas fabric to "set." The girls excitedly informed me it was time to pick a dress.

We walked down the hall, Shay and Arie giddy, and me quickly feeling like I was in a beauty montage from one of my chick flicks.

Cue the pop song as I tried on different outfits. Although I knew as soon as we entered the "dressing room" this wasn't going to be quite like that. Gorgeous fabrics hung everywhere I looked, sheer silks and cottons in every color imaginable. I didn't see one dress, just the raw materials everywhere.

The scent of peach still hung in my nose as I gravitated toward a lightweight rich cream colored silk draped over chair.

"Perfect," Shay and Arie said in unison.

The dressmaker came in shortly and I stood still as he ripped the fabric and twisted, draped, and wrapped it carefully around my body. I stood in awe as he worked silently and masterfully creating something beautiful from nothing but a large piece of fabric. When he was finished, the girls escorted me back to my room to finish my hair and makeup. I may not have felt like a Caelun before, but I sure felt and looked like one now.

THE DINNER.

I stood in the opened doorway in awe as I looked out on the outdoor dinner setting. It was breathtaking. Before me, in the middle of an expansive colorful garden, was a small exquisite table glowing in candlelight. The suns were setting, so there was still plenty of light, but the candles provided quite an ambiance. My father and aunt were already seated at the table, and seemed to be in a heated discussion. I didn't want to intrude, so I turned to leave, but not before my father noticed me.

"Eden. You look beautiful!" He rose and walked toward me, arms outstretched.

"Thank you . . . King Samuel." Nothing else felt right. Father. Dad. Hey Daddy-O. He smiled back at me understandingly.

"Please come, have a seat while we wait for Marek and your friend."

"Wow," someone whispered behind me. I turned and could not stop the immediate smile that spread across my face taking in the Caelum edition of James. Standing in front of me, shirtless, his skin glowed flawlessly, and stood out being much lighter than everyone else's skin on the patio. His broad shoulders and chest slimmed down to the deep blue piece of fabric wrapped around his waist and cascading to the floor. His warm brown eyes, same color as his hair, sparkled as he looked at me. He reached for my hand.

"I like yours better." He winked at me, took my hand in his and spun me around.

My creamy dress was loosely draped, one shouldered, and clung perfectly in the right places. My upper body was covered in the gold painted flowers, and my makeup was simple with flecks of gold around my eyes, which had turned a light shade of purple since my arrival in Caelum. My hair, at least the white part, was dyed a light rose gold color. The short side of my hair had been braided against my head and the longer side curled and hung loose. I only felt slightly uncomfortable being so dressy. James being in a man-skirt lightened my mood and made me feel more relaxed. James and I'd forgotten about everyone else on the patio when I noticed Marek's facial expression looking at my father. I glanced at Samuel nonchalantly and saw something unsettling in his eyes. His suspicion about James and me was confirmed, and he wasn't happy about it.

Marek cleared his throat. "Let's all sit and eat. I'm starving."

As I sat between James and Marek, I glanced across the table to see my aunt Vera's eyebrows raised over a disapproving look, immediately changing to a smile as we made eye contact. I smiled back, wondering what her and my father had been discussing when I first arrived.

In the middle of the table was a huge, perfectly browned, cooked bird, begging to be carved, complete with different breads and cooked vegetables covering every square inch of the table. Every person had three different glasses: one for water, one for a non-fermented cocktail, and the last for an adult beverage—the last tasted like wine, but felt much stronger. It was apparent that Caelun's had an appetite for food and drink. As the dinner began, Marek was the first to start talking.

"Father, I'm sure you have many questions. Where would you like us to start?"

"Well, of course I want to know how you found your sister," Samuel said as he cut a huge piece of meat off the bird. "But first, I need to know what happened to you Eden. Where have you been?" He looked at me, his eyes honest.

I launched into Ava's story and mine as Rosalina told me. I recounted their friendship briefly before I went into her hospital stay when I was born. I watched the tears form in my father's eyes as I explained my birth and my mother's death. I explained my adoption and my adoptive parents. He would occasionally ask a question, but for the most part, he listened. When I got to Eric and Gabby, I knew it was going to be an important moment, telling him I had a daughter. I took a deep breath and just said it.

"After about a year of being married, we had a daughter named Gabrielle."

I watched two completely different things happen simultaneously. My father burst into laughing and crying, and I saw a deep sense of dread flood my aunt's face. Feeling super uncomfortable with the rising tension of competing feelings, I smiled and glanced at James, who put his hand on my leg under the table in a knowing, reassuring way. He felt it, too, even in an unknown language. He knew I'd told them about Gabby, having heard her name. Marek was fork deep into a potato casserole and didn't seem to notice anything.

"I have a granddaughter?" Samuel cried. I smiled at him, loving how deeply he felt everything.

"Yes, and she is sweet and wonderful and incredibly gifted." I ate a bite of some sweet carrots. At this point, Samuel already knew I was a widow, so I skipped up to my trip to Italy and meeting

THE DOOR KEEPER

Rosalina. Something made me feel uneasy about sharing too much at this particular table, so I only hit the highlights: that Rosalina had Ava's key, she gave it to me, and told me how my mother died.

Now we were getting to the hard part. James.

Marek, James, and I decided to be completely honest about our adventures in other worlds, but I kept feeling warning bells in my head. Something about the way Vera stared at James and me made me feel very uneasy. So, instead of being one hundred percent honest, I left out many details, including me going to Terra Arborum and my reoccurring dreams. Marek looked at me questioningly, but I kept on. I told Samuel and Vera that James and I met while I tried to use the door on his property. I told them he confided in me that he was a Door Keeper, I told him my story, and we grew close. I explained to them that the more time James and I spent together, the more his story intrigued me. Considering I had never met my own biological parents, his story resonated with me.

As soon as James's father entered the conversation, I felt a tangible shift around the table. We left the safety of telling my story into the grim reality of Door Keeper politics, and I felt the difference. Marek had warned me how passionate my father felt about this issue, so my guard was up, and I tread as lightly as possible. I was brief, but honest, about our travels to Palus. I told him about our troubles and our run-in with Sapp Junior. I felt James' nervous tension bubble up next to me, knowing what we were talking about without understanding the words. I told them about how we escaped, and Samuel listened without interrupting.

I paused before launching into how Marek found me to give my father a moment to respond to our infractions. I knew I had to face it head on and see what James and I were up against. Samuel looked down at his hands, thinking. He suddenly raised his eyes to mine, his expression grim. A chill ran up my spine, realizing this may not be as easy as I'd hoped.

"I'm sorry about James' father." He turned his attention to James for the first time since we had sat. "James, I am sorry about your father."

"Thank you, sir."

Samuel was speaking English. I wasn't sure if that terrified me or comforted me. My father continued.

"But that is no excuse for your behavior. Grief is a part of life, son. I should know. You must pick it up, carry it, and move on. Your actions in Palus did not just affect you, or my daughter; it could potentially affect the entire balance of the different worlds. Palus is one of the most unstable worlds, and not a part of our peaceful alliance. They will interpret any act against the Palun people as an act of war. I hope you fully understand the predicament you have put me in."

"I'm afraid I don't fully understand, King Samuel. Or at least I didn't before. I assure you, after everything Eden and I went through in Palus, I do now, fully understand why traveling through doors is frowned upon."

"Forbidden," Samuel inserted sternly.

"Should it be, though?" I asked carefully.

"How dare you say that?" Vera spoke for the first time, her face contorted.

"Vera." My father raised a hand at my aunt.

"I'm sorry." I looked at my father sincerely. "I don't mean to be disrespectful to you, I know I'm new to all this. I just wondered if my mother would agree with this law."

Vera couldn't control herself. "Your mother died because this law wasn't in place. Her disregard for all of our safeties put your father and this entire kingdom through unnecessary pain." I couldn't miss her venomous tone when she spoke of my mother.

"Enough, Vera." Samuel's hand was up again.

I eyed my aunt carefully. Something dark ran deep within her, and I knew it was most likely going to be my largest obstacle in Caelum.

My father looked from me to James, and back again, clearly thinking about how to proceed.

"Marek, I assume that you found your sister in your search for James."

"Yes, she was at his house," he answered, and as I tried to catch his eye, he looked from Samuel and down to his drink. It felt as though I'd lost him as an ally at the table. I looked back to Samuel. Both suns had fully set by this time, and candlelight created an ominous vibe in an already ominous moment.

"Eden, I gather that you and James are in a relationship," he said flatly.

"Yes, Father, we are engaged to be married." I finally acknowledged our father daughter relationship . . . manipulatively. A desperate attempt.

"You want me to grant him clemency," he said slowly, and looked at me directly. Holding the gaze of his stormy eyes, I answered.

"Yes . . . although, I'd like to know clemency from what, exactly."

"Mercy is mercy . . . regardless of the punishment." He did not hesitate. "Very well. James, due to extenuating circumstances, and your admission of guilt, as well as repentance, I hereby grant you clemency for your infractions. You will not be held accountable for the laws you have broken. Now . . . who wants dessert?"

THE PAINTINGS.

I wanted to relax. We accomplished what we came for. I wanted to feel good about it, but I just couldn't. Something didn't feel right. Everything seemed beautiful, lighthearted, and joyful on the surface, but the deeper things went, the darker they felt. Marek left before we finished dessert, which, not surprisingly, included fruit. He didn't even look at me once after the conversation about my father pardoning James.

James and I walked hand in hand through the fruit orchard in the shallow sea after dinner. The water was warm, glowing an eerie shade of blue under the three moons' reflections. The only things we could hear were the faint sound of the wind blowing through the trees and the swishing our feet made moving through the water as we walked. The trees cast perfect dark shadows across the bright water, creating an illusion of a two-dimensional orchard on the white sand under our feet.

Occasionally we would hear the splashes of the blue swans off in the distance. Neither of us said anything, yet I knew both of our minds were full of things to talk about. I wasn't the only one that felt what happened earlier. King Samuel may have pardoned James with his words, but neither of us felt that we addressed what needed to be addressed. I looked at my fiancé, a deep crease between his eyebrows, his lips slightly pursed. His face looked how I felt. Even amidst the tense thoughts that plagued us both, I couldn't stifle the chuckle that rose in me when I saw he had tucked his long skirt up between his legs so he could walk in the water.

"I know you aren't going to make fun of me. Let me remind you, this is all your fault." He pulled my hand and flung me around to face him. I wrapped my arms around his bare waist.

"I know, I'm sorry." The reflections of the water bounce off his face. "You do look super cute, though. I think you might need to bring this home."

"Home?" His eyes grew serious. "After being here, do you still consider Georgia your home?" It was a genuine question.

"James, Georgia . . . Earth . . . it will always be my home. That's not going to change." I surprised myself with the certainty I felt. James smiled and looked over the top of my head at the expansive, hauntingly turquoise sea.

"This ain't a bad second home, though. I could imagine us vacationing here in the winter."

I laughed, then asked him the question I'd been wanting to ask since we left dinner.

"I don't feel as though anything was truly resolved tonight . . . do you?"

James pulled away and looked back toward my father's house.

"I think there is more going on than we know. I'm not sure what all happened during dinner tonight, but peace wasn't one of the emotions I felt. Something weird is going on with your aunt. I don't like the way she looks at you." He turned back to face me. "I think we just need to be on our toes, and hopefully tonight I can talk to Marek. Whatever it is, I know we can handle it. A little family drama never hurt anyone."

I wasn't so sure.

✣ ✣ ✣ ✣ ✣

Three of the most beautiful women I'd ever seen sat around the table where we had eaten dinner earlier that evening. I recognized the table and garden immediately. It must have been early morning—the chirping of birds sang through the air, and the light was bright and fresh. The ladies sat while talking around the table, sipping tea and eating small pastries. I heard her laugh before I recognized her. It sounded just like mine. She sat at the head of the table between the other two. Her hair hung loose and wavy, her face was clean and fresh, her eyes bright lavender.

"I had the dream again last night," she said, her facial expression changing.

"Is that why you asked us here?" The woman to her left sighed, annoyed. "It's just a dream," she added, rolling her eyes. I recognized the harsh yet stunning features immediately. A younger version of Aunt Vera.

The youngest, seemingly angelic woman put her hand on Ava's. She looked at my mother, but addressed Vera. "You know dreams are more than that in this family, Vera. Ava, what do you make of it?" Her voice was soft and sweet.

"I don't know. I've dreamt of the future before, but this felt different." My mother put her hand under the table. She glanced down, and that's when I noticed she was pregnant. She continued, "Every time I have this one, I feel a deep sense of grief . . . of guilt."

From my viewpoint, I seemed to be standing under one of the fruit trees in the garden, by the house. It felt just like all my other dreams. I was a spectator, and was keenly aware I was visiting a moment that I was not invited into. Another lucid dream, powerless to intervene or wake up. I just had to watch.

THE DOOR KEEPER

The youngest of the three stood up and walked toward me. She stared past me, at the ocean. She closed her eyes, same color as my mother's, and inhaled slowly.

"What do you think, Mae?" my mother asked.

The woman's eyes were still closed, as though she was trying to concentrate on something unseen.

"What does your gut tell you?" the youngest asked.

"That this dream is not the future," my mother said sadly. "That it is just wishful thinking."

"What are you saying?" Vera interjected with a high voice.

"I'm saying that I'm afraid my and my daughter's futures aren't together," Ava whispered, softly crying.

I was listening to the conversation at the table, but I couldn't take my eyes off of Mae. She stood in front of me, calm and still. I saw so much sadness in her face. But suddenly, out of nowhere, a very slight smile peaked in the corners of her mouth. She opened her eyes, once again looking out onto the vast ocean behind me.

"Vera, we need to allow Ava to feel what she needs to. Only she knows the path ahead of her. We are here to love and support her. She is our Queen, our Door Keeper . . . and our sister. Besides . . ." Suddenly Mae's eyes cut right to me, like she could see me standing in front of her, and I knew instantly she knew I was watching. "I think Ava is right, her daughter is going to be everything we need her to be . . . perhaps, even more."

My eyes opened. My heart was pounding. The breeze blew off the ocean through the open window and chilled my sweat-glistened skin. My mom knew? She had another sister? Where was Mae? I had too many new questions, and not close to enough answers. I threw the covers back and walked to the window. That had felt so real, like I was there. All my dreams felt that way, but this was different. Had Mae actually seen me?

Then the more pressing questions rose like a flood within me. Was it possible that my mother knew she was going to die? Had she seen it, or dreamt it? I looked back at the painting on the wall over my bed. Her painting. It was incredible, how similar our styles of painting were. Bold, whimsical, with distinctive brush strokes. Shay and Arie told me earlier that night the flower was called Elisium, which translated into "paradise" in English. Which was ironic, considering that was close to what Rosalina named me.

Rosalina. Gabby. I pictured them floating on a small gondola in Venice. Gabby eating gelato and Rosalina spoiling her rotten. I missed her already.

I pulled the picture down off the wall and walked over to prop it up on the other side of the room so I could see it in the moonlight. As I turned it around to place it, I noticed something written on the back.

I miss you already.

I had just thought this about Gabby. A mother's thought for her daughter. My eyes filled with tears. I immediately knew it was intended for me. She absolutely had known. My heart ached. I sat on the edge of the bed, staring at my mother's writing, and wept. I wept for her, for me, for Gabby, for Marek, and for my father. I wept for her own grief, and having to carry the knowledge of what could never be. I wept until my body ran out of tears. I sat there, motionless, my feet cool on the hard stone floor, the front of my silver nightgown wet with salty tears. Suddenly, I remembered. Her paintings were all over this house. I replaced the painting back over the bed and quietly crept out of my room. I walked down to the main gathering room, where I had first seen my father. There were six of her paintings in this room. I anxiously looked behind every one of them.

I love you, my darling.

Trust yourself.

Be bold and brave.

I am so proud of you.

I am always with you.

Eden, you will build the bridge.

The last one took my breath away. She knew my name. Tearless, I just sat in the dark silence. Eden, you will build the bridge. What did that mean? Was this the destiny she talked to Rosalina about? I sat looking at all of the paintings' backsides, stunned.

I felt his presence enter before I heard him.

"I would ask how you knew, but I am no longer surprised by the intuition of the women in this family."

I turned around and looked at my father.

"She knew." Not really a question or statement, yet a little of both.

"Yes, she knew." He sat down next to me. "I tried everything to keep it from happening, tried to keep her safe, but . . ." He trailed off, then continued. "I was going to show you these tomorrow. I knew they were meant for you. Of course, I never thought you were alive to see them. How did you know out about them?"

"I had a dream." Something stopped me from telling him specifics. I wasn't ready to inquire about Mae.

He smiled. "Of course you did."

"Did my mother have a lot of dreams?" I probed, already knowing the answer.

"Yes, she did. She had them most every night. Some were of past events, some of the future, and some were just wild fiction." He smiled. "Almost every morning, she would tell them to me. The mornings she didn't, I knew it was something she was trying to interpret or process. I wasn't prepared when she told me of her reoccurring dream with you, the one she knew would never actually happen. It was the first dream she ever had indicating she was going to die." His eyes fell.

This was the dream Ava referred to in the dream I'd just had. A dream within a dream, how very Inception. I started to feel like my life was becoming the script of that very movie.

"In it, you were young, about ten years old, and you were together on her favorite lake . . ." He was telling me the dream, but I didn't need to hear anymore. I already knew this dream. My heart started to pound when I realized I had been having the very same dream that my mother had. Samuel was mid-sentence when I interrupted him.

"We were skipping rocks." I looked into his eyes. He didn't say anything at first.

"She told me that she heard your name be called, and you broke into tiny particles and floated away, that you didn't belong to her. You belonged to someone else, somewhere else. Somewhere far away. And she knew . . ." He choked back a sob "She knew the only way you wouldn't belong to her is if she were dead."

That confirmed it, the dream wasn't me and Gabby like I'd originally thought. It was me and Ava. The confirmation brought me little comfort as I looked at my father. I could see and feel how difficult this was for him to tell me. I wanted to believe everything my father said so badly, I wanted to cry out and tell him every little detail, and ask every single question that burned in my belly. But something kept me from it. I tried to remember that I didn't know this man, not really. But listening to him talk about Ava this way, it wore away at my defenses. Despite thinking I had none left, my eyes expelled one more tear. As it ran down my cheek slowly, I said the only thing I could muster.

"I'm sorry."

"Eden, it's not your fault." He wiped my tear. "We each have a destiny, we each have our own path. Unfortunately, yours wasn't with your mother, your brother, or me. But that has all changed now. Tomorrow, I will show you all around your new home." He grabbed my hand, kissed it, and stood.

"Tomorrow, I will show you and James all of Caelum."

THE BLACKSMITH.

Samuel's use of the word "home" wasn't lost on me. Rosalina's warning replayed in my head. *The two can't co-exist, there is a reason there are doors between them and Door Keepers to guard them.* Within twenty-four hours of being here, both James and my father had used that word: home. I meant what I told James, Earth would always be where I belonged. But I began to wonder how my father would take that news. Hey, Dad, nice to meet you after thirty years. Sorry you thought I was dead. Just here to visit, see ya later. Something told me he wouldn't take it very well. Then there was the statement about trying to avoid Ava's predicted death . . . what exactly did he mean? He said he had tried to keep her safe. I would have to tread lightly, and work out the best way to proceed. We hadn't really discussed an exit strategy. I knew I had a couple of days to figure it out, but I needed to talk to Marek.

Turned out Marek was MIA.

My two new gal pals, Shay and Arie, came into my room early morning to bring me my clothes for the day. A simple wrap around my chest and long, lightweight skirt, both a bold shade of charcoal grey. Dark leather rope sandals matching my skirt wound up my ankles. The peach color in my hair had mostly faded and was replaced with small purple flowering vines woven into a few braids. I asked the girls to take me to Marek, but was told he was already gone for the day. Instead, they escorted me back to the table in the garden for breakfast. As I entered the courtyard, the early morning suns' rays felt glorious on my skin, and the warmth instantly energized me. The bird's melody transported me back to the dream the night before. But instead of my mother and her sisters, James sat alone at the table. Pastries, fruits and creams, and multiple smoked meats sat untouched in front of him. His bare chest glistened with a recent application of his cactus sunscreen. He smiled and rose as I approached.

"I'm not sure I'll ever get used to seeing you like this. You look amazing."

I returned his smile and sat next to him.

"Well, I'm not sure I'll ever grow tired of your compliments." My tummy growled. "I love that Caelum loves food as much as I do." I dug into the scrumptious looking feast. James didn't waste any time, not knowing how long we'd be alone.

"Marek didn't come back last night."

"Really?" I asked with a full mouth of sausage.

"Really, and it kind of worries me. He left in a hurry last night after dinner."

"I asked to see him this morning, and Shay and Arie told me he was gone for the day." I scrunched my eyebrows and stopped eating. "We need him on our side, James. I don't think we can do this without him. Rosalina told me she felt he was conflicted, between our father and me. And if that's true, it looks like he's picked a side." I became increasingly worried.

"What do you mean 'picked a side'? I thought we were good? King Samuel pardoned me. I know that there is tension, but I thought for the most part we are in the clear?" James looked unsure.

"I just need to see Marek," I answered, not wanting to get into everything I had been worried about the last few sleepless hours.

My father walked into the courtyard as the words left my mouth. His face was bright and excited. He was wearing a pale green skirt, his seemingly standard uniform, making his eyes look more green than grey. Any trace of the sadness the night before was gone. His arms were opened wide like he was welcoming us all over again.

"I'm sure we will run into your brother sometime during our tour today." He laughed as he spoke. Next, he spoke English to James. "We'd better eat up, we have a long day planned." He smiled at James and picked up huge slice of a cake-type pastry. Once again, I felt something uneasy about his cheerful attitude.

"Yes, sir." James joined my father and dug in.

We finished breakfast as Samuel started telling us about his world, specifically their food. They grew and raised everything they ate. They made most everything by hand, artistry and craft being central to their core values. As James and I had already figured out, most people had a trade that was passed down from generation to generation, and the culinary arts were no different. Everyone from millers, to farmers, to cattle ranchers, butchers, bakers and chefs. They were all specialists, and performed each task with great pride in their work. What surprised us though, was there was no monetary system. Everyone traded goods and services. Because most families had one trade, there was no competition. So butchers traded meat for flour, millers traded flour for veggies, etcetera.

That idea carried over into the entire economy. Loggers traded wood for art, food, or clothes. Seamstresses traded clothes for the services or goods that they needed. However, this wasn't always the case. My father explained that many, many years ago, Caelum used money, much like we do on Earth. Money led to greed, and greed led to a loss of pride in their work. People became more consumed with how much money they made on something, rather than the quality of their work. On the verge of a civil war between villages, all the Kings and Queens united and abolished currency of any kind. The only currency allowed was trade. It only took one generation for things to stabilize. James and I were impressed.

Caelum was made up of hundreds of villages spread across different islands. Caelum was about 100 million square miles, about half the size of Earth. My father was King over a tenth of that, which was made up of about twenty different villages on that many different islands. Each island had a representative of the King or Queen to help run things smoothly. But for the most part, each village worked independently from one another.

Samuel walked us around, showing us where people lived and worked. He introduced us to the sweet family that raised and took care of the many fruit orchards. It was amazing to hear about how they cross-pollinated and created new fruits. We met the potter who created every gorgeous platter, bowl, or goblet that we'd used since arriving.

As we walked through the streets, it was clear that the Caelun people respected and revered my father. My presence seemed to bring raised eyebrows and a lot of whispers. Although everything seemed peaceful and easy in the village, something felt off. It just felt like something was missing, and I couldn't put my finger on it, until I met the blacksmith. We stopped by his house because Samuel needed to inquire about an order he placed to repair one of his fences. As my father explained something to James about the metal in Caelum, I followed the glow from the fire into the back room. The immense heat from the roaring fire licked at my skin. I saw a man hunched over an anvil with a large hammer in his hand, working a red-hot piece of iron. He stopped and looked up at me, his head turning to the side, as if puzzled.

"You must be the 'Eden' I've heard so much about." His voice sounded like it was drug through gravel. He laid his hammer down and stuck the iron back in the fire. As he stood, I saw soot streaked across most of his skin not covered by his leather apron. He was much older, his long white hair pulled back and French braided. Deep creases wrinkled his face.

"Yes, I'm Samuel's daughter."

He approached slowly and thoughtfully. "I'm Mac. They said you looked like your mother. They were right." He eyed me.

"Who said?"

"Everyone," he said simply.

"Well, thank you?" I said, uncomfortable.

"You're welcome." He kept staring at me.

"Well, I should get back. It was nice to meet you, Mac." I turned to leave.

"Nothing has been the same since your mother died." I stopped in my tracks.

"What do you mean?" I asked carefully.

"When she left and never came back . . . something else left with her." His voice softened.

"What else left?"

"Joy . . . as well as the hope that it would ever return."

For whatever reason, in that moment I saw it. I knew what was missing. Joy. Laughter. Happiness. I recognized reverence and respect in people's faces, but nothing much past that. Instead, I felt an underlying sense of melancholy. A sadness.

"Well, maybe you can bring it back to our kingdom, who knows? Maybe there is hope after all." He smiled in a way that still looked sad. "You can tell your father that I will have these bars for the prison finished by tomorrow." He turned and walked back to what he was doing before.

"Prison bars? I thought he was repairing a fence."

"Prison bars, 'fences'. . . same thing."

THE FRIENDLY COMPETITION.

Well, that wasn't the most encouraging thing to hear. A prison? Anxious to learn more about this, I rejoined James and my father. Happy to leave the ominous blacksmith's place behind, we moved outside the city toward the mountains. They steadily rose, spearing clouds as they climbed higher than the white cumulus masses could. The sky was bright blue, and the heat white hot as the afternoon suns' rays gained strength. We followed a path into a shaded wooded area, and I immediately noticed James' relief, his cheeks red under the excursion beneath the suns.

My breath caught when I noticed the trees that provided us with the welcomed shade. I couldn't pick out two trees with leaves the same color. I stopped walking and looked up to the tree directly overhead. The bark was a dark reddish brown and the leaves seemed to glow a burnt orange, almost as though they were on fire. I slowly started walking forward. The next tree's leaves were a deep, rich, almost velvety purple. I caught up to James and my father, but I couldn't concentrate on what was being said. These trees enamored me. Blood red, lime green, pale yellow, chocolate brown, dark pinks, some colors I didn't even have names or words for. I couldn't contain the excitement that bubbled within me. It felt like I was seeing trees for the first time, and they were glorious.

Samuel explained the Caelum seasons to James when we heard loud yelling and crashing of metal. Totally engulfed in the beauty around me, the sudden noise startled me. People were obviously fighting in the distance, but then I saw my father's smile.

"Don't worry, it's just some friendly competition." He looked back at us and waved us to follow him.

A smile broke out on James' face. Competition was his favorite game. Me, not so much. I'd rather just sit there and enjoy the trees. James quickened his pace to catch up to Samuel. Men. When we reached the clearing, I finally saw the commotion. In the midst of the colorful foliage, there was a large circular dirt floored arena surrounded by a log fence. There were about two dozen men and women scattered around the giant circle watching the two in the middle, fighting.

It took only half a second to recognize the larger of the two men fighting. We approached as Marek gracefully unarmed the younger man. As the crowd cheered, my brother picked another opponent. I realized it was a lesson. I could hear him explaining moves and asking questions as he attacked or defended. He was very quick, the huge ornate sword he swung moved faster than my eyes could follow.

"I thought Marek was the only warrior?" I asked my father.

"He is, but sword wielding is a sport here. We hold tournaments regularly, and Marek likes to teach. He's the best in our province."

"That doesn't look like a sword," I responded, my eyes growing wide.

The "sword" he referred to looked more like a weapon of death, not of sport. I couldn't imagine the time and effort that went into making one. The blade was very wide and grew wider toward the end of the blade. There was a curve at the end, making the sword look more like a large, deadly, flat hook. It must have been at least four feet long, the handle longer still. As I watched Marek, I could see the handle was shaped so you could hold it with both hands. The thing looked like it weighed a hundred pounds.

As Marek spun and swung the weapon around with perfect control, I could see it in his eyes again. The tension. The war within. Looking at him now, in his Caelum garb, swinging hooked sword and stopping before he sliced his opponent's clean head off, it was hard to see Gabby's uncle. It was difficult for me to see him as the same man who laughed and tickled Gabby until she couldn't breathe, or entered a room with her hanging off of his flexed arm. I could barely recall them eating ice cream together on the front porch. I tried to remember what it felt like to cook with him in the kitchen, laughing, and dancing to current pop songs. I didn't recognize this man, and I didn't like it. I needed to find my brother again.

Before I even knew what I was doing, I entered the ring.

"Brother!" I called out.

I heard James call after me, and I didn't turn around for fear of what I'd see in his eyes. Honestly, I was afraid I'd chicken out.

Marek and his current arena adversary stopped fighting as I approached. The surprise on Marek's face was the first glimpse of the man I recognized. Then the small smile that spread across his face revealed just a bit more of him.

"I heard you like to teach." I raised an eyebrow at him.

"You wanna play with this?" He raised the blade to my throat, and everything in me recoiled in fear. This was my freaking nightmare. He continued with the fat hook blade resting under my chin. "You hate knives, Eden." Like he was telling me something I didn't already know.

"I hate anything that slices." I said, trying to calm myself. "But that doesn't stop me from cutting veggies in the kitchen."

"Okay." Marek lowered the blade and looked me in the eye. I saw a sparkle there, and it fueled me to push through my fear. He looked down at the hook-blade he held, and then back to me. His mint green eyes were soft as he held out the handle in my direction.

"It's only right that you learn with this."

"Isn't that yours?"

"It was Mom's."

Standing close to the blade, I noticed for the first time the blade was inlaid with a beautiful golden tree. It reminded me of the tree branches that were on the door leading into Caelum. I grabbed the weapon. As my hand enclosed the cold steel handle, my eyes involuntarily shut.

When I opened them, I stood alone in the enclosed circle. The suns were in different positions in the sky, and leaves had fallen off the trees, currently blanketing the empty arena. I heard a child laugh behind me and turned around. There he was, maybe five years old, chasing her around, carrying a tiny sword. His brown hair was long and wavy, just like Gabby's. He laughed wildly as he chased her. Her lavender hair flowed out behind her, leaves crunching under her bare feet. She squealed in pretend horror and then stopped, facing him, wielding the very hook-blade that was in my hand.

Now, Marek, she said, *you must remember what I taught you if you want to get better.*

Trust yourself, his tiny voice answered.

What else? she asked.

Be bold and brave, he laughed. I watched as he lifted his sword toward her. She blocked, spun, and he returned her gentle attack with a block of his own. Time stood still, and it seemed like hours while they played together. My heart swelled with emotion watching my mother teach my brother.

Finally, I turned back to face him, now a man, staring blankly at me.

Although the hook-blade looked like it weighed a hundred pounds, it felt extremely light in my hands. Marek slowly lifted his blade up across his body in a ready position. *Trust yourself,* she had said. So I did what felt natural. I held it up like a baseball bat, even choking up on the handle.

"You sure you want to do this, sis?" Marek whispered.

"She taught you . . . now you teach me."

"Don't worry, I won't hurt you. Just do what comes naturally," he said gently.

His blade swung so fast I only heard the swoosh it made as it ripped through the air. My hands flew up, holding the blade straight down, shielding my body before I realized what happened.

Clink.

My feet were wide and helped take the blow, and somehow I held strong. My muscles seemed to have a mind of their own as I pushed the blade out and away from me, pushing his sword up and out. The sound of the metal scraping as our blades ran along each other rang in the air as I returned to my start position. Marek stood, arms out, with a surprised look on his face. The arena was silent.

"*Woo*! That's my fiancée!" James yelled, breaking the silence. Marek's face broke into a large grin.

"Not bad." He went back into his ready position, swung in the opposite direction, I blocked once again.

Clink.

I pushed back. Marek immediately swung his entire body to attack again, but I was already there. Instead of blocking, I swung the hook-blade upward as he sliced toward me, pushing his blade up. I ducked under it and his arm, landing with my hook blade pointed to his back. Marek faced my father and James, and I saw them staring at us with crazy looks on their faces. Their faces probably matched mine. How was I doing this? Marek spun around in a blur, crashing his blade into mine.

Clank.

"How did you know Mom taught me?" He huffed.

Scrape. Clink. I spun and swung under his sword again.

"I saw it, when you handed me this thing," I exhaled.

Our blades were stuck in an X, him pushing against me and I against him.

"Of course you did." He smirked. "But did you see this?"

He swung his blade in a circle and took my feet out from under me. Laid flat on my back, his laugh echoed in my ears.

Not for long.

I swung my leg up and out and caught him right at the ankles, bringing him down to the ground.

Thud.

I rolled over and jumped back up, thrusting my heel on the handle of his weapon, kicking it away. I carefully laid my hook-blade under his chin and looked down at my smiling brother. Now this man, I recognized. His eyes, his entire demeanor, were the ones I'd gotten to know and love back on Earth.

"Don't you dare disappear on us again. Whatever you are fighting against, it's not me, understand?" My voice was firm, but my eyes sincere.

His smile faded. "Yes."

I removed the blade and held my hand out. He grabbed it and stood in front of me.

"You're a natural with that thing. You should keep it, she would want you to have it."

"Thanks, Marek."

"Are you kidding me right now?" James ran up, fake hyperventilating. "Who are you and what have you done with my girlfriend?" He took the hook-blade from me and held it out, inspecting and admiring it.

"That was impressive, Eden." My father looked proud. "Your mother was one of the best sword fighters I'd ever seen. There must me some of her magic left in her weapon." He seemed to be half-kidding.

I wasn't so sure it was a joke.

THE CONFRONTATION.

As we walked back to the house, James walked ahead with my father, and Marek and I hung back. I didn't say anything, afraid to damage the seemingly fragile relationship between us.

"I'm sorry I disappeared last night," he said, looking up at our father and James. He paused a beat, then continued, "It's been quite a while since I've been home, and I needed to see some people."

I didn't push his explanation. If I'd learned anything about Marek, it was he was a closed book until he decided to open.

"It's okay," I lied. Truth was, I couldn't stand not knowing where he stood. I decided to test with something safe. "What's up with Vera? It's obvious she doesn't like me."

"Aunt Vera was always jealous of Mom. Ava had everything she had ever wanted: husband, family, basically the entire kingdom. Everyone loved her. You just happen to represent that. I wouldn't take it personal."

"It seems like more than that." I looked at him. My brother just shrugged and kept walking. Alrighty then, next subject.

"I met the town's blacksmith. He said he was working on prison bars for Samuel, but father told me he was checking on a fence. Does Caelum have a jail?" I asked, hoping for more information.

"Of course." Marek looked at me, surprised. "Caelum isn't perfect. We have crimes, and the criminals have to be put somewhere."

"So that's all it is?" I knew I pushed too far as soon as I asked.

"Eden, not everything is a conspiracy." He rolled his eyes, annoyed.

"I know, I'm sorry. I just feel so uneasy. I can't pinpoint it, and it's driving me crazy." I said, attempting to be honest with him. He seemed to soften, and glanced up at James and Samuel once again before he spoke.

"Hey, why don't we spend some time together tomorrow? Just you and me. I have somewhere I want to take you." His whole demeanor seemed to change.

"Okay." I looked at James. "I guess James could find something to do."

"Sure. I can arrange for him to have sword fighting lessons tomorrow with some friends who are almost as good as me."

"He'd probably love that." I finally relaxed a bit. I didn't love the idea of separating with James while here, but maintaining trust with Marek was important. And tomorrow would be the perfect time to talk about how to leave without causing too much trouble.

"So it's settled. Tomorrow, you and I will have some sibling bonding time." Marek elbowed me in the side.

We all needed to clean up before dinner that night, so in typical Caelum fashion, we all went to the bathhouse for a body soak. It quickly became one of my favorite things. This evening I went for the lavender and honey combination. I'm pretty sure I fell asleep in that hot tub of goodness. James and Marek both went the citrus route. The whole room smelled delicious. Shay came in and repainted my golden tattoos, and Arie brought in a long string of peach Elisium flower petals to weave in my hair. After we finished, we moseyed down to the dressmaker for tonight's attire. I could really get used to this. Marek's invitation for the following day had relaxed me, and in good spirits, I chose a luxurious golden silk fabric for tonight's dinner. The dressmaker, silently, ripped and braided the fabric to create long golden ropes. He draped, tucked, and stitched to reveal the most unique dress. Three braided ropes draped over each shoulder, crisscrossing over my back. The hem was so long it dragged along the floor, but he assured me it was intended, with nothing but a nod. I had yet to hear the dressmaker say one word.

That night King Samuel surprised us all with a dinner on the shallow sea. I'd never seen anything like it. The table was about a hundred yards from shore, and looked like it was floating out in the middle of the water. Lights were strung along poles all around the surreal setting. Samuel told us earlier that day that Caelum only used solar power for electricity, making sense considering they had two suns.

Tonight's dinner was more than just our family. Samuel invited a couple of his closest friends, as well as giving me two invitations. I invited Shay and Arie, the only two friends I'd made since being here. Marek also brought a couple of friends he wanted to introduce to James. Everyone was laughing and in good spirits as I looked around at the eclectic group of us. Perhaps the blacksmith was right, maybe I could help restore the joy that was lost when my mother died. I thought it might just be possible, until I saw my Aunt Vera. She brought up the rear of the pack, alone, and armed with a sour expression. If joy reminded her of Ava, she was obviously going to have none of it.

The twelve of us walked out into the water and approached the most amazing banquet table spread I'd ever seen. The sixteen-foot-long wooden table was covered with colorful fruits and veggies, meats and pies, cakes and cobblers. Two equally long benches sat on either side. The salty breeze provided a steady flow of cooler air in the already perfect dusk weather. I looked up to see the colors beginning to form along the edges of the skyline, a sign the suns would be setting soon. There were six poles coming up from the white sand that held up the hundreds of string lights that draped around and over the dinner table. The lights reflected off the bluish water under our feet, creating an almost magical feeling, as if we were standing on the stars.

I sat in the middle of the table, Shay and Arie sitting on my left side, James on my right. Marek sat down next to James with his friends. My father, his advisors, and Vera sat on the other. The evening's soundtrack was the soft lapping of the water's ebb and flow, only interrupted by bursts of laughter. As the suns set, and the food slowly disappeared, the conversation turned from separate group chatting to the telling of stories to the entire table. Marek told us of one of his most exciting tournament wins, I told several different stories about Gabby, and my father told us about when he met my mother for the first time. It was one of the most wonderful, relaxing moments I experienced since we'd arrived in Caelum. After everyone was full and satisfied, my father stood and raised his glass.

"Tonight, I want to celebrate the return of my daughter, Eden. Her return reignites our Caelum traditions and marks the beginning of a new reign. Caelum will once again, have its Queen!" He raised his glass.

I felt a huge brick drop in my stomach. So much for wonderful and relaxing.

Everyone raised his or her glasses except me.

"To our Queen!" He smiled looking down at me.

Queen? What was he talking about?

"To our Queen!" everyone echoed, except Aunt Vera and myself.

My body felt stone cold. James, having no idea what was being said, looked at me, his face suddenly draped with worry. He could see the wild panic in my eyes. I made sure I thought in English before I spoke so only my father, Marek, James, and I knew what was being said.

"What are you talking about?" I looked up at the still smiling King Samuel. His smile slowly faded as he realized I wasn't in a toasting mood anymore. He looked around at the rest of his guests and continued in Caelun.

"Thank you all so much for coming tonight. I think my daughter and I should have some time to discuss what this means for our family. May you all have a lovely rest of your evening," he said cheerfully, dismissing everyone from the table. All the friends and new acquaintances rose, hugging us, laughing, and left. Everyone seemed unaware of what had just happened, beside those of us who remained. I noticed that Vera sat unmoving at the far end of the table, looking as unhappy about this as I did.

There were many emotions rushing through me at the moment. Frustration and confusion seemed to be the two predominant. I decided to address the confusion first.

"What exactly did your toast mean?" I started, making sure it was in English so James could understand everything.

"There is something I haven't told you."

"Ya think?" I shot off, standing and walking away from the table.

"Eden, I'm sorry, I just got caught up in the moment. Why don't you sit and I'll explain everything." He looked at me calmly, so I sat back down.

His eyes were soft as he took a deep breath. "I'm not the rightful King of Caelum. Well, let me rephrase. I am, but only because your mother died."

"I don't understand. Weren't you the king before she died?" I asked.

"Yes, but I wasn't until I married your mother."

Marek spoke up. "You see, Eden, I'm not heir to the throne. You are." He looked at me with a sympathetic smile. I was trying to wrap my brain around this when I felt James' hand on my back. I couldn't find any words, so thankfully James interceded.

"So your royal line is passed down through the women?" he asked, verifying what we were already realizing.

"Why didn't you tell me?" My question was directed to Marek.

"We were trying to work through a lot as it were. New family, new world, one you hadn't even been to yet. How was I supposed to tell you it was your birthright to rule it?"

It was true. That might have been too much. But I needed to tell them the truth—I didn't want to rule Caelum, my home was Earth. They had expectations for me I was not ready, nor would ever be ready, to meet.

"Dad . . ." I looked to my father. "Dad . . . I . . ." *Can't. I can't,* is what I needed and wanted to say.

"This is what you were born to do, my daughter." My father reached across the table and took my hand. His hands were warm. James' hand warm hand rested on my back. So it had begun, the tug of war between worlds.

I knew this wasn't what I wanted, and despite what my father said, I knew it wasn't what I was born for. But I also knew I couldn't tell him that right now. I needed to gather my thoughts and figure out how to proceed. I needed to buy some time. This was far more difficult and complicated that I thought it would be.

"Can I please think about and just . . . process this?" I looked around the table.

"Of course, Eden, of course." My father squeezed my hand and let go. "I'm sure you and James need to discuss this. After all, this affects him, too." He nodded at James and then left the table, Vera following closely behind. She hadn't said a word the entire night.

Marek stood. "We can talk about this more tomorrow. I'll come get you at first light. I'm sorry again, Eden, I know this is a lot. But it will all be okay, you'll see." With a reassuring look, he turned and followed Samuel and Vera, leaving James and I at the table alone.

"I'm not so sure." I looked at James.

"One thing is for sure, that was unexpected." His soft brown eyes were wide. "Queen Eden." He bowed his head and chuckled.

"How can you joke at a time like this? James, this complicates everything."

"Only if we can't change it."

"Change it? Change thousands of years of lineage and tradition?" I raised my eyebrows skeptically.

"Well, it's obvious where Gabby gets her dramatic flair." James smiled.

"I'm not being dramatic!" I answered somewhat dramatically. "Gabby . . . do we even have any idea what this means for her? She doesn't know any of this exists yet, and now she's already in line to be a freaking queen," I spat out, unable to believe my own words. How was she supposed to?

"Eden." James straddled the bench and faced me. He placed both of his hands on my shoulders. I turned my body to face him. The light's reflections danced in his eyes. It reminded me of the night we were tied up in front of the bonfire in Palus. It reminded me of everything we had been through together. I suddenly felt bolder, braver.

"Eden, I love you, and I'm with you. Regardless. Marek is right, this will all work out. Tomorrow go, and between the two of you, figure out a plan. And once you do, let's get out of here, because I wanna get home and marry you!" He hugged me tight. I thought of us and Charlie and Gabby being a family. At that moment, I knew he was right. I would figure it out. I had to, too much was at stake. Then a soft laugh rose in his bare chest.

"Although . . . we could always stay. King James does have a nice ring to it. I'm a progressive guy, I can handle marrying into the throne."

"You are such a dork." Then I kissed him hard, mostly to shut him up. Mostly.

THE BURNING QUESTIONS.

It was dark, the suns had set hours ago. The three moons' reflections shimmered on the water and seemed to follow us with every step. Her light violet eyes turned down, watching her feet as they moved cautiously through the shallow sea. They were bare, moving slowly, almost dancing as they glided through the glowing bluish water. She wore a simple white silk nightgown that dragged behind, floating on the saltwater. One hand cradled her large protruding belly, the other gently laid over it. She cried softly and sang in a whisper. Her hair hung loose and long, with silver strands braided throughout.

"Mom?" I reached out to her.

She didn't answer or respond.

I stopped walking alongside her. I looked down and was wearing the same gold dress I wore at dinner earlier. A dream. She continued on, her back to me now, hair glowing in the moonlight.

"Eden, my sweetheart."

My pulse quickened and I ran to catch up to her.

"Yes, Mom?" Of course she wasn't talking to me. At least not the me standing next to her, but the one growing inside of her.

"I'm so sorry we can't be together." Her voice was barely audible. "I know this is the only way to fix everything, to undo everything I've set into motion." She rubbed her tummy. My back tingled, like I felt it where I stood.

"You will bring us together. You will be the balance, the bridge. I'm just so sorry I won't be there to help you . . ." She trailed off.

I suddenly knew where we were, where she was going. I saw the door to Earth in the distance.

"But I promise you, when the time is right, you will know what to do. You will have everything you need to accomplish what you need to."

Unable to contain everything I felt, I reached out to her and cried. "Mom, what am I supposed to do? What is my destiny? How could this have been better than us not being together?" I knew it was useless. I knew she wasn't really there.

But she stopped.

She turned and looked toward the world she was fleeing from, the village no longer visible.

"I have seen it, sweetie." She glanced down toward me in her womb, stroking her belly softy. With every stroke of her hand, I felt it where I stood. She continued, almost as though she knew what I had asked. "You will need her, and you will need him. They will make you stronger, and you will need all of that strength for what is to come. None of it is possible if we stay. I'm so sorry. I love you, sweetheart. I promise you, I will always be with you. You will never be alone."

I froze and couldn't follow when she turned and continued walking. I watched as her figure slowly shrank into the horizon, toward the Door that would separate us forever.

"Mom." A tear rolled down my cheek as I heard the door open and close.

After waking up, I lay in bed for hours, unable to go back to sleep. Not only had she known she was going to die, she had consciously made the choice. She had known I needed to grow up on Earth. Had she seen it all? Was she talking about Gabby? Is that who I needed? And the man . . . James? I dreamt almost every time I slept here, every dream only confusing me more and revealing more heartbreaking realizations. She had lied to Rosalina. She hadn't come to Earth too late in her pregnancy by mistake, she had come on purpose. But why? What had she set in motion? What was I supposed to fix?

That morning, I couldn't shake the visual I now had of my mother leaving. It also changed the emotions that now accompanied my dream of her dying during childbirth. I couldn't wrap my brain around the strength and bravery it took to walk into death knowingly. She said I would never be alone. I looked at the painting that hung on the wall, knowing the message on the other side she had left for me. She had taken measures to make sure I felt her presence, and that was comforting.

The only thing Marek had told me about today was to wear my swimsuit. So I decided on just that and a wrap skirt. I assumed we would spend most of the day outside, and I welcomed a day of Caelum's suns' rays. I sat in the courtyard, journaling what I had dreamt the night before, wishing I had a chance to tell James about it. But that would have to wait until tonight.

When Marek entered the courtyard, I closed my journal and tucked it in my bag. As he got closer, I noticed dark circles under his eyes. In the almost four months we had been together, I'd never seen him look so rough. I joked as much and he completely ignored me. He didn't look me in the eyes until we walked out of town, when his entire body seemed to relax. He asked how I slept and gave him a half-truth.

"Not the worst night sleep I've ever had." I shrugged.

"Yeah, me neither." Definitely his half-truth, by the looks of him.

Neither of us said much as we walked further from town. Everything was uncharacteristically bright in the early morning suns. The grass was especially bright green, almost lime, interspersed with purple flowers everywhere. Trees were still glistening with dewdrops resting on their multi colored leaves. Birds chirped loudly, ranging in frequency and tone. Some seemed to carry messages of urgency and some sweet melodies of rest. I tried to pick out one bird from the other, but the sheer amount of them made it impossible. We came upon an open field where teams of beautiful horses were grazing. There were at least a dozen, all varying in size and color, from light and dark brown, black, white, reddish, and everything in between.

"We have a long way to go. Pick one," Marek said nonchalantly.

"Pick one?" I raised an eyebrow at my brother.

"Sure. We don't keep specific animals so that they can remain free. But in exchange for their freedom, they allow us to ride when we need to."

"Seems fair." I shrugged. I walked toward the group of wild animals timidly. Marek approached a huge dark chocolate brown horse with a blonde mane. The horse broke away from the rest and walked to him like he had been expecting him all morning. I watched my brother pull his long skirt up between his legs and effortless swing up on the mammoth beast. Oh, boy. This should be fun.

I slowly took in all of the horses before me, realizing it was probably important to pick the right one. It didn't take long to realize which one she was. She was sleek, and she was gorgeous. Her body was jet black, her mane crazy long, thick, and silver. Every strand of her mane and tail looked like thin yarn. Her eyes were dark grey and stormy, and never left mine as I slowly approached her. Her face and backside were covered in white freckles resembling the stars sprawled across the night sky. She lifted her chin as I reached out my hand, inviting me to introduce myself.

"Well, hello there, black beauty." I instantly loved this creature.

"Her name is Nox. And one guess who she let ride her the most."

I grinned, not needing to answer him. The connections between my mother, this world, and myself were no longer surprising. Trying to imitate my brother's movements, I hoisted up my skirt, grabbed Nox's mane, and tried to lift myself onto her back. I wasn't graceful, nor did it work. I tried again to no avail. Marek started laughing, but then stopped when Nox kneeled, allowing me slide on with little effort.

"She must have felt bad for you," Marek teased.

"Or she's just a sweetheart. Aren't you just a sweetheart?" I moved into my baby voice, the one I slipped into when talking to cute dogs back at home.

"Come on." My brother laughed. "Let's get going."

After a hug of gratitude around my new friend's neck, I gently grabbed Nox's mane and we started on our journey.

THE JOURNEY.

We rode through the rolling hills and pastures laden with succulent flowers for an hour before we came to the shallow sea on the other side of the island. Marek didn't hesitate as he galloped straight into the six-inch turquoise blue waters. I followed behind him, avoiding the spray of warm salty water and sand he left in his wake. The suns were high in the sky by this time, and I felt my eyes adjust to the bright reflections bouncing off the water in every direction. When we first entered the sea, there was clear, crisp horizon in every direction. Within minutes, giant lone trees popped in and out of my line of vision.

Nox ran fast, seeming to love the water. For the most part, we ran side by side, with only the wind and splashing water as our soundtrack. Every now and again Marek would speed up and cut us off, spraying us with saltwater. Neither Nox, nor myself minded though, being wet felt good in the wind. At one point, Nox veered away from Marek and toward a large flock of blue swans, spooking them. I found myself surrounded by a hundred giant birds, all taking flight at one time. I couldn't even see Marek through all of the flapping feathers. The swooshing of the wings reminded me of Strix and our day together in Terra Arborum, which felt like lifetimes ago. We galloped along with the gorgeous creatures for what seemed like a full minute before they rose above my head.

We rode through the shallow sea for another hour before we came to a huge island covered in steep mountains that shot straight up from the sea, cutting through and rising above the large white cumulous clouds attempting to impede their growth. I looked at my brother and he smiled, nodding to a shore in the distance. We changed course and headed for the small shore. As we approached, I saw a steep crevasse in the mountain range that looked like a path between two mammoth boulders. We slowed down as we reached land, careful of the trees that surrounded the shore.

Marek led the way as we entered the tall and narrow cave-like structure. Thankfully, it was large enough to bring our horses. When I could finally see what waited on the other side, my stomach dropped. Every part of my mind screamed in recognition of this place. Outstretched before me was a huge glass lake reflecting the expansive mountain range surrounding it. Just off the shore on one side of the lake were two oversized boulders with pastel colored veins running throughout. They were small enough to climb upon, but large enough to give the perfect view of the expansive, pristine lake.

This was the place in my dream. This was the future that Ava knew she could never have. A future that we could never have together. My eyes welled up for the umpteenth time since my arrival in Caelum. Marek came up beside me and put his arm around me. I had told him my dream, he must have known this was the place.

"I wanted it to be a surprise," he said simply.

"Mission accomplished." I smiled. Suddenly, all I wanted was to go get Gabby and climb these boulders with her and teach her to skip rocks. Maybe the dream could be about us, after all. Maybe the dream could represent hope of our future together, and not the despair of losing it with my own mother. As much as I wanted to be with Gabby in this moment, I knew I had so much to figure out first. There was no way I was bringing her into this world before I had a plan, or before she was ready.

"Come on, Eden, let's make some real family memories that aren't dreams," my brother yelled over his shoulder as he ran toward the lake.

THE BONFIRE.

We spent the afternoon swimming, diving off cliffs, skipping rocks, and eating fish Marek caught. There were also fruit trees around that provided us with mid-afternoon snacks. Nox and Marek's horse, who I decided to nickname Cocoa, grazed leisurely around the island while we swam. It was a perfect day, with no cares in the world—Caelum or Earth. Of all the days being in Caelum, this was the one it felt most like home. I wished James could have been with us, but I understood that Marek wanted to be alone. I knew we had some family business to discuss.

"I have one last surprise for you." Marek carried an armload of fish.

"I hope it's that you are going to make a fire and cook those." I eyed the huge dead fish staring at me blankly.

"Something like that."

I followed him on a path through some trees for about ten minutes. We came upon a clearing with a rock cliff face in the distance. There were subtle stairs jetting out from the wall, and we carefully climbed them to an overhang. The rock overhang provided the perfect view of the lake above the tree line. The suns began to set over the mountains, and the colors that sprang up throughout the sky reflected off the lake. It was a beautiful sight. I peeled my eyes from the perfect picture long enough to see Marek building a fire on the ledge. There were two square rocks that made perfect seating around the fire pit. I sat and helped him get it started. We sat in silence for a while, cooking the fish, and watching the suns set.

Finally I spoke up. "This is awesome, Marek, thank you."

"This was it, you know." He looked at me with sincerity.

"What?"

"This was my dream. The one I had before I found you. The one I told you about at James' house."

The fire at his secret place. That's right.

He continued. "Now I feel like it was sign. Like something was telling me to find you, or maybe it was just preparing me to find you."

"Maybe. I've been having a lot of those lately." I smiled.

"Either way, I never would've thought it was the future. If I'd known, it would have brought me so much hope."

"Well, maybe now you know that, you can have hope. Maybe you can look at all of your dreams that way now."

"I think the blacksmith was right. I think that is your purpose. You have already brought back so much joy to this place. And it's only been a couple of days." Marek glanced at me.

I knew it was time to talk about what we needed to. "Marek . . ." I started.

"No, just hear me out, Eden," he interrupted me. I nodded. It was the least I could do. He took a deep breath.

"I'm sorry I didn't tell you about your birthright. I should have told you sooner. I felt like everything with James and Gabby just made it all so complicated, and I didn't want to make things harder."

"I get it. It's okay." I let him continue.

"I know that it's going to be difficult, and a lot to process for everyone, but Caelum needs you. It needs you desperately. I think you need to consider staying. This should be your home."

Oh no. I did not expect this from him.

"Um..."

"I know what you are going to say, Eden. 'What about Gabby?' But Gabby was made to be here. This is her home as much as yours."

"No, Marek, she's not. Eric was from Earth, and he was her father. She has just as much a right to grow up there as here. Not to mention what James has come to mean to her . . . and to me."

Marek looked down to the fire.

"What about what I mean to both of you? Doesn't that matter?"

"Of course it does." I put my hand on his arm. "You coming into our lives has meant more than I could have dreamed of. But Marek, it doesn't have to be one or another. I don't think it *can* be one or the other. We have to work out a way it can be both."

We need a bridge between worlds. *You will build the bridge.* Ava's words echoed in my mind.

Marek looked resigned. "Well, we don't have to decide anything tonight. Let's talk tomorrow with James, and I'm sure we can work out a plan." I saw something flash in his eyes as he said it, like he didn't believe it. I was slightly bummed at the prospect of another night without an exit plan to go home.

Every day in Caelum, I felt Earth and Gabby slip a tiny bit further from my grasp, and it was starting to worry me.

THE SHOCK.

Despite the suns having already set, the ride back was enjoyable. The moons' reflections off the calm smooth sea provided plenty of light for us to navigate back. Everything felt cooler and calmer under the night's sky. Nox looked like a night shadow riding under me, almost invisible. Marek and I rode back in silence, still processing our conversation around the bonfire. Even with that unexpected turn, I couldn't wait to talk to James and tell him about everything we had done that day. Not to mention we needed to regroup and strategize our exit. As wonderful as today was, and however much I loved learning about Ava and my family, it was time to go home. I needed to see Gabby. I felt our old lives dissipating, and it frightened me.

We went ahead and rode Nox and Cocoa into town since it was already so late. We entered the courtyard and I hopped off my new friend, letting him roam and munch on some of the fruit trees. Our father came out to greet us.

"Welcome back! I trust you both had a fun day of adventure." He was smiling, looking back and forth between us.

"It was great, Dad, thank you," Marek answered, not making eye contact with him.

"Marek, thanks for today. If you'll excuse me, Father, I'm going to go find James and tell him all about it." I smiled at my brother and nodded to my father.

"Actually, I'm afraid you two missed a little excitement while you were gone." Samuel reached out his hand to stop me.

"What happened?" I asked, suddenly worried something had happened to James.

"Well, the Door Maker got us a message from James' brother, Charlie. Apparently, there was a trespasser trying to open the door on James' property and there was an altercation. Charlie was hospitalized, and James left to tend to him."

"What?" That couldn't be right. "James left Caelum?" I felt shocked.

"I'm afraid so," Samuel answered. "He wanted me to tell you he was extremely sorry, and he will be back as soon as he can."

This didn't feel right. James wouldn't leave without talking to me first.

"He knew you would be upset, but he also knew you would understand that if it were Gabby, you wouldn't hesitate."

He was right; I knew James would understand if I had to leave suddenly to be there with Gabby. In normal circumstances, I wouldn't have thought twice about it, but this was hardly a normal family visit. After our conversation last night, it was hard for me to believe he would just leave me here alone. Maybe he thought Marek and I had a plan. Either way, James shouldn't have to be alone.

"I should go and be with him. He probably hasn't even left Italy yet." I moved away from my Father and headed toward the door.

"Actually, the Door Maker's message arrived just after you both left this morning. I'm sure he's already on a plane." I looked at my father and over to Marek, who was still fiddling with Cocoa. I walked over to the table and sat, feeling defeated.

"Is Charlie okay? Did Gio's message say anything about how he is?"

My father simply shook his head. "I'm sorry, it didn't."

This was not what I expected tonight. I didn't like the idea of being here when everyone else I loved was in another world. I was terribly worried about Charlie. I also knew that James' leaving meant I had lost my only other ally in Caelum. If I were going to get home, it would have to be on my own. Now, more than ever, I knew I had to.

Later that night, I stood in front of the large open window facing the sea. The breeze blew lightly on my face, bringing with it its salty taste. It felt just like I was back in Positano, and James and I were dancing to the music in the restaurant the night he proposed. James. I still couldn't shake the feeling something was off, him leaving was not his MO. I looked down at my ring and slid it off. "In every world." I looked down at my long white silk nightgown, like the one Ava wore when she left that night, pregnant with me. This would make a lovely wedding dress. Simple, elegant, comfy. I missed James already. I missed having someone to process this with.

What had he said last night? He's with me, regardless. Then, right after he said that, he leaves? It didn't make sense. He always told me that we were stronger together; he said it when I thought about coming here without him. So why would be go home alone? Why wouldn't he wait for me? If Charlie was really hurt, James could have waited for me, and it would have been our perfect way to leave Caelum without objection. James was too strategic and too smart to waste that opportunity. Which led me to the only conclusion.

It was a lie.

Maybe my father pressured him or threatened him to leave. That was the only explanation. I lay in bed, restless, until I couldn't wait any longer. I had to figure out what was going on, and I couldn't let another minute go by without finding out the truth.

Once I had made the decision to get up, get dressed, and figure out what was really happening, two things happened simultaneously. First, I realized I had immediately fallen asleep. Second, I knew I was dreaming because I was no longer in my room. I roamed the main corridor of the house when I heard voices. I couldn't understand what was being said, so I moved closer to eavesdrop.

"She's going to figure it out," said a muffled voice.

"Not before what is needed to be done, is done." A different voice.

"Dad, I'm not so sure about this."

Marek.

"Well, son, it doesn't matter what you think. You follow my orders, do you understand? I am your father. Your king."

Samuel.

The suspense was killing me. I knew they wouldn't see me, so I entered the room so I could see and hear better.

"I will not lose my daughter again. I will do whatever it takes." Father was sitting at a table, head in his hands.

"You will lose her if she hates you," Marek countered, standing next to him.

"Eden will come around, you'll see. When she sees Gabby here, happy and thriving, she will relent."

Oh my God, what was he planning?

"I think you underestimate her love for James."

"Once Eden understands and has taken her place as Queen, we will think about allowing James to return."

"Return? He's here, or do I need to remind you what you made me do?" Marek retorted.

"It had to be done." Samuel's face was calm. "It is best for everyone."

Oh my God, what did he do?

"Just go get my granddaughter." My father looked Marek in the eyes. "And bring her home."

"Why, so you can throw her in prison with James?" Marek said sarcastically.

What? Prison?

"How dare you talk to me like that!" Samuel stood, his voice rising as well. "Are you afraid your sister is going to be angry with you? This is bigger than her, or you, or James. This is our kingdom. And I will not allow our kingdom to suffer because we are afraid of what your sister might think!" He was furious, but he sat and regained his composure. "Eden will come around, I know it. Now go, before she finds out what we've done with James, and that you are going to get Gabrielle."

Marek turned to walk out the doorway, defeated, and suddenly stopped short.

He looked up and locked eyes with me.

"Damn it. I think it's too late for that."

THE BETRAYAL.

I woke up crying. How could he? How could my own brother do this to me? I knew he was already here. Whatever I dreamt must have just happened, I knew that much. I sensed his presence, his shadow, lingering in the corner of my room. But I needed a minute. I needed to compose myself before facing my betrayer.

"How did you do it?" Marek whispered.

I didn't answer.

"How did you dream in real time?" he asked again.

"Is that all you have to say to me?" I lay still in the darkness, my eyes still closed, tears streaming slowly. He didn't answer.

"How did you know I was there?" I asked.

"You're my sister, I always know when you're dreaming. We are connected."

"Obviously not." I choked back a sob.

"What do you want me to say, Eden? He's our father."

"I want you to grow a pair and stand up to him, or grow a brain and think for yourself!" I shot up and out of bed, beyond furious with him.

"Easy for you to say, Eden. You haven't had to deal with him grieving your whole life!" he shot back.

"How can you do this to me? To us? To my family . . . after everything you've seen back on Earth. We were happy, things were fine."

"Well, they weren't fine here. They haven't been fine here for as long as I can remember. And if you need to make a sacrifice to bring stability and peace back to our kingdom, then I'm sorry Eden. But you just need to suck it up."

"Suck it up?" My voice raised an octave. "Suck it up? You are talking about kidnapping my daughter and ripping away her choices. You have thrown my fiancé in prison! Marek, do you hear yourself?" I was losing control.

"This is happening, Eden." He looked at me calmly. His light mint eyes seemed to glow in the dark room. He was no longer torn. Anything tying him to me was gone.

Something snapped within me at that moment. I saw Gabby's face. Heard her easy laughter and felt her naive innocence. Brother or no brother, I was not going to allow him to take the most important thing in my life and put her on a path she was never destined to be on. I didn't need Ava, Samuel, Rosalina, or anyone to tell me that. It was not time for her to enter this world yet, and there would be hell to pay for anyone who tried to drag her in before she was ready.

I reached under my bed and pulled out my mother's hook-sword that Marek had given me. The moons' light bounced off of it, projecting a bright light on the ceiling. My brother's face was stoic.

"Eden." He looked at me like a I was a petulant child.

"Marek. If you think I'm going to let you take my child, you are insane," I said calmly.

"This is going to happen, you might as well—" I cut him off with a warning.

"Stop. Saying. That. The fact that you think this is actually going to happen shows how little you know me, how much you underestimate me and what I'm capable of." I glared, moving into ready position.

"And the fact that you think you can stop me shows how much you overestimate your very limited abilities." Marek pulled his sword out of its sheath.

Just two hours ago we were eating caught fish over a bonfire, laughing, and joking together. Now we were at war. My heart already grieved the loss of my brother.

"I don't want to hurt you, Eden."

"I don't want to hurt you, either," I said simply, a single tear escaping before I could stop it. "But Gabby is my life, and I will do what is necessary to protect her."

"You don't need to protect her from me. I want what is best for her."

"No, you don't!" I spat bitterly. "You don't get to say that. You haven't earned that right."

We were on either side of my bed, facing each other, swords drawn. Marek was dressed to enter Italy, me in my nightgown. If I didn't stop him, Marek would have Gabby back here by morning. This was it. What it had all come down to. He wasn't going to back down, and neither was I. I knew I couldn't hurt him, but I had to disarm him and keep him from the Door home.

I stepped around my bed and swung my sword out and around in the opposite direction, catching his sword in my hook and pulling it towards me.

The metal scrapped, sending a chill down my spine.

He countered by spinning and swinging outside, extending his arm and bringing his weapon around fast. I blocked and used his momentum toward me to uppercut his chin with my elbow and knee him in the gut.

Chaos followed the clashing of our swords.

I fought him with everything I had. Not just physically, but emotionally. Everything that raged inside of me. My insides screamed at him with every punch, every swing of my mother's weapon.

He pushed me against the wall, attempting to knock the hook sword from my hand, to no avail. Vases crashed on the floor. Using the bed as a springboard, I kicked him across the face. He retaliated with a blow to the side of my head with the butt of his weapon. Swinging wildly, he sliced the picture Ava painted hanging over my bed. The ripping sound of the canvas stopped me cold.

"This is why she left. He wouldn't let her do what she needed to." I huffed, unable to breathe in enough air to quench my need for it.

"What are you talking about?" my brother gasped, looking for oxygen himself.

"Marek, this is not what Mom wanted." I exhaled and spat some blood out of my mouth. I couldn't stop the tears from flowing. "Can't you see that?"

"No, how would I know what Mom wanted? She left me. I've only ever known what Dad wants. I've done his bidding my whole life. And right now, all he wants is you, here."

"It doesn't have to be that way anymore. Of course he thinks that is what he wants. He's scared. He doesn't know there is a better way."

"Eden, I wish there was another way. But there isn't." He sighed and dropped his weapon.

"Marek, listen to me. If Ava wanted me to be Queen, she would have stayed. Everything would have worked out that way if she had. The point was that I wasn't supposed to be here. That's why she left. She left knowing what would happen, she sacrificed herself!" I was sobbing, trying to stay rational.

"Stop. Stop trying to confuse me."

"No. Ava was Queen, this is her kingdom, her wishes should mean more than Samuel's. She wanted me to build a bridge between worlds, not Caelum's queen. That's why she wanted me to be born and raised on Earth, to bring the two together." I had finally caught my breath, and a glimpse of the truth.

Marek looked into my watery eyes; his were full of doubt.

"You would say whatever you needed to stop me, that's all I know for sure."

"No," I cried, realizing I was not going to change his mind. I couldn't beat him with the sword. My only chance was to get to Gabby first and run. But then I'd be abandoning James. I couldn't think about that right now. Gabby came first, and I must protect her.

I knew I couldn't outrun Marek. Suddenly, I knew what I needed to do.

Without warning, dropping my sword and grabbing my key off of my nightstand, I turned and jumped out of the open window. I landed on the roof of the building beneath my father's house, and rolled down the pitch, grabbing the edge before I fell off. I dropped carefully to the ground, looked up and saw Marek looking down at me out of the window, then he disappeared. I ran as fast as my bare feet could carry me, until I saw her. Nox had run around the corner and dropped to the ground immediately upon seeing me. I jumped on her back and we took off down the stone path toward the shallow sea. Toward Gabby.

The wind was stinging my eyes we were running so fast, my nightgown sailing out behind me. I didn't turn around until we reached the sea. Marek was nowhere to be seen. I squeezed my legs tighter, urging Nox to run faster, afraid Marek was closing in. I knew I was getting closer to the Door when we passed one of the giant trees I remembered on our way in. I glanced behind to see Marek on his horse, gaining speed. Within minutes, he was on top of us. He jumped from the back of his horse, knocking me from Nox. We landed hard in the wet sand. I rolled, jumped up and started running. Marek ran up behind me, kicking my legs out from under me, causing me to fall into the warm shallow water again.

"I won't lie, you are putting up a better fight than I thought you would."

As soon as the words left his mouth, I punched him hard across the face. He swung, discombobulated, and I ducked, missing his attempt.

"Stop!" he yelled.

"Leave Gabby alone." My hand throbbed and my mouth tasted salt, from a combination of tears and the sea.

I tried punching him again, but he blocked and kneed me in the side. I fell on my backside into the water, then swung my leg, taking his out from underneath him. I hopped up and ran, adrenaline fueled, toward the door. I was so close.

"Eden!"

I pulled my key off my neck and got it ready before I got to the door. I saw it growing in size in front of me. Almost there. I reached out, grabbing the door frame, swung around and inserted the key. I paid no attention to where Marek was until the door was opened. I felt him grab my nightgown when I leapt through the door. Forgetting that there were stone steps and water gushing down them, I slipped, hitting my head on the way down.

THE OTHER SISTER.

There were no dreams this time. There was nothing to distract me from the truth. I had failed. I was locked underground in a prison cell while Marek went to collect Gabby for my father like she was a tax owed to him. What was I going to do?

I looked around at the small cell my brother left me in. I came to on a small bed in the corner with a pillow and blanket. It was significantly cooler down here than above ground. The dark stone walls were bare and cold, same as the floor I stood on. I reached out and clung to the very bars I watched the blacksmith forge. How ridiculous. So much for bringing the joy or happiness back to this place. Forget laughter, the only thing I could muster was anger. How could I have let this happen? How could I have foolishly trusted my 'family'?

My nightgown had dried, but the dirt and grime from my feud with Marek remained. I paced my cell for over an hour. I couldn't help but wonder if Marek had reached Gabby yet, or if her and Rosalina were still in Venice. That would at least buy me a few additional hours to figure out how to fix this. I knew that Marek knew Rosalina's plans for Venice, and would know where to find them. How would he get Gabby from her? I knew he wouldn't hurt either of them, but he wouldn't need to. Rosalina would trust Marek when he lied to her. Some fictitious story of me being hurt and needing Gabby. I grew more upset with every passing minute. And where was James? Was he okay? I couldn't imagine what it took to get him in a jail cell. I tried not to think about it, but of course I couldn't stop myself.

Suddenly I heard steps from outside the dark room. I rushed to the door to see a giant man dressed in the same warrior garb Marek had worn before. He was older, tall, and wide with golden tattoos covering every inch of bulging muscles. His white hair was cropped short, same as his beard. His eyes were hard and he wore a deep scowl. In one hand he held a long weapon that reminded me of the ones I saw in Palus. He stopped in front of me, and muttered something I didn't understand.

I took the only chance I might get.

"Sir, I'm Eden, King Samuel's daughter. I'm not sure what they told you—" But he growled and cut me off before I could say anything else.

"I don't care what they told me. And I don't care what you try to tell me. I only care what she says." And with that he pulled out a large key and opened my cell door.

"Back up, girl." He eyed me. Once I was an acceptable distance back, he stepped aside to reveal who was standing behind him.

It was her.

Mae. My mother's younger sister.

She was beautiful, and looked just as angelic as she had in the dream. She wore a simple light purple dress, the same shade as her eyes. Her dark grey hair hung down past her shoulders, loosely curled.

I was stunned into silence, unsure if I was still awake or had fallen asleep and was dreaming again.

THE DOOR KEEPER

She glided straight to me and raised both of her hands to either side of my face. The warmth from her hands radiated on my cheeks and slowly warmed the cold, damp room we both stood in. The guard closed the door behind her and locked it, but it didn't matter. I knew everything would be okay. I knew there was a reason I was here, and that Mae held the answers I needed. Her eyes held mine in their tight grasp. She had my mother's eyes.

"Eden, I have waited such a long time for this moment."

"Mae?"

"Yes." She smiled. "Don't worry, child. I will explain everything. Here, please sit down." She gestured to the bed. Her angelic presence felt absurd in this jail cell.

"I will start where we left off, after you saw us chatting together that morning at breakfast." She laid her hand on mine. I wanted to ask her how she knew about that, to ask if she'd seen me that morning like I thought she did. I wanted to ask her what she was doing here. Where she had been this whole time? But I couldn't muster a single question aloud. Somehow, I knew I'd learn the truth eventually, and that was enough for the moment. She continued.

"Your mother had the skipping rocks dream for weeks. It took her a long time to tell your father about it. As you can imagine, when she did finally tell him, he didn't take it very well. Your father loved your mother fiercely, and the idea of losing her drove him mad. He tried to reason with Ava, but she was stubborn. She knew what you needed to be, and what you needed to become it. Even though she was willing to sacrifice herself to give you that, your father was not. And when she wouldn't recant her plan, your father kept your mother in the house under lock and key."

"He locked her up?"

"Yes, he was distraught, desperate, and didn't know what else to do. He was terrified to lose her. For himself and the kingdom."

"Sounds familiar."

"Fear has an incredible stronghold on your father. He has lost himself in it. He is no longer the man Ava married, but even so, your father is not the enemy. He just needs someone to remind him what hope looks like, to free him from the man that grief and fear has turned him into. To restore him to the man he once was. He needs someone who will not give up on him." She looked me in the eye as she said the last sentence.

"How did she leave then?" I asked, ready to hear the rest.

"I helped her." She smiled sadly. "She knew I believed in her, and that I would help her do anything she needed to restore the peace between worlds."

"What happened? She told me she set something in motion. What is it exactly I am supposed to fix?" I couldn't stop myself.

Mae smiled at me. "That's another story for another day. But the short story is that your mother crossed into a world and created a situation that led to unrest and the potential for future conflict."

I nodded, already feeling like I knew where that story would lead. But I had to keep focus on the task at hand, and right now, that was learning the truth.

"I lied to your father and told him that I agreed with him about Ava staying in Caelum and you following in the footsteps of our ancestors. I convinced him to allow me to take her to our home village and try to change her mind. Instead, I freed her and took her to the edge of the shallow seas and said goodbye."

She looked down at her hand on mine and her voice was shaky.

"I don't regret it. Even now, after everything. I know it was the right thing to do. Ava was my best friend, and I would have done anything for her. Saying goodbye was the hardest thing I've ever done, but I trusted her . . . and I still trust her decision.

"It was several days before your father learned the truth, and by then it was too late. Vera was the one to figure it out and told Samuel what I had done. Grief stricken and heartbroken, he brought me before the court and sentenced me to life in prison. I've been here ever since."

My heart sank when I realized everything Mae had given up for my mother. What she had sacrificed to ensure that her plan was carried out, and that I became whatever it was I was supposed to become.

"You've been in prison this whole time?" I couldn't believe it.

"Yes, my darling. But don't feel too bad for me. My cell is much nicer than yours. It's more of a suite, and I have a private courtyard that I can visit on occasion." She beamed like that was somehow good news.

"How can you be in such good spirits? You've been in jail over thirty years!" I looked at her, unbelieving her cheery attitude.

"Because, my dear, prison cells can't hold me . . . or you for that matter. Especially in our dreams. How else do you think I brought you here?" Her lavender eyes sparkled.

THE DREAM THROWER.

"What do you mean?" I looked at my aunt with wide eyes.

"In our family, our streams of consciousness overlap. They transcend time and space. Your brother had the dream of you because I threw him the dream of the future. You had the dream of Ava giving birth to you because I threw you there. The same way I threw you everywhere else. It was my only way to reach out to you and prepare you for the truth." She smiled at me in a way that made me laugh.

"You *threw* me to those places?"

"Well, in a manner of speaking, yes. I am a Dream Thrower. I can throw people's consciousness' to places and times that I choose. Those whose minds are open to receiving them, anyway."

"Wait," I interrupted my aunt. "Does that mean that all of the dreams I had growing up, they were you?"

"Not all of them, only the ones in the past year. Anything you saw of your mother's pregnancy or delivery was me. I was trying to lean you in Ava's direction. All of the dreams you had growing up, of these flowers for example," she said, referencing my tattoo, "they were from your own ability. You have your own gifts in the subconscious realm. I can only enter willing minds; however, I think you may be able to enter any mind you wish. I tried many times to reach out to your brother, but the dream of you was the only one he would receive. Your father has conditioned him to resist his consciousness being contacted. At least, from *me*."

I smiled at my aunt, already knowing where she was going.

"But he sees all my dreams."

"Most of them, yes. He has yet to see one of your mother. If we can find a way to throw him into one involving her, I think we can make him understand."

I thought about that. The only problem was that he'd been brainwashed not to trust anything about Ava's decision or what she wanted. There had to be another way. I knew immediately what I had to do.

"No. Marek believes he is doing what is best for Gabby and for Caelum. We have to figure out a way to show why my growing up on Earth was vital, why it was important, why it was necessary. I know where you need to send me, what he needs to see.

"Send me back to Gabby's birth."

I lay back on the bed as Mae sat next to me. Within moments, I had succumbed to sleep. The next moment was incredibly surreal.

I was standing off to the side of a large hospital room, every shade of beige imaginable. People in scrubs scurried everywhere. I didn't need to count to know how many there were: twelve. I remembered the sense of panic in the room as the doctors realized Gabby was stuck. I watched the wonderful mom who raised me pacing back and forth on the other side of the room, praying out loud, knowing the situation was dire. I lay on the hospital table, bright light shining between my legs, exhausted from the three and a half hours of pushing with no progress being made. Eric stood next to me, dripping with concern, and stroking the top of my head, encouraging me the best way he knew how.

Doctors and nurses were rushing to and fro, trying to decide the best course of action to save the baby and me. She had been stuck in the birth canal too long; she had to come out now. In a last ditch effort before they wheeled me back to surgery, two nurse midwives positioned themselves beside me and placed their knees into my stomach, pushing down and out, finally pushing Gabby free.

She was white and lifeless, arms hanging limply toward the floor.

The doctors and nurses immediately rushed into action, shoving a breathing tube down her throat and pumping her full of life. I stood off to the side, my eyes stinging with tears and the memories of watching my little girl be born, dead. I looked at myself laying on the table, not understanding what was happening, relieved she was out, but knowing something was wrong. I watched Eric hold my hand tightly, afraid to leave my side.

I walked over to the incubator where my precious, helpless, baby lay, full of tubes, wires, and monitors. Then I watched the moment I only heard about until now. She reached up and grabbed the breathing tube and pulled it out, breathing on her own. Clear as day. I laughed, while crying, as I watched my five-minute-old baby defy the natural laws of this world.

Then there was a steady montage of doctors telling Eric and I that she wouldn't breastfeed, or go home with us, and everything that may be wrong with her. She breastfed, went home with us days later, and turned out in perfect health. Finally, the dream ended with Gabby a week old, sleeping between Eric and me in our bed. Eric, Earth. Me, Caelum. And Gabby, the perfect balance of both.

THE PRODIGAL BROTHER.

"How will we know if it worked?" I sat up slowly, fresh tears falling down my face.

Mae's eyes were soft when she answered. "We won't. We just have to hope." I groaned. Hope seemed too hard a task while sitting in this dungeon.

Over the next twenty-four hours, I told Mae about my life growing up, Eric, Gabby, my journey to Italy, and everything with James. She already knew he had been imprisoned and assured me he was safe. Something about Mae kept me calm in the face of so much uncertainty. I had a million questions, yet Mae's company kept them all at bay. At one point, I finally asked her about it.

"Why am I not worried more?" I looked at her over our lunch served by the strong brute we had as our guard.

"Why am I so happy to be here, with you, in jail?" She responded with her own question.

"I have no idea," I answered truthfully.

"You've heard people talk about your mother's joy. She embodied it. It flowed through her and into everyone she encountered. She has passed it onto you. Well, I embody hope. It flows through me in the same way. It is why Ava came to me to help her."

"What does Vera embody?" I asked cautiously.

Mae's face became serious. "Vera embodies peace. Which is wonderful and important. But without the balance of joy and hope, it can succumb to fear. Which I am afraid it has. With only Vera by his side, your father has come to value peace over all else, and striven for it at all cost. At the cost of many others. The only problem is you can't will or strive your way to gain peace, and you definitely can't purchase it at the expense of others, that's not how it works."

Mae didn't need to explain that part to me. I had already seen his willingness to sacrifice my mother's, Mae's, and my freedom for the sake of 'peace'. It wasn't hard to imagine that if he would sacrifice the freedom of those he loved, he would easily justify taking the lives of those he didn't.

Yet it was difficult for me to stay angry at my father after hearing everything from Mae. I felt extreme pity. This was man who had lost everything he held dear and was reacting in the only way he knew how. But I was resolved to show him a different way, I was resolved to change it, to fix it. I knew that Mae had spoken the truth, and if I could get to Samuel, somehow I would make it all right again. I realized that whatever my mother had planned for me was more than about this, but it was the place to start. I couldn't bring peace between worlds until there was peace here. Real peace, not built in fear, but peace rooted in joy and hope.

I stood up and walked toward the bars that held us prisoner. I turned and looked squarely at my aunt.

"I already know the answer to this, but do you think I can actually change his mind? He has lived this way for thirty years, I'm not sure his long-lost daughter has enough influence to change something so deeply rooted."

A deep, recognizable voice spoke behind me. "Maybe and maybe not, but all of us together might."

Marek. I jumped at the sound of his voice behind me. I turned to see him standing, holding the bars, his eyes swollen and face ruddy from crying.

"Eden, I'm sorry."

"'Eden, I'm sorry I kidnapped your daughter' or 'Eden, I'm sorry I lost my mind for a minute and will never think of doing something so stupid again?'" I glared at him.

He sighed and looked down at his feet before he looked into my eyes.

"I'm sorry I lost my mind for a minute and will never think of doing something so stupid again." As he spoke the last part, he unlocked the cell and opened the door.

I exhaled as I realized that my beautiful daughter was safe with Rosalina back in Italy. I walked toward my brother and punched him in the face as hard as I could before I collapsed in his arms and embraced him.

"I deserved that," he whispered.

"Damn right you did." I sobbed in his shoulder.

"I promise I'll never lie to you again."

"That would be nice." I sighed. Marek pulled back and walked over to Mae.

"Mae, I'm so sorry. Can you find it in your heart to forgive me?" Mae stood and looked up at Marek with grin.

"Lucky for you, Marek, hope and forgiveness go hand in hand. I always knew you would come around. It just took thirty years." She laughed lightheartedly like she wasn't talking about being in prison most of her life.

"I assume you saw the dream?" I asked my prodigal brother.

"Yes, I actually was outside of where Rosalina and Gabby were staying in Venice. I was watching them through a window from the canal and your dream just popped in my head. After I saw you, Eric, and her sleeping in your bed, I opened my eyes and Gabby was laughing at something Rosalina had said. I'm not sure what happened, but I could see it, Eden. I saw the best of Eric and the best of you in her. I could see the best of both our worlds. And what you said about Ava telling you to build the bridge, it was like it all clicked. It was as if Gabby was a physical manifestation of it, of what is possible if we just allow it."

He got from the dream exactly what I hoped he would. He saw that Gabby was the whole point. She was the reason I needed to live on Earth. It was the only way to bring us together.

Suddenly Mae spoke up. "Alright, if we are going to do this, we need all the help we can get. Let's go get James."

THE REUNION.

We walked through a maze of dark corridors, most of the cells without any occupants. After descending a flight of stairs, we turned and found who we were looking for. He was lying face up on a bed with his bare arms crossed over his chest. He looked healthy, and I didn't notice any obvious signs of struggle. I walked slowly to the bars, unable to take my eyes off him.

I missed him more than I realized.

"I'm not hungry," he growled, totally unaware of who was standing at the door.

Marek unlocked and opened the gate that divided us.

"Really? I'm freaking starving." I almost laughed. James jumped up and flew into my arms.

"Eden, oh my God!" I could barely breathe, he squeezed me so tight. "Are you okay? What the hell happened to you?" He looked down at my still muddy white-ish nightgown.

"In my defense . . ." Marek started.

Pow!

James punched Marek right across the face, same place I did. Marek groaned, sighed, and held his cheek.

"Yeah, okay. I deserved that, too."

"You deserve more than that, Marek, how could you?" He got in Marek's face and I saw the anger building, so I stepped in between.

"Listen, James, we've all been through a lot this past week. Marek understands now, we are all on the same side."

"Eden, his puny friends drugged me! He knew that was the only way to get me in here."

"James, I'm sorry," Marek said earnestly. "I'm serious. I know now that my father is wrong, and this is not what my mother wanted. I'm with you guys, for real. I want to fix everything."

Mae walked up to my brother and put her delicate hand on his arm.

"Marek, if you want to fix everything and make everything right, you know what you need to do." Her eyes pleaded. Marek's eyes hung heavy when they met James', then mine.

"Yes, I know." He put his hand on Mae's. "James, you need to follow me."

We followed Marek down another long hall and down two more flights of stairs. We came to a well-lit room with prison bars. But this room had furniture and a wall of books. An older gentleman around the age of sixty sat on an oversized chair, reading. His hair was long and wavy, a darker brown with salty grey throughout. His beard was thick with matching patches of grey. His eyes were a warm chocolate brown with wrinkles around the corners. He concentrated on what he was reading with a deep crease between his brows.

James' body went stiff. Slowly, a deep quiver rolled through him. His eyes were wide in recognition. I glanced to the man reading in the cell, a recognition of my own forming. Not of someone I'd met before, but someone I could see in the future. James, or maybe Charlie.

Oh my God.

I barely heard James' inaudible whisper.

"Dad."

And as if on perfect cue, Jay looked up from the book he was reading at the group of people standing before him. His eyes moved from one person to another, until he noticed his son.

Disbelief flooded his face.

"James?"

"Dad!" At this point, Marek had unlocked the door and James rushed through, embracing the man he had missed the past fifteen years.

"I can't believe it is actually you," Jay cried.

James was crying and beyond words.

"Well, we have as much time as we need to catch up." Mae walked into Jay's cell. "Why don't we all have a seat?"

It felt like years ago James and I set out to find what happened to his father in Palus, and it almost killed us. Here we were, months later, sitting in a Caelum prison cell, next to him. It was unbelievable, but unfortunately, his story was *very* believable.

Jay told us what happened fifteen years ago. He was helping Squash in the war against General Sapp, making about a trip a month to bring supplies and other items they needed to win the war. One day, the Door Maker summoned him. Not expecting anything out of the ordinary, he made a routine stop to visit him in Italy, on one of his trips home from Rio. Jay had known about the law forbidding the crossing of worlds, but he had made a promise to assist in the war and knew that much hung in the balance.

Samuel was waiting on him at Gio's house. After confronting Jay about his transgressions, he demanded his key or consequences. He wanted to make an example of Jay so that no other Door Keepers would break the law he had instituted. Considering Jay's family had kept the door for hundreds of years, that was not something he was willing to give up. Samuel had him arrested on the spot and brought back to Caelum, where he had remained since.

"I would have lost hope completely, but Mae visited my dreams shortly after I arrived." He nodded towards my aunt. "It's nice to meet you in person, by the way." He smiled. Then he turned his attention to me. "Mae told me of everything that had happened with your father and mother. She also told me that you would come one day to free me. It made it easier, somehow, knowing that it wouldn't be forever. But I have to admit, I had no idea you'd bring James along." He smiled at this son, but then sadness flooded his face. "I'm sorry about your mother. I miss her every day."

"You know she died?" James looked down.

"Yes. Mae was kind enough to allow me into her dreams every now and again. Mae threw me into her last dream before she died so I could say goodbye."

I couldn't keep the tears from flowing down my face. What an incredible gift Mae had, to be able to transcend time and allow people to say goodbye. I thought about how wonderful it felt to see my mother each time, and the closure it allowed me, even having never met her. Even if Mae was right and I had it too, I didn't know how to use it, or control it. Feeling sentimental and caught up in the moment, I leaned over and hugged Jay.

"I'm so sorry this happened to you. I'm so sorry that my father put you here and took you away from your family. I can't believe you sacrificed fifteen years."

"Eden, being a Door Keeper is in my family's blood. As much as it pained me to be away from James and Charlie for that long, I knew that Door Keeping was their future, even long after I am gone.

Yes, it might have been easier to give up the key and go home, but easier isn't always what is best. I wasn't willing to risk my children's futures, and neither was your mother."

I pulled back and looked my future father-in-law in the face.

"My mother?"

"Yes, I met her once, right after your brother was born." I looked at Marek and he seemed equally as surprised. Jay continued, "She was actually the person who brought the threat in Palus to my attention. Squash was a friend of hers."

Every time Jay mentioned Squash's name, my heart sank a little bit. So many people had given up their freedom and their lives for James and I. My mother, Mae, Jay, and Squash had all sacrificed for us, and the growing debt was becoming hard to bear. Suddenly, Jay looked at me very carefully and intently.

"Do not misunderstand, Eden. None of us gave up what we did for *you*." James looked at me questioningly, but I was only looking at Jay. He spoke slowly. "We did it for what you represent, our future. You, James, and even Gabby . . . you are our children. You are our legacy. If we can't sacrifice for that, or for you, then *nothing* is worth our sacrifice."

I was immediately filled with understanding. Of course he was right. Just days ago, I was willing to fight Marek to ensure Gabby's safety. The love for our children and their future will drive us to sacrifice anything asked of us, even separation from them.

I looked back at Jay with gratitude in my eyes. "How did you know that is what I was feeling?"

"It's just a knack I have for reading people." He smiled. "Although, I haven't used it in a long time." His smile reminded me so much of James'. So did his uncanny ability to read my mind in certain situations. But most everything else about Jay reminded me of Charlie.

I couldn't stop the smile that spread across my face when I thought of Charlie learning that we had found their father.

"I can't wait to see him either!" Jay beamed.

"Why do I never know what any of you are talking about?" James laughed, but with a hint of frustration.

"Charlie," I said with a grin.

"Charlie." James smiled his father's smile. "Dad, I think it's time we get you home."

"Son, I can't imagine anything more wonderful."

"Wait." James turned to me. "Eden, we'll stay until we figure this out with Samuel."

"No, James, not this time. It's time we each take care of our own families. Get Jay home to Charlie, and I will take care of my father."

"*We* will take care of our father." Marek stood up. "I've spent my whole life carrying the weight of his fears, and it's time to be free from them."

"And it is time for me to face Vera. We will go together." Mae stood as well.

"It's time to make everything right again, to make everything you all have sacrificed worth it." I stood, joining the rest of my family. "But first, I think I need to get out of this nightgown."

THE FUTURE.

The prison guard, who had apparently fallen in love with my aunt many years ago, had two horses ready for James' and his father's journey to the Door leading home. We stood outside in the courtyard where my aunt had made her home the past thirty years and said goodbye.

James held me tightly and whispered. "Hey, remember what I told you the night before I got thrown in your father's prison?"

I chuckled at the absurdity of that statement. "Yes, you told me to figure it all out so we can go home because you wanna marry me." I looked up at him.

"Well, it's still true. And yes, I still don't have your father's permission, but we do have mine now." He smiled down at me. "Seriously, Eden, thank you. I can't believe he is alive. I can't believe we have him back."

"I'm not sure there has *ever*, in the history of in-laws, been more drama between two families than ours." I smiled half-heartedly. James laughed.

"Definitely not true. Romeo and Juliet. Never mind, bad example. Like I told you, we can make it through anything as long as we are together. Whether or not you make peace with your father; *we* will always be a family. You, me, Charlie, and Gabby." Then he kissed me softly. When he did, I saw a flash of something. Like a picture was in front of my eyes for a moment and then was ripped away. It was all of us, sitting on a blanket by the lake back home in Georgia. We looked so happy, eating a picnic lunch, spring blooming all around us. Gabby was holding an adorable chunky little baby in her lap . . .

"I love you," James whispered in my ear, snatching the picture away.

"I love you, too," I replied, distracted by what I had seen. James let go of me and got on his horse.

"Please be safe, and I'll see you very soon," he called out as they started heading down the trail toward the shallow sea.

"Of course, you, too." I waved back at him. I turned, anxious to ask Mae about what had just happened.

"Mae, I just saw a flash of something. What could it have been?"

"It could've been anything. It could have been a wish, a hope, a dream, or your future. It's up to you to interpret. We just purposefully used your ability to manipulate dreams for the first time. Your ability has been building up the past thirty years. We technically just opened the dam, so you may have an abundance of things pouring out of you as a result."

Marek entered with full warrior garb on, complete with his weapons. He handed me Ava's hook blade.

"Don't try to kill me with it this time, okay?" He chuckled.

"What's with all this?"

"We have to be ready with everything. We have no idea how Samuel will react to this betrayal. He is expecting me to arrive with Gabby tonight, and instead I'm showing up empty-handed, with you and Mae free. Let's just say that he and Vera will probably not take it very well."

"Marek is right, Eden." Mae stepped next to me. "There is a small chance we may have to take the kingdom by force."

"Take the kingdom?" This surprised me. "I don't want the kingdom."

"I know, but if he doesn't relent, we will have to take it to ensure he doesn't keep coming after Gabby." Marek's voice was stern.

"It won't come to that," I responded.

"Of course we hope it doesn't. But if it does, you are the rightful Queen, and you can claim it at any time. And I don't think he will deny you because it is, after all, what he wants," Mae said thoughtfully.

"But that's not what I want. Trust me, it's not going to come to that." I grabbed Mae's hand. "If you have shown me anything, it is to have hope."

"Well, you bring your hope, but I'm still bringing my sword," Marek retorted.

"Oh, you better believe after all we've been through, I'm covering all my bases." I winked at my brother, hook blade in hand.

THE JUSTIFICATION.

My father stood on the edge of a cliff overlooking the shallow sea. He was, of course, anticipating the arrival of his granddaughter. His hands held behind his back, his dark silhouette against the colorful sky. The suns were setting, and the winds blew his hair back and over his shoulders. Vera stood beside him, his loyal companion. Her thin silhouette looked frail next to my father's wide, regal stance. Her hair was pulled back in a large bun of braids, her long gown blowing in the breeze behind her.

I waited behind them watching them for a minute before I announced my presence. My hair was loose and free from any Caelum adornment. I wore the clothes I had entered this land in, making sure I separated myself visually from the land my father so desperately wanted me to rule.

I didn't think about what I was going to say, I didn't plan a speech. I didn't argue with him in my mind or try to justify either of our actions. I closed my eyes and did, however, remember Gabby's favorite poem. *Just buckle in with a bit of a grin, just take off your coat and go do it. Just start to sing as you tackle the thing that cannot be done, and you'll do it.* I pictured my beautiful daughter reciting it to me with her big smile. I opened my eyes, looking and my father, and just thought about how I would have felt in his place. How I would have felt if the person I loved most in the world left me purposefully and took away my unborn child? It would have driven me mad. Perhaps even made me desperate enough to arrest innocent people, kidnap, and live in fear of it happening again.

"What have you done?" My father didn't turn around. He just watched as James and Jay rode their horses through the shallow sea toward the Door that led them home. Vera spun around, glaring at me as I approached.

"You little wretch, after all your father has done for you," she spat.

"Quiet." I raised my mother's blade and rested it under her chin. "You've done enough damage. Thankfully, you aren't my problem. You're hers." I nodded behind me to Mae coming up the hill.

"Mae," Vera gasped.

"Yes, your very own sister you left to rot in prison. I'm sure you have a lot of catching up to do." I removed my sword. "Now let me talk to my father." I turned toward him, but not before Vera reached out and grabbed at me.

"You won't get away with this. You aren't half the woman your mother was!" she growled. Something deep welled up inside of me as my body and mind took control and did what came naturally. My hand blocked her grabbing me and, as my arm straightened out in her direction, I felt a warm sensation moving through my arm toward my hands. I instinctually knew it was energy, a dream more specifically, I could expel to her at any moment.

"No." My voice was calm and steady. "I am exactly half the woman my mother was, and my other half I received from your King. And I was raised by two people on Earth who taught me more about grace, selflessness, and forgiveness than Caelum ever could have. I have become exactly who she wanted me to be, no thanks to you. The only reason my mother died the way she did was because you forced her hand. And for that, your punishment is to witness what you put her through." And with that I released the energy stored in my body and watched as Vera's eyes glazed over, and the emotions of the dream she was living through enveloped her face. The dream I dreamt so many times over the past year. The dream of my birth and my mother's death. After it was over, she crumpled to the ground with a cry and sobbed softly.

I turned my attention to my father, his face wracked with sadness. Despite everything, I knew this was never what he wanted. I was, after all, more like him than I cared to admit.

"I understand what drove you to this, Father," I said simply. "But Gabby is not yours to take."

"But *you* were. You were mine. And she took you from me."

"She did what she thought best for all of us, for the kingdom, for the worlds."

"She was wrong."

"Well, I know she wasn't."

"She wasn't wrong, Dad." Marek came up beside me. "Eden is what Mom wanted her to be. The bridge between worlds. Gabby is just one result of it. I understand what Mom saw now, the importance of it."

"Marek, after all we have been through together, how can you do this? Ava left us both." A tear ran down Samuel's face.

"Mom just didn't leave us Dad, she left everything. She sacrificed everything for this. We can't stand in the way of that. She deserves her wishes to be honored."

"I refuse to believe that!" My father raised his voice and lost his composure. "I refuse to believe that Ava dying was the only way."

I watched a broken man attempt to scratch, claw, and grasp at any last bit of understanding. None of that would bring the peace he so desired. He had lived the past thirty years in fear, without hope and without joy. His joy was dead, and his hope had been locked away. I remembered what Mae had said about balance. I turned to her behind me. She had crouched down with her hands on Vera's shoulders. Mae looked into my eyes and nodded. I had to restore the balance. I had to restore what he had lost so long ago, in order to free him.

"Dad, remember when I found Mom's messages to me behind the paintings? You told me we all have a destiny, and we all have our own path. You were right, mine wasn't with you, but it can be from here on out, if you let it.

"I don't blame you for what you did. If I've learned anything over the past week, it is that we will do anything for our children, our legacies, our futures. And while misguided, I know that is all you were trying to do. I forgive you. We all forgive you. When Mom died, you lost your joy. When you imprisoned Mae, you lost your hope.

"And now, I will give both back to you."

I closed my eyes and asked for what I needed. I'm not sure who I asked, but I felt it bubble deep from within me, until it rose to the surface. I felt it as it moved down my arms toward my hands. I opened my palms facing outward and slowly drew them up and around my sides. The energy left me as I did. I opened my eyes and watched our surroundings melt away. The suns blurred until they disappeared, the cliff melting into a stone floor. The trees of the forest behind us morphed into the fruit trees in the garden. Music started playing, and people were dancing all around us, twirling, singing, and laughing. The sweet smell of flowers and fruit filled the air. The sky was bright in the noon day suns. I heard Marek expel a curse word under his breath next me and looked at my father, whose face matched the surprise I felt. Mae was still bent over Vera, but surrounded by children dancing all around them. Vera slowly lifted her head, shocked at what transpired.

Mae lifted Vera to her feet and they made their way to the three of us, standing off to the side of the colorful party. We all startled when we heard his voice, booming over the party.

"Welcome, everyone. What an incredible day today as we celebrate the new Queen of Caelum!" Everyone cheered as we watched this version of my father address the party. James and I stood next to him, beaming brightly. James' arm was wrapped around my waist tightly, and Charlie stood next to him with an adorable curly haired little boy, about Gabby's age, on his back. Marek stood on the other side of Samuel, grinning from ear-to-ear. I looked around, trying to find Gabby in the midst of the party, but I didn't see her. A small wave of panic went through me . . . until I saw her come through the door.

She was so incredibly gorgeous. Her long chocolaty hair flowed loosely curled, with strands of flowers woven throughout. Her large crystal blue eyes shone bright against her dark skin. Her cheeks had lost their baby fat, but I still had to fight the urge to run up and kiss them. Her long, light pink, flowing gown was simple and elegant. The intricate tiny crown placed upon the top of her head was a light golden bronze.

She was a beautiful young woman, and she had become Caelum's Queen.

THE REALIZATION.

Within seconds, it all melted away, and we all stood where we did before entering the vision. My father stood before me, looking at me disbelievingly.

"You did that? What was that?"

"It's the future, if we stay on the path we are currently on. The one Ava set in motion when she left," I answered, unsure how I even knew the answer.

"It's true." Mae stood and put her hand on Samuel's shoulder. "Eden and Gabby will be everything we need them to be . . . maybe even more." She winked at me. She had said that in the dream she threw me into, the one when I saw her for the first time.

"That was crazy," Marek said, shaking his head. "Did you see us? That was in the future?"

I watched the realization land on Samuel's face. Everything he wanted and desired: family, joy, Caelum's rightful heir on the throne. It was all possible if he were patient, if he trusted Ava. I put my hand on his arm.

"Dad, if you let us go, we will come back to you. This story is so much bigger than us, or Caelum, and we have to let it play out the way Mom wanted. If you do, then what you saw will happen. Everything will be as it is supposed to be."

"That was everything I have ever wanted." He sighed. Tears streamed down his face. "Eden, she is beautiful. Gabby. I can't wait to meet her, whenever you are ready." His grey watery eyes met mine. "I'm so sorry."

"Dad, it's okay." I embraced my father, for the first time truly knowing and understanding him.

"Welcome back, Sam." Mae smiled at my dad.

"Mae, I'm sorry for what I have done to you. You didn't deserve the anger and blame for what happened, and I took it out on your anyway."

"You were heartbroken. We all were. Grief does terrible things to people." Mae turned her attention to Vera, still crumpled on the hard ground. "As does jealousy and manipulation, sister. You will pay for what you have contributed to this situation, Vera, but it will not be by Eden's hand or mine. It will be by your own mind. You will have to live with the nightmares and dreams that follow today, I'm afraid. Truth and reality can be hard pill to swallow for those who have avoided it their entire life."

"Indeed," Samuel said. "I'm afraid I will also share in that sentence. I'm sorry I ever doubted Ava."

Mae took Samuel's arm and led him down the hill back toward the house. "Perhaps we can find a way to bring you some closure."

I stood on the edge of the cliff overlooking the suns setting low on the horizon. The reflection of them shone brightly on the water. For the first time I sensed what had been missing here: peace. The absence of conflict. I reflected on what Rosalina had told me before we left. She said that sometimes you had to work through the conflict in order to remove it. She was right. Everything had been put on the table, our fears, regrets, guilt, hopes, and dreams, and we worked through it.

This whole time I had been searching for my mother. Every door I went through: Terra Arborum, Palus, and now Caelum. It was all to

THE DOOR KEEPER

learn about her and where I came from. In attempting to find her and about my past, I learned about my future. All of this searching brought me back to the one thing I'd had all along. Gabby. It was all a giant circle. My mother left me so I could have my daughter. My mother sacrificed herself for the legacy she would leave behind. That's when I felt it. My being a mother was never in competition with my destiny or being a Door Keeper, it relied on it. They were interchangeable, one and the same. There was no choice to be made; I understood that now. My fulfilling the destiny my mother talked about was also my fulfilling my role as a mother, preparing Gabby for her future. If I failed at one, I would fail at the other. Something important grew inside of me upon this realization. Determination. I was more determined now, more than ever to give Gabby whatever she needed to grow into the queen she would one day become.

Marek came up and stood beside me, staring off into the horizon.

"You were right," he said simply.

"Which time?" I smiled.

"When you said I underestimated you. The way you got through to me, the way you got through to Dad. You were right. Gabby was never going to leave Italy. What you did back there, it was incredible, Eden."

"It was almost unbelievable."

"Did you see how beautiful Gabby was?" He trailed off. "What are you going to do now?"

I turned to look at my brother. "I'm going to go home and give her exactly what our mother wanted for me. And one day, when she is ready, I'm going to tell her about all of this. But for now, I think we both have a lot of growing up to do."

THE WEDDING.

I stood on the veranda overlooking the Spiaggia Grande and Santa Maria Assunda. The sun shone bright, highlighting all the bright colors of the villas stacked around me. It had been a month since our return from Caelum and I still thought about it every day. I imagined standing on the balcony at my father's house overlooking the shallow sea. Our worlds were not that different. The salty air and steady breeze from the ocean both reminded me of the other. I turned around at an audible gasp behind me, smiling.

"Oh, Eden. It's perfect." Rosalina stood in the doorway of my bedroom with her hand covering her mouth. "You look beautiful." I decided to wear the dress that my mother had gifted Rosalina on one of her visits. A beautiful royal blue silk dress with braided accents and a plunging neckline. Rosalina giving me this dress and the key launched me into this life, and I felt it only appropriate that it launched me into my next adventure.

At that moment, my adopted mother, Evelyn, and Gabby came in the room, hand in hand. My mom wore a huge grin only surpassed by the squeals of Gabby's excitement.

"Mom, you look *so* pretty, but look at what Poppy brought me!" She twirled the perfect peach and cream dress Samuel had brought her from Caelum. Although no one but those who had been there knew where the dress was actually from. He had it made specifically for her, for this occasion, and she loved every minute of it.

"Oh, sweetie, you look so beautiful! I love the flowers." I smiled at the crown of Elisium's in her hair. If she only knew . . . a crown of Ava's favorite flowers, fit for a future Queen.

"Now, this is what I have been waiting for. Eden, it's all so amazing, I can't wait." Danielle joined the group, wide-eyed. There we all stood together, old and new friends, in the room that started it all. My mom, Rosalina, Danielle, Gabby and I all piled into a car and left for La Sponda. All of the men were getting ready at Le Sirenuse, the hotel were La Sponda was located. When we arrived, the girls left me alone in the foyer, but not before many kisses, hugs, and tears.

As I stood there, excited for this new chapter to begin, the two men responsible for me entered together. The man who raised me and gave me everything I ever needed or wanted approached me first.

"Dad." I smiled.

"Hey, sweetie. You look wonderful."

"Thank you."

"I want you to know how proud I am of you, and how excited I am that James is joining our family. I had the honor of giving you away to Eric, a memory I will cherish forever. I think it is only right that Samuel get that same honor today."

"You sure, Daddy?"

"Of course I'm sure. I'll see you down front. I'll be the one trying to keep your mom from crying too loud." He winked, kissed me on the forehead, and left me alone with Samuel.

I barely recognized the King of Caelum in his navy blue Italian suit. He tugged on his sleeves, obviously a little uncomfortable in so many clothes.

"I am so grateful you found your way to someone so worthy of being your father." Samuel smiled sadly.

"I was very fortunate." I looked at the door my dad had exited through.

"Thank you for allowing me to be a part of today, Eden. Are you ready?" He extended his arm to me, and I took it gladly. I looked down to take a moment and noticed the gorgeous turquoise tiles beneath my feet. They reminded me of walking in Caelum's shallow sea.

When we entered through the archway, the view before me took my breath away. James had rented out the entire restaurant for the day, and added even more flowers to the already expansive variety of climbing vines. Three violinists played the wedding march in the corner, harmonizing beautifully. Standing along the edge of the railing were all of the people I cared about. Gio stood in the center as our officiant, dressed in a handsome suit. Charlie looked dashing in his wedding attire standing next to Jay, the best man. On the other side of the aisle were Danielle and Gabby, both barely able to contain their excitement.

Sitting in front of the wedding party were my parents, Marek, Aunt Mae, Rosalina, Patrick and Emmie.

Then I locked eyes with him.

The man I didn't know I needed or even wanted, until I saw how life could be with him. We could have survived without each other, but that was the beauty of our relationship. It wasn't out of necessity or desperation that we loved each other. We had both lived complete lives without the other and had tried life alone. Sure, it was easier. There was no one to fight with or argue with about the small or large things; but the truth was, I'd rather fight with him about which ice cream to buy than eat my triple-chocolate-overload alone.

He wore a light blue button down shirt with dark grey dress pants. His smiling, warm chocolate eyes were deep and watery when

THE DOOR KEEPER

I approached. My father stopped me before I reached him and whispered in my ear.

"You deserve all the happiness that this world—or any world—has to offer."

"Thank you, Father."

I turned all of my attention to the man I would forever call my husband. It was a short ceremony, and we wrote our own vows. We had to be careful what we included since half of the wedding guests didn't know about Door Keepers, Doors, or the worlds beyond them. So, the first night of our honeymoon, we wrote down the vows we would have said if we could have.

After the ceremony, we all ate and drank together. The food was incredible, and our champagne glasses stayed full. After a large dinner, we had music playing, complete with dancing and much laughter. Charlie and Marek had a dance off that had everyone in stitches. I'm pretty sure Charlie had been watching instructional dance videos on the internet to prepare. Some of his moves were pretty impressive. I stood off to the side, watching Gabby and Emmie twirl in circles and dancing their little hearts out when Samuel approached.

"I can see why she liked coming here. It's quite enchanting."

"Yes, it is. There is even so much more beyond Italy. This is just a tiny slice of Earth. There are thousands of cultures and people groups completely different from this," I replied.

"It's hard for me to fathom."

"I can imagine." I smiled.

"I wish your mother could have been here today." He sighed looking out over our friends and family dancing. Marek had just picked up Gabby and was spinning her around. "She would have loved to have seen us all so happy. Celebrations and parties were always her favorite."

"Don't you worry, she saw it." Mae had walked up beside us. Samuel and I both looked at her, puzzled.

"You're surprised?" She smiled. "She knew much more than you know. Why do you think she gave Rosalina that dress?" She laughed lightheartedly and left to join the circle of dancers.

My father and I just looked at each other and laughed. It warmed my heart to know that my mother saw me so happy. I hoped it helped her with the difficult choices she had made. James danced up to me, twirled, and then offered me his hand. I, of course, took it gladly. We made our way to the dance floor.

"Well, Mrs. Musgrove, how are you feeling as a married woman?" His eyes sparkled.

"Well, Mr. Musgrove, I am feeling quite content and satisfied so far." I smiled.

"Oh, honey. You won't know satisfaction until tonight." He winked and I laughed. We enjoyed the company and atmosphere until the pastel colored sky turned a dark blue. As the night was winding down, I was cooled, sitting under one of the lemon trees by the pool on the terrace when Marek walked up.

"I think you are going to have a tough time prying Rosalina away from James." He laughed and I looked behind him to see her dancing with James, her head resting on his chest, looking very content herself.

I laughed. "Actually, she was swooning over our dad earlier. I think she might prefer Caelun men."

"We haven't had a chance to talk much since everything happened." He sat next to me, sinking his already bare feet into the pool. "How are James, Charlie, and Jay doing?"

"They are actually doing great. Charlie was over the moon, as you can imagine. Jay moved back in and will live with Charlie when

THE DOOR KEEPER

James moves into our place. They have all three been inseparable, making up for lost time. When everyone arrived in Italy, Samuel went and saw Jay to make amends. It's hard to make up for what he did, but he has humbled himself enough to try. Thankfully, Jay had a long time to work through everything in his own heart, and he understands what losing everything can do to a person. I think everything is going to be okay."

"It's amazing, with everything we have been through, that we are all here together, celebrating. I think Mom would have been proud." He put his hand on mine. Then on cue, as though it were scripted, I saw her. She was on the other side of veranda watching everyone dance. I could barely see her through our family dancing between us, but it was her. She wore the green dress in the photo I had of her with Rosalina, with the matching green foliage woven throughout her long, white hair. She had one hand covering her chest and she was laughing. We locked our lavender eyes, smiled at each other, and then in an instant, she was gone.

THE EPILOGUE.

As I read the last sentence, a tear lands on the page of the book laying in my lap. It isn't the first and I'm sure it won't be the last. She was there, at the wedding. My brain is having a hard time computing everything. I look up at the geese settling into the lake. Or are they blue colored swans? My eyes are playing tricks on me. How am I supposed to even know what is real anymore? How am I supposed to believe any of this?

Yet, I know it's all true. Of course it is. Not only does it make sense, but it fills in so many gaps and holes I have. I remember most of this like it was yesterday. I flip the pages in the book back to the night Marek arrived at James' house.

"Later that day, Gabby and I sat at the table with Charlie and James. Gabby was delighted to find out Charlie was James' brother. Charlie had hung out with her for me multiple times at the gallery through the building process. After a nice dinner, Gabby convinced him to go outside and make some videos, although it didn't take too much convincing. After James and I cleaned up the kitchen, we sat in his living room and cuddled on the couch."

Yup, exactly as I remember. What in the world? Or should I say, what in *what* world? This ginormous journal recounts everything as

I remember, but it just all feels so unbelievable. But what if it is true? What if everything in this book is true? If it is, the better question is, why am I reading about it all in this journal?

Suddenly, I'm afraid I already know the answer.

I walk inside the house to the person waiting for me to finish. His feet are kicked up on the arm of the couch and he's snoring. I sit down by him and gently wake him. He has been waiting for about twelve hours for me to read the whole thing. His eyes open.

"Hey, I'm done." I look down at the book I'm gripping tightly.

"Are you okay?" He sits up with a concerned look.

"I don't know, it's a lot to take in," I say honestly. "Charlie . . ." I look him in the eyes so he can't lie to me. "How long has she been missing?"

"A week," he said solemnly. "I'm so sorry, Gabbs."

I look at my uncle who has been more of a big brother to me over the past seven years, and set the book in his lap.

"So this . . . this is all real?" I glance at the book.

"Every word of it."

"Why did you give it to me? Why didn't she tell me all of this?"

"This was her way. It was a lot to process, and your mom found the best way was to journal. So one day, she decided to combine all of her journals together for you. She didn't want to miss any details or leave anything out. She was planning on giving it to you on your eighteenth birthday."

My eighteenth birthday is in two weeks.

"I'm assuming the fact that Dad left three days ago had nothing to do with joining Mom in Tokyo, and her extending her trip." I'm also now figuring out that Mom's trips around the world had little to do with her curating the art gallery, and a lot more to do with being a Door Keeper.

"No. When Eden disappeared, James freaked and reached to your uncle. She was following a lead about a disturbance in Palus. It was a routine scouting mission and one night she just vanished. So James went after her."

"Why are you telling me all of this? What can I do?" I was on the verge of tears. My family is in trouble, and I can barely grasp what is happening.

"Because I'm going after them, and I need you with me," he answered.

"Me? I can't be of any help. I just found out about all of this," I countered.

"Gabbs, you may have just found out about all of this, but your mother has trained you for this since she discovered the truth. Everything she has done has led you to this moment. You have Eden's gift, you already know that. And I need your connection with her to find them. I can't do this without you."

My mom loves dreams. She loves to talk about them and analyze them with me. Now I know why. As soon as I read about her dreams in the book, all the ones I've had over the years popped into my head. Maybe Charlie is right. Maybe together, with his lifetime of Door Keeping experience and training, and my connection to Mom in the subconscious, we can find them.

"Okay, she said in the book that once she used her gift intentionally for the first time, everything came flowing out of her. Maybe we should do the same thing," I said, starting to buy into this crazy idea.

"I asked your mom once how she pulled certain moments out, or how she knew where to throw people in dreams. She said she just asked herself to find them. So why don't we start there?" Charlie got up and rearranged the pillows on the couch for me.

"Shouldn't be too hard, I'm flipping exhausted." I mustered a smile at my uncle. He had come over last night and I ended up reading all night. I lay down and pictured my mom's face. Her dark skin and light, stormy, grey eyes. Her longer asymmetrical bob that brushes the top of her collar bone, next to her tattoo. The way her whole face lights up when she laughs.

"Mom, where are you?" I whisper under my breath as I drifted off to sleep.

My body instantaneously freezes. I'm standing in the middle of a blizzard, not able to see but a couple feet in either direction. Large white snow chunks blow in every direction. It's frigid and unbearable. I can't stop shivering, and the chattering of my teeth is the only thing I hear over the wind. Suddenly, I see black figures approaching from behind me. They're massive, slow moving creatures. They have long fur that's coated in snow, and carry large weapons. They drag a smaller creature behind them, hands bound, it's fur covered completely in snow. When they grow closer, I can see skin peeking out from beneath the fur coat's hood. It's her. Her skin is bright red, wind burned from the blizzard. She stops cold, then turns her head toward me.

"No! No, baby, wake up. You've got to wake up." She tries to run to me, but the giant monster pulling her yanks her, causing her to fall flat on her back. She gets up and starts toward me again.

"Get Marek, tell him they are taking me to the Apex. The Apex, Gabbs. Don't forget!" I can barely hear her over the wind.

"Mom! What is happening? Are you okay? Tell me what to do!" The tears freeze on my face.

"Just tell Marek and stay home. Take care of JJ. I love you, baby. Now wake up!" She's crying and begging me. The huge beast hits her across the face, knocking her down.

"Mom!" I cry. I run toward her and cup her bruised face in my hands. Her body is ice cold. She opens her eyes slowly and smiles at me. "Wake up, sweetie." Then she slaps me with the remaining strength she has left.

"Mom!" I sit straight up. Charlie is next me in seconds.

"Are those tears *frozen* on your cheeks?" he asks, eyes wide.

"We have to call Uncle Marek, I know where Mom is."

Acknowledgments:

The person who deserves my gratitude and thanks first and foremost is my husband, Andy. You have always given me the space and freedom to pursue my dreams and wild, crazy ideas. Thank you for always listening to me talk about whatever scene I was working on at the time, and for giving the Serenbe its name. Thank you for inspiring James and giving me such rich material to pull from when writing. You will always be my absolutely favorite person.

To my beautiful children, Eli and Peyton. For inspiring me, challenging me, and pushing me with your very existence to be my best self. You have taught me the importance of telling our stories and the impact it can have on the people around us. Both of you inspired Gabby's character and thanks for making it so easy.

To my Mom and Dad. You both have always encouraged me, loved me, and supported me. I couldn't ask for better parents. Thank you for always being my number one fans.

To my siblings: Mayhay, Age, and Matt. Mayhay, you have been my best friend my entire life and I couldn't be more grateful for you. Boys, y'all taught me how to have fun dancing. You three make up the other sides of my Parker box; together, we are a stronger.

Thank you to Royal James publishing for giving me a chance, and allowing me an opportunity to tell this story. Nichole, I'm sorry for driving you crazy with my many emails, thanks for your patience with me. Major gratitude is owed to Cindy, my editor, for making this manuscript *so* much better. Thanks for adding the hundreds of commas, and spaces between my many dot dot dots.

To my Beta Readers:

Lydia Mays: You were the first person to fall in love with these characters as much as I did.

Tara Bruce: I wear the key necklace you gave me most days. You read the book exactly like I hope everyone does, with joy and enthusiasm.

Bonnie Clark: NO ONE, I repeat no one has encouraged me through this process more than you have. I'm so grateful to be your book buddy.

Maureen Goodwin: Your thoughtful feedback brought a new insight and perspective to this story. One I wouldn't have had without you.

Natalie Deviez: You are my Danielle. You are one of the people who have influenced my own personal story and the story of my family the most.

Kayla Stagnaro: Your support in transitioning from COLORS to writing meant more than you know.

Chantel Adams: I miss our long traffic filled car rides together. You are a great person to debrief with.

Melanie Dale: Your feedback as a writer was invaluable and you also brought a new perspective to the narrative that was much appreciated.

Cori Turner: Thank you for taking COLORS so that I could pursue this. You are a huge part of this actually happening.

Jessica Stewart: Thank you for being there when the first page of this story was written, sitting amongst the Christmas trees and creepy elves.

Jen O'neill: We have walked through so much together and there is no one I'd rather walk along side with.

Esther Clark: Your excitement about this story re-energized me on the days I dragged and thought it sucked.

Alexis Polston: Thank you for your love of chocolate. (And for taking time out of your crazy college life to read this book!)

Jeremy Kirby: Thank you for being the only man to beta read this whole thing through. I toned down some of Earth's clothing descriptions just for you.

To the two amazing ladies that helped me with editing my first drafts. Lydia, for helping me develop characters and plot. Kara Chatham for helping me realize I apparently hate commas.

Special thanks to Jennifer Schuchmann, Lydia Mays, and Holly Crawshaw for your early publishing/writing/editing advice. Hollywood, your advice is the reason this thing actually sold, I'm completely convinced of it.

I am in debt forever to Meghan Brim, who's immense and never ending talent created the most gorgeous book cover I've ever seen. Your art deserves to be seen by the world(s).

Special shout out and thanks to my old small group. Jen O'neill, Amy Bennett, Jen McGhee, Becky Bennett, Kim Minick, and Rachael Melton. We have shared things together that few women have and I will be forever grateful for our memories. Wanda Forever. Girls, look out for her in the sequel.

To Plywood People: The lessons, community, and friendships that you fostered well surpassed COLORS. It influenced almost every decision I made writing, editing, and publishing this book. I am genuinely grateful for my Plywood community in Atlanta.

To the sweet family who owned the door on the edge of the field. Thank you for inspiring this entire story and even more amazingly, thank you for letting me have the door.

Abba, I feel like you are probably getting sick of me saying thank you. But just humor me for the thousandth time, because I want/need to do it publicly. This story, this book, my entire life wouldn't exist without you. Everything I am experiencing right now is immeasurably more than I could have ever imagined. You planted dreams and talents in me as a kid and waited ever so patiently for me to re-discover them. Thank you for every blessing, every hardship, every lesson, and every joy; because all of them inspired and helped create the person I am today. Thank you for being my muse, because everything I do, or have ever done, have been inspired by you.

It's all yours, that is why it's always in all caps.

About the Author:

Steen was born and raised in Woodstock, Georgia. While she has only recently discovered her passion for writing, she has always been an artist and a storyteller. A couple of years ago, a story idea gripped her and wouldn't let go until she wrote it all down. The Door Keeper is her debut novel and she can't wait to pursue all the other stories that have built up in her over the last three and a half decades.

When she isn't writing, reading, painting, or baking, Steen enjoys spending time binge watching TV shows with her husband and playing in the pool with her two children at their North Georgia home.

For more information or questions, feel free to contact Steen!
Email address: thedoorkeepertrilogy@gmail.com
Social media:
    Blog: thedoorkeepertrilogy.com
    Twitter: @steenjones
    Instagram: @thedoorkeepertrilogy
    Facebook: facebook.com/thedoorkeepertrilogy
    Goodreads: steenjones

Made in the USA
Charleston, SC
06 March 2017